WHEN WE WERE INFINITE

KELLY LOY GILBERT

SIMON & SCHUSTER BFYR

New York   London   Toronto   Sydney   New Delhi

SIMON & SCHUSTER BFYR

An imprint of Simon & Schuster Children's Publishing Division
1230 Avenue of the Americas, New York, New York 10020
This book is a work of fiction. Any references to historical events, real
people, or real places are used fictitiously. Other names, characters, places,
and events are products of the author's imagination, and any resemblance to
actual events or places or persons, living or dead, is entirely coincidental.
Text © 2020 by Kelly Loy Gilbert
Jacket illustrations © 2020 by Akiko Stehrenberger
All rights reserved, including the right of reproduction in
whole or in part in any form.
SIMON & SCHUSTER BFYR is a trademark of Simon & Schuster, Inc.
For information about special discounts for bulk purchases,
please contact Simon & Schuster Special Sales at
1-866-506-1949 or business@simonandschuster.com.
The Simon & Schuster Speakers Bureau can bring authors
to your live event. For more information or to book an event,
contact the Simon & Schuster Speakers Bureau at 1-866-248-3049
or visit our website at www.simonspeakers.com.
Interior design by Lizzy Bromley
The text for this book was set in Bell MT Std.
Manufactured in the United States of America
First Edition
2 4 6 8 10 9 7 5 3 1
CIP data for this book is available from the Library of Congress.
ISBN 978-1-5344-6821-4
ISBN 978-1-5344-6823-8 (eBook)

FOR MY PARENTS,
AND FOR AUDREY,
ZACH, AND DASHIELL—
MAY YOU ALWAYS FIND
MUSIC IN ALL THE
NOISE SURROUNDING YOU,
AND MAY WHATEVER SONGS
YOU BRING THE WORLD
BE STRONG AND KIND
AND TRUE.

Dear Reader,

Please be aware that *When We Were Infinite* contains content that may be triggering. For a list, please see the bottom of the following page.

When We Were Infinite contains the following content that may be triggering: a suicide attempt, conversations about suicide, instances of suicidal ideation.

PROLOGUE

WHEN JASON WAS VOTED onto Homecoming court the fall of our senior year, it both did and didn't come as a surprise. It didn't because Jason was attractive and talented and kind (I, of all people, understood his appeal); it did because he generally disliked attention and, for that matter, dances. And because I often thought of the five of us as our own self-contained universe, it was a little jarring to have the outside world lay claim to him like this. Netta Hamer, the ASB president, made the announcement at the beginning of lunch one day, when the five of us were all sitting together in our usual spot. We were, of course, as delighted as Jason was visibly mortified—he tried to pretend he somehow hadn't heard, which meant that now we weren't going to shut up about it—but we couldn't have known then how that night of Homecoming would turn out to be one of the most consequential of our friendship.

"For the record," Sunny said, "I do think it's a tradition that needs to die, like, yesterday." Sunny was the ASB vice president, which she'd described as the group project from hell. Associated Student Body officers ran all the dances, and Sunny had tried, unsuccessfully, to do away with the dance royalty. She had been on the Winter Ball court her freshman year, the same year as Brandon—in fact, since Grace had been on the junior prom court last, I was the only one of us five who'd never been chosen. "You parade around a bunch of random people and it's just like, hey, look at these people who haven't even accomplished anything specific! And it's so weirdly heteronormative."

"Ooh, true, but I can't *wait* to see Jason get paraded," Grace said, clapping her hands. "Jason, do you get to pick out theme music? I hope they make you wear a *crown*."

"Should I buy a new phone?" Brandon said thoughtfully, dangling his old one in front of Jason's face. Jason kept eating, glancing past it into the rally court. "Will all the many—and I mean *many*—pictures I'm going to take fit on mine, do you think?"

Jason balled up his burrito wrapper and arced it into the trash can a few feet away, then pointedly checked his watch. "Oh, don't be so modest," Brandon said, grinning hugely, knocking Jason a little roughly with his shoulder the way boys did with one another—some boys, anyway, because I'd noticed Jason never did that sort of thing, even in jest. "You're going to be so inspiring."

"You know, honestly, I think it's kind of nice," Grace said. "Everyone here is too obsessed with accomplishment. It's nice to have one thing that's just like, *You didn't do anything to earn this! We just like you!*"

"Mm," Sunny said. "That's a pretty idealistic way to say a bunch of underclassmen think Jason's hot."

Jason choked slightly on his water, but recovered. Brandon gleefully pounded his back.

"Little emotional there?" he said. "I get it, I get it. Big moment for you."

"Jason," Grace said, biting the tip off her carrot stick, "would you rather falsely accuse someone of cheating off you and they fail, or have every single Friday night be Homecoming for the rest of your life?"

"Oh, come *on*," Jason protested, finally, "what kind of sadistic choice is that?"

The rest of us cheered. "Put it up here," Brandon said to

Grace, lifting his hand for her to high-five. "You broke him."

Would You Rather was Jason's game. He used to come up with the questions when we were waiting in the lunch line, or walking to class: *Would you rather badly injure a small child with your car, or have a single mother go to jail for hitting you with hers?* Once Sunny had told me she imagined Jason played it alone, testing himself with all kinds of ethical dilemmas, which I believed.

We were all laughing. Jason said, "When I'm king and I'm looking over my list of enemies, I'm definitely remembering how none of you but Beth were on my side."

Actually, I hadn't joined in because I was imagining the night of Homecoming, how inside the music people would twine their bodies together and whisper secrets, how maybe on some certain chord Jason might look my way and want that with me, and I was afraid if I said anything now I might give myself away. I had been in love with Jason nearly as long as I'd known him. It was the only secret I'd ever kept from my friends.

I was about to chime in, though, when Eric Hsu came over. Later, after all the ways things came apart, I would look back at this moment as a warning, a kind of foreshadowing of what I let happen.

We mostly knew everyone in our class—we were a school of about two thousand and Las Colinas was always in the lists of top-ranked public high schools, which meant that years into the future we would still have a sleep debt and self-worth issues and nightmares about not having realized there was a back page of a calculus exam. Eric was the kind of person who would definitely pledge some kind of Asian frat in college, and Sunny and I had once clicked through his tagged pictures to confirm that he was in fact flipping off the camera in every one of them. (Also, he had the third-highest GPA in our class.) Eric's eyes were bloodshot, and when he came close he smelled like pot. Jason cocked his head.

"You all right there?" he said. Jason had a way of being on the verge of a smile that made everything seem like an inside joke you

were in on with him. It made other people think they shared something with him, that they knew him well, although that usually
wasn't true.

"Yep. Yep," Eric said. "Doing pretty good."

"Yeah? What's, uh, the occasion?"

"Just working on my stress levels," Eric said. "We're just all so
stressed *out* all the time, you know?" Then, apropos of nothing,
he turned and peered at me.

"Hey," he said, "I want to ask you. How come you never talk?"

The five of us looked at each other. "Excuse me?" Sunny said,
a little sharply. "What's that supposed to mean?"

"Beth never talks to the rest of us. But then I see her sitting
in your little huddle here and she's all—" He mimed what I think
was supposed to be mouths opening and closing with his hands.
"How come?"

It was true that outside of our group I was much quieter. I'd
overheard various interpretations about what my deal was: that
I was boring, or stuck-up, or a bitch. Still, what Eric said wasn't
the kind of thing people said to your face. It was jarring for a lot
of reasons, but I remember it for one I wouldn't have anticipated:
how truly, utterly impervious I felt. Eric could say whatever he
wanted about me. I was always invincible with my friends.

"You are high as fuck, buddy," Brandon said, clapping Eric on
the back, and there was an edge to his tone. "Maybe you should
go home."

"Well!" Grace said, when Eric had wandered off. "That was rude."

I smiled. It seemed, at the time, like a small thing that would
become one of our *remember whens*. But later it would feel like a
relic from a different life, back when we could just root ourselves
in the moment and not have to brace so hard against the future.
And I would wonder if there had been signs I should've seen,
even then, that could've changed how everything went after.

"I'm just not as dazzling as the rest of you," I said, which felt true, but I didn't mind. I knew from them how someone could shift through the wreckage of your life and pull you from the rubble as if you were something precious. That was worth being the least dazzling one—it was worth everything.

"Selling yourself a bit short there," Brandon said. "I bet you could absolutely murder a crossword puzzle if I put one in front of you right now." Since finding out a few years ago I loved crosswords, he'd always teased me about it. "If anything says *dazzling*, it's absolutely crossword puzzles."

"Beth, of course you're dazzling," Grace said.

"It's fine. At least I don't have to be on Homecoming court."

Jason laughed at that. Later that day, though, as we were packing up after rehearsal, he turned to me.

"You know," he said, "silence isn't the worst thing in the world."

He meant it kindly, in case I was still worried about what Eric had said, which I wasn't. We were musicians; we were intimate with silence. Mr. Irving, who conducted the Bay Area Youth Symphony, or BAYS, as we called it, always said silence was sacred: it was in that space that whatever came before or after was made resonant.

But I had always known silence—as fear, first as that catch in my mother's voice and my father's stoniness in return, and later as all those throbbing empty spaces where he used to sit or sleep or keep his computer and his gaming things. I had known it as the possibility of emptiness, as something I was trying to shatter each time I picked up my violin.

There was so much the five of us had lived through together, so much we'd seen each other through. But in the whole long span of our history together, this was the most important thing my friends had done for me: erased that silence in my life. In the music and outside it, too, we could take all our discordant parts and raise them into a greater whole so that together, and only together, we were transcendent.

I always believed that, in the end, would save us.

AROUND DUSK in Congress Springs, when it's been a clear day, the fog comes creeping over the Santa Cruz Mountains from the coast, shrouding the oaks and the redwoods in a layer of mist. The freeways there tip you north to San Francisco or south to San Jose, hugging those mountains and the foothills going up the coast on one side and the shoreline of the Bay on the other.

It was still late afternoon the day we were heading up through the Peninsula to SF for our annual Fall Showcase, and sharply clear-skied, which made it feel like the blazing gold of the oak trees and the straw-colored grass of the hills had burned away all the fog. It was October, and we were seven weeks into our school year and ten weeks into our final year in BAYS. Sometimes I wondered about early humans who watched the grasses die and the trees turn fiery and then expire, if they thought it meant their world was ending. That year, because it was our last together, it felt a little like that to me.

So far just Sunny and Jason were eighteen and could legally drive the rest of us around, so Sunny was driving; I was sitting squeezed in between Jason and Brandon in the back seat, Grace in the front, my whole world contained in that small space. Jason, Grace, and I all had our violins on our laps so Brandon's bass would fit in the trunk with Sunny's oboe and her stash of Costco almonds, and I was holding my phone in my hands because I was hoping to hear back from my father.

"Is that a new dress, Grace?" Sunny said as we passed the Stanford Dish. Sunny wasn't sentimental, but when she cared about you, she followed the things in your life closely, almost osmotically. "It's cute."

"Thanks!" Grace said. "I thought it might work for Homecoming, too."

"Except that Homecoming will never happen," Brandon said, waggling his eyebrows at Sunny in the rearview mirror. "We're all waiting for Jay's big moment, but the end of the world will come, and there we'll all be staring down the meteor, poor Jason waiting in his crown, and Sunny will be complaining how Homecoming *still* hasn't—"

"Brandon, don't bait her," Grace said, at the same time Sunny said, "Okay, but seriously, I don't understand how everyone here can have a 4.3 GPA but be so massively incompetent in basically every other area of life." Homecoming had been repeatedly pushed back this year—now it was after Thanksgiving—because the other ASB officers had taken too long to organize everything, which Sunny had complained about both to us and to their faces for weeks, even after Austin Yim, the social manager, told her she was being kind of a bitch.

"Anyway," Sunny said, "if Homecoming does miraculously actually happen despite the rampant incompetence, I bet Chase will ask you, Grace."

Grace made a face. "I don't know. He still hasn't said anything about it."

Grace had had a thing lately for Chase Hartley, who hung out with a somewhat porous, mostly white group of people who usually walked to the 7-Eleven at lunch and stood around the little reservoir there. Even though she and Sunny and I would spend hours afterward dissecting their hallway conversations or messages and parsing the things he said to figure out whether he was into her, I was privately hoping that he wasn't. The last time she'd had a boyfriend—Miles Wu, for a few months when we were sophomores—she would disappear for three or four days in a row at lunch with no comment and then show up the fifth, smiling brightly, as though she hadn't been gone at all. But then again, Grace and Jason had very briefly gone out in seventh grade before I'd known them, and so it was always a little bit of a relief when she was into someone else.

"Chase seems exactly like someone who wouldn't think about it at all until the last possible minute," Sunny said. "Why don't you ask him?"

"We were all going together, right?" I said. "We could get a limo or something."

"Maybe!" Grace said brightly. "I'll see what happens with Chase. Or he could come with us. Brandon, you're going, right?"

I didn't want Chase there—I wanted just the five of us, cloistered from the rest of the world. It was only fall, still blazingly hot in the afternoons and still with the red-flag fire warnings and power blackouts in the hills to try to keep the state from incinerating, but already I'd begun to feel the pressure of the lasts—the last Fall Showcase, the last Homecoming—before the universe blew apart and scattered the five of us to who knew where.

"Are you kidding?" Brandon said. "Like I'd miss Jay's big coronation?"

"My what?" I felt Jason turn from the window to look at us. Brandon grinned.

"Nervous about tonight?" he asked Jason. I was leaning forward to give them more room, and with Jason behind me I couldn't see his expression, but I could imagine it—mild, guarded, the way he always looked before a performance, or a test at school.

"No," Jason said. "You?"

We were all a little nervous, minus maybe Grace. Brandon laughed, then reached around me to smack Jason's thigh. "Liar. And no, I'm not nervous, but I'm not the one with a solo."

"Eh," Jason said, "not a big solo. I'm just tired."

I wiggled back so I was leaning against the seat too and could see them, and Jason shifted a little to let me in. "You didn't sleep?" I said.

"I did from like twelve to two and then like four thirty to six."

That was the worst feeling, when you couldn't keep your eyes open any longer but you had to set your alarm for the middle of the night to wake up and finish schoolwork. I was drowning in homework and would be up late tonight too. I said, "Were you doing the Lit essay?"

"Nah, I haven't even started. I had a bunch of SAT homework."

"Did you guys hear Mike Low is retaking it?" Grace said, rolling her eyes. "He got a fifteen ninety, and he keeps telling everyone there was a typo."

"He asked me to read his essay for Harvard this week," Sunny said. "Did you guys know his older brother died in a car accident when we were little?"

"His brother?" Grace repeated. "That's so horrible."

"It is, but also—I don't know, I thought it was kind of a cop-out. The essay, I mean."

"Whoa," Brandon said. "That's pretty cold, Sunny. His *dead brother*? How is that a *cop-out*?"

"Not in life, obviously. That's beyond horrible. But his essay just felt like . . . playing the dead brother card to get into college? I don't know, if someone I cared about died I don't feel like I could turn it into five hundred words for an admissions committee."

"Gotta overcome that white legacy kid affirmative action somehow," Brandon said. "Okay, but also, can we go back to the part where you said writing about his family tragedy is a cop-out, because—"

"Let's help me pick a topic first," Sunny said. "I literally have nothing like that. My essay is just going to be Hi, I love UCLA, I'll do anything, please let me in."

"That's where some of your friends are, right?" Grace said.

Sunny had a group of queer friends she knew from the internet. Most of them she'd never met in real life, but one, Dayna, lived in LA and Sunny had met up with them the last time she'd gone to visit her cousins. They'd made her an elaborate, multi-course meal of Malaysian dishes and taken her to an open mic night. Sunny had been enthralled by their friends—Dayna had had to leave home after coming out to their parents, and had built their own kind of family in its place—and also radiant with joy, sending us probably a dozen video clips of the performances and pictures of the food, but when I said it sounded romantic she'd said it wasn't, that she wasn't Dayna's type and they were just generous and open that way. I thought she might like them, but she always brushed it off. I followed some of her friends on social media—most of them didn't follow me back, which was fine; they were important to me because they were important to her—and I always wondered if she ever told them she felt out of place with us, or she didn't think we understood her.

"Just Dayna, but they'll probably be somewhere else by then for college," Sunny said. "It was more just—I swear sometimes Congress Springs is like so aggressively straight, or maybe that's just high school, and I loved the whole scene there."

She'd talked about wanting to be in LA for years now. As for me, all I wanted in life was what we had now: our Wednesday breakfasts and study sessions and hours holed up at the library or a coffee shop or each other's homes, the performances and rehearsals together, how at any given point in the day I knew where they were and probably how they were doing. For years I had harbored a secret, desperate fantasy that we would all go together to the same college. I would give anything, I would do anything, to matter more to them than whatever unknown lives beckoned them from all those distant places.

"What are you guys writing about?" Sunny asked.

"I have nothing to write about," Brandon said. "I'm boring. My life is boring. I would've thought by now I'd have, like, done something for the world."

"That's because you lowkey have hero syndrome," Sunny said.

"What? I don't have hero syndrome."

"Okay, then would you rather date someone you didn't like or someone who didn't need you even a little bit?"

"Someone who didn't need me."

"Really? There would be nothing at all to fix in them? They wouldn't be even the *tiniest* bit better off being with you?"

"She's got a point there," Jason said to him, amused, and Brandon flicked Sunny lightly in the shoulder. "Okay, fine, touché."

"I kind of thought about writing about that article on moral luck," Jason said. "I forget who posted it. Did you guys read it?" We hadn't. "It was about how maybe whether you're a good person or not comes down to luck. Like if you hit someone with a car and it was an accident, you aren't guilty, just morally unlucky. Or, like—maybe you would've been a decent person if you grew up in, I don't know, California today, but instead you were born during like, the Roman Empire, and so you became some bloodthirsty soldier instead."

"Isn't that basically the Just Following Orders excuse?" Sunny said. "Anyway, *plenty* of people are born in California today and aren't decent people."

"Right, sure," Jason said. "I mean, you read the comments section of basically anything and you're like, cool, half the people here are fascists. But I think the part that gets me is more the opposite. Like what if you tell yourself you're a good person but then when it comes down to it, if you'd been born into slightly different circumstances you'd also go around crucifying people or whatever? So then you were never really good, you've just been morally lucky all along."

"Nah, I think you'd hold out," Brandon said. "You would've been a blacksmith or something. A doctor."

"A Roman Empire–era doctor sounds basically as bad as a soldier," Grace said.

"*You* would've been a soldier, definitely, Sun," Brandon said, and Sunny laughed.

Nestled in the car there with all of them that day, I thought I'd write about them, maybe, and what they meant to me. They were the truest thing I could think to tell anyone about my life and about who I was.

My phone was still quiet when we got to the theater, and I checked my email again, just in case. Three nights ago I'd been up past two in the morning working on an email to my father. He almost always stayed up late gaming, or at least he used to, and so while I was writing I imagined him awake too, twenty miles away. Usually I didn't invite him to things, because even if he did come, which I doubted he would, it would be unbearable if he didn't have a good time. But this was our last Fall Showcase and my first show as the second-chair violinist, and so I'd thought—*why not?*

We got there at the same time as Lauren Chang and Susan Day, the third and fifth violins. When they said hi, Jason switched on a smile, what I always thought of as his public mode, and reached to hold the door open. They were midconversation, and Susan was saying, "Actually, it's pretty impressive what you can accomplish just to trick yourself into having self-esteem," and Jason laughed.

"That's the most inspiring thing I've ever heard," he said, and Susan blushed, pleased. When they went ahead of him inside, though, he was serious again. He caught my sleeve just before I went through the door.

"Hey," he said quietly, "did you hear from your dad?"

I shook my head, and Jason winced. "I'm sorry."

"It's all right."

"I mean—it's not."

It was loud when we arrived backstage, everyone spread across the risers. Jason and I took our seats at the front. Tonight's was just a brief solo to introduce himself as the concertmaster—his more important one was later in the year—but earlier that week I'd noticed he'd bought gold rosin for his strings, something he'd always scorned as a waste of money.

"Did your parents come, Jason?" I asked, and then immediately regretted it. We all knew better than to ask about his parents.

He took a moment to answer, arranging the music on his stand. "They might've," he said, politely. "I'm not really sure."

"I'm nervous," I said quickly, to change the subject. "Especially about the Maderna. Are you?"

"Nah, it's so self-indulgent to be nervous." Then he winced. "That, ah, came out wrong. I didn't mean you."

"No, it's all right."

Mr. Irving was making his way to the front of the risers, his shock of frizzy white hair tamed slightly for the occasion. Jason studied me for a moment, then offered me a smile—his real one, the corners of his eyes crinkling. "You let people get away with too much."

When we filed onstage, it was immediately warm under the lights, and bright enough that you couldn't make out individuals in the audience. And even though it was stupid, I let myself hope. But of course my father wasn't out there watching. It was a weeknight, and in San Francisco, after all.

Mr. Irving held his arms up, waiting. Then he lifted them and the music began, like a thunderclap, and we were inside it.

We played our full set: a Handel, a Maderna, a Chopin. When it was time for Jason's solo, the violins lowered our instruments.

As I watched him, my heart thudded. He took a deep breath, then he straightened and drew his bow forcefully across his strings.

His style was so different from mine; I always thought of myself as slipping into a piece. Jason broke in like he was shattering glass. But then, right before the coda, I heard him start to falter—just slightly, on that run of grace notes—and I looked, alarmed, at Mr. Irving. In an orchestra, you learn to hear that point when things escape the conductor's control, like an old cup you can fill without watching because you know the pitch change just before it overflows. I held my violin in my lap and watched Jason, willing him to stay with Mr. Irving. He held on. I smiled at him, relieved, but he was absorbed, and didn't see me.

When we came back in, it took a beat for us to meld cleanly together again, and I couldn't quite hear myself. Sometimes, on a piece that was especially comfortable to me, I would lift my bow slightly above my strings so that just for a few seconds my motions produced only silence, so that when I started playing again I recognized the tiny change in sound.

I was tempted to fall into that indulgence that night, to hear whatever difference I made, but I knew I couldn't. There was, after all, an audience, and in music you could be a lot of things, but selfish wasn't one of them.

I woke exhausted on Monday. I was desperate to sleep more, like every morning, but instead I dragged myself out of bed to shower and do my makeup and hair and brows. I could hear my mother getting ready for work, the pipes groaning when she turned on the shower. We lived in one of the older houses in Congress Springs, a dark two-story with reddish carpet and no air-conditioning, built seventy years ago back before the family diners and the feed shop and the Olan Mills studio gave way to tutoring centers and Asian markets, before white parents started holding town forums to discuss how the schools had gotten too competitive. Most adults here worked in tech, but my mother, who had gone to Lowell and then Berkeley and probably expected a brighter future, worked at a bank near downtown for what seemed like, based on how much she worried about bills, not very much money.

While I waited for my mother to be done with her shower—there'd be no hot water if I turned mine on at the same time—I checked my phone, and there was an email from doug.claire: my father. I opened it, my heart stuttering.

Sorry to miss the show, he'd written. *I'll come next time if I'm free.*

You can read so much into so few words; you can conjure whole universes. And I let myself, my mind wandering, until my phone buzzed. It was Sunny, a message to me and Brandon and Grace: *okay, who's seen the review?*

When I went downstairs, my mother had arranged a place setting for me: a bowl of jook carefully covered in tinfoil, a glass of milk, and a section of the newspaper, folded open. There was a note next to my bowl in her neat, small handwriting: *Dear Beth, drink ALL the milk. Here is an article about your show.*

Maderna's *Liriche Greche* was an ambitious piece for sixty teenagers to attempt, even under the direction of celebrated veteran Joseph Irving. When the Bay Area Youth Symphony gave its anticipated Fall Showcase, the program offered a promising and impressive selection.

While the music was technically proficient—the young musicians have clearly been hard at work—at times the sound tended toward the deconstructive, occasionally to the music's detriment. The most technically demanding section of Chopin's Prelude 28, No. 4 was played nearly exactly as it was written on the page, with little to offer by means of interpretation or emotion. It was a surprising showing from Irving, who usually favors emotional movement over structure and rigor.

Principal violinist Jason Tsou, a senior at Las Colinas High School in Congress Springs, delivered a skillful if emotionally stunted solo. The evening's one high point came with Tsou's mastery of the spiccato. In Tsou's case, perhaps the attractive glow of future potential excuses last night's performance.

——RICH AMERY

By the time my mother dropped me off at school, Sunny, Grace, Brandon, and I had already been messaging about the review for nearly an hour. It was a cool, clear morning, mist still clinging to the foothills rising out past the track and baseball fields. The trees by the parking lot had littered layers of red and gold and orange leaves everywhere, small sunsets that crackled under your footfall.

Sunny was waiting for me by the math portables, eating her daily breakfast of almonds and dried cranberries out of a Stasher bag, which she held out to offer me. "You think Jason's seen it yet?"

I ate an almond with exactly three cranberries so I wouldn't mess up Sunny's almond-to-cranberry ratio. "My guess is yes, by now. He probably went looking."

"It wouldn't surprise me if he was expecting it to be bad." She glanced behind her as we started across the rally court to our lockers. "After we dropped him off last night, Brandon said last week, he and Jason were at the gym and something happened, like Jason messed up or couldn't finish his—what do you call them? Reps?" Sunny hated the gym. "And he got mad and threw his weights across the floor. I think Brandon's kind of worried. He said he feels like one of these days Jason's just going to snap."

"Snap in what way?"

"He didn't say. And then Grace, naturally, laughed it off and told Brandon he worries too much." Sunny rolled her eyes. "I know Grace doesn't physically believe in things going wrong, but—"

"What are we talking about?" Grace said, smiling, materializing in front of us as we approached our lockers. Brandon was with her, drinking coffee from his Hydro Flask.

"Your relentless and extremely unfounded optimism," Sunny said, reaching for a sip of Brandon's coffee.

"Are you still talking about the review?" Grace said. "He said he could tell we'd been working hard, didn't he? I think he was trying to be nice."

"Trying to be *nice*? Okay, I mean, would you rather sleep through the SAT or have to tell Jason to his face that he sounded emotionally stunted?"

"Did he say anything to you about it, Brandon?" I said.

Brandon raised his eyebrows. "What about any of your interactions with Jason makes you think he would see it and, what, call me? Text me emojis about it?"

"It's better than if he just doesn't talk about it with anyone."

He laughed at me. "You really didn't grow up in a real Asian home, huh? Gotta work on that repression."

"Brandon," Grace scolded. She knew about that twinge in my chest I always got whenever someone commented how Asian I wasn't. It marked my lack of wholeness, how visibly I never quite belonged. My mother had grown up in the Sunset District in San Francisco, the daughter of parents who'd run a laundry service and preferred not to talk about their difficult pasts, and she spoke Cantonese but had never taught me or sent me to Chinese school. She'd married a white man—my father was a fourth-generation Idahoan before he moved here—and our last name was Claire. Sunny and Brandon and Jason's families were all from Taiwan—Sunny and Brandon were both born there—and sometimes it seemed like everyone but me knew the same places to eat in the night markets in Taipei, the same apps you used for group chats with your cousins overseas. Grace's family had been here for four generations, and every year her huge extended family went on cruises together and all wore matching jerseys with NAKAMURA on the back. My mother was an only child and the daughter of only children, and so I didn't belong to any family in that same way in any country. I belonged, instead, to my friends.

"So you think Jason's upset?" I said.

"I think it's going to really fuck him up," Brandon said.

"Do you think there's any chance at all he'll think it wasn't that bad?"

Brandon snorted. "None."

We found Jason by the poster wall outside the cafeteria with Katie Perez, the senior class president. They were hanging a sign among all the others advertising service club activities: a used graphing calculator drive, a gun violence walkout, a climate change march. He looked pleasant and nonchalant, although he always did in front of other people. Sometimes when I saw him, the angular lines of his face that were always both familiar and elusive to me, something inside me went off like a camera flash.

"DIY pumpkin porg making, huh?" Brandon said, reading Katie's poster.

Grace squinted. "What's porg? Is that like a health food?"

"From *Star Wars*," Katie said. "That was the fundraiser we all voted on, remember?"

Jason laughed, handing back her masking tape. "The representation the people demand."

"Yes, the people don't realize how much work it's going to be to get a million, like, pumpkins and googly eyes," Katie said. "Okay, I'm off to copy more flyers. Thanks, Jason."

And then it was just us. I knew Brandon was probably right, but if Jason brought up the review, it would mean it was okay. We could pick it apart and strip it of its power; we could drown it out with all our voices instead.

We waited to see what Jason would say, trying to pretend we weren't.

"I'll be honest," he said. "Porgs are the only part of *Star Wars* I *would* expect you to know about, Grace." So he wouldn't say anything, then, which meant neither would we.

AT THE END OF rehearsal the Wednesday before SAT IIs, Mr. Irving asked if any of us seniors were planning to audition for music programs. My heart skittered, the way it did just before flipping over a test sheet to start an exam, and I willed Jason to raise his hand.

He didn't. I knew the rough sketch of the future he'd methodically planned for (Berkeley, med school, a cardiac fellowship), and I'd always known none of my friends would continue musical careers after BAYS, but still I'd always hoped somehow it would be different for Jason. He was easily the most talented of the five of us, and it felt extravagantly wasteful to abandon that. We'd never once had a principal violinist who considered BAYS the end.

After rehearsal, Mr. Irving asked me to stay. When the room had emptied and he was still perched on his stool, he smiled at me and said, "You know, I've been thinking it would be well worth your time to apply at places like Curtis or Jacobs. Maybe Berklee or something like the New England Conservatory as backups."

I was startled. I hadn't raised my hand during rehearsal to say I was auditioning; Mrs. Nguyen, the private teacher I saw once a week, had asked whether she should save room in her schedule for extra lessons to prepare for auditions, and I'd said no and assumed the matter was settled. I knew it would be something of a stretch, but I was hoping for Berkeley—my father had always wanted me to go there like he and my mother had, and it would mean, most likely, being with Jason. "Oh—well—"

"You'll probably have to go out of state to land anywhere worthwhile."

"Right, of course. I just hadn't—I hadn't really thought—"

"You aren't considering it? There's not a single school of music that would tempt you?"

He was watching me closely. The lights were hitting too brightly on me, and I started to answer, then stopped. I could've told him the truth, which was that no, it wasn't something that had ever felt like a real option. Or I could've told him the other truth, which was that I fantasized about it in the same way I fantasized about, say, being with Jason, or my father moving back home. I could tell him that if I thought too hard about the future I could get lost in the grimness of a world without violin, where my life would just be some exhausting job that made billionaires richer while people starved and the planet spun toward immolation, but that for as long as I could remember I'd kept a framed picture on my desk of my father and me from when I was a year old, where he was sitting at his computer with me on his lap, *Call of Duty* on his screen, and we were wearing matching Berkeley shirts and both of us were beaming.

But those things would disappoint him, and I never liked to give people the answer they didn't want from me. "Maybe if it were, like, Juilliard—not that I'd get—"

"Juilliard's prescreen deadline is coming up," he said eagerly. He and his husband had both gone there; he spoke of it often. "Have you given any thought to a possible audition repertoire? I don't know if you've looked at Juilliard's requirements yet—for the Paganini, I think you might consider the Twenty-First. And for the concertos—do you know Zwilich?" He got up from the stool and pulled a folder of sheet music from his bag. "Why don't you take this home and see what you think of it. I thought it would be perfect for you."

I stayed up late that night messaging with Sunny and Grace (Sunny had been arguing with her parents, and Grace was having bad cramps), and they asked what Mr. Irving had wanted to talk to me about. I told them, but then accidentally turned my phone on silent and fell asleep before I saw a response, so in the morning Grace's message was waiting for me: *Oooh, you should go for it!!! You would love that.*

I told Jason about it as we were walking to second period, and something changed in his face when I did. "You're applying?"

"I wouldn't be able to go," I said, suddenly embarrassed. "Well, I'll never get in, either. I just didn't want to say no to Mr. Irving."

"He asked you?"

"Did he ask you, too?"

"No."

"He probably assumed you are since you're the first chair. I think all the other ones have at least auditioned."

"Maybe," Jason said. I couldn't quite parse the tone of his voice, and I hoped he hadn't taken it as an accusation.

"Have you ever thought about applying?" I said. "Just—to see?"

He was quiet awhile. "It's probably not a good idea."

I imagined him packing away his violin for the last time, shoving it under his bed. "You don't think you'll miss it?"

"I'll probably have to do molecular bio or something for med school."

That wasn't actually an answer, but also the expression on his face wasn't exactly an invitation. "Right."

"That's cool you're doing it, though." He held open the door for me. "I bet you'd regret it forever if you didn't."

We spent most of Saturday taking and then recovering from taking our SAT IIs, and Sunday we spent five hours studying at Brandon's house, making a pilgrimage halfway through to load up on snacks. But then on our way to Ranch 99, when we passed Target, there was a sign saying you got a gift card if you got a free flu shot, and Brandon flipped a U-turn, saying, "No, come on, we're doing it, it'll be good," when Sunny told him it was the randomest idea he'd ever had. So we all got our matching flu shots and our five-dollar gift cards, then had a contest to see who could buy the best snack with it in five minutes. Jason won with caffeinated bulgogi-flavored beef jerky, except then it came out that actually it had cost nine dollars and Sunny said, "Jason, we trusted you! Automatic disqualification," and Jason said, "How much do you think it should cost? You don't think people should be paid a living wage to make your novelty foods?" and Sunny said, "The rules very clearly—" and Jason said, "Okay, capitalist," and yanked the bag away, and bits of caffeinated beef flew all over and we had to brush them from our hair. He was laughing, we were all laughing, and I thought how impossible these moments would be to ever explain to someone outside of us, let alone ever replicate.

The next morning before school, Vikram Reddy asked Teri Ma to Homecoming with a flash mob of people from choir. He'd written an original song that name-dropped not only Teri and the different friends they'd be going with but also, somehow, transpiration and factor markets and *Bodas de Sangre*, which we were reading in AP Spanish. We all circled around to watch, and it was stupid, but when they were finished and Vikram dropped dramatically on one knee and we all applauded, I imagined Jason asking me.

Of course that wouldn't happen. But the five of us could go, and we could make it something special and memorable we did as a group. I could imagine all of us caught in the rhythms and the shine of the night, the way it felt sometimes at one of our performances except that we wouldn't all disperse afterward. Maybe the night would make things feel different to Jason—would make *me* feel different to him somehow.

At home that evening, I looked up limousine rentals. It would be nearly a hundred dollars for each of us, which was a slightly terrifying number. But I thought about how in a limo we'd have our own small world, and I would pay anything in service of that.

For dinner, my mother had made steamed pork cake, and when I came downstairs with my laptop she'd spooned a portion onto a plate for me with broccoli, spinach, and rice. She would have liked for us to regularly sit down and have an uninterrupted meal together, I knew—sometimes, wistfully, she'd mention it— but most nights I was doing homework and she was answering emails or paying bills or cooking for the next day, which she was doing tonight. She pulled a cutting board from under the sink and a knife from the block on the counter, gently nudging jars and bottles out of her way to make room. My father had hated all that clutter. *Just throw it away and buy a new one if you need it,* he'd snap sometimes when he was clawing his way through the refrigerator looking for jam, or digging through all the pens in the kitchen drawer to find one that still worked.

"Is that homework?" she said, pausing her mincing ginger to take a bite of pork cake, when I set my laptop down on the table. She'd never been a good multitasker, and whenever she tried to eat while she was doing something else, she always timed it wrong and opened her mouth before she'd even picked up her food so that for a few seconds she sat slack-jawed, her mouth gaping. I looked away. I hated thinking how that might have repulsed my father.

"It's planning for Homecoming."

"Oh—are you going to Homecoming? I would have thought it had passed by now. What are you planning?"

"I was just looking at different limo companies."

"Oh, Beth—limos are so expensive. I can drive you there. I don't think teenagers should be spending all this money on extras for dances like this." She went back to chopping. "While we're on the topic of money, though, I'd like to have a discussion about your plans for next year. Is there a good time we can—"

She always tried to schedule things like this. "Why don't we just talk about it now?"

"Well—all right, there were some things I wanted to prepare first, but I suppose—" She set down her knife and wiped her hands, then came and sat down next to me, too close, and opened her laptop.

I felt myself resisting. So far I'd avoided the topic of next year with my friends, but they were who I wanted to map out the future with, not my mother with her spreadsheets. But also—I felt this was a conversation my father might want to be present for. Berkeley was one of the only things he'd consistently talked to me about when I was growing up.

My mother typed something, her brow furrowed in concentration. Sometimes, when I let myself notice, she seemed so tired and frayed to me, so fragile, and I wondered whether she missed my father still, whether she felt as alone inside the house as I did. When I was a child, we'd been so close—at night she would come crawl into bed with me if I had a bad dream. She'd kept all the drawings I used to proudly give her, framed around the house like a museum of a past life.

"I think we should talk about finances first." My mother angled her laptop so I could see the file, rows of color-coded numbers that jumbled when I looked at them. On her background, there was a COUNTDOWN TO ASHEVILLE! widget. We were going this summer to celebrate my graduation, my eighteenth birthday, and her forty-fifth birthday. She'd been planning already for over a year. Whenever I opened my email, she'd sent new articles like *Ten Vistas You Absolutely Must See on the Blue Ridge Mountain Parkway* or pictures from restaurants: fried chicken, barbecued ribs.

"As you can see," she said, "it would be advantageous to go somewhere with lower tuition, so I think staying in-state makes the most sense. But I haven't spoken with your father yet about his contributions, so—"

"What do you mean his contributions?"

"Well, I expect that he'll also contribute toward your college fund."

My skin felt tighter around my rib cage. "I don't want him to pay for any of it."

She looked at me, puzzled. "You have to report his income on your FAFSA anyway. Of course I've always expected—"

"I don't want to ask him for anything."

"You don't have to ask him, Beth. I'll speak to him about it."

I felt my voice rising. "I don't want to use his money."

She tapped her fingers on her keyboard lightly and blinked at the screen. "Well, I don't know if—"

"I'll stay in-state and go to a public school. It's fine. I wanted to go to a UC anyway."

"That's fine if that's what you want to do, but it limits your options so much to—"

"I'm not going to use his money."

She started to say something, then stopped. I could tell she wanted to ask me why. Finally, she said, "It's good to keep your options as open as possible."

"That isn't an option for me."

"Beth, I've always worked hard, but my salary isn't—"

"I'll just stay in-state. It's fine." My heart was starting to race. "Is that all? I have a lot of homework tonight."

Maybe because she was tired she didn't press it, or maybe she planned to come back to it later. "Well, I—I suppose that's all," she said. "For now."

My parents met at UC Berkeley. They were in the dorms together as juniors, and one night my mother was cooking in the communal kitchen, soy sauce chicken in foil and (because she believed in eating at least two different vegetables every night) dau miu and bok choy, and she offered him dinner; three years later they were married. Once upon a time they delighted one another and they were happy.

Before he'd left, when they were fighting all the time, I'd read all the articles I could find on things like *How not to drive your boyfriend away* and *Why he's thinking of leaving you* and *What makes marriages fail*, because I knew that when I was older I wanted it to be different for me. For a girl, it seemed, the dangers were myriad: you talked too much, or not enough; you let yourself go or your makeup looked too harsh; you didn't have enough sex; you nagged him or made him feel emasculated or you weren't fun. How did people ever stay together? And how would I ever learn to be good enough, to somehow avoid whatever it was my mother had done? I'd become so conscious of all the things she was doing that might drive him away—her hovering, the way she would press her lips together and look upset for hours on end when he was trying to play his video games, how she would make demands of him and not stop when it was already clear he was increasingly annoyed. It felt unforgivable that she hadn't tried harder.

Back upstairs, I closed and locked my door and went back to the limo website. When I was fourteen, my mother had signed me up for a credit card in the name of financial health, and I used it to put down a deposit for the limousine rental for the night of Homecoming. It was so much money it made me feel a little sick, but I'd be paid back for most of it, and it would be a special night, an important one for us. And I knew from watching my mother what could happen when you squandered your chance to hold on to someone.

THE FIRST OF our college apps were due at the beginning of November. Eric Hsu figured out some hack to add most of the senior class to a WhatsApp group he named *Rager!!!!*, and we used it to complain en masse when for a week straight probably a third of us all set our alarms for two a.m. to wake up and work on our essays—you'd pick up your phone at three in the morning and there'd be fifty new messages, which was gross but also kind of nice. After the five of us turned in our first applications, Mrs. Nakamura sent us cookies via Grace, triangles made to look like college-y pennants with each of our names written in icing, like this was supposed to be a celebration. But each application—BU, Stanford, Princeton, Cornell—represented a different shade of separation: Would you rather lose the people who mean most to you to a redbrick campus with fall foliage and snow, or to a campus studded with palm trees by the ocean? Would you rather their new world be full of thirty thousand potential friends to replace you with, or an intimate four thousand?

Wednesdays were late start days, and for years now we'd had standing plans to meet at Grace's before school for breakfast. Mrs. Nakamura was a real estate agent, and their house always looked Instagram-ready—Brandon had joked once that cooking in their kitchen made him feel like British bakers were waiting to judge him. That week we made ricotta pancakes, a recipe Sunny wanted to try. She and Brandon mixed the batter, and then Jason meticulously flipped them while I sliced strawberries and Grace whipped cream. Sitting at the Nakamuras' kitchen island, the light streaming in through their windows and our silverware clinking softly against the plates and my friends all laughing together, I thought how cruel it was that no one in the world could stop this all from ending.

"It'll be better than you think, Beth," Grace said. "You're still thinking about next year, right?" She reached over the bowl of strawberries to pat my hand. "Everyone ends up loving college. You will too."

"Speaking of," Sunny said, before I had to answer Grace, "Except not speaking of, I just didn't have a good segue, who wants to go to something next week with me?"

"I do," Grace said. "What is it?"

"It's this thing on Tuesday at the LGBTQ Community Center downtown. Crafternoon."

"Me," Jason said. "I love crafts."

She raised her eyebrows. "You love *crafts?*"

"Like friendship bracelets and popcorn strings and yarn balls? So meditative. I love that shit."

"Sun, I didn't know there was an LGBTQ center in Congress Springs," I said.

"Yeah, I've been wanting to go for a while. I kind of want to meet people."

"I'll be your wingman," Brandon said.

Sunny rolled her eyes. "Who has time for a relationship? No, just meet other queer people."

"What about the GSA?" Grace said. "Didn't you used to go?"

"Mrs. Welton asks me that literally once a week." Mrs. Welton was the vice principal who advised the ASB and also the Gender and Sexuality Alliance. "I went like four times. And every time she'd give me this huge weepy hug and tell me to call her Mama Kat, which, ew. She definitely thinks it's like, my parents don't know and are going to disown me. One time she started telling me how she knew honor was an important value to my family."

"Ooh, like she just watched *Mulan*?" Grace said, laughing. "Who else was in the GSA?"

"Mm—Liam Chadwick. Missy Straub. Then mostly younger white kids you probably wouldn't know. Oh, that one junior girl that hangs out with Chase's group. Emma something. Moffat? They're all great, but honestly, it's like eighty percent Mrs. Welton talking about her gay son and then crying and telling us all we're beautiful the way we are. Which—thank you, I know that. But I want to meet like—other Asian and POC queer people. One of the times I went I said we should talk about intersectionality and race and Mrs. Welton literally was like oh, no, we don't see color here."

"Gross," Brandon said. "Let's all go with you."

"Boo, I can't," Grace said. "I promised my mom I'd help her stage. The rest of you go."

Sunny made a face. "I can't show up with three straight people. I'm picking Beth."

Brandon pretended to be wounded, but maybe he wasn't completely pretending, or maybe I was just projecting—I thought it would be better with all of us, because everything was; because we had such limited time left for that.

The day of Crafternoon the next week, when it had started to get cold again and the hills had turned brown as all the grapevines in the vineyards dropped their leaves, I was walking with Grace at the beginning of lunch. In AP Gov, fifth period, Mr. Markham had gone off on a bizarre tangent about Kennedy's assassination, and as we left class together afterward, Grace had said, "Okay, ooh, this will be fun—which conspiracy theory is everyone in our group?" and now she was trying to convince me that Brandon was The Government Faked the Moon Landing, and we were both laughing, and so I didn't notice right away that Chase Hartley was waiting in front of her locker with a bouquet of red roses.

My heart sank. I did not want Chase Hartley in our limo, Chase Hartley around for the whole night of Homecoming. When Grace saw, she put her hands to her cheeks.

"Chase!" she said, almost scoldingly. "Are these for me?"

He handed them to her, a little sheepishly. "Yeah, I wanted to ask you—you want to go to Homecoming together?"

Grace was so delighted I felt chastened that my initial reaction hadn't been to share in her happiness. She stood on tiptoes to fling her arms around his neck, and the cellophane around the roses crinkled between them. He patted her on the back a little awkwardly and said, "Okay, awesome, well, uh—I guess we'll—talk about details and stuff later?"

"I give it a two," Brandon said, when Grace recounted the story. "Maybe a two-five. Zero points for creativity, but I'll give him the two for at least buying flowers ahead of time."

From where we were eating lunch, we could see Chase across the rally court, drinking a bottle of something unnaturally blue. The five of us had been eating in the same place since we were freshmen, a gap between two cement planters at the edge of the rally court across from the gym. The campus had been built to look like someone's idea of an East Coast school, brick buildings and ivy everywhere, except the hallways were outdoors because it was California, and the murals on the gym walls were all of apricot orchards and a giant pitchfork, which was, inexplicably, our school mascot.

Grace readjusted her flowers. "I thought it was sweet. He looked nervous. He used the word *awesome*."

I tried to avoid looking directly at Jason, worried that my

longing would be nakedly visible if I did. "So—Chase will come with all of us, then?"

"I guess so? Or I guess I'll see if he wanted to go with his friends."

"Are we all going with dates?" Brandon said. "Maybe I'll ask—"

"I don't think we should," I said quickly. "We were going together, right? I got us the limo."

"Oh," Grace said, frowning a little, "you did? I didn't realize that was something we were definitely doing."

"I thought we—"

"Come on, Nakamura, go big or go home," Brandon said. "It's Jason's big night, after all."

Jason rolled his eyes. "Beth, how much do we owe you?"

"You can pay me after." I was afraid to tell them how much it cost, but it would be easier, afterward, if the night went well; hopefully either Chase wouldn't come or somehow wouldn't ruin everything, and it would be a good memory, and it would be worth it.

Sunny wanted to leave a little early for Crafternoon to make sure we weren't late and the whole time we were driving Grace messaged us screenshots of her and Chase's conversation, which was almost exclusively him flirting in a way that felt entirely devoid of substance. I wrote back *lol* and 😍, but as we walked into the building, I said, "I think I'm a bad friend."

"Why?"

We were in a big room papered brightly with posters and paintings, split into different zones: couches, coffee station, bookshelves, a grouping of tables where the craft was set up. We were a few minutes before it was supposed to start, but it had the feel of a room where people had been hanging out for a while. There were maybe twenty people, a diverse-looking group. As we stood there, unsure where to go, a smiling Black man wearing dangling plasticky rainbow heart earrings came over to welcome us.

"I'm Robert," he said. "You folks haven't been here before, have you? Important question—how do you feel about Perler beads?"

There were two clusters of people bead-making and talking animatedly with one another, and a few people looked up and smiled at us, but after we finished talking to Robert, Sunny led us past them to an empty table. Tubs of Perler beads were set out along with squares of parchment paper and a mismatched selection of irons, and someone had made a sample set of rainbow earrings like the ones Robert was wearing. Something about the way the papers were cut—clearly by hand, but also carefully—made my eyes well up. I think it was imagining someone taking that care for Sunny.

"Should we go sit with other people?" I said.

"Maybe in a little bit." Sunny pulled out one of the plastic pegboards and ran her finger through the beads. "So how come you're a bad friend?"

"You don't want to talk to anyone?"

"Yeah, I will. What were you saying earlier, though?"

I told her how my initial reaction to Chase hadn't been happiness for Grace, how even now I wished we didn't have to factor him in. It was funny thinking sometimes how much Sunny used to scare me before we were friends—part of the reason I told her everything was that I always trusted that our friendship would matter more to her than even the worst things I told her. "On a scale of one to ten, how guilty should I feel?"

"Like a negative four."

"Really?"

"I don't think we're required to, like, hardcore ship her and Chase just yet. He has to prove himself first. Also—" She made a short line of blue beads. "I feel like at least eighty percent of the guys who think they're in love with Grace couldn't tell you the first real thing about her. Like, they're like, *ooh, she's so cute and bubbly*, and they build some whole fantasy around that."

"Yeah, but it's not just that I'm worried he isn't good enough for her." Although I was; there was no one like Grace, and she deserved more than grocery-store roses by her locker. "It's also that—you know how it is when you have some specific hope about how something's going to go?"

"Yeah, I don't think you have to beat yourself up over not actively fantasizing about riding in a limo with Chase Hartley for Homecoming," she said. "You're just lowkey type A about some things, which is fine. Like—birthdays and stuff."

"I'm type A about birthdays? That makes me sound incredibly fun."

Sunny laughed. "Fun is overrated. You just always want to make sure everyone's happy. Seriously, Beth, don't worry so much. In fact, if anything, you should be pettier. Like, in life."

I didn't want to be pettier. I wanted to be open and generous and uncomplicated, welcomed and embraced by the world. I wanted to be, I guessed, more like Grace—as easy as Grace to love.

"Anyway," I said, "You didn't come here to talk about straight drama. You should go meet people."

She immediately pretended to focus on her beading. "Everyone's so much older."

People did look older, but not impossibly so. "What about those people over on the couch?"

"They're probably in their twenties. And they all know each other already, and also I'm sure they have more important things to talk about than my extremely bland high school life. I don't even know what I'd say."

It was so unlike her to be insecure. "But you were so excited to come. You shouldn't come all the way here and then not meet—"

"Actually, I think I'm ready to go," she said, pouring her beads back into the tub and standing up abruptly. "Ready?"

"Wait, Sun—"

"It's fine. I'll come another time. Come on."

A few people said goodbye as we were leaving, and I saw Robert register us walking out. He rose to catch up, but Sunny ignored him. In the car, I said, "Are you okay?"

"I'm fine." She made a face. "Ugh. I don't know what's wrong with me."

"Nothing's wrong with you at all. Was it not what you wanted?"

"No, it was exactly what I wanted. That's the thing."

"Well, it's hard to meet new people."

She handed me her phone to put on Google Maps—we always teased her for how she always got directions even to places she knew well in case there was traffic—and a message popped up, from her friend Dayna: *Hey Sun, I'm thinking of you. You got this. I'll check in w you after to hear how it went.*

"I had this really stupid argument with my mom last week," Sunny said, backing out of the parking space. "I've told her like three times what pansexuality is and the other day she was like, okay, well, why don't you just wait to see who you marry, and then it doesn't matter who else you like?"

I winced. "I'm sorry. What did you say?"

"Nothing. I tried explaining why that's not how anything works and then she was like, well, it doesn't matter now because you're not going to date anyone of any gender until you're thirty. I was like, okay, Ma, fine, my sexuality is I need to get into college. But it's been messing with me. Like, obviously being in a relationship or not doesn't change anything, and I know that, but then I also started spiraling over like—*does* it count if my life is basically indistinguishable from a straight person's life? I guess I just started worrying I was a fraud, or not queer enough, or something. And I told myself I'd magically fit in in the right queer space that wasn't our GSA and then everything would make sense, but then today was like, perfect, and I didn't even know what to say to anyone."

"They would've loved you," I said. "You should go back. They'd be lucky to have you. Anyplace would."

She made a grumbling noise, but it was tinged with affection. Still, the rest of the drive she was a little sad, so I was too. Every summer we went to Pride in SF with her—this year Brandon had flown home two days early from his family vacation to be there— and it was always electric and beautiful just to be there together, and I didn't feel useless in the way I did now. I wished I knew all the right things to say.

Or maybe my wish was bigger than that; maybe it was more about the pressing sense of insufficiency. I wanted her to have everything, and I wanted us to be home for her—not her non-queer friends or her in-person friends or her friends from home; her friends, full stop, without qualification. I wanted to always be enough.

For Thanksgiving, as we'd done the past six years, my mother and I went to Boston Market. Before we'd left, I'd spent ten minutes staring at my open closet, trying to decide whether it was worse to look like I'd just rolled out of bed or like I had actually gotten dressed up to go get takeout. *Oh, tough call,* Sunny said, when I messaged her and Grace about it. *I think dressed up.* My father usually went to Idaho for Thanksgiving. I'd texted him earlier that day with a picture of my common app, and I'd edited the picture so UC Berkeley was highlighted. He'd written back right away: *great news, keep me posted.* Then he added, *See you for Christmas Eve, if not sooner,* and all day I carried that around with me, the *or sooner* clanging against my heart.

My mother and I selected two servings of turkey and four side dishes. When we got home, I set the bag down on the table and started to open it, but my mother said, "Oh, Beth—let's at least put everything on plates."

I closed my eyes so that I wouldn't glare. "Why?"

"It'll look nicer. Here, bring the bag back into the kitchen. It'll feel more like Thanksgiving this way."

She plopped all the side dishes onto salad plates and arranged them around a mini pumpkin she'd bought the week before. She'd gotten a bottle of sparkling apple cider, and she poured some in wineglasses as we ate.

"I thought," she said, and cleared her throat, "that it would be nice to say what we're thankful for."

I chewed a piece of turkey. It was dry and salty, tough between my teeth.

"I'm thankful for a stable job and a roof over our heads and food," she said. "And for Asheville to look forward to. And most of all, I'm thankful for such a wonderful, beautiful daughter." She smiled at me. "A beautiful daughter almost in college."

I swallowed the turkey and reached for my cider. My face was burning. I should have watched more carefully when my father was still here, I told myself. I should have watched exactly what she'd done to drive him out, so that I could make sure I never made the same mistakes.

"What about you, Beth?" she said softly. "What are you thankful for?"

I looked at her smooth, pale face and tried to picture my father looking at her the same way, noting her short eyelashes and the way her skin without blush was flat and shadowy, the wrinkles forming under her eyes. I felt something ugly bubbling up. "My friends."

"Ah," she said. "Of course. You're a very good friend to them too." She studied a few stray kernels of corn on her plate and pushed at them with her fork, then looked up at me.

"Your friends . . . ," she said, and her voice trailed off as though inserting a comma, beginning a list.

I stood, pushing my chair back so it probably scratched the hardwood floor. "I'm finished," I announced, though half my plate was still uneaten. "Thank you for dinner."

She let me go. Later, I heard her washing the dishes downstairs. Much later, when she was in her room for the night, I was hungry and came downstairs to the kitchen, and when I opened the refrigerator I saw she'd neatly piled all my leftovers in a covered bowl and had affixed a little Post-it note on top that said *Beth*. I stuck everything in the microwave and burned my tongue on my first bite.

THE SUNDAY AFTER Thanksgiving was Brandon's eighteenth birthday, and for the rest of our lives I would think of that day as a curtain, coming down and dividing our lives into two acts.

It was a beautiful fall day, all the Liquidambar trees lining the streets and the grapevines up in the foothills blazing red against the sharp blue of the sky, and in the morning Grace and I spent two hours drawing and cutting out clothes that looked like Brandon's for dinosaur figurines to wear. In eighth grade, we'd found *The Adventures of King Brandon and Prince T-Rex* in Brandon's room: a comic book he'd made when he was six, in which he was, basically, stronger/more powerful/a better basketball player than anyone else (dinosaur or human) in the land, and we'd been so amused by it that Sunny had made copies for the rest of us. We used to pull them out sometimes at lunch to read aloud while Brandon glowered at us. We'd made little King Brandon and Prince T-Rex figurines by copying the drawings onto Shrinky Dinks, and each year on his birthday we decorated his locker with them. One year, King Brandon and the dinosaurs were eating a box of cookies Grace had baked; another year we did a beach theme, with real sand in a tray. Tomorrow, the dinosaurs would pretend to be Brandon: they would listen to the music he liked, and wear clothes like his, and we were going to get supplies at the restaurant tonight, like chopsticks and napkins with the restaurant's name, at his birthday dinner.

This year Brandon wanted to eat Korean barbecue because he was doing some kind of complicated, protein-heavy diet, so we were going to go to Gajung Jip. Brandon was driving Jason and me. He picked me up first, and when I got in he said, "Congrats on being my inaugural I-can-drive-people-around-now ride," and then we drove the seven minutes to Jason's. At Jason's, the door was open a crack. We knocked and no one answered, but Jason was expecting us, so we pushed the door open and went in.

When we entered I felt my shoulders tightening and my arms pulling in like a shield across my chest. Maybe it was the vibrations in a raised, strained voice, or maybe rage has its own frequency and physical texture. Or maybe I saw Jason and his father faced off the way they were, in the living room, before I even fully registered it.

Even now, I remember the way it smelled in their home that day, a mix of meat and white pepper and bleach; I remember the pile of newspapers lying by the doorway next to the shoes piled around the shoe rack, the television playing a Mandarin station in the background. I remember that it was cold inside their house and that I wondered distractedly if they, like my mother, refused to turn on the heater, and I remember the jeans and pale yellow sweater Jason was wearing, the sweatpants and faded black long-sleeved shirt his father wore. And I remember how it felt like my organs were being wrung and twisted, a trembling that emerged from somewhere inside and radiated all through me.

Jason had turned to look when we entered, but Mr. Tsou hadn't, and for a moment absent of logic, I thought, *Maybe they didn't notice us.* His father was breathing heavily, a raspy sound, and when he spoke to Jason again, his voice was careening out of control, almost yelling. He stepped closer to Jason, who took a step back.

His father broke off. There was a moment of suspension, a moment of waiting, when it seemed as though things might veer off their set trajectory—as though his father might still calm himself, might leave, or might instead erupt. I felt the weight of awful possibility.

Brandon felt it too. Carefully, he stepped forward and positioned himself so that he was in front of me, and just after he did, Jason said, "Dad—" his voice high and afraid, and then Mr. Tsou struck him, hard, across the face. Jason stumbled backward, his feet making a syncopated, staccato thudding sound on the hardwood floors, before he lost his balance and fell. His father lifted his foot and kicked Jason in the side so that Jason crumpled, the way a sheet of newsprint catching fire seizes and pulls in on itself.

He stood over Jason for a moment, breathing hard, his hands clenched in fists. And then it was as though he saw Jason for the first time, lying twisted on the floor like that and breathing fast and shallow: Mr. Tsou started, leaning backward, and a look came across his face as though he might be sick. He turned away from his son and left. We listened to the sound of his footsteps falling down the hallway, a door closing somewhere in the back of the house, and then there was a terrible quiet.

My throat seemed to be catching each breath halfway down so that every attempt at oxygen died somewhere in my throat, and I was growing a little light-headed. The room was wavering around me, arcing and flattening itself out like a cat.

Brandon composed himself and recovered before I did. He reached down and offered his hand, but Jason pushed himself up and stood, unsteadily, on his own. He breathed through his nose, each breath shaky, like his whole chest was trembling. I thought of all those joints and tendons and veins under his skin, how precisely they were arranged and held together.

"Jason," Brandon said, "are you okay?"

"Yep," Jason said flatly. He coughed twice and then reached up and wiped his forehead; he was sweating, his skin gleaming, and there was a red mark like an ember glowing on his face. "I'm fine."

"That was fucked up," Brandon said desperately. "You aren't—you're not hurt? Or—"

"I'm fine."

"No, really, that—" Brandon laughed nervously, a strangled, high-pitched *hhhhuhhh* sound I'd never heard from him before. "Jason, I had no idea it was that b—"

"Let's just go," Jason said, impatiently. He straightened and strode toward the door. "We're going to be late."

We steadied ourselves, remembered that Sunny and Grace would be waiting at Gajung Jip. And I thought—wildly, graspingly—that maybe he was all right after all. Maybe he was used to this; maybe it was something, like extreme temperatures, to which you could learn to adapt. Because we'd seen Jason slip away before, pull back inside himself, and he wasn't doing that now. He wanted to go with us, to be around us. Somehow we would make this all right.

Walking outside, it was like small earthquakes kept erupting underneath us; my legs kept threatening to give out, and my balance was wrecked, like the earth wasn't holding steady where I needed it. When I glanced backward at the house, I couldn't focus, and I would have sworn I saw a movement in the curtains.

In the car, Brandon clutched the steering wheel with both hands until his knuckles went pale and said, "Jason, I should've—I don't know. I should've done—"

"What restaurant are we going to again?" Jason said. "I'm kind of in the mood for Japanese."

"That sounds great," I said quickly. I was sitting in the back, and I leaned forward toward him, but he didn't turn around. "I'll call Sunny and Grace and have them meet us. Where do you—is there anywhere you'd want to go?"

"I don't really care."

"There's that sushi place by school," Brandon said. "Or we could get ramen, maybe, or whatever you want. That izakaya. Anything."

"That's fine," Jason said. "Anything's fine."

Brandon met my gaze in the rearview mirror. I'd never seen the same fear in his face. "Ebisu?" he said.

"That's perfect," I said, when it was clear Jason wouldn't answer. Grace and Sunny were probably at Gajung Jip already— it was about ten minutes south—and I texted Grace. *Can you meet us at Ebisu instead? I'll explain later.* I knew Grace wouldn't mind, but Sunny might. It was incomprehensible that their lives, these past moments, had gone on as usual, that they had no idea what had happened. I wondered how many times Jason had thought that about all of us.

Sunny and Grace were already at Ebisu when we got there. By then the mark on Jason's face had faded so that he looked more flushed than injured, but Grace peered at him and said, "Jason, what happened to—"

"Whoa, Grace, new sweater?" Brandon said quickly, loudly, even though she was wearing a wide-striped hoodie that had been one of her staples for years.

Grace looked at him strangely. "No?"

Our waitress, a pretty, soft-spoken Japanese girl several years older than us, led us to a table near the front. Jason studied the menu in front of him, quiet, his hands folded in his lap. I watched him breathe, watched the steady, measured rise and fall of his chest. I thought how if he were badly hurt or if he were going to have some sort of breakdown, he wouldn't be breathing like that; it would be raspy, or erratic. We were good for him, I told myself—he was drawing strength from having us near.

"So why'd we have to switch restaurants?" Sunny asked after we'd ordered, looking across the table at the three of us. She and Grace were seated on the other side like an interview panel. "Brandon, I thought you wanted barbecue."

"Japanese just sounded really good," Brandon said quickly.

Sunny raised her eyebrows. "Maybe next time it'll sound good before we've already put our names in at Gajung Jip."

"Yeah," Brandon said, "maybe it will."

The waitress returned with steaming bowls of noodles. When she set Jason's in front of him, he frowned. I saw she'd brought him tempura shrimp udon instead of the vegetarian he'd ordered.

Jason shoved himself back from the table and slammed his palms against the edge so hard that the teacups rattled and spilled. All around us, heads swiveled to look.

"Are you fucking *kidding* me?" he snapped.

We stared. Under the table I felt a knee knock against mine. I knew without looking it was Brandon's.

"It's okay," I said quickly to the waitress. "He can have mine." I'd ordered the vegetable udon too, and I slid it across the table to Jason. My hands trembled, and the broth sloshed over the edge. "Jason, here."

The waitress looked shaken. She started to say something, but Brandon said, "No, no, it's fine. It's fine." He smiled weakly at her and she hurried off, glancing back over her shoulder once.

Both Sunny and Grace were still staring at Jason. *I should have told them,* I thought, *somehow,* and I tried to catch Sunny's eye, to signal that she shouldn't say a word to him. But Jason was staring back at her as though he was daring her to say something.

She leaned forward toward him, her eyes narrowed. "Jason, what's wrong with you?"

Brandon said, quietly, "Sun." He tried to shake his head at her, but she wasn't looking at him.

Jason said, coldly, "What?"

"What do you mean *what?*"

"I mean," Jason said, "are you saying you take issue with something, Sunny?"

"What do you—"

"Really, Sunny?" Jason said. He was smiling, a scary tight smile, his eyes hard. "*You* of all people are going to try to tell me off right now?"

"Aaaanyway," Brandon said. He tried to laugh.

"No, really," Jason said. He pushed himself back from the table again and crossed his arms over his chest, and his expression, the clench in his jaw and his narrowed eyes, were so hostile that for a moment he looked just like his father.

"I want to hear this, Sunny," he said. "I want to hear how you—*you*, of all people—can try to take some kind of high road here. Really, tell me."

"Jason—"

"Or maybe you want to talk more about Mike Low's dead brother making it harder for you to get into college? You know why people always say you're such a bitch, Sunny?"

It felt like someone had injected me with ice, or liquid nitrogen; I felt a sharp cold leaking through me. Sunny looked frozen too. "Jason, what's—"

"Does anyone else see the irony here?" he demanded. He stretched out his arms like a question mark. I couldn't look at him. I wanted to find Sunny's hand under the table. "Does anyone want to tell me I'm wrong? Because I think we all know Sunny—"

"You guys!" Grace said suddenly. "There's a Band-Aid in my soup!"

I wrested my gaze from Jason and Sunny and turned to Grace, blinking. It felt like I imagined it would to manually shift gears, to jerk mechanics into place. Grace held up the Band-Aid with her chopsticks; it was wrapped in a hollow ring, used.

"Man, disgusting," Brandon said, and his voice cracked.

"Wow, Brandon," I said. I tried to keep my voice light and mocking, though I wasn't someone who had ever been good at teasing and perhaps now I was coming across badly, not jokingly at all. "How old are you turning—thirteen?"

I'd startled him; his eyes opened wider, a little. But he forced a smile and a quick, barking laugh. "Beth, I give you a ride, and you break my heart," he said. He held his fists next to each other in front of his chest and pantomimed snapping something—his heart, I supposed—in two.

Sunny said nothing. I willed her not to cry.

The moment was long over, was beginning to fade into another, but I said, "Yeah, you know me." After that none of us could think of anything to say, and the quiet settled in around us like ash. I looked sideways at Brandon. Beads of sweat had broken out on his forehead, just below his hairline. Across the restaurant, the door opened, and we heard the little bell above the door jingle.

Jason stood. His chair screeched across the floor as he pushed it back. "Excuse me," he said, and for a brief, terrible moment I thought he was going to leave, that we'd have to follow him, to force ourselves on him, but we watched him go to the back of the restaurant toward the restrooms instead. When he was out of earshot, Brandon let out a long breath, his shoulders slumping. To Grace, he said, "Thank God you had that Band-Aid in your soup."

"It was mine," she said. "I dropped it in when no one was looking."

Brandon laughed, a little hysterically. Sunny didn't laugh with him.

"Sun," I said, "are you okay?"

She swiveled her head toward me, but her eyes didn't quite follow. "Is that what you all think of me?"

"Sunny, no, you know better," Grace said quickly. She reached up and brushed Sunny's hair across her forehead, the gesture soothing and motherly. "I don't know what's wrong with Jason, but you can't listen to—"

"I know people say that about me," Sunny said, slowly, as though she hadn't heard Grace. "But you guys *know* me. I thought Jason—"

"Sun, when we went over to Jason's, his dad—things were really bad." Brandon swallowed, then looked at the table. It was selfish, but I wanted him to keep talking. If he didn't, then Sunny would turn to me, would expect me to fill in, and I didn't feel like I was getting enough air to talk. "He didn't mean it. Don't take it personally."

She surprised me; she sat back, and said, quietly, "Okay." Watching her close her eyes and breathe deeply, her breaths a little jagged, I reminded myself that she and Jason had been friends longer even than I'd known them—that friendships didn't happen by accident, and that whatever reasons Sunny and Jason were friends already still held true. She wiped her hands on her napkin, then blotted at her eyes. I reached across the table to pat her hand.

Grace said, "Is he okay, Brandon? Do you want me to call my mom?"

But then we glanced up and Jason was walking back toward us, and my heart clanged like a bell against my rib cage, and I said, "We'll tell you later."

Things were better when Jason came back; for the rest of our meal, he stirred at his soup and smiled vaguely at things the rest of us said. It was Grace who carried the conversation that day, chattering about how impossible it was to shop for her little brother for Christmas. Sunny was quieter than usual, but I saw how she made an effort, forcing herself to laugh. And I loved her for showing that sort of grace without yet knowing why it was being asked of her.

We finished eating. Most of us had barely touched our meals, except for Jason, who had eaten the entire contents of his bowl, even the sweet potato, which I knew he hated. After we paid the check, Brandon lingered a moment, and as the rest of us were walking away I saw him slip a few more bills under our receipt.

In the car, Jason closed his eyes and leaned his head back against the headrest. It was almost suffocating being there, the silence. When we'd pulled out of the parking lot and back onto the road, Jason murmured, his eyes still closed, "I'm sorry."

"What? Why?" I said quickly, and at the same time Brandon said frantically, "No, no, nothing to be sorry about."

Jason didn't answer. I hoped that he knew we understood, that this wasn't something he'd hold against himself.

"Jay, do you want to crash at my place tonight?" Brandon offered. "If you wanted to—"

"No, I shouldn't. But thanks." It was the last thing he said that night except for *Thanks for the ride* when Brandon pulled into his driveway.

"Here," Brandon said, "we'll walk you." Jason paused, but he let us; we got out of the car and walked on either side of him to the front step. We watched him unlock his door and go inside, and we watched the light in the entryway go on and then switch off again.

Just before getting into the car, I looked back toward the house. I don't know what I was expecting to see, but for some reason I felt uneasy about it being there behind me, something like how my mother warned me once, when I was younger and we'd gone to Santa Cruz, *Never turn your back on the ocean.* I twisted my head to look over my shoulder, and for just a moment, I saw Jason's mother with her face nearly pressed to the window, watching the two of us make our way to the car. She looked small there, swallowed by the window and the fabric of the curtain, and something about the way she'd been watching us made me think she'd been home listening all that time.

———•◦•———

After Jason disappeared inside, Brandon backed out of the drive-way, drove the length of three houses, and then pulled over and turned off his car. The silence swirled in around us and descended, coming to settle on our shoulders.

I wasn't ready to go home yet. There was still so much for the four of us to talk about together. But Grace had curfew, and Sunny's parents had already called asking where she was before we left the restaurant, and my mother had sent me a message, too (*You should get a good night's sleep before school starts again!*—which seemed like a missive from another universe altogether).

"God," Brandon said at last. "We shouldn't have gone in." He turned his head toward the window, the tendons in his neck jut-ting out. "Or I should've—God, I can't believe I just stood there."

"You couldn't have done anything, Brandon. If Jason wanted your help, he would've said so." But I heard again how much it had taken for Jason to say *Dad*, and I knew it wasn't true; he couldn't have asked anything of us at all. "Do you think it's like that all the time?"

"It didn't feel like that was the first time, did it?"

My hands were shaking, and I pressed them together. I closed my eyes. When I opened them again, Brandon was still staring out the window.

"Jason's dad thinks he's wasted his shot at college," Brandon said, mildly, like we were discussing a news article over lunch, and I was jolted—I'd forgotten, in the moment, that of course Brandon understood everything Jason's father was saying. "He thinks Jason's been selfish the past four years. He thinks he's a failure."

"He thinks that about *Jason?* How can he say—"

"My dad can be like that too," Brandon said. "I mean, I don't know, you come here and you've made all these sacrifices and you want to prove yourself and you've worked hard your whole life, and if your kid doesn't live up to that, it's like, what's your problem?" His voice was very flat. "It fucks you up to hear it, but I get it, you know? But my dad's—he's not like that."

"Do you think Jason's mad at us?" I asked.

Brandon shook his head. "I don't think so," he said. "I just wish . . ." He trailed off.

I asked, "What?"

"Nothing," he said. "It just—God." Without warning, he balled his hand into a fist and slammed it so hard into his dashboard that it sounded as though something—plastic, bone, I wasn't sure—had cracked. The sound reverberated off the walls of his car, and I felt it pass through me like a current, like a finger grazing across a power strip's exposed prong.

"Brandon," I said, "you're bleeding."

He looked down at the line of blood trickling from his knuckles. "Fuck," he said, calmly, as though it were the requisite response. I handed him a tissue from my purse, and he pressed it to his knuckle. I watched the little splotch of blood seep through.

We stayed in his car like that for a long time, neither of us speaking. Brandon wadded up the tissue and stuffed it in one of the side pockets on the door, and I thought he might say more. But he was quiet, and it occurred to me to wonder if he was waiting for me to talk too. At last, he said, "It's late."

It was. He started the car and pulled back onto the road, the engine detonating the quiet. We drove past all the other long driveways, the lights shining from all the huge, looming homes, and when we passed the strip mall with the tutoring center and real estate office on Via de Valle, there were still cars in the parking lot, and it was inconceivable that in the outside world nothing had changed. When we passed the row of Victorian homes off Willys Drive, I glanced at Brandon's hands on the wheel; his knuckle was still bleeding. I drew in a deep breath.

"You know," I said, "I think for Jason, just knowing that you're there makes a huge difference, and—"

"That's not enough," Brandon said tiredly. "You know it's not enough."

He made a left turn onto my street. As we passed under a streetlight, the yellow glow flickered in through the window, and in that quick flash of illumination I thought I saw his eyes pooling, small streams reflected beneath them. But it was dark, and I was still reeling, and so I never was quite sure.

The four of us had agreed to talk the next morning, and we met at Brandon's at six. In my jacket pocket, I had the dinosaurs, although I knew already we wouldn't use them today, that it wouldn't feel right. We were all quiet, bleary-eyed from the hour, and Brandon shut his door and motioned for us to keep our voices down so his parents wouldn't hear. In his room, there were clothes strewn everywhere and notebooks scattered, like always—"Do you just, like, randomly strip wherever you're standing?" Sunny had said to him once—and today the mess was somehow comforting. Brandon looked awful, though, dark circles ringing his eyes. I knew I did too.

We'd all been up late messaging. It had started as a group chat minus Jason, so Brandon and I could tell them the whole story, which we'd done haltingly, clumsily, and then when Sunny and Grace had gone to sleep Brandon had called me.

"Just checking on you," he'd said. "You think you'll sleep at all?"

"No, probably not."

He'd sighed. "Yeah, same. You doing all right, though?"

I didn't bother answering; he knew the answer anyway. "We should've done a sleepover or something," I'd said, even though there was zero chance any of our parents would've allowed it on a school night. But being alone here in my room in the dark of night was physically painful—my chest hurt. Already I was dreading hanging up.

"You want me to stay on the line?" he'd offered. "I can just go on speakerphone and be here in the background while you try to sleep. Virtual sleepover. I'll probably just binge-watch Netflix anyway."

I had felt completely alone before in my life and I would never forget what it was like, but my friends were the reason I could sometimes almost forget. It should've been Jason he was waiting up for, not me, but the night felt bearable knowing he was there, the murmur of his show coming softly through the phone until the call had dropped around three.

"So," Brandon said now, wadding up a shirt next to him on the floor and then sending it flying toward his closet, "what should we do?"

I had been awake the whole night agonizing over that. Everything you do, and everything you don't do, is all woven into the narrative of your life; each choice you make sets the future in motion, even (and perhaps especially) if you don't feel it at the time. Each action or inaction is a thread pulled into the greater whole. Dozens of times all night, I'd started to message Jason, and then stopped myself. If I wrote to him and he didn't reply—it would kill me. It was better to not try.

"We'll just have to really be there for him," Grace murmured. She yawned hugely, and then rubbed her eyes. "We'll have to be real friends for him. I'm sure he needs friends right now."

Sunny shot her a look that was equal parts impatient and affectionate. Brandon said, "Okay, but aside from that—I mean, should we tell anyone?"

I said, "Who would we tell?"

"I don't know. I was thinking about it all night. Some adult?"

I wasn't the kind of student who was close to any of her teach-ers. I could've told my mother, I suppose, but what could she have done? I imagined her indecision, the hapless, feckless worry that would exude from her, and it felt worse than doing nothing.

"I'll probably tell my mom," Grace said.

"Don't tell your mom yet," Brandon said. "Just—wait on it, okay? What if she wants to do something about it?"

"Did you tell your parents?" I asked him.

He shook his head. "They kind of know Jason's parents."

I said, "Should we call the police?"

"You can't call the police," Sunny said immediately. "We're, like, white-adjacent, maybe, but I still would never call the cops on a POC. You think they're on your side? How do you picture that going, exactly?"

I hadn't thought of it like that. My father had called the police to our house once, when a neighbor crashed their car into our mailbox, and they'd been friendly and polite. One had given me a See's lollipop. "Right," I said quickly, embarrassed. "True."

"Maybe it doesn't matter whose side they're on," Brandon said. "There's no way what happened wouldn't count as assault, and—"

"Well, my parents go too far sometimes too," Sunny said. Sunny fought with her parents all the time. When it was really bad, she would storm out and wind up at my house or Grace's and spend the night because she refused to go back home, and I'd sit up with her when she was too upset to sleep. She had a much older brother who'd bought a multimillion-dollar home in Palo Alto at twenty-five, and she'd told us she thought her parents had always wanted another son just like him. "It's definitely messed up, but I would never want anyone to call the cops on them. I promise you Jason doesn't want his dad getting arrested."

Brandon said, quietly, "You weren't there, Sun."

"Okay, well, what do you think your parents would do if someone called nine-one-one on them?" she said. "Can you picture that going even remotely well? Is there any universe where their response is *Oh, okay, it's clear we messed up, and now we're committed to being better going forward?* They'd flip out, right? And who are they going to take it out on?"

"I mean, maybe if they—I don't know—"

"If they what? Arrest his dad? That sounds like a great solution for someone with an anger problem. What happens when he comes back home?"

"What about, like, firefighters?" Grace said. "You know, the ones where you can drop off a baby at the fire station."

Sunny snorted. "Okay, and then what—they sic their fire hoses on his dad? What do you think happens when you call someone? Like, what exactly is the endgame here?"

"The endgame is for this not to happen to him again," I said, and there was a sharpness in my voice. I tried to soften it. "What about Mr. Irving?"

Sunny made a face. "He's probably some kind of mandated reporter or something. Plus, Jason would still have to face him three times a week afterward. You know he'd hate that."

"He knows Jason, though. Maybe he could talk—"

"Mr. Irving is great and all, but he's—" She looked to Brandon for help.

"Right," Brandon said. "He's just not—he wouldn't understand," and too late I realized what they meant. Inheriting my father's face, my father's name, meant I could sometimes forget or fail to notice things they couldn't, like that overconfident way Mr. Irving would plunge ahead when he couldn't pronounce someone's name because he never asked first, and how once when Seoyun Kang corrected him, he'd said jovially, "I might never get that right!" and then never even tried; how sometimes if we weren't in our assigned seats, holding our instruments, he'd mix us up, or how he'd sometimes slip into those same coded words our white teachers used—the *pressures at home*, they'd say. The *cultural differences*.

"Right," I said quickly, and I was ashamed that I hadn't seen it that way sooner. It wasn't the point of the conversation, I knew that, but that circle drawn around them, me outside it with my naive ideas about telling Mr. Irving or calling 911—it stung.

"What about his sister?" Grace said.

Brandon made a face. "Evelyn?"

"They're close, right?"

"Yeah," I said. Evelyn was at Berkeley now. She and Jason were just eighteen months apart, and she'd graduated the year before, so we used to see her a lot at school. I found her incredibly intimidating. She was beautiful—she looked a lot like Jason—and aggressively good at things, like school and singing and public speaking. Also, no matter how many times I'd interacted with her, I could never tell whether or not she knew who I was. She was the only person in Jason's family he ever talked about. "Maybe we could tell her and she could talk to him."

"Talk to who," Brandon said, "their dad?"

"To Jason," Grace said. "Do you think he'd tell her on his own?"

"Yeah, I doubt it. What's there to say? She probably knows, anyway. It didn't really feel like that was the first time."

"Also, Brandon's scared of Evelyn," Sunny said. I think it was supposed to be a joke, or at least said jokingly, but she couldn't quite make the words come out light enough.

"She's definitely scary," he said. "But also I just don't really see it solving anything."

"So I guess—what do we think's going to happen?" Grace said. "What are we solving? Like, do we think his dad's going to really hurt him? In a dangerous way? And we're trying to stop him? Or—what?"

"That's not—that's not really the point," Brandon said. "It doesn't have to get worse for it to be awful. It's already awful."

"But do you think it's actively *dangerous?*"

Brandon looked at me. I knew he was thinking what I was—that of course it was dangerous but also that the word felt all wrong there, that our whole conversation felt so sterile and lifeless held up against last night.

"Honestly—maybe not," he said. "But it's hard to say. And anyway, I just don't think that matters as a standard."

"Okay, well, then, I think—" Grace started. She cleared her throat. "I just think maybe we're making too big a deal out of this. I mean—maybe it's not like it happens all the time or maybe it's not like this huge thing that always happens. And everyone gets mad sometimes, and—"

"You've got to be shitting me," Brandon said. "Maybe we're making too big a *deal* of this? Grace, you weren't there."

"Well, I was there at dinner when he blew up."

"What's your point?"

"My point is that was really awkward, but now it's over. So maybe whatever happened—maybe it's better to just not dwell on it. Was it really *that* bad?"

Grace always liked easy things, the world scrubbed off and sanitized before it was handed to her. I knew that about her, and it was even comforting sometimes, but it would take me a while before I forgave her saying that.

All the same, though, I didn't like the expression on Sunny's face. Brandon said, "It was worse. The hell, Grace, seriously? It was horrible. I can't believe you'd say that."

"I'm not saying it wasn't bad. I'm just saying maybe now it's over, and we don't have to sit here talking about whether we're going to call the police. Maybe we can just try to be there for him and try to be the kind of friends he needs right now. That's all I'm saying."

"You don't think that's exactly what we're trying to do?" Sunny said.

Grace put up her hands. "I just think—"

"Okay, well, what you're thinking—"

Don't be angry at her, I pleaded silently with Sunny and Brandon, even though I was maybe a little angry myself. We couldn't afford a fracture between us right now.

"But it's basically what you're saying, isn't it?" Grace said. "That it's not bad enough to where you'd want to call the police. So I'm saying, if that's true, let's just try to be his friends."

That wasn't what we were saying, of course. What we were saying was that there weren't options that felt like they fit into the situation; there weren't resources or adults who we felt we could trust. Which wasn't a measure of severity at all; it was just a reflection of the way the rules weren't built for us, the world not designed for us. It was terrible, and we could do nothing. There was nothing for us to do.

JUST AFTER I'd been accepted to BAYS in eighth grade, my parents' fighting had started to take on a new tenor. It was different than at Jason's—no one touched one another; it was like force fields around each of us—and it had its own presence in the house, like a sibling. I would wake up each morning with a stomachache.

My friends had all known one another a long time, but I was still new then; my friendship with them felt tenuous, and it was in the midst of that fighting that I first went to one of their houses. I had a group project with Brandon and Jason, and the three of us went to Brandon's after school.

His house was on a quiet side street backdropped by the hills, and his room was messy in what felt like a very boyish way to me. When we went in, he swiped at a mass of basketball shorts on his bed and said cheerfully, "Sorry about the mess," even though I didn't think he really was. He opened a Spotify playlist on his laptop, and then his mother called him from work, and while he sat there saying *uh-huh, yes, no,* he opened *Faster Than Light* and started playing, and my stomach flipped over.

He hung up. Onscreen, a hole was blown into the side of his ship, and his movements got more frantic and exaggerated. "I always die," he said, ducking and swerving like it would help somehow. "We're losing oxygen."

"Sometimes you can seal them off into a different part of the ship," I said.

Brandon looked up, startled. "You play *FTL?*"

"I—play it sometimes."

He died, turned all the way around, and appraised me, a game-day grin spreading across his face. "You been holding out on us, Claire? What are you, some kind of gamer girl?"

"Um—" My stomach twisted like a skein of yarn.

"Because that's awesome. Just so we're clear."

"I'm not very good. I play sometimes with my dad, that's all."

"Jump in," Brandon said.

"I—that's all right."

"Come on," he said, smiling, and I tried frantically to decide whether *I'd rather not* felt like too assertive a thing to reply. Finally, I repeated, "I'm really not that good."

"Don't be so modest," he said. "Come on. Let's see what you've got."

"Well—okay," I said. "I can try. I might die, though." I'd tried to hold my voice steady, but I'd slipped a little at the end, and Brandon's smile never wavered, but Jason—something made me think he'd caught it.

"Come save me." Brandon slid his keyboard over to me. It made a scratching sound across his desk the way it did when my father did the same thing.

Sometimes, growing up, my father had acted like dads did in books or movies—he'd bring home trinkets for me, or he'd come to my shows or back-to-school nights or take us hiking at Sanborn Park. Mostly, though, he played video games.

He could slip so effortlessly in—it took seconds—and then he was gone from us the rest of the night. We could never hold him the way his screen did. He'd play all weekend and all evening, sometimes skipping dinner. Sometimes my mother would ask him to play less and he'd go cold and quiet, but he'd do it for a few days, and they'd argue the whole time. And then he'd go back to playing and my mom would watch, a tightness like a mask over her face, and he'd pretend not to notice her. Or maybe he really didn't notice; maybe the screen's pull on him was that strong. When you tried to talk to him while he was playing, his voice was louder and brighter, and his answers to you never quite made sense. Once I was telling him about a coding lesson we'd done at school—I'd thought he'd like it; I'd been excited to tell him—and my mother said quietly, judgment seeping from her tone, "Can you put that down and listen to her?"

He liked obscure, process-oriented games where you built something, a house or a rocket ship or an army. The summer before I started BAYS, he'd played *Don't Starve*, and that was the game I always thought of as a turning point. My father despised what he called girl toys—dolls, princess things, anything overtly feminine—and wanted me to be a devoted gamer instead. But I was clumsy and lacked the instincts, and my mind wandered. I couldn't lose myself in all the false worlds the way he could. He would flinch at each of my mistakes, his voice rising, until he'd commandeered the keyboard again and I stood next to him, inadequate and cast out. But when we'd played *Don't Starve*, something had happened. We were trying to defend ourselves against the hounds that appeared periodically when I'd said, "If we led them to the Treeguard, would they attack each other while we escaped?"

My father had stared at me. "Beth," he said, and the way he'd said my name was like an embrace. "That is a *stellar* idea."

Everything changed after that. He bought a small monitor he spent hours setting up in my room, and he made a Twitch channel so we could livestream ourselves: a father-daughter gamer team. When I was good enough, we'd go live. And in the midst of all their fighting, that would be the thing, unlikely as it seemed, that would hold us together. If I could live up to the dreams he had for me, it would keep him rooted here with us.

Faster Than Light was one of the games I had struggled with. There were so many moving parts to keep track of, and the rebel forces were relentless; you had to make decisions and make them quickly, and I kept losing the crew or the ship.

Brandon was still multiple waypoints from the Federation, and he'd lost some crew members in the blast. I tried to get the survivors all to another part of the ship to seal it off so they wouldn't suffocate; then I could send them out to attack. But I was still frantically trying to find a way to make repairs when there was another weapon strike, and I died.

I sat back heavily. I was sweating. It was just—with Brandon and Jason watching, it was so much pressure. I wasn't cut out to do this for a live audience. My father wanted this so badly, I knew, but I was going to let him down.

"Sorry," I said. My voice came out strangled. "I'm not good at—"

"Whoa, whoa," Brandon said, grinning. "It's fine, Beth. I would've died anyway. Here, try again."

"It's okay."

"No, come on, I'm impressed you even got that far. Let's try it."

I felt like I might throw up. "No, really, that's all right."

"Just go back to—"

Jason gave him the tiniest shake of his head, almost imperceptible, but Brandon saw it and went quiet right away. He reached out and pulled his keyboard back.

All the muscles in my chest squeezed together. This was just a game to him; I'd made too big a deal out of nothing. "I didn't mean—"

"Hey," Jason said abruptly, reaching out and kicking Brandon in the calf, "you got anything to eat?"

"Yeah, probably."

"Can you go look?"

"Yeah, yeah." Brandon got up, abandoning the game. A few moments later, we heard the refrigerator door open.

"The thing about Brandon," Jason said mildly, reaching for Brandon's mouse and closing the game, "is you can always just tell him to shut up if you don't want to talk about something." He didn't look at me, and when I replayed that moment later it was that part that struck me. Because if he had, it would've felt accusatory, or at the very least searching. I recognized that he was being careful with me. And I thought two things then: that Jason had understood that there were things I couldn't talk about, and that it was because there were things he didn't talk about either.

We were young, we didn't know each other all the way yet, and it was a small moment, and maybe one Jason didn't think of again. But if I had to pick a single moment when I first knew I loved him, it was that day.

Before Brandon's birthday, I would've said that rage in a person has to go somewhere—that it's not an element you can keep dormant inside you, shielded from the greater world. Because we were all enraged, at Jason's father and at a world that wasn't designed to protect us or give us options or a way out.

But at lunch that first day back, I looked down at the sandwich I was eating and thought how it would become the glucose flowing through my bloodstream, the amino acids that would form my cells, and what had happened with Jason felt that way too, as though it had become a physical part of me: tangible and permanent, a sharp cold feeling in the abdomen and a wavering of the heart, an extra weight to carry around like so many new cells. Some things don't spill over; instead you absorb them, and there's nowhere for them to go.

I would've done anything for him; any of us would have. But

we found ourselves doing very little. He didn't want to talk about it, that was obvious, but he also didn't want to, say, borrow notes or copy homework or go out at night or even snap at us, take his anger out on us, as he had with Sunny in the restaurant.

That evening, my phone on loud in case he called, I finally thought of something I could do for him. It was small, and it was frivolous. But I remembered how when we were freshmen we'd gone to watch the choir performance, because Evelyn was in it, and they'd done a truly haunting version of "Hallelujah" that Jason, who normally didn't love the song, had really liked. He'd mentioned a few times over the years that he'd always tried to find a violin version of the arrangement, but he never could. I knew he was still probably thinking about it because he'd mentioned it again just a month or so ago, when we'd heard the Jeff Buckley version playing at Squishy when we'd gone to get boba, and so that day I thought—what if I wrote it for violin and recorded it for him?

I found a video of the performance on YouTube, and all week I worked on it, first transcribing the arrangement as best I could for violin and then making a recording of it. At various points during the arrangement, there were as many as five different parts at the same time, and I played all of them, recording and then playing with my recording so I could eventually cover all five. Three nights in a row, I only got a few hours of sleep, and I almost didn't wake up in time for Wednesday breakfast at Grace's.

I finished the recording late that night, technically Thursday morning, the day before Homecoming. I wanted to give it to him in person—I wished I had some kind of tangible, physical version of it—and I wanted us to be alone, or at least as alone as you can ever be on a campus with two thousand people. The closest I could come was between first and second periods, when we always walked together. He was wearing his glasses instead of contacts that day, which usually meant he was tired, and it made his jaw and cheekbones look more angular. Sometimes being close to him made me feel a kind of physical unraveling, like parts of me came loose and I felt fluid, like magma. It felt then like if he brushed against me, or leaned into me, I would ignite, but he never did. I was always nervous he would notice. But also, I guess, I was nervous that he never would, that it would be a secret I'd have to keep forever.

We were already past the library when I finally worked up the courage to say, "I have something for you."

He raised his eyebrows. "Oh?"

"I, um, made something."

He gave me a little smile, one that might've been amused. "You made something?"

"Yeah. I'll send it to you." I took out my phone and forwarded him the email I'd sent myself with the file attached. It was always loud in these passing periods, all two thousand of us charging around the campus at once and that crush of overstuffed backpacks, but still I could hear my heartbeat in my ears. "It's—well, you can listen to it."

"Should I listen to it now?"

"If you want."

He pulled his phone from his pocket. Listening to it—it was too loud for me to hear his phone—his expression changed. "You made this?"

"Yeah."

"How did you even find it? I've been looking for this forever."

"I wrote the parts."

"You *wrote* it?" He listened a few more seconds, then he slipped his phone back into his pocket without finishing, and I knew he recognized it for the gesture it was. "It must have taken you forever."

"I wanted—"

There was something in his face that could have been wariness, or could have been a warning; I couldn't tell. My voice caught. I wanted things to be better for him. I wanted him to tell us when they weren't, and I wanted him to let us in; I wanted to do something, anything, for him. But I saw the way he went tense—if I said those things, they'd glance off him, come skittering back to me scraped and raw.

"I wanted you to have it," I said finally. "I thought you might like it."

"You really didn't have to do anything like that," he said. "This is—probably one of the nicest things anyone's ever done for me. So it figures it'd come from you." I forced a smile, and blinked a few times until I trusted myself not to cry.

I told myself maybe tomorrow night would mark a turning point—we could ride around all night in the limo together, and maybe, in our own private world that way, it would be different. He would feel all the ways we cared about him and, for the first time, open up.

All the things Jason kept from us—if it were me, I was certain I'd have to tell them to someone or they'd corrode me from the inside out. He never seemed to need people the way I always did, that bottomless gaping hole of need inside me. But I wanted him to need me, because the people who need you don't throw you out or leave you, because they can't.

I thought that, anyway. Maybe it was even partly true.

Jason was gone at lunch that day to finish a lab report. When the rest of us had gathered, squinting against the November sun, I said, "So what's our plan for tomorrow night?"

"Yeah, I don't think Jay wants to go to Homecoming," Brandon said.

Something twisted in my chest. "That's what he said?"

"What do you mean, he doesn't want to go?" Grace said. "People will be expecting him."

"I mean, they'll be expecting him to, what, smile for a couple pictures?" Brandon said. "You know he doesn't give a shit about that. I think the odds he wants to, like, get dressed up and pretend he's into it, plus ask his parents if he can go, are basically nil."

"We can just all not go, then," Sunny said. "If he doesn't want to, we can stay home and hang out together instead."

"Don't you have to go?" Grace said.

"I mean, they'll be kind of pissed if I don't, but what are they going to do? I hate Homecoming anyway."

I felt knots tie in my stomach, felt the night I'd been clinging to start to disintegrate. "It's just—I did get the limo already."

"You can cancel it, though, right?" Sunny said.

"Maybe—"

"Let's cancel it, then, yeah?" Brandon said.

I looked at Grace. "Do you think Chase—"

She made a face. "I guess I could tell Chase I can't go."

"You don't think he'll be upset?"

"I mean, probably he will be, but I'm sure if I explain—"

"No, you can't explain," Brandon said. "Just tell Chase you have a migraine or something."

"A migraine definitely makes it sound like I'm ghosting him."

"Make up something else, then."

"I'll feel so terrible."

"Yeah, but how much fun are you going to have anyway?" Sunny said. "If the rest of us don't go, and then what if something happens with Jason? I'm going to get a lot of shit from ASB for not going either, but, I mean, it is what it is."

"You don't think we should just go and then, I don't know, keep our phones on in case he calls? I mean, if something else happens, I don't know how much we could do anyway."

"That's not really the point," Brandon said. "I just don't think we should all go without him. And I think we should make it clear we're there if he needs us."

"Yeah—" Grace sighed. "Yeah, I guess I'll tell Chase I can't go. I just feel bad."

I called the limo company as soon as I got home that afternoon to cancel, but the man I spoke to said it wasn't possible—
that because it was less than forty-eight hours' notice, I would
be charged in full.

My heart flipped over inside my chest. "That's five hundred
dollars," I said. "But the deposit is only—"

"Sweetie, if you read the contract, you agreed to pay in full
with less than forty-eight hours' cancellation. You still want to
cancel? You're paying either way."

My hands were shaking when I hung up. Maybe Brandon
was wrong and Jason was still planning on going after all, so I
wouldn't cancel just yet. And if we didn't go—what would I do
with a five-hundred-dollar credit card bill? I wouldn't tell my
friends about it, I decided, and I would count it as a small sacrifice I could make for Jason. I'd find a way to pay; I was pretty sure
you had twelve months, it was just that the interest ballooned
while you waited and then you owed more. But Jason would
insist on paying me back if he knew, and certainly I couldn't take
his money for my mistake.

I was stopping by my locker after fourth period the next day
when I heard someone calling my name. When I turned to look,
Chase Hartley was loping after me.

"Hey," he said, when he caught up. "I wanted to talk to you.
You have a second?"

"Um, sure."

Chase reached up and pushed his cap back. He'd been moving
quickly, but he didn't seem at all winded. "So—did I do something to piss Grace off?"

Maybe the question shouldn't have caught me off guard, but it
did. "Oh," I said, stupidly, "what do you mean?"

"You heard she's ditching me tonight, right? You're her friend, so I figured you'd tell me why so I can make it up to her."

"Um—" I looked helplessly toward where the junior class officers had set up the Stress-Free Zone cart, with its free stress balls and Ziplocs of homemade glitter slime, in the quad. "I don't think it was you. It's just—something happened, kind of not to do with Grace, but we all have to—it's just something that came up."

"But like what came up?"

"I can't really say."

"What, Grace told you not to?"

"Um—did you try talking to her?"

"No, because I didn't want to sound like a jackass if I did something hella obvious to piss her off and had no idea. That's worse, right? When you're like, all good here, all cool, and someone has to spell it out for you."

I felt a stab of guilt. It would be one thing if he were rude or demanding or hostile, but he wasn't—he seemed sheepish, maybe, but also sweet, in a way that surprised me.

"I really don't think it was you," I said. "I mean—I *know* it wasn't. She was excited to go, and she thought your flowers were really sweet. It's just that—she was needed elsewhere."

He didn't bother to hide his skepticism. "She was needed elsewhere specifically tonight from seven to ten p.m.?"

"Not just tonight. A lot of times, but—including tonight. Are you still going to go, do you think? With your friends or anything?"

"Ah—nah, probably not. All right, well, I'll see you." Then he added, not quite matter-of-factly, as he was already turning to go, "I already got her a corsage."

I couldn't think of what to say in time, but maybe still he saw me look panicked. It seemed so much worse when boys or men were sad, people who, like Chase, probably didn't spend much time that way. So I almost told him how much Grace liked him, and I also almost told Grace he'd come to talk to me. But I worried maybe that would just push her closer to him, maybe it would make her change her mind about going that night, so I didn't, in the end.

All day I held out hope that maybe Jason did still want to go, but then all day he didn't mention it, and I was afraid to push him by bringing it up, especially since no one else was. After school, Sunny, Grace, and I went to Brandon's. We'd stay there all night, we decided (I told my mom I was at Sunny's), and we'd check in with Jason to see if he wanted to come too. Or if he was still planning on going to Homecoming, we'd all go. I kept watching the clock—if I didn't call by six, the limo would show up. I felt awful about the money going to nothing. Every winter, I gave as much as I could to the National Honor Society's canned food drive, and I felt sick thinking about how many cans the five hundred dollars could've bought.

Brandon had grabbed a bag of shrimp chips from the kitchen and one of the washed takeout-container-turned-Tupperwares of cut fruit that their cook had prepared and set them on the floor along with some juice boxes of chrysanthemum tea. I sat on the floor, leaning against his bed. His comforter was a generic dark plaid, probably something his mom had gotten at Costco, and it was soft against my cheek. Sunny sat across from me, our legs touching, occasionally making a show of sweeping articles of clothing out of the way. I pictured Jason alone in his house.

"You think we'll ever turn out like that?" Brandon looked up at the ceiling, stretched out on his bed. On the wall above him, there was a poster of Yao Ming and Jeremy Lin he'd put up in elementary school and never taken down. "Like his dad, I mean. It really gets me when I think about our parents having friends. Because then it's like, you know, that's going to be us someday."

"I don't think our parents have friends like we're friends,

though," Sunny said. "Their friends are kind of interchangeable. Someone to get dinner with, someone to have over for parties, all that."

"Do you think any of his dad's friends would say something to him?" I asked.

Brandon snorted. "Have you ever . . . met an adult?"

"If it were one of you guys—"

"It will never be one of us," Sunny said. "We won't turn out like that."

"Do you think his dad expected to turn out like that, though?" Brandon said. He was still staring up at the ceiling. "No one has kids thinking, *okay, great, someone I can treat like shit.* And it's not like it's always awful with them, you know? Sometimes his dad takes him to concerts or ball games or things. And if you ever talk to him, he comes off as a nice guy. His friends probably think he's pretty great."

"So, what, that excuses it?" Sunny said. "It's fine to commit a little domestic assault if every now and then—"

"Lay off, Sunny, come on," Brandon said sharply, sitting up so swiftly it made me jump. "You think that's what I think? You really think that?"

"Well, you just said—"

"I said what? I said it was fine to watch my best friend get roughed up while I just stood there like an asshole? You think I liked that?"

She looked away and didn't answer him. She hadn't expected that vehemence, I don't think, although to be honest I hadn't either. But I understood where she was coming from—that need to be the one most bothered by something, to prove yourself.

After a while, Brandon said, "Obviously, it doesn't excuse it. If anything, it makes it worse. But my point, if you'd just listen for like eight seconds, is that you never know what's going to make you snap and maybe we actually could turn out like that, who knows. I don't think anyone can say they're like some inherently good person and there's things they would just never do, so they never have to worry about it. It's like that whole moral luck thing Jay was talking about."

"I don't think that's true," Sunny said. "I think you can decide there are things you'll never do, and then you just . . . don't do them."

"Yeah, okay, sure, but say something happens? You get mugged or something or your kid gets sick or—I don't know, you lose your job and your house. Then what?"

"Then I'll still somehow manage to cope with it by not assaulting someone? Those all still sound like excuses to me, Brandon."

He made a frustrated noise and looked to me for help. A sharp ache flickered through me at losing this forever after graduation—my role as the mediator between them. Having people who I knew well enough to mediate.

"It's not an excuse," I said quietly.

"I know it's not an excuse."

Grace was always better at defusing these small tensions. Sometimes I wondered if it came so naturally to her because she never quite felt them the way I did, not as deeply, and they didn't have the same hold on her; they were easier to break. But Grace had gone to the bathroom and so she'd missed this turn in conversation, and in a way I was glad; the talks you have depend so much on who you're with at any given time, and maybe if she were here we'd be talking about something that mattered less.

Brandon said, "My dad—after he first came here, he did his residency in this small town in Michigan and people were really horrible to him and he got really jaded. My mom talks about it sometimes, but he never does. She said she's never seen him the way he was when they lived there. And sometimes I think about—did Jay ever tell you his dad was supposed to be a doctor too? He did med school and everything. That's why he came here. But now he does insurance or whatever, which feels like, I don't know, an f-you to what he actually wanted. And I always wonder if it was really bad for him and that scarred him somehow."

"Does it matter, though?" Sunny said. "Everyone has bad things happen to them, so—"

"You haven't. You said so yourself when you were complaining about not having anything to write in a college essay. When you think about how easy your life is compared to your parents', don't you feel kind of guilty about it sometimes?"

She sighed. "What's your point?"

"I just—I'm worried we're not that different. Everyone likes to think they're a good person, but maybe it's just that some people's circumstances never make them prove it. And with Jason, I mean—I just stood there."

"You're not a bad person, Brandon," I said. "You're completely different."

"Hey, I'll take it," he said, and he grinned. It almost tricked me into thinking it wasn't forced.

It was nearly five thirty. Brandon picked up his phone and glanced at it, and Grace came back into his room then.

"Did we hear from Jason yet?" she said, settling down cross-legged onto Brandon's bed.

"Nah, that was just Leo."

"What'd he want?" I said. Leo was Leo Lim, who Brandon played basketball with. He'd always been fairly close to Leo and a few other guys, Tim Parrish and Bentley Look. The season was about to start, and I'd never liked basketball season because Brandon would get absorbed into Leo and the others for nebulous basketball-related reasons. Would it be like that this year too?

Brandon put his phone away. "Ah, he just wanted to see about working out tomorrow."

"Text Jason again," Grace said. "Or maybe I will. If we're all here together, he should at least come hang out. We could watch a movie or something."

She messaged, and we waited a few minutes again. And it was fine, probably—he'd mentioned earlier in the day he'd been up late cramming for the AP Econ test (we all had) and it wasn't unlike him to go home and crash before dinner. It was unlikely that he was in any kind of peril.

I told myself that, anyway.

"It'll be awful next year," I said. "It's hard like this, when he's close by and we're all together. But if we're all in different places, and there's no one near him—"

"Ugh, don't say that," Sunny said. "I already feel guilty we're just, like, hanging out while he's doing who knows what."

"Maybe next year," Brandon said, "we can like—have some schedule to make sure he pings us regularly or—"

"Or what if we all tried to stay together next year?"

They all turned to look at me, startled. My voice had come out in a flood, surprising even me. I hadn't planned to say this now.

I had said it, though, and so I kept going. "Because if it's just Jason alone—what if something happens, and we're all hundreds of miles away? I think we have to all stick together."

"How would that work, though?" Grace said.

"Well—he wants to go to Berkeley, right? So we can all apply there, and then maybe also we can apply nearby just in case—like weren't you going to apply to St. Mary's, Grace?" It was surreal to be actually saying this aloud. "Or we could do community college a year and then transfer. It's much easier to get in as a transfer." Jason and Sunny and Brandon were practically guaranteed admission. I was a maybe, but hadn't I been working hard all my life?

"That's—an interesting idea," Brandon said, slowly.

We all looked at one another. I couldn't feel my hands.

"I think we should do it," Grace said, impulsively, surprising me. "I think you're right, Beth. And we're lucky we're in California and there are so many good options here. There's

USF right across the Bay too. I was thinking of applying there anyway."

I could hardly speak. "Really?"

Brandon said, "Sun?"

She was methodically picking lint off his comforter, not looking up. "You really think it will make a difference?"

"I mean, that's hard to say, but what I do think is probably what he's been going through has fucked him up more than any of us have ever realized. So."

"Well," she said, "if that's true, I mean—okay, sure, if it works out that we all get in there, or close to there, okay."

"Even if it's not LA?"

Sunny shrugged. "Yeah, I mean, then it's not LA."

"Should we ask him first?" Grace said. "Are we even telling him about this?"

"No, no, we definitely can't tell him," Brandon said. "He'd for sure tell us not to. I wouldn't put it past him to like end up going somewhere really random just to make sure we didn't feel obligated to go there too."

"Yeah, he would totally do something like that," Sunny said. "Okay, so, what, then—we just pretend like we're applying normally to throw him off?"

"I mean, my parents are going to make me apply normally anyway," Brandon said. "My dad is all in on the college tour trip. But we'll just—we'll go through the motions and all, but—here we are. Yeah?"

"Here we are," Sunny said.

In the kitchen, we could hear one of Brandon's parents opening the fridge. I felt like if I moved I would break the spell.

"Okay," I said. "Well—okay."

"Then we're all in," Brandon said, and thumped me on the back in a way that felt distinctly basketball-y. "I feel like we should like commemorate it somehow."

I could hardly breathe. I couldn't believe what had just happened. The thing that I had been most dreading—it no longer existed. It was worth the canceled limo, worth whatever it would take for me to pay the fee.

We took a selfie. I imagined showing it to Jason later, revealing how all along we'd known we'd do this for him. Then Brandon wanted to post it, and he and Sunny argued over whether or not it was a good idea ("It's definitely like *look at us all hanging out without you!*" Sunny said, "Which is like the opposite of our point, isn't it?"), and I needed to find a way to sneak into a room where they couldn't hear me and call the limo company, but still I couldn't keep the smile off my face. It was the first time maybe all year that the future felt like a beam of light instead of a black hole.

I had been so happy—I was still so happy—but all that weekend when I practiced there was a physical, heavy grief that crept down my arms to my fingertips. Because it was official now: I wouldn't keep playing after this in any real capacity, and a life without violin, when I thought too hard about it, felt colorless and bleak. But I told myself this was a small trade-off; the best part of music had always been that we did it together. And I'd never truly expected to play past high school anyway. The things you dream about aren't the things you expect to actually have.

Maybe it wasn't just that, though, my sadness; maybe it was also that it wasn't right to feel happy about promising to stay together when the reason we were doing it was what it was. Would you rather all of you split up forever, or Jason suffer? They were inseparable now, what we were promising and what he was facing, and to view the future together as an uncomplicated gift would be to answer that one wrong.

AT REHEARSAL on Monday, Jason heard me warming up with the Zwilich Mr. Irving had given me, and when I put my bow down, he said, "So is that one of your audition pieces for next year?"

"Oh—no, I just liked the piece. I'm not auditioning anymore."

"Oh, what?" He frowned. "Not at all?"

"I didn't think it made sense."

"Ah." He leaned closer. It was noisy in the room, everyone playing all at once, and he had to duck his head and speak almost directly into my ear for me to hear him. "I've been thinking of it. Auditioning, I mean."

"Really?" I was more than a little startled, for many reasons, not least of which that it was nearly too late. The due date for audition recordings was less than two weeks away. "Like, to a lot of places?"

"Nah, more like—going for broke. I was thinking I'd just do Juilliard. I doubt I'd get in, and it's not like I'd go even if I did, but, I don't know, I guess I just want to see how it goes."

Immediately, before I could stop it, my mind flooded with images. I saw the two of us rehearsing together late at night in the practice rooms, all the noise of the city stilled around us; I saw us in the dorms I'd been looking up online, tucked away on the tenth or eleventh floor with the cityscape framed outside the windows, reams' worth of new sheet music filling the bookshelves. I saw us standing onstage in recital halls.

"Do you think there's time?" I said. "To get the recordings together?"

"Sure, I mean, there's over a hundred hours in a week if you don't sleep. And I was looking at the requirements and it wouldn't mean learning more than one new piece."

"Well—maybe I'll do it with you," I said. "If you wanted, that is."

"Yeah?" He pulled back a little and studied me. "The thing is—it has to stay quiet. I wasn't even going to tell Grace or Brandon or Sun."

"Oh," I said. "You don't think they'd want to apply too?"

I knew as soon as I said it there was no chance. And Jason, of course, was too polite to say they'd never get in.

"It's just if they happened to say something and their parents overheard, and then somehow word got back to my parents—"

It was true that my mother rarely talked to other parents, had never been a part of the unofficial Asian Parents' Network that traded gossip and recommendations for restaurants or tutors or summer camps. Mrs. Nakamura wasn't really either, though, and I doubted Sunny or Brandon would say anything, especially if he told them not to. But I didn't want to question him or start some other conversation that might somehow change the course of this one, so I said, "Right, definitely."

There was almost nothing I didn't tell them, especially Sunny. And it was outside of what we'd promised one another. But if there was a minuscule chance—

I was good at hiding things. Maybe that was something Jason and I had always shared.

MY MOTHER came into my room the next evening as I was practicing the Paganini for Juilliard. It was storming outside, the rain coming in sheets against the windows and filling the creeks that veined through our neighborhoods, and I craved being at Grace's house in front of a fire.

My mother sat on my bed and waited for me to pause, and I felt myself going tense with her there. Lately she was hovering more than usual. Sometimes in the evenings I'd see her looking through all the college brochures that came in the mail, and when I could sense she wanted to talk about them, I would go upstairs.

I was frantically trying to get all the pieces ready in time to make my prescreening recording—Jason was right that we could meet the requirements mostly with pieces we already knew, and I could carve time from all the nighttime hours I'd usually be sleeping—but I was keeping the application a secret from everyone, my mother especially. She would ask too many questions, and she would want to talk about money again, and she wouldn't understand why I was doing it and also why I wasn't trying to audition anywhere else. She would like it, I knew, if I applied to music programs, and she wouldn't understand that it was more important to stay with my friends. When I put my violin down, my mother said, "That was so lovely, Beth."

"It was just warming up."

"Well, it sounded beautiful. You've been working so hard lately on your violin. What's it for?"

"Just some difficult pieces."

"For your next concert?"

I nodded.

"Well, I hope you get more sleep, because it already sounds lovely," my mother said, then splayed her fingers out on her kneecaps and took a deep breath. I simmered with impatience. Each minute I wasn't playing felt irretrievable and precious.

"Your Gong Gong and Po Po," she said, "have told me that they would like to contribute to your college education."

"Really?"

"It wouldn't change the situation too drastically, but I think it could be a good opportunity for you. And also for them, I suppose. It would make them feel involved, and it's something good they could do."

I wasn't close to any of my grandparents. My father's father had died when I was three, and his mother hated phones, so I'd only ever talked to her when I went to Idaho. Before my parents divorced, the three of us used go up to the city some weekends to eat dim sum with my mother's parents, because my father loved dim sum, and for a while after the divorce my mother still used to take me with her to see them. Mostly they'd talk about adult things, or sometimes they would rehash or pointedly not rehash the same fights they'd probably had all through my mother's life, but my grandfather would play tic-tac-toe with me or do math tricks on the paper placemats and my grandmother would grab my hand and press gifts inside, lai see or sometimes gold jewelry in zippered fabric envelopes from the jeweler's, and then fold my fingers closed over them. My mother didn't talk about her par-

ents' pasts often, but I knew they'd been hard—as a child my
grandmother had lived in another family's kitchen as domestic
help, and my grandfather had been born to a sixteen-year-old
who eked out a living picking fruit. They were financially comfortable now, but my mother had once told me that had come too
late; they'd been marked by the difficulty of their earlier years in
a way money couldn't assuage now.

For the past few years my mother had been going less often
and without me, saying she knew I needed to study or practice
violin. I could've gone anyway, but I never had, and when she
came home and seemed sad or agitated I never asked her about
it. I always hoped someday to forge some kind of real relationship with them, though. Asian grandparents were everywhere in
Congress Springs, clustered together on playgrounds and pushing strollers in the store, speaking in Tagalog or Korean or Urdu
even when their grandchildren were clearly only half Asian. I'd
always wished I had that kind of grandparents, the ones who
taught you to slip into other tongues and other worlds as your
birthright.

"All right," I said.

"They'd like you to come and have dim sum with them so you
can tell them about your plans."

"Okay."

"I thought maybe we could go on Christmas morning." My
mother hesitated, then added, "I know it's Christmas, but it's just
dim sum."

She was making such a big deal of things. I was supposed to
see my father for Christmas Eve, which was our tradition, but my
mother and I never did anything on Christmas morning that I'd
be especially sad to miss. "I already said okay."

"Good. It's settled, then." She stood up. Just before she reached
the door, she turned back and added, "It's just one meal."

"She always overreacts," I told my friends as we were walking into Sandwich Station at lunch the next day. I'd been up all night working through the Paganini and then the Zwilich, and I was so tired the bright yellow walls with their menu photos throbbed in my peripheral vision. We'd gone off campus because Brandon wanted their meatball sub, and the sidewalks were littered with acorns and fallen branches from the storm. "Shouldn't she be trying to get me to have more of a relationship with them? My grandparents are the only family we have, and I haven't seen them in literally years."

The bell above the door dinged. It was a cramped place with a counter and just two small tables, and we'd barely beaten the lunch rush. "Beth, you order," Sunny said. We'd always suspected the man who usually worked at lunchtime didn't like Asians. (Grace thought we should boycott, the same way we did the chicken place a few doors down ever since Sunny told us what the National Organization for Marriage sticker on their cash register meant, but Sunny, uncharacteristically, overruled a boycott of Sandwich Station; she loved their eggplant wrap.) I put in their order, and then we waited by the door. Lunch was short; we'd eat in the car going back.

"Your grandparents are the ones who gave you all your jewelry, right?" Sunny said. "Like that jade bracelet you have and the gold necklaces? And that diamond pendant?"

"Yeah, most of it. So with things like that—I think in their way they probably care about me."

The place was filling up; we were pressed more tightly against one another to make room. Jason unwrapped one of the cinnamon mints in a bowl by the door and popped it into his mouth. Grace said, "Do you and your mom talk about them a lot? Like, does she tell you why she doesn't want you to see them?"

"No. Sometimes I think the only way she knows how to respond to conflict is to cut people off. Or cut them off from me. She never tries to work things out or like—change herself, she's just done."

"I don't know," Sunny said, thoughtfully, "I don't really get that vibe from her. The fights you guys have are the opposite. Like her wanting to go over the same thing a million times. And then how you said when you were younger she used to make you practice asking for things at restaurants or whatever because she thought you should be more assertive—I bet that's because she always worried she wasn't assertive enough herself or something."

"And look at you *now*," Brandon said, nudging me. "Ordering all our sandwiches like a goddamn *boss*."

I rolled my eyes. "Maybe that's it, though. She has some weird view of standing up for yourself where it just means you leave."

I heard myself say it and wished immediately I'd phased it differently. *I didn't mean you, Jason,* I wanted to say. *You should leave; you should do whatever it takes.* He was leaning against the wall and watching the man behind the counter, fiddling with the mint wrapper in his fingers. Was it my imagination that he was trying to stay on the outskirts of the conversation? I shouldn't have brought up fighting with parents.

"It's always so surprising when adults are dysfunctional about things," Grace said. "It's like, you've had almost fifty years to figure this out!"

"Really, that surprises you?" Brandon said. "I mean—adults are generally not great."

That seemed safer, talking about adults in general and not parents in particular. "Well," I said, "they did give us income inequality and a bunch of wars, so there's that."

"Don't forget gun violence," Sunny said. "Their gift to our generation."

"And a planet that's going up in flames!" Grace said cheerfully, popping open her Sanpellegrino. "Would you rather die of a preventable illness because not enough people gave to your GoFundMe, or bake to death?"

"Bake," Jason said. "Then at least other people don't have to sit there refreshing your page and feeling shitty when the numbers aren't high enough." He hoisted himself off the wall. "I think that's our order."

It was louder and more crowded inside now. Jason went to the far end of the counter and came back with just four bags. "I think he forgot yours, Beth," he said. "I'll tell him. What'd you get?"

"Oh, I didn't order anything."

"You didn't get anything?" Grace said. "You love their caprese sandwich."

"I'm not that hungry."

"What do you mean you aren't hungry? This isn't some weird weight-loss thing, is it?" Sunny said. "Friends don't let friends diet."

"No, I just don't really feel like eating." I was trying not to spend more money. I'd gotten an email last night about my credit card statement, which I'd deleted in a kind of panic. I was pretty sure I had already missed the payment, but I was too scared to log in and check.

"Maybe you're getting sick," Grace said. "You've been staying up so late all week."

When we went back outside, someone called, "Jason!" and we turned and saw Whitney Lim and Tara Tu from school coming across the parking lot. Tara was tall and willowy and a little exhausting—someone who would sidle up to you and ask how you were doing so that when you reciprocated she could launch into an extensive detailing of her latest drama. In middle school we'd briefly had one of those friendships where we wrote each other notes on elaborate Asian stationery before she'd moved on to someone else. When they came onto the sidewalk, Tara said, "So why weren't you at Homecoming?"

Brandon visibly flinched. I remembered too late Tara had been paired up with Jason that night for the Homecoming court— they were supposed to be announced and walk onto the dance floor together.

"Oh," Jason said. He rubbed his hand over his jaw. "Yeah."

We'd studiously not mentioned Homecoming around him since it happened; we'd pretended it had never existed. But we'd heard how they'd announced his name and then there was a long silence, and then all the other ASB officers were mad at Sunny for not having warned them he wasn't going. I'd overheard speculations about his absence (he'd gone on a bender, he thought Homecoming was lowkey homophobic and wanted to support Sunny), but things moved so quickly in high school I'd hoped people would move on without anyone ever saying anything about it to him.

He hadn't asked if the rest of us had gone. But it would be like him to feel guilty for not honoring a commitment.

"I had to walk all *alone*," Tara said. "Everyone was talking about it. Where were you?"

"You guys better hurry and order," Brandon said. "It's hella crowded inside."

"So crowded," Grace agreed brightly. "Their fries are so good. I should have gotten some. Have you had them, Tara? They have some spice on them that—"

"Is everything okay, though?" Tara said, coming a little closer to Jason. She was wearing Birkenstocks that dragged loudly against the concrete. "I was just telling Whitney you wouldn't stand us up without a good reason."

"Yeah—" Jason said. "I fell asleep, actually."

Tara laughed, a surprised bark "No one called you or anything?"

"My phone died."

"But how—"

"Okay, well, it was great talking to you guys!" Grace said, and reached out her arms to herd us toward Sunny's car. "I have to go see Mrs. Chang before the bell rings."

In the car, Jason said nothing. All our attempts at starting some other conversation died out, and even with my arm and leg pressed against his, he felt unreachable. When I was small, my father had liked building elaborate sandcastles with me, and I thought back to how carefully you had to watch yourself around them, how if you touched them even gently they would crumble, because it felt like that now with Jason. He didn't take out his sandwich. We went over the freeway overpass, past the turnoff for his house, and still the silence carved itself between us like a canyon.

When we pulled into the student parking lot, Brandon cleared his throat.

"Jay, you didn't win, by the way," he said. "I know you were probably wondering."

Jason looked at him like he'd forgotten he was there. "I didn't win what?"

"Homecoming king." He reached across me to clap his hand on Jason's knee. "Sorry, man. I know how much it meant to you."

Jason stared back, blankly. My heart pumped a surge of electricity, a flash all the way to my feet.

"But you're Homecoming king in our hearts," Grace said. "In my heart every day is a Homecoming parade just for you. Also in my heart you're definitely wearing this super-elaborate, really regal crown."

"Is there a scepter?" Sunny said. "It feels like there should be."

"Anyway, it was probably rigged, so you shouldn't feel too bad about it," Brandon said. "But we're all here for you in, you know, your time of loss."

Jason's rib cage pressed against mine each time he drew a

breath, each time he shifted in his seat. Brandon's grin wavered. I couldn't bring myself to join in the joke. Because if it was the wrong move, if it upset him, then I would be implicated in it too.

Be all right, I said to Jason silently. *I would give anything for you to be all right.* And maybe it was just that I wanted to believe it, but when his eyes met mine it seemed he knew what I was thinking.

Then he laughed. It was his real laugh, all the lines in his face softening, and the relief was like a downpour. I held that close all afternoon, dizzy with hunger from skipping lunch.

On Thursday, when we didn't have rehearsal, Jason came over after my lessons with Mrs. Nguyen so we could listen to each other's repertoires.

For the Paganini, he'd chosen No. 5, perhaps the most technically difficult, and I watched his fingers fly so fast they blurred, his veins tracing rivers across the backs of his forearms. The way he looked playing made me ache, and I always wondered if he glanced up and met my eyes if he'd be able to tell how I felt. It was, I realized, the first time we'd been truly alone together since the day at his house.

When he put his violin down, it took me a little while to find words. He was sitting next to me on our couch, and if I shifted just a few inches over, I would be touching him. Finally, I said, "I've always liked that one. It's so—so dramatic."

"I can't get the ending right." He half smiled. "Can't stick the landing."

"What was wrong with it?"

"I don't know. I keep rushing, for one thing, and then I get all caught up in the tempo and it goes kind of flat."

"I don't think it goes flat." I reached up to push my hair behind my ears. Did he feel anything too, being alone here with me like this? Maybe I was imagining that things felt different. "If you got in—do you think there's any chance you'd go?"

He stacked his sheet music neatly on the stand. "Probably not."

I'd known that already, but still something flattened in my heart. "You don't think you'd like New York?"

"No, I've been there. I like it a lot. When you walk down the street and no one knows you—you're so anonymous. No one's paying attention to you at all."

Was that what he wanted? It was the opposite of what safety felt like to me, which was being known, surrounded by those you knew. "That part feels a little overwhelming."

He smiled in a different way—sort of, I thought, affectionately. "It doesn't seem like your type of place, no. I always pictured you somewhere—smaller. Somewhere where you have to notice more."

"What do you mean notice more?"

"I mean—I just think you have to be a certain kind of person to appreciate somewhere like Congress Springs the way you do." He considered it for a moment. "And I don't mean someone like Grace—Grace is going to be happy wherever she goes for the exact opposite reason. I mean I think you notice more deeply."

A warmth spread through my chest, that sunburst of recognition when someone you care about shows you some way they've held a space for you in their heart. Without warning, I felt my eyes well up.

He deserved all the best things. He deserved all the best from us.

"I keep thinking—" He tapped his fingers against my music stand. "I keep thinking about that review."

"The one from our fall show? Jason—it's not even worth thinking about. Seriously, you should just forget it."

"It isn't like he was wrong."

"He *was* wrong. He—"

"It's fine. It's pointless to try to just forget what your flaws are. You'll never change if you just brush it off any time someone criticizes you."

"I mean, okay, that's fair, but I don't think he was ever right to begin with, so—"

"If someone says something negative about you and it bothers you, it's because they're right. Like if he'd said, *welp, you missed all the notes and you couldn't handle the tempo,* I would've shrugged it off because it's wrong on its face."

"That isn't how criticism works."

"No?"

"It's not like the worse it feels, the truer it is. It doesn't work that way."

"Maybe it's not quite that simple. But when it stings in a specific way, it's because it's real."

I knew I wouldn't convince him. But I understood in that moment what this audition was to him—why he was going through all the effort when he knew it wouldn't matter in the end. It was another chance to measure himself and, hopefully, not come up wanting. He had something to prove; he had a wrong to right.

I wanted to find something to say to that, something that would be soothing and would also tell him, maybe, how I saw him, but before I could think of what, he leaned back and rested his hands on his knees. "All right, Claire, you're up."

In a way, Jason was always the audience I imagined playing for, so I was nervous, but it went away as I played. Every piece was like that—each one offered you a purpose. But also, today I wanted somehow for him to hear what I felt for him, to hear all those things I'd never been able to tell him.

"You're doing something really interesting with that one," he said after I ran through the Paganini. It was the one I felt least confident in. "It sounds—it sounds kind of angry."

"Really, it does? Angry how?"

"Why do you say it like that?"

"Say it like what?"

"Like it's this horrifying possibility."

"I don't mean to sound angry." Mrs. Nguyen would always frown when she thought I was making a facial expression that might distract an audience, when I looked unhappy or too intense. *Audience don't want to see you angry*, she'd say, tapping my forehead. *Very distracting! Not like a lady. Everyone want you look pleasant. You try smile more. Relax your face.*

"You think there's something wrong with being angry?" he said.

"I'm really not, though. I'm just playing."

Jason picked up the sheet music and ran his finger across, then stopped when he came to the third variation. "These bars here," he said. "If it were me, I think I would've toned them down, but—"

"I'll try that next time," I said quickly.

"No, that's not what I'm saying. I'm just saying I would've been more—I don't know, restrained, and I think that's less interesting than what you're doing with it. It kind of elevates the whole section."

I felt myself blushing. "That's nice of you."

"It isn't. I'm just being honest." He started to say something, then stopped. Finally, he said, "Sometimes I think you don't—I don't know. I think you don't say everything you're thinking. You do this thing sometimes where, like—I don't know, you say the right thing, but then I get the feeling it's not actually you."

"What do you mean it's not actually me?"

"I don't know, exactly. But then sometimes when I listen to you play, it's like—oh, okay, there's a lot more going on than what you ever say."

He dropped his hand from the music stand, and when he did, his arm brushed against mine, and instead of moving it away he left it there.

For one moment, we both paused. He felt warm and solid against me. In AP Bio, we'd just done a study on plankton whose phosphorescence made trails across the sea, glowing in the darkness of the depths like the northern lights, and Jason touching me, his arm bare and against mine; it felt like that. I felt the heat of that movement in streaks across my skin.

And then, so quickly, he yanked himself back. I couldn't read the look on his face.

"Sorry," I said, and my voice came out high-pitched, and he said, also quickly, "No, no, it's fine," and then he picked up his violin case again, not for any discernible purpose, but maybe—I thought—just to have something to do with his hands. "You want to run through it again?"

And there was something about the way he jerked back that stunned me. Because of all the times he'd ever touched me, it had always felt so deliberate; he had been so measured and in control. This was different. This time it felt like he'd been startled, like he'd caught himself—like if he hadn't been careful, something else would've happened, like this would have gone further.

I REPLAYED that moment between us a thousand times afterward. Had I just imagined it? Because the next day he was so blandly ordinary toward me; all day I felt certain that if I'd said, *Jason, did something happen between us yesterday at my house?* he would have stared back blankly, or perhaps even with pity. I felt, all day, an enormous amount of doubt—how was it that in the moment I'd so misjudged what had happened, or what hadn't? How had I felt something that might not ever have been there?

At rehearsal that afternoon, we worked through the andante in Mahler's 6th. We'd all kind of hated Mahler ever since learning how he'd forbidden his wife, Alma, from composing and had instead made her go on long, silent walks with him so he could daydream about his own compositions, which is to say that it wasn't anyone's favorite piece. But it also wasn't especially complicated to play, at least not the first violin part, so it was more than a little surprising—shocking, actually—when on our first full run-through Jason stumbled over a few notes and then lost his place entirely.

I didn't want to turn and look at him in some kind of obvious way, but when I watched him out of the corner of my eye, he was gripping his bow so hard his veins were jutting out of the back of his hand and his forearm, and for just a moment, before he wrestled it back under control, his expression was furious. Something vital in my chest, some organs and viscera, squeezed into a tight fist.

"I've been having a hard time with that one," I said to him when rehearsal was over and we were packing up. It wasn't true, but I wanted to hear what he'd say to that.

Jason smiled, a polite smile that was the opposite of an invitation. "You sounded good."

Obviously I couldn't say *Well, you didn't.* "Do you like that piece?"

"It's all right. What about you?" He reached out to take my bag of sheet music—our bags were all heavy, especially mine because I always took too long to weed out the pieces we were finished with—and hoisted it onto his shoulder, and I don't think he noticed that he hadn't waited for my answer before he said, "Ready to go?"

I could feel him close off as soon as we got outside to where Sunny and Brandon and Grace were waiting for us, and I recognized the way he did it: like it was a relief to him, and he'd waited this long only out of courtesy when it was just the two of us. As we all walked to the parking lot together, I watched him closely. What if something had happened—what if his parents had found out about Juilliard somehow? Or what if he'd changed his mind?

"Everything Mahler wrote is always like, ooh, I'm going to *compose,* the world is my *symphony,* I'm a *man* and an *artist.* It's gross we've probably played more things in BAYS by him than we have by women," Grace said. "Like, really gross."

"So we still hate Mahler, huh?" Brandon said.

"What do you mean *still?*" Sunny said. "Team Alma all the way."

"Alma was also not the greatest person in the world," Brandon said. "Not that she deserved that or anything, just I don't think there are exactly heroes in that story."

"Uh, what do you mean there are no heroes? Alma trashed her shitty husband for fifty years after he died and couldn't defend himself and it took historians years to realize she was making stuff up."

Brandon laughed. "Well, when you put it like that."

Jason had stayed quiet the whole time. We passed the portables and the tennis courts, and when I saw his car right at the edge of the parking lot, my heart sank. I felt desperate to keep him here longer, for him to talk to us.

"What's everyone doing tonight?" I said. I looked at Jason when I said it, but I don't know if he even heard.

"Oh, it's going to be a wild Friday night," Brandon said. "You guys start reviewing for the Bio final yet? I think I'm going to go pound some caffeine and hole up in the library. Anyone want to come?"

"I will," I said. I always wished we'd do that kind of thing every night—it always felt like a waste whenever we were all doing the same thing, like studying or eating, at the same time but separately.

"You got any new crossword puzzles?" Brandon said. "Hook us up. We'll make it a real party."

Grace said she'd come after dinner, and Sunny said she'd get more done if she stayed home, and Grace said, "Oh, come on, it'll be fun," and Brandon badgered her until she finally said, "Okay, fine, but I hate the library," and Grace said, "You guys can come to my house. We can bake something. Or my mom will bake us something," and through that whole exchange too, Jason said nothing.

When I said, "What about you, Jason?" he startled. From the blank, distant expression on his face, he could've been somewhere else altogether.

"Grace's tonight?" Brandon said. "Studying? Baking? You in?"

"Ah—" He forced a smile. "You guys have fun."

I watched him as he walked to his car. When he got in—I don't think he knew I was watching—he slid into his seat and then closed his eyes, and he sat there like that, alone, for a long time. When I drove away with Sunny, he was still there.

That night at Grace's, I told them how off Jason had seemed at rehearsal, and I asked if they thought we should try to call Jason's sister. We were in Grace's family room, Sunny and me curled up on the soft gray couch with our laptops, Brandon with all his notes spread out across one of the ottomans, Grace attacking her history book with a highlighter. Mrs. Nakamura had started decorating for the holidays already; three wreaths hung on the wall by the door, and on the mantle there were tall glass apothecary jars all filled with different gold baubles: gleaming Christmas ornaments, tiny wrapped gifts, glittery fake pinecones.

"Do we even have her number?" Sunny said. "It's not like we can get it from Jason."

"It's in last year's BAYS directory."

"Oh, right." She smiled a little. "Of course you still have that."

"Yeah, I don't know," Brandon said. "Like, is calling her actually going to help in some concrete way, or are we just trying to prove something to ourselves, you know? Because—"

He paused, because Mrs. Nakamura had come in with a plate of cookies that she set down with a flourish on the coffee table.

"This is an experiment," she said. "The other day I made dough and froze it, because is there anything worse than when you don't have time to bake but you just really need a cookie? So you have to tell me how these are." Then while we ate them (they were excellent), she sat next to me on the couch and stayed to talk, and then Grace was yawning and Mrs. Nakamura said she thought it was obscene for high school students to do schoolwork after nine p.m., so we all packed up to go.

But the whole way back and especially at home I was uneasy. I made up an excuse to message Jason and didn't hear back, which hopefully just meant he was sleeping, but I couldn't stop all the what-ifs from blooming like algae into an opaque, toxic cloud.

I would give anything to be with him right now. I felt the few miles between us, all the closed doors and all the hours until Monday, as a lump in my throat. And for a few minutes, I let myself imagine a world where instead of being alone tonight we were together, and I let myself imagine having some solid and undeniable claim on him, one that meant he wanted me there and welcomed me into all those shadowy places he never let anyone follow him into. I let myself imagine us lying together in the dark.

But I wasn't with him, and I didn't have that claim, and he was out there somewhere and I didn't know whether he was all right and it was unbearable. It wasn't quite ten—surely not too late to call a college student. I looked up Evelyn's number.

She picked up, which surprised me a little. She'd never struck me as the kind of person who'd take calls from random numbers.

"Evelyn?" My voice came out higher-pitched than I meant, even higher than what Sunny referred to as my customer service voice when I was talking to people I didn't know as well, and I cleared my throat. "This is Beth Claire. I don't know if you remember me—I'm one of Jason's—"

"I remember you."

"Oh—great. Um, I wanted to talk to you because—well, as Jason's friends, we've just been—we've been a little worried about him, and we thought—"

"Why?"

"There was kind of—" I swallowed. I sat down on my bed. I could hear my pulse thudding in my ears. "After Thanksgiving, we were at your house, and there was kind of an incident with your dad. And then today, he just seemed—"

"What do you mean an incident?"

I somehow hadn't planned to have to say the words aloud. "Your dad hit him," I said finally. "It was—it was pretty bad." She didn't answer, and I felt the words start to choke me. "But then today he seemed maybe kind of like he did that day, a little bit."

"Did something happen today?"

"I'm not sure."

"Then what exactly made you so worried?"

What was I supposed to say—that he'd made mistakes while playing? All those things that meant something in our world, that I was attuned to because I cared about him, wouldn't translate into anything I could say to his sister on the phone. "He seemed upset."

She was quiet a long time. Finally, she said, "Did Jason ask you to talk to me?"

"No, but—"

"Okay, so—I'm not really sure what we're doing here."

"We were just worried about him."

Her voice was sharp. "Well, what do you want me to say?"

What did I want her to say? That she would know some way to fix things, I guess. Or that somehow things weren't as bad as they seemed, or that there was some reason I hadn't considered that, actually, Jason would be fine, or that I didn't need to worry because she was going to do x, y, and z.

The silence on the phone splayed out, miring us inside it. My face was burning. Maybe I'd said everything wrong. Sunny or Grace or Brandon should've called her instead. After a while, when I'd run through all the other impossible options, I said, "I guess I just thought maybe you should know."

The panic set in as soon as I hung up. My hands were shaking. It was hard to remember how just a few minutes ago it had felt like a good idea somehow to call her. Was she going to tell Jason I'd called? He would be furious; he would definitely consider it a betrayal. I'd been counting on her knowing that and caring enough about it not to tell him, but maybe that had been foolish.

Also, I'd counted on the call being worthwhile. I could live with the unpleasantness as a sacrifice I'd make if it did something for Jason somehow. But obviously that had been naive.

But maybe Brandon had been partly right—maybe it had been for my own sake that I'd called her. Maybe deep down I'd never expected her to fix it; maybe I just wanted to mark us as caring and involved, doing everything we could. Maybe I'd just wanted an outside witness to how deeply we cared for him.

That was where Brandon had only been half-right, though. Because I think then I still thought that the sheer force of caring could somehow be enough—that it would matter, that it would change things, in the end.

I told my friends about the failed phone call, but I told them not to tell Jason. He never mentioned it, which I hoped meant Evelyn hadn't told him, but I couldn't be sure. He also, of course, never brought up any of the rest of it himself, not Brandon's birthday or the day at rehearsal, but on Monday we were sitting in our usual spot at lunch, and just before the bell rang Jason cleared his throat.

"Also, uh," he said, and reached into his back pocket and pulled out his wallet, "this is from my mom." From inside his wallet he pulled out four sealed red lai see envelopes with gold embossing, and he handed one to each of us.

"Ooh!" Grace said. "I love Lunar New Year!"

I was surprised. It was something Grace's mother might have done—the way she sent cupcakes for Grace to give us on Valentine's Day and homemade mochi for New Year's. But we hardly knew Jason's mother, and unlike Mrs. Nakamura, we almost never saw her, and Lunar New Year was almost two months away.

I never knew the correct way to open gifts like that, when the gift was clearly money—it felt strange to open it in front of whomever had given it to me, but equally strange to simply pocket it without looking. So I looked around at the others, but they seemed as lost as I was.

Finally, Grace smiled, a little awkwardly, and slid open the envelope. Then she jerked back, visibly startled.

"Jason," she said. She shook her head. "She shouldn't . . ." She trailed off, and Jason looked away. The rest of us peeked inside our own envelopes. There were two hundred-dollar bills inside each one.

Brandon stuffed the money back in his envelope, out of sight, and he held the envelope gingerly between his thumb and forefinger. "Jason, it's too much," he said. "We can't—"

"It's fine," Jason said, a little shortly.

"But Jay—"

"Just—she wanted you to have it." He was sitting cross-legged, and he clapped his hands loudly on his thighs. It made a hollow sound, like punctuation—an ending. "So," he said, then stopped.

All I could think was how that was nearly a thousand dollars between the four of us. I couldn't remember the last time I'd seen Sunny at a loss for words like this. She had her lips pressed together, and she was blinking quickly, her envelope on the ground in front of her.

Jason cleared his throat and then folded his arms across his chest, not looking at us. Brandon reached up and rubbed his temples with his thumb and forefinger, and then dropped his hand heavily. My fingertips felt icy, tingling and numb.

Finally, Grace said, "Well, that was nice of your mother."

"Mm," Jason said.

"Yeah, tell her thanks," Sunny murmured.

"Yep."

Brandon was still holding the envelope so it dangled from his fingers, wobbling. He looked a little pale.

"Well!" Grace said brightly. She straightened and slipped the envelope inside her backpack, out of sight. "You know what you can do with two hundred dollars? I heard an ad on the radio last night, and did you know for two hundred dollars you can have someone supposedly name a star after you? My mom and I were laughing so hard. They send you some dumb little certificate, which I don't know how you could ever prove which star it was because who's even in charge of naming stars? Would you rather spend two hundred dollars to have a star named after you or—I can't even think of another option."

Jason laughed gratefully. "How do you know they aren't just renaming the same star every time?" he said, and Grace said, "That's probably exactly what they do," and Sunny said, "That assumes there's even one star they're somehow in charge of," and Brandon said, laughing, "Man, you guys are all so *cynical*," and Grace said, "If you give me two hundred dollars, I'll print you a certificate right now that says any star you want is now the Brandon Lin," and it was okay, we were okay—the moment had passed.

Still, all that day it was as if the envelope throbbed there in my backpack, like surely everyone in class could see. I thought about my credit card bill, but you weren't supposed to send cash in the mail, and my mother always took my cash to the bank to deposit for me and I could never explain to her where this much had come from. So I gave the money to the NHS food drive, but sometimes even now I remember Jason's mother's face in that window, shrouded by the curtains; I remember everything that happened after, and I wish we'd never taken her money.

I **STILL** hadn't told my mother about Juilliard, so when I turned my application in Tuesday after school I put the fee on my credit card, which still had the balance for the limousine rental. For my essay, even though I knew it would upset him if he knew, I'd written about what had happened with Jason on Brandon's birthday. I couldn't shake the irrational anxiety that somehow he'd see it.

I messaged him right after to ask how everything had gone. He didn't write back all evening, and I spent it in a quiet state of panic, worrying that somehow his parents had found out or that he'd changed his mind altogether. Around midnight, though, he finally wrote back: *I guess fine. You?*

It would be weeks before we heard anything, and in less than a week we had finals, and then it would be the holidays and winter break, and so I thought violin would recede into the background for a little while. But the next day, at the end of rehearsal, Mr. Irving did something that stunned us: he announced that the violin solo in Mendelssohn's Violin Concerto in E Minor, the one we'd play in less than two weeks at our winter show, would be up for audition this year.

Everyone who wanted to audition, he told us, would play it next Monday at rehearsal. There was a silence, and then whispers, and as we put away our instruments Jason's face was carefully neutral, his movements very precise. Everyone knew that was supposed to be Jason's solo. We'd been working on the piece for weeks now—Mr. Irving had adapted the arrangement so that only the second movement was written for a solo, so we'd been rehearsing the first and third—and it had been assigned since the beginning of the year. Probably, knowing Jason, he'd been practicing it for months.

"That's weird he decided to do it as an audition," Grace said after practice when we were all walking together to the parking lot. I stiffened; I'd thought that all of us would politely not mention it. Because without any explanation, what else were we supposed to assume except that Mr. Irving was somehow disappointed in Jason? "And it's so last-minute, too."

"Yeah, what the hell?" Brandon said. "Did he ask you about that, Jay?"

"No, he didn't say anything." Jason shifted his violin case to his other hand. "But of course it's better to hold auditions. That's more fair."

We were at the parking lot, and Brandon offered to take me home. From the window, I watched Jason walk to his car, holding his violin under his arm like a bulky package. I wished I could go with him; I wished he'd go with us. I said, "You think he's upset?"

"Probably," Brandon said. He looked tired, and maybe a little worried, too. "But then knowing Jay I also could see him legitimately thinking it's fair. You know? If he deserves it he'll get it, and if not then he shouldn't have had it to begin with."

"I guess maybe. I just—I'm imagining him at home thinking Mr. Irving thinks he's not good. Or obsessing over the times he made mistakes, or that review."

Brandon winced. "Yeah, I could see it going like that, I guess. Or, I don't know, maybe it's the opposite and he has bigger things to worry about."

"Well, that's not exactly better."

"But then—I mean, you talked to his sister, right? And she thought everything was fine?"

"She was annoyed I called. I'm not sure those are the same thing." I watched the band room, the office, the gym go by out the window as we left campus, the view jostling as we went over the speed bumps at the exit. "It's weird, though—I mean, the violins aren't bad this year or anything, but I wouldn't say over-all this is the most talent we've ever had. It's not like when we did the auditions for the first chair it was even that close."

"You going to audition for it?"

"Oh, I—what? I don't know." I felt myself reddening. I suppose the question shouldn't have startled me—I was the second chair, after all—but there was something embarrassing about saying I might want it, like putting on makeup in public or admitting you were on a diet or saying you liked someone who probably didn't like you back.

But still. Maybe it was because there was nothing more I could do about Juilliard now but wait, or maybe it was because I knew Juilliard wasn't a possibility anyway, but when I pictured telling people *when I was younger I used to play the violin*, the future felt like something to suffer through. The truth, which was as difficult to admit as desire always was, was that I would love to play the solo; maybe it would be something I could hold on to when everything was over.

"Why wouldn't you?"

"I don't think I'd be very good," I said. "But also—" I hesi-tated. "Do you think it would bother Jason? If I did?"

He thought about it for a while. He turned right onto Bubb and slowed to a stop at Columbus, then shrugged. "If anything, I think he'd think it was weird if you didn't. Don't you? You know how much he hates when anyone lets other people win."

"You don't think it's—I don't know, doubting him somehow? Or pretentious, kind of?"

"I mean, I don't know what the hell Mr. Irving is thinking to just throw it out there like that, and if Jason ever needed a good year it's right now, but if everyone else is auditioning, it just looks weird if you don't. And anyway, Beth," he added, "if I'm being honest, Jason has to know you have a shot. It's your kind of piece, I think. When it comes to, like, musicality and expression and all that, I think you might be the best."

I wondered, I had always wondered, exactly what Jason's talents meant to him. Sometimes it felt like he held those things apart and didn't let them touch the core of himself, maybe in the same way he held people distant sometimes. Because I'd never seen him seem truly proud of himself, I'd only seen him duly satisfied; if he got back a test with less than an A, he'd leave it on his desk like a self-reproach, but when he did well he barely glanced at the papers before stuffing them in his backpack. And he was so humble, always more excited about someone else's accomplishments than his own.

But maybe he needed those things—the first-chair position, his grades, his SAT scores—so much that he kept that need locked away. Maybe it was like how vital and fragile it felt when Brandon used the word *best* to describe me. I had never been the best at anything. But when he said it, I saw how it could reshape the world around you, place you somewhere different inside it—how everything else could pale next to it until that felt like the most or the only crucial part of you.

That year a cold front blew in in mid-December. In the mornings, lawns glinted with frost, and the sunlight when it came was thin, and every night when I'd message with my friends for a while before going to sleep I'd huddle in bed, my phone glowing in my blanket cave. One evening at dinner, my mother pulled her fleece tighter around herself and said, "It makes you wish you could fast-forward to summer in Asheville, doesn't it?" That week we turned in the rest of our college apps, and now it was like being on a plane: I'd been strapped in and propelled from the safety of land, and could only wait to ride it out. I was nervous all the time. The three biggest threats that I saw to our promise were these: that I didn't get into Berkeley, because it would mean there was nowhere at all in Northern California I could reasonably go (even Davis was nearly two hours away); that Jason or one of the others got into an Ivy League and wouldn't turn it down; or that Sunny decided to just do what she'd always said she wanted to and go to LA.

And then, of course, there was Juilliard. But maybe it didn't make sense to even think about that.

I asked Sunny, one night when we'd gone to get boba for the caffeine so we could stay up late studying at her house, if she thought it would be hard to turn down LA. Jason had tutoring and Brandon was at the gym and Grace was helping her mom stage a house in Los Gatos, so it was just the two of us.

"Just because it's the thing you've always wanted," I said, as we were driving back to her place. "Like, do you think you'll be a different person without it? Or you'll look back and think you made a mistake?"

"I mean—yeah. There'll always be a part of me that regrets not going, I think. But also—" She hesitated. She circled her straw around the bottom of her cup. "I keep thinking about what Jason said to me that day in the restaurant. Do you remember that?"

"Oh, Sun, you can't let that get to you." I hated the idea of her thinking about that. "It was just an awful night. He didn't mean it."

"It's just—when it's like, a random person you don't care about, it's whatever, but when it's one of your best friends who you've known basically all your life—I care what Jason thinks about me, you know?"

"I'm *sure* if you asked him right now he'd say something totally different. You can't keep thinking about it like that."

We were in front of her house, and she parked and turned off the car but didn't get out yet. "It's just been on my mind a lot. Like I think you—you're naturally a good person, but I always feel like there's something inside me that doesn't let me—put other people first in the same way you do. Like I don't have that nurturing or giving side of me. And I always try to tell myself it's just that I'm ambitious, but I don't think that's all of it. I think you can be ambitious but still a good person, you know?"

I realized two things then: that on some level I'd been waiting for a way to tell her about Juilliard, and also that maybe I would never be able to. "Of course. Sunny—you are a good person."

"But maybe all this time I've been so focused on my own stuff and meanwhile Jason was like living his own nightmare, and I had no idea. Have you noticed all the new stuff he's had lately?"

"What do you mean new stuff?"

"Like a bunch of new clothes, and he got an Apple Watch."

"Did he?" I hadn't noticed.

"And I'm pretty sure his phone is new too. And after that money his mom gave us—his parents must have gotten him all that, right? Or maybe his mom? And it makes me sick thinking about them just, like, buying him a bunch of shit. I think it just scares me because we've all worked so hard here and we're going on to the next thing and I worry it's like, I'll poison the rest of my life because yeah, I was 'successful'"—she put air quotes around it—"but then I had bad morals. So I think this will be good. It's something we can all do for him and each other and I think that's important, right? And I think I'm definitely a better person with you guys than, like, in ASB, so there's that."

"Right," I said, and made myself smile like my stomach wasn't in knots. "That's the most important thing."

I just wouldn't think about Juilliard, I told myself. And it mostly worked, because I was so focused then on practicing the Mendelssohn solo feverishly for the BAYS audition, and something was happening: I was falling in love with the piece. I'd found recordings of it and was listening to them every night as I was studying for finals, trying each time to notice something new. I heard the surprise of the rising and falling, the marching sound of the call and echo, how inside those ominous, imperious chords there were little hints of uncertainty, notes that felt like, if you let them, they might take off in another direction altogether.

I wanted this solo. I wanted it to be mine.

Sunday night before the audition, I stayed up until three in the morning playing and replaying, willing my fingers to remember these patterns. It would be awful to look back and see all the mistakes or roughness I should have worked harder to smooth out. But I tried to tell myself that these many hours, all these practices leading up to this, had been worth it whether or not I got the solo. Music is a mirror: It waits quietly for you, and when you come to it, you appear temporarily inside of it, you insert yourself there and mold yourself and the piece to fit, and in the best times, you then go away with new insights about yourself.

But in all of it, all the practicing and the longing, all the work, I was uneasy with myself. Because what I was doing, when it came down to it, was plotting against Jason—planning on and working out ways I could see him fail.

The next day, everything was one long distraction from the afternoon. When auditions started, I was careful to keep my expression neutral and clap politely when each person had finished. It was strange listening to others playing a song I thought of now as mine. But it was difficult to concentrate on the other auditions anyway, because all I was doing was waiting for my own turn.

When Mr. Irving called on me, my pulse tingled in my fingertips. Next to me, Jason whispered, "Good luck," and I smiled back, and I rose, and lifted my violin.

When I started playing, I felt immediately all those many hours that I'd spent practicing. Of all the metaphors we'd been given over the years, I had thought of music as many things: as an escape, as a mirror, as a voice, and even, when I was lonely, as a friend. I had never before thought of it as a magnet. But playing that day, everyone turned to listen to me, it was exactly that: The very sound pulled my arms into motion, set my body swaying gently, and drew to me every single person in that room.

And then, suddenly, it was as though no one else was even there. For the first time, I didn't care what it sounded like to those around me. It was all so beautiful, so haunting and consuming, that I wondered if perhaps, this whole time, I'd had things wrong. Maybe the audience wasn't my concern after all; maybe the reviews didn't matter, or the applause, or even the long dissections afterward of what we had and hadn't done well. And maybe whatever it was I managed to impart to the audience was unimportant. Maybe music, the very best music, was selfish, and maybe all of it—the practicing, the many many repetitions, those flashes of inspiration and this, this revelry—was for *me*.

I could have played for hours. I drew out the last note as long as I could, my arm taut, and I felt myself drift back into the room.

And then I stopped. In the stillness, in the way all those around me held themselves motionless so they didn't break that silence I had created, I felt for the first time as though I understood what music really was: It was the work of sifting through all the long, tireless, tedious hours for these single moments of grace.

When I sat back down, my heart was pounding. I was too nervous to look at Mr. Irving. Jason whispered, "Beth," and I turned. He rested a fist on his chair, so that only I could see it, and gave me a secret little thumbs-up and whispered, "Oh my God."

And then it was his turn, and he stood and lifted his violin. I sat back and listened, my own violin stilled in my lap, and heard the piece I had just played take on new dimensions, twist and change until it was almost another thing altogether. When afterward I whispered, "That was amazing, Jason," I had to force the words, and I wondered whether his own congratulations to me had come easily to him.

I watched Mr. Irving for signs—if he inclined his head toward me or toward Jason, or if he held eye contact with one of us a second longer—but he gave away nothing. Brandon always said Mr. Irving would be a poor poker player, the way he reddened when we kept making the same mistakes or couldn't stop beaming when he was pleased with what he'd heard. But during auditions he was always like this: unreadable. "I'll let you know my decision Wednesday."

After rehearsal, Brandon had tutoring and Sunny had a group project, and Grace's family always ate dinner early. In the parking lot, after they had all gone, Jason turned to me.

"You want to go get coffee or something?" he asked. He was tapping his fingers on his case, like he was jittery. "I feel like I've got all this adrenaline."

I laughed, but it made me kind of sad, too. "Coffee will help?"

"Dinner, maybe?"

"That sounds great." I was still trying not to spend money, and also I was supposed to go home for dinner, but this felt more important than either of those things. I texted my mom to tell her I'd be home later and then turned off my phone before she could call and ask a hundred questions about where I'd be. Jason patted his pockets and made a face. "I think I left my wallet at home. You mind if we swing by real quick?"

He opened the car door for me, and I tried to look nonchalant as I buckled my seat belt. It had been a long time since Jason and I had done anything alone together like this—something that could, if you squinted, look like a date. But it wasn't, was it? It was a dinner between friends; it was last-minute, not something Jason had planned for.

Except I kept feeling it again, that rush of heat when he'd touched me at my house, that moment of electricity before he'd pulled away.

When he got into the car and closed the door behind him, the sounds from outside cutting off abruptly, the air going past my ears was warm and close and we could've been the only two people in the world. He turned on the car and backed out of the parking space, his arm draped over my seat. I sat very still.

"Does knowing all this is the last time make you wish it would be different next year?" I said. The piece had made me even more wistful than usual about what we'd be leaving behind. "Even just a little bit?"

"I never said I didn't wish it would be different."

"What do you mean?"

He considered that. "Well—it was always supposed to just be a hobby. Make me well-rounded, all that. My mom pushed for it. But then I wasn't awful at it, and now it's probably the thing in my life I'm best at. And I guess it's where I feel most like myself. It's just—it's hard to give that up."

"That's why you wanted to apply to Juilliard?"

He didn't answer right away. "I wanted to do it with you," he said finally. When he said things like that—how was I supposed to take it? It was the matter-of-factness that always threw me, how dispassionate it all seemed, as though whatever was between us was already settled somehow. "And also—"

He hesitated. I said, "And also what?"

"It's—kind of my one big rebellion. You know."

I didn't. "What do you mean?"

"I wasn't supposed to fuck around with music programs at all. I mean, it's violin. I wasn't supposed to actually, you know, care

about it. And I *really* wasn't supposed to want to do it forever."
He smiled, an unhappy smile. "You want to know something stupid? I used to want to be a famous violinist when I was a kid. I always thought I'd be so happy if that was the thing I got to do every day of my life."

"That's not stupid."

"Maybe for someone else it wouldn't be. I just—I guess when you're a kid it takes you a little while to learn what you can have and what you can't. You think if you want something, that means it's possible. Sometimes I kind of miss that. I think my whole life I've just—it's stupid, but I think I've always let myself pretend maybe it wasn't really going to be over. I guess this way I could keep pretending for a little while longer."

I had played violin with—and often right next to—Jason for six years. And yet that was the first time I understood that it wasn't about proving something to himself after all. I had been so wrong about what it meant to him.

"Maybe you still could, though," I said. "I mean, I'm sure you'll get invited to audition, and even if your—" I had been going to say *even if your father.* "Even if you aren't supposed to. You'd be out of the house, so—"

"So—what, exactly? I couldn't pay for it, for one thing. Plus it just—it just wouldn't be worth it."

"It's your life, though."

He smiled. He didn't answer. I waited, and eventually I realized that had been his answer, that for all I wanted to push harder, for all the possibilities this could've opened up, there was a finality to it. There was a growing ache in my chest. Finally, I said, "So what will you do?"

"I'll do what I'm supposed to. I'll go to Berkeley if I get in and do, like, bio or something. Then I'll go to med school."

"Do you think you'll be happy?"

"Probably not, no."

"Jason—that's horrible."

I wanted to say so much more than that. I wanted to say that he deserved better, that he deserved the world, that I was so sorry about everything. That I would do anything for him. That I loved him.

I didn't say it, though. And he shrugged.

"It's life," he said. "It is what it is." Then he said, abruptly, "Sometimes when I think about the future—"

When he didn't finish, I said, "When you think about the future, what?"

"Nothing. It doesn't matter. People have it much worse."

We were on his street now, and as we approached his house I wondered if he was thinking what I was—that it was the first time I'd been back here since Brandon's birthday. I was pretty sure it was the first time any of us had been back.

When we pulled into his driveway, he shifted his gears and idled the car and turned to me. "I'll just be a second," he said, his voice flat and very polite. "You're okay just waiting out here?"

"Definitely," I said, also politely, though it wasn't, of course, a question.

"I'll leave the heat on." He got out, and I watched him jog up to the front door and disappear inside.

I was chilly waiting, even with the heat still running, and I wrapped my arms around myself. I knew he'd come back out, that nothing bad was going to happen. But still, it felt like a long time that I was waiting there for him, watching the minutes go by on his clock. There weren't many, four or five, but still I was relieved when the door opened again and he stepped out.

"Sorry about that," he said, getting back in. "I guess I was driving all day without my license, too."

"Wow," I said, mildly. "Good thing you didn't get pulled over."

"Yeah," he said. "Good thing."

He pulled out of his driveway, looking over his shoulder, and while he was still twisted away from me like that I cleared my throat.

"Jason," I said, "are things any better at home?"

We were so infrequently alone together. With the others there, Jason could have ignored my question completely, been silent and trusted that someone else would pick up the conversation so that I wouldn't feel as brushed aside and didn't have to bear the weight of his silence. But if I asked now and he said nothing, it would be worse, and more hurtful, and I knew he wouldn't do that to me. Still, my heart was racing. I knew, too, that maybe it wasn't quite fair of me to pick that moment to ask.

He turned back, facing forward, and pulled onto the street. I waited. He pulled up to the stop sign at the end of his street and braked carefully, looked both ways, and then continued on, both hands firmly on the wheel. I waited still, my palms damp. Jason stopped again at the light on Arroyo, flicked on his blinker, and stared straight ahead. I pretended to watch as the cross traffic went by. When the light changed, he pulled forward, his foot light on the gas so that we crossed the street slowly.

Finally, he cleared his throat. "Not really, actually," he said.

"Jason, I'm sorry. Is there anything we can—"

"Look, Beth," he said, "I'd rather not talk about it. Okay?"

It wasn't fair to be stung. If anything, he'd spoken gently. But I sat back, quietly, and thought how he could have at least taken his eyes off the road a moment, just turned once to look at me.

Mr. Irving called me the next night at home. I was in my room because my mother was irritated I'd been out and hadn't answered her call—"Something could've been wrong, Beth, and I would've had no way to get ahold of you!"—and when I picked up the phone and heard his voice on the other line, I knew.

"Beth," he said, and I could hear the smile in his voice. I felt like something floppy and deflatable, a balloon maybe: All the air whooshed from my lungs at once. "Congratulations. I'm giving it to you."

As soon as he hung up, I wanted to call one of my friends. Sunny had been messaging me all night to see if I'd heard anything yet. But I knew she'd have a barrage of questions—it was how she reacted to news, wanting to know everything all at once—and I wasn't ready for that yet. And Grace was so effusive with her celebration that it could feel like an unprincipled happiness. I so rarely heard her allow for possible unpleasant outcomes, or to focus on the worst parts of a thing, and because of that sometimes it was hard to take her happiness seriously, or to let it mean very much to you—if I called her now, she'd be excited and breathless, she'd shriek congratulations, and she wouldn't want to talk about what this meant for Jason. And Brandon—Brandon would know exactly what it meant for Jason, so I couldn't expect him to be happy for me.

I tried to imagine Mr. Irving making the announcement tomorrow: to have everyone turn and look at me, to have them all know, in unison, that I'd been not just good, but the best. I felt like someone else altogether.

I went downstairs to get a drink, and my mother, who was washing dishes, looked up when I came into the kitchen. Sometimes when she saw me she slumped a little in relief, like maybe she hadn't quite expected me to be there after all, and when she did it I tensed involuntarily in response, the two of us an inverse equation.

"Who was that on the phone, Beth?"

"Sunny," I lied. I turned quickly, so that my hair ducked in front of my face. It seemed mean that I'd lied about it; my mother would be overjoyed to hear about the solo.

Would it be worse, I wondered, to pretend it didn't mean that much to me, to try not to gloat in front of Jason, or would it be worse to make it clear how much I'd wanted this? I thought back to the way I'd felt—weightless almost, my whole body light and buoyant—just before that last note, and how that feeling had stayed with me long after.

But all night I thought of Jason pretending not to care, making himself congratulate me. I thought of him going home to live with the loss.

When Mr. Irving answered his phone later that night, his tone was clipped. It was after ten, perhaps too late to call someone his age.

"It's Beth again," I said. I tried to steady my voice. "I've just been thinking, and I think that Jason should have the solo instead of me."

I was a little dizzy, and I was suddenly overcome with a terror of my mother overhearing. I looked up to make sure my door was closed, and Mr. Irving said, "Excuse me?"

"I don't think I should play the solo," I said. "I think you should give it to Jason."

Mr. Irving cleared his throat. It was always horrible being on the phone like this, where you couldn't pause and think about your answers, where you were so exposed.

"You know, Beth," he said, a little sharply, "this audition was for you. I always give the solo to the first chair, but I did it differently this year because, frankly, I thought you'd play it better, and you did."

I closed my eyes, took steady breaths. I couldn't cry. "It's just that I know how much this means to Jason," I said, "and I think he needs it more."

I heard my mother's footsteps in the hallway, her quick, uncertain gait, and my heart quickened as she came closer. I listened to her pause outside my door, and then continue to her own room.

"You realize," Mr. Irving said at last, "this will be our

best-attended show of the whole year. This is a big deal, Beth. You never know who might be there."

"I know," I said. My throat seemed to be closing, and I could just force out a whisper. Did he think I didn't know that—that this was easy for me?

"You're absolutely sure," he said.

"Yes. I'm sure."

"You're turning it down."

"Yes." My voice was giving out, my throat clutching at my vowels, like it wanted to stop me.

"Well, all right, then," Mr. Irving said. "Don't say anything to Jason. I'll announce it tomorrow, and he'll find out when everyone else does."

It was still early enough that he could have called Jason that night, if he'd wanted to. And so I thought he was waiting to tell Jason because he was giving me time to change my mind. I thought about it, wavering, when I picked up my violin again that night and felt a desperation to play that piece, just for pleasure, while it was still sort of mine. I looked at the clock and thought how it wasn't too late yet; I could still call Mr. Irving back, or go in early to rehearsal the next day and tell him I'd made a mistake. Even the next day, when we arrived at rehearsal, I thought how no one knew yet, and it wasn't too late.

Right before Mr. Irving signaled for quiet, I looked at Jason. All day he'd been withdrawn; all day he'd seemed nervous. He looked up—our eyes met—and he gave me a quick, reassuring smile. "Good luck," he whispered, and I had to look away. The room was thick with its waiting, and there was a burning like hunger in my chest.

When Mr. Irving announced it would go to Jason, I was careful to look surprised, but not sad. I wanted Jason to turn to see me, to know I was happy for him.

From a distance, if you were in the back row with the percussion or maybe off on one of the far sides like the flutes, it probably seemed like Mr. Irving was looking at Jason. But he wasn't; he was watching me, waiting to meet my eyes, and when I looked up he gave me a slight, quick nod. I don't think anyone else saw it; it was subtle, and no one else would have known the context. But I saw, and I understood then that he hadn't waited to announce the solo because he was waiting for me to change my mind—if that had been it, he would have asked me again if I was sure, and he wouldn't have reminded me, at the end, that I had chosen this. That little look he gave me told me that he'd waited to tell Jason so I could see this: Jason's shoulders slumped in relief, his smile like curtains opening and sunlight spilling across a bare hardwood floor.

OUR WINTER show was at a church in Portola Valley the Saturday before Christmas. School had just gotten out the day before—it had been a crush of finals and projects and papers due; Grace had messaged us one evening in tears from the stress—and Jason had been reserved and distracted all week, especially at rehearsal. Later, of course, I would look back and agonize over what I might have missed, but at the time I thought he was nervous about his solo. But, as expected, it was very good. He stood near Mr. Irving in the front so that his shadow from the stage lights fell across me and he was a silhouette to me, backlit, as he played. He played flawlessly and precisely, his strokes steady and sure.

Just as he got to the final strains, just as the rest of us had lifted our violins and flooded the room again with our sound, someone in the audience broke into applause. It sounded like someone pounding on a door, breaking into some sacred private moment, and I stiffened—clapping after a solo was even worse than clapping between movements—and it made me stumble and, for two beats, lose my place.

But then, for a moment—just a moment—I could pretend, if I really tried, if I blurred my vision so I lost sight of Mr. Irving and of Jason, flushed and hiding a smile before me, that that applause was for me, that it was my music that had moved someone to forget themselves and to break the audience's code. For a measure, before I returned to my immersion in the song, I let myself pretend.

When it was over, when we'd finished that last fermata and the lights in the audience had come up just slightly again so we were no longer cocooned up there in that brightness, I was watching not Mr. Irving, and not Jason, but Jason's father, in the front row of the audience. And when we lowered our instruments, when Mr. Irving reached up and wiped his forehead, shining under the lights, and when Jason exhaled, I was still watching his father and wondering if perhaps he had been the one to applaud. Because even before Mr. Irving held out his hand toward Jason to acknowledge the solo, Jason's father—who must have arrived at least half an hour early to secure that seat—was beaming and clapping loudly and speaking excitedly to the people around him, motioning occasionally toward the stage, and in that moment what I imagined him saying was, *Look, up there, that's my son.*

For Christmas Eve that year, my father was going to come and get me. I hadn't seen him in a year, since last Christmas Eve, when we'd gone to eat at a Korean barbecue place one of his coworkers had recommended, and afterward we'd gone to Rancho so he could take pictures. It had been crowded, and I kept hoping we'd run into someone I knew, someone I could introduce to him, but it had mostly been older hikers. I'd been stiff and anxious, second-guessing everything I said and fumbling my answer when he asked what I was playing (I'd answered for BAYS, but he meant video games, which seemed obvious in retrospect), but toward the end of the hike he'd been pleased with his pictures, showing them to me almost shyly, and his happiness had been a treasure I'd carried around with me for weeks.

We'd planned to go to lunch, and all week I'd been checking the weather report four or five times a day to make sure it wasn't supposed to rain, just in case he wanted to go back to Rancho, too. The day before Christmas Eve, a package I hadn't ordered showed up on the doorstep, and when I opened it, it was a heavy-duty raincoat from Sunny, with an accompanying note that said *fingers crossed for no rain, but just in case!!* On Christmas Eve, I woke up before dawn and then the day was too charged and promising to sleep any more, so eventually I got up. I had six hours before he was supposed to come still, and none of my friends were even awake to talk with. I made coffee and thought about making some for him, too, but decided against it because it would be cold by the time he came and he'd always been particular about coffee. He'd always liked brownies, too, so I decided to bake some. My mother came downstairs a little after seven. "What does it smell like in here?" she said, looking around happily. "Are those brownies? How festive!"

While they finished baking, I changed my outfit twice and wrapped the gift I'd gotten him, an antique book of black-and-white photos of UC Berkeley. By then the brownies had cooled, and I cut them carefully and messaged Grace, who I knew would be awake by now, for advice on how to make them not like they were from a grade-school bake sale. She sent me a picture to copy from Pinterest, and I folded them up in parchment paper, then hunted around until I found some leftover ribbon in one of the junk drawers and tied the ribbon around them to make a neat package. Then I decided it would look better with a label, so I untied the ribbon and wrote *cocoa brownies* in my neatest handwriting on a slip of paper, punched a hole in it, and retied the whole thing. My father had always appreciated clean, attractive packaging.

I realized too late I should've saved some for my mother. But then it was just a few minutes before he was supposed to come and I didn't want him to catch me in the middle of unpacking and repacking again.

Our home phone rang ten minutes after he was supposed to

pick me up, and right away I knew. I let my mother answer the phone and let her come find me in my room, still holding my purse and the book and the brownies on my lap.

"Hi there," she said. She tried to smile. "That was your dad."

I stared at her. A little ringing, a high-pitched shriek of tinnitus, started in my ears.

"It turned out he had a meeting," she said. "An emergency meeting. They had an internal launch last week, and there was a bug and it's losing them money every minute—he couldn't miss it."

"Oh," I said. I turned away from her. Now I could hear my own pulse, a rapping sound over the ringing.

She reached out, tentatively, and tucked my hair behind my ear. I pulled back, tossing my head so that my hair fell back where it had been. She dropped her arm quickly to her side.

"Let's go get lunch," she said. "We can get anything you want."

"I'm not really that hungry."

"You don't want to eat?"

"No, I'm not hungry."

"We could get Thai food," she said. "That's your favorite. Or we could get—"

"I'm not *hungry*," I snapped. "And that's not even my favorite."

She blinked; I'd stung her. "Beth," she said, "I'm sure he really did want—"

"It doesn't matter."

"I just think—"

"I said it doesn't *matter*." She hovered, her arms halfway reaching out, and I said, sharply, "I'd just like to be alone."

She closed her eyes, tightened her mouth—she looked as though she were in physical pain. She stepped back and turned around and went out the door, and I watched her go, my arms crossed over my chest. After she'd gone, I flung my father's book to the floor and watched as it thudded to a landing on its side, the corner denting. I could hear my mother's footsteps hesitating down the hallway, on the stairs.

Talking to Jason was the only thing I could imagine helping, but when I wrote to him he didn't answer, even though I held my phone and looked at it for a long time.

Unfairly, maybe, I was hurt that no one else had checked in to see how it had gone. I tried to tell myself it was for the best, because I couldn't imagine admitting to them that my father hadn't wanted to come see me. With their happy families, the Christmas bustle—they would think I was pathetic, and I would cast a pall over their day.

When I went downstairs a few hours later, my mother had made a tableau on the kitchen counter: the newspaper flat before her in a way it never was when she actually read it, a full cup of tea that had cooled. When I saw her waiting for me like that I felt guilty, not at all like a person whose father might treasure her company.

"Are you hungry?" she said. She tried to smile. "I made noodles. Or there's some char siu bao in the freezer. I could warm one up."

"I—okay." I still wasn't hungry, but I knew she'd feel better if I ate. "Are the noodles still warm?"

"I'll warm them." She stood up quickly and went to the fridge, pulling out a covered bowl. She poured the contents into a pot on the stove and turned it on. It was more dishes that way, but she always thought food tasted worse when you heated it in the microwave. She stirred carefully with chopsticks, leaning over the stove until steam rose from the pot, as I waited.

"Thanks," I said, when she lifted the noodles back into the bowl and set it in front of me. I ate a few bites, chewing more than I needed to. "These are good."

"Oh." She waved a hand dismissively. "Too salty. I put too

much oyster sauce." She pulled out her chair and sat down next to me, watching me eat.

"Beth," she said softly, "I'm sure he really did want to come." She reached for her cup and tilted it so that the liquid inside swirled around, and she watched the little whirlpool she'd formed. "It's hard for him to show things, you know. He gets nervous. And I think he wishes he saw you more, and then he feels guilty when he—"

"What else did you put in these noodles?"

"Garlic." She set her cup down, and she looked sad. "Lots of garlic. I can make more if you want."

"No, I'm full."

"They say garlic boosts the immune system," she said. "I don't want you to get sick and be—"

My phone buzzed. My heart skipped, expecting Jason, but it was Grace: *How's your dad?? Did you guys go to Rancho? Are you still with him? How did it go?*

It was only because coming downstairs to see my mother waiting for me like this had hollowed me out, and only because it was Grace, that I wrote back that he'd decided not to come. Six seconds later, my phone rang.

"Come over," Grace said immediately when I picked up. "Come have Christmas Eve dinner with us. Do you need a ride?"

My mother took me. She had mentioned earlier that it might be nice to make hot chocolate and watch Christmas movies when I got back from seeing my father, but when Grace invited me she said nothing about that, and I tried not to think of her waiting at home alone that night. On the ride there, I kept my phone in my palm, but Jason didn't write back. Twice my mother opened her mouth and then closed it again, the roundness of it making me think of a fish.

When I went inside, Mrs. Nakamura gave me a long hug.

Their house glowed, adorned with endless white Christmas lights. There were painted wooden snowmen by the entryway and pine wreaths on each door, a full-size tree in the front room and a little one with handmade ornaments by the TV, and a fire gleaming and flickering in the living room. Upstairs, in Grace's room, there was a surprise: Sunny and Brandon were there.

"What are you guys doing?" I said. "Aren't you supposed to be doing family stuff?" Sunny's relatives were in town—she had three cousins all crammed into her room—and every year on Christmas Eve, Brandon's family had crab and prime rib.

"Grace told us about your dad," Sunny said, and she looked (maybe predictably) enraged. Brandon said, roughly, "You deserve better than that, Beth," and Grace folded me into a fierce hug. My eyes welled up. I couldn't speak. They'd dropped everything, had left their family obligations without notice, to be here.

When she stepped back, Grace said, "We'll have a better time without him." She motioned toward her desk, where she'd arranged a plateful of baked goods: English toffee, Mexican wedding cookies, peanut butter brownies, variations on granola and chocolate and cake and caramel, and two tall glasses of milk. And—I'd just noticed—there were carols playing from her laptop, and a pop-up card next to the cookies with shiny red cut-out letters: MERRY CHRISTMAS, BETH!

She turned to smile at me, and I thought of her that day in eighth grade before we were friends turning around in the lunch line with that same smile, the way she'd said, *It's Beth, right? You're in BAYS with us!*—that moment I thought of now as the beginning of my life, the beginning of everything. My throat tightened, a lump forming. And I thought, for the thousandth time, *Why me?*

MY MOTHER and I were still having dim sum with my grandparents Christmas morning—she had reminded me about it at least once a day for the entire week beforehand and knocked to make sure I was awake Saturday morning—and when I still hadn't heard from Jason by then, I told myself it was because it was Christmas, that everyone was busy. I'd sent him a Merry Christmas message, but he was neither a holiday nor an emojis person, and so it wasn't entirely unusual for him not to respond. And I'd overslept, and my mother was anxious about us being on time, so my mind had wandered a little. As we were leaving, my mother had looked at me. "That's what you're wearing?"

I was wearing jeans and a striped sweater and the jade pendant my grandmother had given me. "What's wrong with it?"

"Nothing, nothing," my mother said quickly, after waiting a few seconds too long. "It's fine."

I messaged my friends on the way there to complain. *What are you wearing?* Sunny asked, and when I described it—she knew exactly what items of clothing I was talking about—she wrote back: 😵 *It's dim sum! It'll be like, grandparents in sweats. You're fine.*

My grandparents lived in the Outer Sunset in the same house where my mother had grown up, a pale blue two-story that touched its neighbors on both sides, part of the block-long continuous row of pastel houses that were all variations on one another: the same second-story bay window protruding over the garage, the same stucco roof. You could stand in the middle of the street and look three blocks down to the ocean. It was perpetually foggy there, gray even when it had been sunny driving in, and all the telephone and Muni lines crisscrossing overhead tessellated the sky. Every few minutes the house would clatter, my grandparents' porcelain rattling in the china hutch, when the Muni rolled by.

My grandparents were very particular about things—even though we always drove into the city, they were adamantly against driving within the city limits and refused to go anywhere they couldn't walk or take the Muni. Today, because they wanted dim sum, which meant the one specific place in Chinatown they liked, we were going to meet them there.

My grandparents were already sitting when we finally arrived at the table, both of them wearing dark windbreaker-type jackets, both a little more severely angled with age. They were short, shorter than my mother, and my grandmother, who had always been small, had lost weight; her jacket puffed around her, and her cheeks were hollowed out. She was wearing, along with her jacket and cheap-looking slipper shoes, large diamond earrings and a diamond pendant and several rings, and there was a Gucci purse draped over her chair. I knew she would stuff creamer and sugar packets from fast-food restaurants into her pockets, she would steal stacks of napkins and plastic utensils on the way out and hoard them so she never had to buy her own, but the purse was probably real. It had been nearly five years since I'd seen them, and I hesitated for a moment, unsure if I was supposed to hug them. My grandmother stood up, smiling.

"So big now!" she said. She stuffed a red envelope into my hand and then closed my fingers around it.

"Oh—you shouldn't—" I said, but she waved me off impatiently.

"Sit down, sit down," she said.

My mother took a deep breath before she sat, radiating effort.

"Beth is wearing the necklace you gave her!" she told my grandmother. "Doesn't it look lovely?" Her tone was all wrong, as if my grandmother had said something unpleasant and she was trying to smooth it over.

"How come it took you so long?" my grandmother said. "You always want to drive all over the place. Takes so long."

"We hit some unexpected traffic."

"Better to walk. Then you aren't always late."

My mother took a long breath and then turned over her teacup, then mine. A waitress came by and said something to me in Cantonese, and I said, awkwardly, "Sorry—" and looked to my mother for help.

"Pu-erh," my mother said to her.

I was possibly the only person in this restaurant who didn't speak any kind of Chinese—at least from a cursory glance, I was the only one who was half white—and I felt the emptiness of it, my own rootlessness. When I was younger and still saw my grandparents I used to wonder if they were different in Chinese. These people who were at best peripheral to my life—I couldn't come from some greater whole without also coming first from them.

"So, Beth, almost college, huh?" my grandfather said. "What did you score on SAT?"

"Oh—I haven't taken it for the final—"

"She has *plenty* of time," my mother said quickly. "Plenty. It's a very complicated process, but we know all the deadlines. She can miss the next two testing dates and still do completely fine. There's also the ACT." Then she started telling them how the scheduling worked and then the differences between the ACT and the SAT, as if there were any way they wanted to know all the minute details. She always did the opposite of putting people at ease, of making a situation feel natural. She could conjure tension where there'd been none.

She would've kept barreling on, I think, but a waitress wheeled a cart to our table, and my mother stopped talking so we could order. As the table filled with bowls and bamboo steamers, jook and dao miu, har gow and shumai and char siu bao, I was suddenly ravenously hungry—it had been years, I realized, since I'd had dim sum. Everything tasted like childhood, the char siu bao pillowy and soft, the tripe crunchy and clean-tasting, steamed with chiles, and I was reaching for another piece of tripe when my grandmother tapped my hand away, clicking her tongue in disapproval.

"You should eat more vegetable. Your mother don't tell you? Boys don't like girls who eat, eat, eat."

My face went hot. My mother said quickly, "The gai lan is delicious. How's the har gow?"

My grandmother sniffed. "Dry."

"Maybe different cook today," my grandfather said.

My mother changed the subject, asking about a memorial service for one of their friends who'd just died, and the rest of them ate, but I was too self-conscious now. Maybe I shouldn't have come after all. My mother picked at a chicken foot and then pushed the bones around on her place, and after a little while she deftly emptied the rest of the platter of chow fun noodles onto my plate and said, "Here, Beth, eat this," and resentment swelled inside me—of all the times for her to suddenly decide to act like nothing was wrong.

"You'll apply to Stanford?" my grandfather said. When he lifted his chopsticks, his hands shook with a tremor I didn't remember from the last time I'd seen them. "What about Harvard?"

"Those are both so expensive," my mother said. "Beth will likely—"

"Not with a scholarship, huh?"

"There are a lot of wonderful options Beth can explore."

"Not good enough for Stanford?" He turned to my grand-mother. "Helen Wong's grandson got into Stanford."

"Gwai lo don't care about grades, that's why," my grand-mother said. "You just have one child, how come she don't do better? Not enough time to help her with grades?"

I looked at my plate and imagined myself telling her how repugnant her comment before had been. My mother said, "Beth has worked very hard in school."

My grandmother clicked her tongue again. "Too bad you already had Beth when your husband left. Otherwise, you start over, find another husband, and then—"

Abruptly, my mother stood up. Some of my grandmother's tea sloshed over the side of her teacup. "We're going to leave," she said. Her voice came out high-pitched and quavery.

"Sit down, sit down," my grandfather said, bewildered. "Look, you knock over Mama's tea."

I expected my mother to sit down, to apologize for her outburst, but she clutched her purse, and her face was red. "Beth, let's go."

I got up. My face was burning as I followed her through the restaurant, weaving through the round tables and all the carts.

In the car, my mother leaned her head back against the head-rest, closed her eyes, and pressed both hands against her chest, wincing like she was in pain. Her hands were plain, without nail polish or jewelry except for the jade bracelet she always wore. I thought of how sometimes when I was younger she would take me with her to get a manicure because she loved for her hands to look nice. They were shaking. Somewhere else in the garage, a car alarm went off.

"I don't know why I always hope for more from them," my mother said, her tone as if she was speaking more to herself than to me. "They're never going to be different than they are."

Walking through the restaurant I had been embarrassed,

but now, unexpectedly, my eyes pricked with tears. My mother deserved better than this. Maybe all along the real reason I'd avoided coming with her to see them was so I could pretend to myself she had parents who cherished her and took fierce pride in even her smallest accomplishments, who saw her as a gift to them and to the world and who made her feel treasured, because the alternative—that there was no one in her life who did that for her, that no one saw her that way—was unbearable to face.

"The world was terrible to them, you know," she said. She jammed her key in the ignition. "It taught them to never let down their guard even with people they're supposed to love. And my dad—he always longed to go to college, and he's very self-conscious about not having an education. They both had very hard lives, and—" Her voice was trembling, and she stopped speaking. The car alarm stopped, and the squeal of brakes ricocheted off all the cement. Then she swiveled herself to face me and touched me, gently, on my cheek. "Beth, I want you to know there was no truth at all to what my mom said. I would do it all again—all of it—to be your mother. You are the joy of my life."

There wasn't any real joy in her voice—she sounded on the verge of tears. I still believed her, though. Maybe that was the worst part.

She didn't wait for me to answer; she turned the car on and reversed, a little recklessly, out of the parking space. On our left was a silver Tesla that had parked a little over the line, and she wasn't really looking over her shoulder at it, and I held my breath, half bracing in case we hit it. We didn't, though; we skirted by it, unharmed.

The whole way back, the silence swelled between us, and by the time we went across the bridge in Hillsborough, where the Flintstone house was, I'd begun rehearsing what I'd say to her when we got home. She should know, at least, that I loved her, that I thought her parents were unfair to her. But when I imagined putting those things into words I felt them wither inside me. I didn't say things like *I love you* to her. I couldn't picture myself trying to describe how it had affected me seeing her near tears in the car.

Still, though, I wanted her to know those things. I wished I was certain she did.

By the time she pulled into our driveway, neither of us had said anything the whole ride. My mom's skin looked blotchy.

"Maybe it's better," she said quietly, "if we don't—involve them in your future. Certainly, it won't be impossible without them. I can look into a different loan structure. And I know you didn't like the idea, but I think I should talk to your father—he'll pay child support through graduation, and there's no reason he shouldn't continue to—"

The words blared in the car like a foghorn. "What do you mean he'll pay child support through graduation?"

"Well, typically—in California, at least—it's until age nineteen or high school graduation, whichever—"

I stared at her. "Don't ask him for child support."

"What do you mean?"

"I mean I don't want him to pay child support."

My mother looked confused. "He already pays child support."

I was hot all over, my skin too tight. "What do you mean he pays child support?"

"Well, that was our agreement—"

"How much does he pay?"

"He pays—" She glanced at me, and then pushed her door open. "Beth, I don't think I understand your concern here."

"All my life you've been asking him for money?"

"We have a court-ordered financial agreement."

"What does he pay?"

"He pays what we agreed—Beth, where are you going? Come inside."

I had always been proud of how little I asked of him and expected of him. I had been available, always, and I had been so careful—so exquisitely careful—to not be clingy or demanding or needy, all the worst things you could say about a girl. I had wanted to be easy. But all this time, whenever I wrote him to invite him to concerts, whenever I asked about seeing him on holidays, and yesterday when he hadn't come, maybe all this time he was thinking *haven't I already done enough for you?* He didn't even live in our house and yet somehow still my mother, who had a job of her own, had continually pressed him for money as though he did. All this time she had been holding him hostage. She had turned me into a monthly burden in his life, a bill to pay along with internet and rent. And she had never told me—she had let me think she was doing everything for me.

"Beth, where are you going?"

"I'm going for a walk," I snapped.

"Why don't you come inside and—"

But I hurried so that I was out of earshot, or at least I could pretend I was, and though I knew she was standing there in the driveway for a long time, debating going after me, eventually she gave up and went inside.

Grace messaged to ask how it had gone with my grandparents. I thought about telling them everything that had just happened, everything my mom had just told me, but what would I even say? Every now and then, Brandon's father took him out of school just to do things like go eat at House of Prime Rib or watch a daytime baseball game, and Brandon joked with him affectionately and asked him for advice. Every year, Grace's family went to Carmel for a week and her father staged the same picture he'd been taking with Grace and her brother since they were infants. When Sunny told her father she was queer, he took her to dinner and bragged repeatedly to the waiter how Taiwan was the first Asian country to legalize same-sex marriage, and when she tried to explain to him that she might not marry a cis woman (or anyone), he told her whoever it was would be incredibly lucky and all he cared about was his children's happiness. It was so different for them. So I walked the neighborhood by myself, forcing myself higher and higher up the hill on Via Colina until my calves burned. Every time I saw an elaborately decorated house, I wondered about the people inside—if they all really loved the holiday that much or if any of them were doing it just to convince themselves they were cheery, to look good to outsiders. But maybe ours was the only unhappy home there.

It was around two in the afternoon when I got back, and I was exhausted of the world and all its betrayals, and because it seemed the cleanest way to escape, I took two Benadryl to fall asleep.

Sometimes when I'd write to my father or sometimes, less often, Jason, I would turn my phone off immediately after and wait as long as I could, holding open all that space for an answer to come back. Then all the time waiting wasn't the same agony as silence, because you could tell yourself it was all possibility instead. I did that now—I turned off my phone, and I left it off all night. And it was partly that I couldn't imagine talking to anyone, but it was also that I did this sometimes—I let my hope accumulate.

So when Jason jumped from the Golden Gate Bridge, it was just after five on Christmas and my phone was off and I was, uselessly, asleep.

MUCH LATER, when I could bring myself to read about it, I learned that the time of free fall from the bridge is four seconds. For nearly four seconds, then, Jason sank through the air, his clothing billowing up above him and the mist from the water rushing up at him like a wave. The way he fell, he would have been able to see the sky above him and the cars barreling over the lanes of the bridge, and he would have passed seagulls hovering over him in their flight. He would have been falling too fast, the wind and the speed and the force flooding his eardrums, to hear the cars or the boats below or the shouting from people who saw him up above. It was clear that day, and cold, and to anyone who witnessed his contortions and wild flailing from the bridge it must have looked as though he were trying to swim.

My phone was ringing—it was Brandon, too early for him to be calling. I was disoriented and at first mistook it for my alarm, thinking it was a school day. It was just before seven the next morning.

He had to tell me three times before it sank in—I kept saying, "What do you mean? What do you mean?"—and then I couldn't speak. He'd opened with "He's alive, but," and I think now how heartbreakingly kind of him it was to do that, that I didn't have to live through his death even for a few seconds before I knew he'd somehow survived.

"His mom called me. She called from his phone, and I thought it was him when I picked up—then she told me—" Brandon was crying. "Fuck, I can't breathe." I could hear him gasping for air. "She said when they pulled him from the water they thought he was dead. He's in the ICU—he broke his ribs and punctured his lungs, and—"

Later, Brandon would tell me how his father had overheard his call with Jason's mother and had gotten on the phone and asked Mrs. Tsou if he could be allowed to speak with Jason's doctor. I think about that now, his father stepping in like that. After he hung up, he tried to give Brandon a hug, but Brandon fought his way out. He was yelling and swearing, and his dad finally grabbed his arms and pinned them to his sides and said, "Brandon, listen to me, listen to me—I talked to his doctor; he's going to be okay."

Which was bullshit, Brandon told me, obviously a cop-out, obviously nothing was okay, but he forgave his father when he saw he had tears in his eyes.

But that was later, and in the moment I don't think it would have mattered if he'd told me. I wouldn't have been capable of absorbing it.

"My dad said he'll be okay," Brandon was saying, and I realized I hadn't heard some of what he'd told me. "He said he'll be in a lot of pain and he could get infections, but it won't—he said when you're young you heal fast and probably he'll be back home in two weeks or maybe even one, depending—"

It was stupid, it was just that my mind was flying wildly around, grasping for solid ground, but all I could think was *But what if we hear back about the Juilliard auditions?* They would have to pause it, I thought. How could the world just keep going as if—

Brandon was saying something. I said, thickly, "What?"

"I said are you okay?"

"Am I okay?"

"Your voice sounds weird. Are you sitting down? Do you—"

I couldn't shut off the tinnitus in my ears. I put down the phone. I sat up and put my head between my legs and breathed until the room wasn't going blurry at the corners anymore.

"We have to go see him," I said when I picked it back up.

"We can't."

"What do you mean we can't?"

"His mom said she'll tell us when we can come."

"But we have to—"

"I know," he said. "I know. But she said"—he pitched his voice higher, imitating Jason's mother—"*This is not party.*"

"But—"

His voice gave out. "I know."

I don't know why it felt like there was nothing else to say. Or maybe it wasn't that, either—maybe it was that there was so much it couldn't fit into language. But as all the air around me went thin like my ribs had shrunk around my lungs, we stayed on the phone, silent and so incredibly far away from him.

It was four days before they let us see him, and in those days nothing else existed in the world. We spent them mostly at Grace's house, showing up first thing in the morning and leaving long after dark. Mrs. Nakamura made us hot cider and cookies, and she'd come sit next to Grace, stroking her hair, and we watched movies and waited to be able to go see Jason. We would sit tangled on the couches or on the floor, our limbs pressed together, and when someone got up to get something to eat or go to the bathroom, I missed their physical presence. Brandon's and Sunny's parents both called them constantly, for no apparent reason, I think just to make sure they were still there, and one night Brandon's mother came to pick him up—that was also different, that his parents didn't want him driving—and she and Mrs. Nakamura talked in the kitchen for a long time, and when I looked in they were both crying.

That morning when I'd stumbled downstairs, my mother hadn't left for work yet, and she'd asked me if something was wrong.

I was immediately on guard. "Like what?" I'd said.

"Well—I heard something happened with someone at your school. Something—someone tried to hurt themselves. So I was just wondering if you'd heard anything about that."

"Where did you hear that?"

"It was discussed on Nextdoor."

His name hadn't been in the news anywhere, and the school hadn't sent anything home, and she didn't talk to other parents from school unless she was dropping me off at someone's house, but I would make sure that didn't happen. I knew she wouldn't hear more details. "Well, I didn't hear anything," I said. "Maybe it was a freshman."

"If you ever want to talk about—"

"I don't," I said, and she'd left me alone after that. Maybe she assumed I was still angry about the child support. Which I was, but it was a suspended anger that hung around the periphery but for right now felt unreachable. I didn't care about my father or my grandparents. When finally I had to go home that day, Mrs. Nakamura saying gently that surely my mother missed me, I felt the absence of my friends like a sickness. I couldn't sleep that night.

On the fourth day, finally, Brandon called to say we were allowed to go see him. Some of my friends' parents—Grace's, mostly—spent a long time debating whether we should be allowed to go by ourselves, or whether they should come, but eventually they softened, and Brandon drove us. We were quiet on the way there, and I leaned my head back against the headrest and closed my eyes. I was viscerally, shatteringly nervous, cold all over and with a sick thrumming in my whole chest. Since we'd heard, I hadn't been able to shake the fear that Brandon's father was wrong—maybe there was a blood clot lurking in Jason's lungs, an infection lying in wait—and I had lived in terror of my phone ringing; at night I would wake up with the horrible certainty something awful had happened, that the way I was feeling was a sign. And now we were going to see him, and as much as I'd been desperate to be with him, I could feel already how it was never going to be enough. What would we say to him? What would I say? All this time we'd been waiting, all the things I wanted to say had been crescendoing inside me, rising to a din. But we could hardly burst in and say *Why did you do it, Jason?* I couldn't stand in front of his hospital bed and look him in the eye and demand *Why weren't we enough to stop you?*

In the parking lot, we were jostled violently going over a speed bump. My eyes flew open. Brandon was driving too fast.

"Slow down," Sunny snapped. She clutched the armrest so hard her knuckles turned white, and when we pitched forward again on the next speed bump she made a gasping, choking sound and grabbed at my arms.

"You know what my dad told me once?" Brandon said. "He said the spinal cord has the same consistency as toothpaste."

I shut my eyes against the image. Sunny said, "That's disgusting."

"That's why you can't move someone after an injury, because if anything touches that cord, it's not springy—you know, it doesn't go back to how it's supposed to be. God," he said, "I just keep thinking about how it's like toothpaste and—"

"Stop the car, Brandon," Sunny said suddenly, urgently.

"We're almost—"

"Brandon, *stop.*"

He slammed on the brakes just in time for her to fling open

the door and retch onto the asphalt, her chest heaving. I stroked her back. She sat hunched for a few minutes, then she sat up and closed her eyes and leaned back against the seat. "Okay," she said, "park."

Inside we walked down the hallway, square white linoleum tiles and a low ceiling, fluorescent lighting. Our footsteps echoed around us, and there was a hum of medical noise: beeping and thrumming. The flickering of lights overhead and the lack of ventilation inside were blurring my vision slightly, dulling the edges so that even when I focused nothing quite held.

At the ICU we had to be buzzed in. My heart was pounding, and I tried desperately to arrange all the words screaming around in my head into something I could possibly say to him, and then there was no more time to think about it because Sunny had pushed open the heavy wooden door to his room and we were there, and there he was.

The first thing I noticed was that so many things in his room were clear: bags of fluid, the tubes of the IV inserted into the back of his hand, and I think I saw those things first because I couldn't look right at him, the same way you can't stare into the sun. There was a tube in his chest, too, clear and rubbery and thick, and when I saw it my esophagus revolted and I gagged. I turned away, ashamed, and then, finally, I made myself look. His face was bruised and puffy, and there was an ugliness to it. All the same, though, seeing him—some small screeching corner in my mind went quiet at last.

Jason lifted his hand a few inches off the mattress in a small wave. When he breathed, it made a wheezing sound. He coughed and then winced and pressed on his chest with his thumb. It wasn't a large room, and it was empty aside from Jason. Were his parents not here with him? They were making him wait here alone?

"You guys shouldn't have come," he muttered, and him saying

that—the rejection of it—would play over and over in my mind for weeks. "I told my parents to tell you not to come."

"Of course we came," Brandon said. "We would've come the second we heard if your parents had let us." He closed his eyes and pressed against them with his thumb and forefinger. His shoulders were shaking. Grace reached out and took his hand—I stared at their hands there, twined together that way—and she leaned against him.

"You should have called us," Sunny said. "We would have done *anything*, Jason. We would have done anything at all."

Jason said, "I know."

Later, I'd read that of all the people who've jumped from that same gap in the guardrails, fewer than thirty have survived. There were a few short articles about Jason in the news, none with his name, but they were easy to find with the right keywords. In one of them, Jason's survival was described as miraculous—miraculous that he managed to right himself so he absorbed the force of his fall feetfirst, miraculous that he didn't die on impact, miraculous that there was a coast guard boat near enough to yank him out of the water, to lay him on the painted concrete floor of the boat and pile heavy felted blankets on top of him. Miraculous that the paramedics arrived when they did to treat his collapsed lung, miraculous that when he went into shock, that alone didn't kill him.

I remember reading that story and how when I put it down my body went numb and my mind went blank, like it was protecting me from knowing any more, from having to think or revisit or argue. It was protecting me, I think, from having to defend to some faceless reporter what it had felt like to see him there, to look at him battered and damaged that way, to understand what had happened to him and how none of us were going to be the same from then on. Whatever it felt like in that room, it didn't feel like a miracle.

Jason opened his eyes again. The left half of his face was

scraped, and his head was encased in a plasticky apparatus that looked vaguely gladiatorial. The sheet was only half covering his chest, and beneath it his skin was bruised deeply, as though someone had dipped a thumb in fingerpaint to smudge rough streaks of charcoal and blue and puce. I watched his chest rise and fall.

"Where are your parents?" Grace said, as though she'd read my mind.

"They're here. They went to go get something to eat in the cafeteria."

"Oh," Grace said, and I could tell she was blinking back tears, and then none of us knew what else to say.

Jason shifted his legs slightly in the bed and grimaced, and for a few seconds the electronic beeping of his heart sped up and then slowed again. I watched the monitor on his IV pole. I was acutely aware that still I'd said nothing to him—I felt that lack as a hollow in the pit of my stomach—but everything I could think to say was so tremendously small.

We stood for a while, the thin, high-pitched beeping of the monitor and the starchy rustling of Jason's sheets the only sounds. I cleared my throat, then wished I hadn't. I trained my eyes elsewhere in the room—on the whiteboard on the wall with YOUR NURSE TODAY IS ANDREA CHONG written on it, the bag of fluid labeled HYDROMORPHONE—instead of on Jason.

"Are you in a lot of pain?" Brandon said.

"What do you fucking think?" He mumbled it, though—the words were sharp, but his tone was blurry and faded. Later, Brandon would tell me his father had explained to him that dilaudid makes you loopy, and he would say that Jason wasn't really himself. It was supposed to be comforting, I think. It wasn't.

He looked at me then. And I was so exposed in that moment, like he could see all my inadequacies, all the things I couldn't say—how if he'd thought we shouldn't come see him here, I'd done nothing to prove him wrong; I was unneeded. I said, "Jason, what happened?"

But then the door to the room opened. Jason's parents came in through the curtain, his mother holding a paper cup of water, and then a step behind them was Evelyn. All of them looked exhausted. It was the first time I'd seen Evelyn without any makeup on, and she looked like a blurred version of herself. She didn't acknowledge me. I wondered if she would. I wondered whether she'd said anything to Jason about me calling her.

"Hello, hello," his mother said, "thank you for coming. Hello."

Jason's father peered at me. I never knew whether he recognized me, if he remembered that Brandon and I had been at his house that day, if it would have made a difference to him either way.

"It's okay, Jason okay now," he said, and he patted my shoulder. "All okay now," he repeated, and dropped his arm. He stared helplessly at Jason there in the bed. "Next year he go to Berkeley, huh? And put all this behind him. Next year, much better."

My heart was pounding. There were words all tangled up inside my throat, waiting to be loosened. *This is your fault* is what I wanted to say, and I wanted to scream it at him. *He would have been all right if not for you.*

Later, I'd learn that Mr. Tsou stayed awake all night sitting by Jason's side, that every time Jason caught his breath in pain his father wept, that when he thought Jason was sleeping he told Mrs. Tsou it should've been him instead in the hospital bed. I don't know if it would've mattered to me then to know that. I like to think it wouldn't have changed anything, that I understood then all the shortcomings of remorse and how impotent it is against the past. I like to think I recognized that you don't have to tell yourself things are fine to make it easier on another person, and that you don't have to turn your heart toward men who are suffering when they've brought it on themselves.

But probably that isn't true of me. After all, I would, at that point, have forgiven my own father everything in exchange for something as small as a phone call.

"Your nurse is coming back," Evelyn said to Jason. "Your friends should probably go."

I wanted him to say something to us with her there—something that would prove to her that we belonged, something to make it so she couldn't fence us off from him the way it felt like she'd already mentally done, as though we didn't matter. But he didn't; he was slipping back into sleep, and he mumbled something unintelligible.

"Thank you for coming," his mother said. "He is very tired. He need to rest. Thank you for coming. Evelyn say he need to see his friends. He is very happy to see you." At the door, she lowered her voice.

"This is private family matter," she said. She tried to smile, and then she reached out and grabbed my hand. I let her, because I didn't know what else to do. "Don't tell everyone, please, okay? This is family matter. Thank you for coming to see him. He will be okay now that you see him."

That night at home I woke up in that porous middle-of-the-night dark because I couldn't breathe. My lungs were nets, the oxygen pouring through them no matter how much I gasped for air, and my heart was sputtering in my chest so I could feel suddenly how incredibly fragile it was. I could feel how it was about to slip out of rhythm and how it could end everything in a single instant.

I couldn't draw enough air to scream for help, and I dragged myself, mostly crawling, down the hall. My mother took me to the emergency room, driving thirty over the speed limit and praying frantically aloud. I didn't have my phone, and all I could think was that I wouldn't get to tell my friends goodbye.

At the hospital, they drew blood and ran EKGs on my heart. Afterward, the doctor came in, a Filipino man in his fifties who carried his clipboard with both hands. He sat down and told us my tests had been normal, which was, I think, supposed to be reassuring, and then asked if I'd been stressed or anxious.

"Their school—" my mother said. "It's very stressful. Other children have—struggled. As a parent, you worry—"

The doctor nodded sympathetically. I'd had a panic attack, he said, and I should exercise and make sure I got sufficient sleep.

We drove back home. The sky had started to lighten, the day rushing toward us before we were ready, and we were both exhausted. I was sick and afraid, my body a stranger to me.

"I hope you know," my mother said, when we passed by the nature preserve on Arguello, "that you can always talk to me."

I said nothing. The sun flickered a peekaboo through the row of redwoods we went by.

"About anything," my mother said. Her eyes were wet. "Anything at all."

At home after the hospital, I went back to bed. I woke up disoriented hours later because someone was in my room.

It was my mother. I squinted at her through mostly closed eyes, and she didn't see me. She was arranging something on my nightstand, and when she stepped back I could see what it was, all set on a tray: a cup of hot peppermint tea, a bowl of jook with cilantro and green onions on top, a vase with roses from the bush by our walkway. She fussed with it, arranging it carefully, and then smoothed the blankets over me and laid her hand gently, so gently, on my hair. I pretended I was asleep.

JASON WAS, everyone said repeatedly, lucky. He had broken three ribs and his collarbone, for which he'd had surgery his second day in the hospital, he had significant bruising, and he'd lost some blood, for which he'd been given a transfusion. But those were, all told, considered minor injuries weighted against what could have been, and after ten days in the hospital, his arm still in a sling, he was back home. We heard not from Jason (I had been faithfully messaging him every day, but I'd never heard back) but from Brandon, who'd heard from his father, who had gone to see Jason's parents at the hospital.

When winter break ended and I went back to school—we all went back to school, even though it seemed impossible—without him, everyone had heard somehow. That first day back, I was staring into my locker, trying to remember what I needed and why it mattered, when Annique Chang and Harish Desai came up to me. Annique looked like she'd been crying.

"Beth, I can't believe it," she said. "I had no idea Jason was struggling."

"Is there anything we can do?" Harish said. "Can we all send him a card or something? Or set up a GoFundMe?"

It felt like being plunged underwater without an oxygen tank—how desperate I was to swim back to the safety of our group, where I wouldn't have to fumble for the right way to explain how awful it would be for them to make Jason a GoFundMe because my friends would instinctively understand.

"Um," I said, "I don't think—"

I couldn't make it through the sentence before my voice gave out, and then I was crying.

"Oh, Beth," Annique said. Her eyes flooded. And I was moved by that but also, maybe unfairly, angry—this was our tragedy; it wasn't hers.

"Aw, you're a good friend," Harish said, patting me on the back, his eyes concerned. "Are you going to be okay? It's good you have Sunny and them."

Everyone was talking about him. And far more intensely than after Homecoming, too, a situation that was probably close to Jason's personal hell. Harish, who was Instagram-famous mostly for being hot and well dressed, filmed himself and a bunch of other people talking about mental health and then posted it all as a series of Insta stories. Teachers urged us in class to make appointments with the guidance counselor if we needed to talk. And rumors swirled about why: he'd overdosed on drugs, he'd run away from home, he hadn't gotten in anywhere for early decision. Knowing they were false somehow didn't help; I felt each of them as its own emergency, maybe because we didn't know, actually, what exactly had happened, or why. And besides that, Jason was in the hospital still, and I could feel each of the miles between us like a knife wound.

There was a new tightness in my throat that had followed me everywhere ever since my night at the hospital, which terrified me because that was what before had bloomed overnight into the panic attack. In class I felt trapped if I had to sit somewhere far away from the door or if the teacher had a strict bathroom policy, and I would run through scenarios in my head—in AP Calc, for instance, what would Thea Rogel, who sat next to me, do if I suddenly slumped over in my chair?

The worst thing, though, would be for something to happen when I was with my friends. I hadn't told them about the hospital. Every time I imagined saying it aloud, speaking it into reexistence, there was that same heaviness on my chest and that same cold torrent of fear. But also, it would be too much to ask of them to deal with right now. At night sometimes I would read about infections that could set in after surgeries, bad reactions to blood transfusions, and I had nightmares about the phone ringing again, the hospital calling, although if something happened they wouldn't call me; disaster could be rising right now. We had not passed through a crisis; we were inside it.

The rest of the world felt fake. The things that showed up in my email—credit card statement notifications, college spam, the B & B reservation my mother made for Asheville—were like postcards from a stranger's life.

We skipped Wednesday breakfast for the first time in years, because it didn't feel right without Jason. In BAYS, Mr. Irving asked if I would act as first chair while he was out. It could've seemed cold, like a replacement, but Mr. Irving's eyes were pained when he spoke to me, and when I talked about it with my friends we understood he meant it more as holding space for Jason, as something I could do for him. And we were grateful for that, not least because it pointed to a future when Jason would return.

But the truth was that since Christmas I'd barely picked up my violin at home. It was a little better at BAYS when it wasn't just me and there was more purpose in togetherness, but even still I felt sometimes that in being there I was wasting myself. Because I was here, in rehearsal, day after day, while I found myself unable to do even the smallest thing for Jason, throwing myself at the altar of something so intangible and so needless and so dangerous as *sound*.

When I was eight, after years of pleading, I'd gotten my ears pierced. I adored my piercings, how grown up they made me look: me, but enhanced. I would admire them in the mirror and carefully sort out my small collection of earrings, and for the first eight weeks, as directed, I'd meticulously turned the earring posts and rinsed my ears with alcohol twice a day. I'd had them in almost half a year when one day I went to remove the backing on my left ear and realized, horrified, that my ear had grown over it entirely. I screamed.

My mother was too afraid to watch and so my father took me to the doctor. He was supposed to be at work, and he was irritated, and I felt the weight of myself pressing against the life he'd wanted. But he held my hand when I cried as the doctor cut into my earlobe, and he patted my hair, and told me I was being brave. He'd never said that to me before. I wanted to keep his praise embedded in my heart. Afterward, the doctor said, sympathetically, to my father, "We see this a lot, you know. Always in young girls—they're vain, you know, want to look pretty like their friends, but they aren't responsible enough to take care of themselves yet." I'd thought my father would defend me—hadn't he just said I was brave?—but when I looked up at him, I saw in his expression that I'd been wrong: he agreed with the doctor after all.

In that moment I saw myself as he saw me, I understood the shape I took in his life: I was, paradoxically, simultaneously too much and not enough. And all my life since then I had tried to rectify that. I had silently taken instructions on how to be better from everywhere I could glean them: when I was a freshman and my locker was next to where a group of senior guys would laugh and murmur things about girls walking by (too much makeup; too small an ass; not enough makeup; too loud; kind of a bitch because she'd turned one of them down). When I saw movies and all the most desirable women had just a few lines. When Isaac Lin asked Melissa Kim out and she turned him down and everyone was mad at her because she'd embarrassed him, and hurt him, and he was so nice. When someone who'd been in BAYS ten years ago ran for Congress, and I watched both pundits and my father declare her shrill.

Back then I didn't think he'd ever leave. We were a family; he was my father; I'd thought those things were immutable as eye color or birthplace. And, too, I'd thought I had learned. When I needed something, I went to my mother, and I tried to get better at the games he liked, and I tried not to ask him for things. I tried to erase whatever parts of me were demanding or needy or disagreeable. I tried to take up less space. I'd thought as I got older it would be better, that I would be better, because of how religiously I had devoted myself to not being the wrong kind of girl. But then he'd left, so I understood that I was not in fact better yet. I was, in spite of everything, the same.

And then, miraculously, with my friends I'd been given another chance. I could be someone else with them; I could be the best version of myself. We could build something that mattered, and I could belong with them, and I could shed the ruinous parts of myself that drove people away from me and give all I had.

But now here I was again. And I knew this feeling with Jason: the damning glare of your own inadequacy, how much you hadn't been enough for someone. You had asked too much and given too little, and you'd nearly lost everything as a result.

One day that first week back, a few other people from our class came to hang out at lunch. Which happened sometimes, but this time it was because they wanted to talk about Jason. They perched on the edges of the concrete planters and talked about whether there were signs we'd all missed, how awful it could be here, whether it might happen again with anyone else. Vincent Wu, who Jason played tennis with sometimes, said, "I heard he's not ever coming back to school."

Sunny frowned. "Where'd you hear that?"

"My mom heard about it."

"But you're not talking to Jason, are you?" I said. "It's just a complete rumor you're—"

"I'm just saying what I heard."

"That's what a rumor is," I said. My voice came out loud.

"Whoa, whoa," he said, holding out his hands, "let's calm down here."

"Little-known fact!" Grace said cheerfully, ripping open the wrapper of her LÄRABAR. "Girls are allowed to say things, actually," and because it was Grace, Vincent laughed and tipped an imaginary hat.

"Jason'll definitely come back, right?" I said when Vincent and the others were gone. Already it seemed an impossible luxury that he used to just be here, with us, all the time.

"Yeah—" Brandon squinted at a big group of sophomores walking by, all with cups of boba from the new place by the freeway. "I do kind of wonder if he just—won't."

"Like, ever?" Grace said. "What would he do, just drop out?"

"I don't know, some kind of independent study or something? I mean, would you want to come back? Everyone here knows too much about everyone else. What if people asked you a bunch of questions or said stupid shit to you, you know?"

"We have to get him to come back," I said. "Can you imagine if he doesn't and we never see him, and he's just at home every day by himself—" I had to stop, the words rising in my throat to choke me. I tried frantically to take deep breaths. *I am fine*, I told myself, *I'm fine, I'm fine, I won't have a panic attack here.* The world was starting to narrow in my vision, but if I closed my eyes they would notice something was wrong. I wondered if they could hear it in my breathing.

"I just remembered I have to go turn something in," I said, and I got up quickly. My voice came out a little strangled, and Sunny peered at me closely, but she didn't press it, and I made it to the science wing bathrooms and hid there the rest of lunch in case I threw up, or passed out, slumped against the metal wall of the stall with my fingers pressed to my wrist to track my pulse.

No one said anything, but something else happened with Grace later that day. I was at my locker after school when she appeared behind me and said, "Why didn't you tell me Chase came to talk to you?"

I closed my locker and turned to her. Chase Hartley felt so thoroughly a part of another, past life that at first I didn't register her meaning. "What do you mean?"

"Before Homecoming," she said. "He said he came to talk to you."

I blinked at her. "Grace, I don't—what are you getting at?"

"I saw him today and it was really sweet, he said he'd been hearing about Jason and asked if I wanted to talk or anything."

"*Chase* asked if you wanted to talk about Jason? To *him*?"

"And then he asked if that had anything to do with why I couldn't go to Homecoming."

"What did you tell him?"

"I said yes. And then he said he asked you—"

"Grace, you told him that?"

"He was really sweet about it. He won't tell anyone." She tightened her ponytail. "But I can't believe you never told me how he came to talk to you before Homecoming, Beth! I felt so bad. I didn't know he was that upset about it. I wish I'd gone with him."

I was having trouble rooting myself in the conversation we were having. Chase felt entirely inconsequential to me, and I had to struggle through the fog around me to remember even having talked with him. "I don't really—Grace, we really shouldn't tell people more about Jason. He'll be so upset when he comes back and finds out there're all these rumors flying."

"Chase won't tell anyone."

"How do you know that? And that's—that's beside the point. I'm sure he wouldn't want Chase to know either."

"I just can't believe you didn't tell me."

"Okay, well, you'd already decided you weren't going, so it didn't feel—"

"Yeah, but if I'd known he was going to be that upset, maybe I would have."

Why were we still talking about him? "Okay, well, I guess I was just more focused on Jason, and considering he almost died—"

Grace looked stricken. I should've been more careful with my tone. I said, tightly, "But since you told Chase everything, he understands now, right? I'm sure it'll probably be fine."

On my way back to the parking lot I was afraid to walk by the science wing bathrooms, because I was afraid if I saw them again I'd panic. So I went through the rally court instead, and I saw Chase there loping across the other end with Jacob Rogel. They were laughing about something together, and I felt a surge of fury. If he knew about Jason, because Grace had told him, what was there possibly to find to laugh about right now? I'd been right about Chase, obviously; Grace shouldn't have told him.

I wanted to be done here. Next year this would all be behind us. We would go somewhere else, away from here, and it would be just the five of us—we could camp out in one of our dorm rooms, and it would be like living together. Maybe some of us could room together—Brandon and Jason could, or maybe Sunny and Grace and I could be in a triple. The only thing that brought me comfort was knowing that we would come out of this stronger. It would bring us together; it would cement things between us permanently. I wouldn't survive it otherwise—none of us would.

The first time I heard from Jason was that night. I was in my room after my lesson with Mrs. Nguyen, which had been a disaster. "Your mother pay a lot for these lesson," she'd told me, not ungently, because it was clear I hadn't been playing. "Is something wrong?" So now I was supposed to be practicing, as I'd promised her I would. I was holding my violin, but when I looked at the string of notes fanned out across the page, at all the half rests standing out like little gravestones, a whole cemetery contained within the staff, I felt that if I didn't stop myself I was going to slam my violin to the floor.

Then Jason messaged. When my phone buzzed where it was charging on my desk and I saw his name, it was like a wave crashing over me, a flash of heat that went from my head to my fingertips. My hands were shaking as I entered my password. He'd written, *how's it going?*

I put my phone on my bed and burst into sobs. I clutched the phone against my chest and tried to regain control. When I could type again, I wrote, *How are you?? How is everything? We miss you so much.*

Eh, hanging in. Kind of bored.

Well, boredom wasn't the worst thing in the world. *I don't know if you got my messages*, I wrote.

Sorry, he wrote back. *I had to get a new phone.*

Of course. I should've thought of that—if he'd had it with him, surely it would've been ruined. All this time I'd been sending messages to no one, and maybe all this time he'd wondered where we were.

It was only later that I realized he still should've gotten all my messages anyway. But I couldn't let that matter—that was in the past, and at least he was responding now.

The next day, which was early dismissal day, he messaged just before the bell rang to say, *what are you guys doing after school?*

We had rehearsal, but maybe he'd forgotten. Either way, we'd skip it, obviously.

On the way there, we talked about what we'd say. Grace wanted to just relax, to try to keep things light, but I thought it was critical to know what had happened and why. And I thought we should know now, as soon as possible, especially now that he was back home and out of the hospital's 24/7 care.

"And he's, what," I said, "at home all day, alone? With his parents? Maybe we could set up a rotating schedule so one of is always with him. But also—I really think we have to find out why he did it. That's the first step."

"You think he'll tell us?" Sunny said.

"As opposed to what—just never telling us?"

"I mean, you know how Jason is."

"He has to tell us. If we don't know what pushed him over the edge, how do we stop it from happening again? We have to find out."

Next to me in the back seat, Grace fiddled with the zipper on her backpack. "Maybe we should, like—try to talk to an adult or a counselor or something? Do you think it's a good idea to try to push him like that?"

You didn't seem to worry about what was a good idea when you talked to *Chase*, I thought. "I'm sure it's not a good idea to just not talk about either."

"I just feel like I don't know the right way to handle things."

There was something clinical in the way she said it. "Well—"

I stopped myself, because I understood something then, all at once, the four of us in the car driving to see him: None of my friends had watched their worlds fall apart before in the same way I had. Because I had spent years of my life dissecting the way things could fall apart, I knew the way a threat could rumble like a fault line when on the surface you could still tell yourself, maybe, that everything was fine. I knew that, I had lived that already, in a way that they hadn't.

And I could use that now, for Jason, and for all of us. "I just think we need to have a plan," I said. "Not just for today, but for—well, forever, maybe. We have Berkeley next year, but for the in-between."

"I guess it's going to be the elephant in the room anyway," Brandon said. "We can just see what happens when we see him. Maybe he'll feel like talking."

"But I think we should find a way to bring it up, just so we know for next time. So there's not a next time."

Brandon hesitated. Finally, he said, "Yeah, maybe, okay."

"So we'll just—we'll wait for the right moment today," I said. And that would be the beginning; the rest, we'd find our way through.

When Jason opened the front door, he had on his glasses and sweats, and his hair was longish and his voice was a little scratchy. Seeing him in person felt like a resurrection.

Everyone gave him a hug, and he let us. Brandon was teary. Jason looked, mostly, tired, although less awful than he had at the hospital—his face was normal again, even though his arm was still in a sling. He moved kind of stiffly, like it hurt.

Immediately when we went inside, the smell of the house, astringent like cleaner, tunneled me back to when we'd been here—a lifetime ago—on Brandon's birthday, and my stomach clenched. Brandon glanced at me, and I knew he, too, was seeing again Mr. Tsou yelling, Jason lying on the ground. We left our shoes by the pile next to the door. It was quiet inside, and as we followed him across the entryway, the marble tiles were cold under my feet. The walls in the entryway were lined with dozens of pictures: Jason and Evelyn as toddlers in a miniature tuxedo and gown at a wedding, Jason and Evelyn in ski gear on top of a mountain, Jason and Evelyn meeting Santa as little kids. Mr. and Mrs. Tsou were in some of the pictures, too.

In the living room, I sat in one of the reclining chairs near the TV, which was as far as possible from where Jason had fallen to the ground. Then I regretted it: Sunny and Brandon and Grace were all on the love seat, and it was small enough that they were pressed together in a way that looked comforting to me. I should've tried to sit with them instead.

"Love the picture of you rocking the Pull-Ups there," Brandon said, smiling a little forcedly, motioning to a framed photo above the fireplace. "Hadn't mastered potty training yet, huh?"

Jason glanced toward the picture but otherwise didn't react, and Brandon went quiet. I could see something akin to desperation in his expression.

I didn't know what to say either. I hadn't expected it to be this hard.

"Listen, Jay," he said, quietly, "I don't really know what to say. Um—but listen, we're all—"

Jason said, "Can you guys do something for me?"

"Anything," Brandon said.

"Can we just—pretend it never happened?"

I thought maybe someone would protest, and when no one did, I thought for a moment that I would. Because not only was it ludicrous that Jason would even suggest it, it also seemed counterproductive. How could we be there for him in whatever ways he needed without knowing the full story?

But maybe Brandon understood something about how much Jason needed that, how much it cost him even to say that much. He said quickly, "Yeah, Jay, of course, of course," and Grace said cheerfully, "Pretend *what* never happened?" Sunny said, "Yeah, definitely" too, and Jason looked to me then, like a question, and when he did I could see it took something out of him.

Of course we couldn't pretend that, not really. The things or the people you try to pretend away are never really gone, just absent—so much glistening negative space, a ghost you're for-ever stumbling over in the hall—and of all the things that have ever haunted me, this is perhaps the one that haunts me the most.

And even at the time I knew it would be like that. Making that promise at his house that day, I knew there would be the night-mares of freefall, the nights I jolted awake drenched in sweat, the panic arising at even the shortest of goodbyes. Freshman year in college: I have my fingers pressed to my wrist because I don't trust my pulse, and a boy who lives across the hall peers at me and says, "Why are you breathing like that?" and my chest squeezes closed like a fist. I am in my TA's office, still wearing the hospital bracelet they put on me in the emergency room to show her as proof of why I haven't been to class, and I can't get a full sentence out without running out of breath but she doesn't seem to notice, and now whenever I'm with other people all I can think about is whether they'd know how to save me. I am awake the whole night struggling to breathe, each minute a year long. I am in the airport waiting to fly back home after Thanksgiving and I nearly black out at the gate, and then I can't move, and I miss my flight. Some-times even now, when I'm crossing a bridge or when I hear the first Christmas song of the year, my heart will start to pound so hard I'm scared it might split my chest wide open, and then I'll be suffocated with the sense that somewhere, hundreds of miles away, something is terribly wrong.

But maybe back then some part of us still thought we knew how to bury things. Or maybe not—maybe it was just that he'd asked something of us when he so rarely asked for anything.

So I said, "Yes." We would do this for him: We would inter that night forever in our past, that past we shared, because he'd asked. Because we loved him; because it was all we knew to do.

WE DIDN'T see Jason much while he was at home, and we didn't hear from him often either. He had appointments, we knew, but aside from that I couldn't imagine how he was filling his days. I was afraid to ask him things directly, and so I didn't ask if he was coming back to school, but with every day that passed it seemed like less of a possibility. I could feel myself unraveling. On weekends and Wednesdays, because we still weren't doing our breakfasts, I could never sleep in. My pants were all loose on me and I always had a headache and I couldn't remember what it felt like to be relaxed; all our old familiar places, BAYS and the rally court and Sunny's car at lunch, had lost their sense of safety.

I was struggling as the temporary first chair—I sounded awful. My friends told me not to worry, that I sounded great, which I knew was a lie. "You're trying your best," Brandon said sympathetically. "Go easy on yourself, you know? It's a lot."

I was checking my email constantly these days—we all were—and I still hadn't heard from Juilliard. Maybe that wasn't relevant anyway with Jason gone; maybe he wasn't in the right place to get news either way, and the five of us staying together at Berkeley felt more vital than ever. And besides that, I still couldn't play at home, and at BAYS it was rote and flat. But I also thought that if we were invited to audition in person, maybe it would give him something—it could be a reason to push forward, remind him who he was.

We'd still heard nothing about auditions by the time Brandon told us at lunchtime Jason was coming back tomorrow. I tried not to let it bother me that he'd told Brandon first, and groped around for relief. Tomorrow! It would be better with him back. We could keep a closer watch over him, and there wouldn't be that emptiness everywhere: in his seat in every classroom, in his seat at BAYS.

"Do you think it'll be worse here?" Sunny said. "At least at home he doesn't have to talk to anyone."

"People will be nice," Grace said.

"Don't you think that's almost worse? If he won't even talk about it with us, how's he going to react when all day it's, like, Eric Hsu or whoever coming up to be like *oh, Jason, I'm so sorry, are you okay?* I think it's very possible he's going to have to relive it over and over all day long for as long as people still think about it when they see him."

"But we'll be here," I said. "We can head it off. We'll be a shield." Coming back would be a minefield, yes, but: Jason was coming back. It was something to celebrate; it was a reason for hope. We would make sure everything went the way he needed, and everything would be good. Everything would be fine.

The morning of Jason's first day back at school, I wore a dress and curled my hair. I was nervous in a physical, all-consuming way. I'd barely slept all night.

I waited by his locker, but I didn't see him before the bell rang, and not knowing quite where he was brought all my thoughts to a yearning, desperate pitch. When I went into first-period AP English, he was there already. He was wearing his glasses, and his hair was a little long, but his arm was out of the sling, and when he saw me come in across the room, he lifted his hand off his desk just a few inches in a small wave.

To anyone else who didn't know us, it would've looked like such a small thing—just a little gesture, daily, banal. But the room that day didn't feel big enough to contain what that wave meant: all the things it encompassed, all those years it held.

All day my stomach had been in knots imagining Jason besieged by well-wishers, imagining what it might take to make him snap. If he could just hold on until lunchtime, then it would be just us, and we could order the world as we needed.

We'd decided we'd have a potluck without calling it that, or calling attention to it; we would, as he'd asked, pretend everything was normal. I rounded the corner to our spot, and everyone but Jason was there already, and my mind was so focused on scanning for him that it took me a moment to register that sitting next to Grace, his backpack slung onto the ground like he belonged there, was Chase Hartley.

When I hurried over, Chase was in the middle of telling a long and detailed story about his dog escaping and ending up at the neighbor's pool party. I looked to Sunny—of all of us, she was the most likely candidate to get rid of him—but then Chase said, "So then we were—oh hey, Jason, what's up? Long time."

I'd been so flustered I hadn't even heard him approach. He sat down next to Sunny. I tried to signal her with my eyes, but she was watching Jason. When I looked at Grace—surely she would tell Chase to leave—she was unwrapping her granola bar, and when she looked up she leaned over and said, "Jason! You're finally back!" and gave him a side-hug.

We'd agreed not to make it a big deal, make him the center of attention. There was a roiling in my stomach.

"Hey, man, it's good to see you," Chase said, holding out his hand for Jason to slap. "I heard you were having a rough time. You just gotta, like—keep your head up, you know?"

For a second an expression I couldn't quite name flickered over Jason's face. I went tense. But Jason smiled and slapped his hand against Chase's. "Yeah, right," he said easily, and then fell quiet again.

The silence stretched. We'd planned to focus conversation on light things—inside jokes, do-you-remembers that would make him smile. I started to say, "Do you guys remember when—" but before I could get any further, Chase said, soberly, "Yeah, my uncle has like really bad depression too. He had to be hospitalized a bunch of times, actually."

"Oh, that's so sad," Grace said. I stared at her, willing her to make eye contact with me. She picked out the dried cranberries in her granola bar, setting them neatly on the cement next to her, and then peered back into her backpack.

"Yeah," Brandon said, clearing his throat, "yeah, that sucks. Hey, so did you guys do the take-home test yet for AP Lit?"

"Not yet," Sunny said. "How was it?"

"I don't know, I haven't done it either."

"Same," I said. "The last one was hard."

"Yeah, it was pretty bad."

We all tried not to look at Jason. He took a long swallow from his water bottle and then put it back down, tapping his fingers against the lid.

I couldn't fathom what Grace had been thinking, or what it would be like to be Chase, to so confidently imagine myself fully welcome in any situation, with any group of people.

"Okay, well!" I said quickly. "I tried this new cookie recipe last night. Anyone want some?"

"Whoa, kind of buried the lede there," Brandon said. "You have cookies, and you've been holding out on us? Oh, I got some of those shrimp chips too."

"Oh right, our potluck," Grace said. She pulled out a Tupper-ware with sliced oranges and strawberries, and Sunny had brought little meatballs on toothpicks. We put them in the middle of our circle, and I rearranged everything just to have something to do with my hands. I still couldn't look at Jason.

"Aw, is this like a welcome-back party for Jason?" Chase said. He reached for a cookie. "You guys are such good friends."

"No, it's just—"

Abruptly, Jason stood up.

"I have to go check on some stuff with Mrs. Kim," he said. "I'll catch you guys later."

"Did you want to eat first?" I said.

"Ah—I'm all right, thank you," Jason said, very politely. "Maybe if I get back before the bell rings."

I looked helplessly at Brandon, but what was there for him to do? "All right, see you soon," Brandon said, and we watched Jason cross the courtyard and head up the stairs at the science wing. I felt like I might be ill. I closed my eyes. My pulse was roaring in my ears.

"Well, that went well," Brandon said shortly. He clapped his hands over his knees, his jaw set. "Good talk, everyone."

"He probably really did have to talk to Mrs. Kim," Grace said. "When you're gone for that long, I'm sure there's a lot to catch up on."

"Yeah," Chase said, "I had the flu in the fall and I missed like four days and coming back was like, brutal. I'm not even in all the AP classes you guys are. These cookies are awesome, Beth. What's in them?"

"Sugar," I said coldly. "Oats. Butter. Normal cookie things."

He looked surprised. "Ah. Well, they're really good," he said, and there was something in his tone—the same measured way my father used to sound when he thought my mother was being unreasonable, and all at once I was so furious it was hard to sit still.

"Why don't you just take them," I snapped. I shoved the Tupper-ware toward him, the bottom scraping against the concrete.

"Uh—I don't think—"

"No, just take them, Chase. You can have them all."

After Chase finally left, awkwardly taking the cookies with him, I felt bad about making a scene, but only a little. Grace looked like she might follow him, but instead she gave him a kiss on the cheek. When he was out of earshot, she turned to me.

"What was that?" she said.

"What do you mean what was that? Why did you bring him here today?"

"He just wanted to eat with us."

"Okay, well, that was truly the worst possible timing imaginable."

"He was trying to be nice," Grace said. "And I really doubt Jason left because of him."

"Really, when Chase wouldn't shut up about depression and hospitals and basically everything Jason told us he wanted to try to forget about?"

"I think he really cares about depression and things because of his uncle. I told him it might be awkward, but he said he didn't mind."

"Who cares if it's awkward for *Chase*, Grace! What were you even *thinking*?"

"Well, you were super rude to him, so maybe he won't come back. If that's what you wanted."

We stared at each other. I never fought with Grace. Then she said, very quietly, "You should've told me he came to talk to you."

Why—so he could come here and ruin things like today? I closed my eyes and tried to smooth my expression so I didn't look as angry as I was. "Okay."

"I just think we can't tiptoe around him forever," she said. "I think we just have to get back to normal. That's what he wanted, right? I think that's what we should do."

I didn't see Jason alone again until the next morning. All last night I'd been planning out what I might say to him, but when we fell into step together, before I could say any of it, he said, "So, looks like Grace has been talking a lot to Chase still?"

"I guess so, kind of."

We were in front of the science wing, and I felt my heartbeat start to rise. I was still afraid to go by the science wing bathrooms, and I couldn't think of a plausible reason to explain why I needed to go around the long way to second period now. When the bathrooms came into view, I stopped walking. Jason glanced at me. "Something wrong?"

"I've just been going around the library instead," I said. "Just trying to get more daily steps in."

I don't think he believed me, but to my relief he didn't make a big deal out of it. As we went by the library, he said, "You think she's happy? Grace, I mean?"

Alarm bells went off in my head. I tried to keep my tone neutral. "I don't know. How come?"

He shrugged. "I think Grace is more complicated than people give her credit for. Like you'd think everything's on the surface, but I actually don't think she's necessarily like that."

"Are you remembering this from when you guys went out?"

I couldn't parse the look he gave me. "I totally forgot about that." (Had he, though?) We went by the drama club's table, where they were selling tickets for *Othello*. A sophomore whose name I didn't know was shouting, "Extra credit in any of Mrs. Neumann's classes if you come!"

Jason said, "She talk about him much?"

"Kind of," I said, then I hesitated. Maybe if the circumstances were different—if it weren't his second day back—I might have pressed him more about what happened, about why he'd done it. Because of everything there was to talk about that day, why was Grace the thing foremost on his mind? Maybe I had totally misread what had happened at lunch the day before—maybe it wasn't the particular things Chase was saying at all; maybe it was the fact of him with Grace. Maybe all that time he'd spent alone at home, all that time I'd been holding him so closely in my heart, Grace was the one he'd been holding on to.

And it was important to know, wasn't it? It felt that way, at least. There was so much we needed to know.

But to be without him for so long and then to be there with him—the sheer fact of him there was overwhelming, the familiar angles of his face, the closeness of his skin near mine, the way that every tiny motion between us crackled like an explosion; we were both amplified, the world distilled into just us two. It drowned out all the sentences I'd been practicing, halted all the questions. There was a stillness, maybe, then, and it was only those times that I felt the disarray of all the rest of it: When I was with him, I understood quiet again because the world finally felt at rest.

And maybe, too, I was just so happy to be with him that I didn't want to risk it. I understood how fragile happiness could be.

Or maybe it wasn't happiness at all, but relief. It's easy to mistake them when that's all you have.

MAYBE IT had been naive to assume that Jason being back meant he'd be back at BAYS, too. But I'd assumed it anyway—I'd thought things would be better then too, that I would be able to play again—and when he didn't come, I was anxious all through rehearsal and the music sounded tinny and chaotic to my ears.

We didn't want to seem pushy, so we didn't ask him, but we speculated about it. Grace thought maybe it was physical-therapy-related, and Brandon thought maybe Jason was under orders to take things slow. But I was worried it was more complicated than that.

I didn't know how to explain it without telling them about Juilliard, though. The four of us were standing in the parking lot after rehearsal; it was winter and dark already, and freezing, and when Serina Kim, a junior from Monta Vista who played flute, stopped on her way out to say hi to Brandon, I wondered if, when she left, I should tell them.

It had been hard for me lately to be at BAYS in a way it never had before. I could play as directed, the requisite notes at the requisite times, but if I ever tried to take it past that, I went hot and shaky and a hardness crept over me. I had always been able to find a way inside the music, but the few times I tried that now it felt like a physical rejection, like trying to join the opposite ends of a magnet.

It made me feel like someone else. I didn't know what was wrong with me.

"I just don't know how you all have time to do BAYS senior year with college apps," Serina was saying. "My parents think I should quit."

"You weren't planning to, like, *sleep*, were you?" Brandon said, grinning at her. "What do you think this is?"

If I didn't know him, I would've believed in his smile, I think. Probably to an outsider, to someone like Serina, who didn't go to our school and maybe hadn't heard about Jason yet, it didn't look like anything was wrong. But maybe it was easier for people to hide things than you'd ever expect.

I shouldn't tell them about Juilliard yet. Not telling anyone was the one thing Jason had asked of me, and besides that, maybe we wouldn't be asked back to audition; I was still waiting to hear. And anyway, Jason was here, so I told myself to be reassured by that.

Until then he wasn't. The day we were supposed to all go off campus for lunch together for the first time after break, Jason didn't show up for school. We all tried messaging and calling him, but he didn't respond.

All day, I kept my phone on in class, which you weren't supposed to do, and by lunchtime I was frantic. Grace and Sunny both thought maybe Jason had appointments and had forgotten to bring his phone, and Brandon was uneasy but certainly nowhere near my level of panic. Somehow that was the opposite of calming, like those dreams where no one believes you that the building's burning.

"You think we should just stay here?" I said. "What if—"

"They wouldn't just leave him alone if they didn't think it was okay, right?" Brandon said. "I mean—he's seeing a psychologist regularly and stuff, right?"

"But that means you trust his parents?" My voice was

shaking. "And we thought he was fine before, too, and—"

"You know," Sunny said, "My friend Dayna said people who survive suicide attempts almost never try again. When the impulse passes, everyone wants to live."

"But they've never even met him," I said.

The bell rang. "Let's see if he's answered one of us by the time school's out," Brandon said. "And then if not, maybe we can go over there. Or I can go over, or something."

"I think even that might be overreacting," Sunny said. "But yes, okay, sure."

I walked with them as far as the library, where we always parted ways, and then I found, all at once, that I couldn't keep propelling myself toward the science wing. The thought of being trapped in the classroom made me want to peel off my own skin. I would be useless in there, I would be basically locked inside, and I couldn't go.

It took me nearly half an hour to walk to Jason's house. His car was parked in the driveway, but no one answered when I knocked.

My vision was blurring, and I thought I might pass out or have another panic attack. Maybe both. But I tried again, and then a few moments later I heard footsteps.

When he opened the door, it was a palpable relief to see him. He was wearing sweatpants and glasses and an old baggy T-shirt, and he looked a little disoriented, but there he was. I willed my heart to slow back to normal.

"Beth," he said. "What are you doing here?"

"Did I wake you up?"

"Ah—"

"I didn't mean to. I just—I wanted to make sure everything was all right."

An almost-imperceptible flicker of annoyance shifted over his face. "Yeah, everything's fine."

"Are you sure?"

"Yes."

"Okay. I just—" It seemed like he should know how terrified I had been. It shouldn't have been that much of a surprise, really, to see me there. "I just wanted to see if you needed anything."

He watched me for a moment, and then he sighed. "You want to come in?"

Inside, he made us both tea. His kitchen was messy, dishes in the sink and on the counter, stacks of papers and bottles of vitamins scattered across the table. He didn't say anything as he boiled water, and I could feel my heart rate picking up at the sense of unwelcome.

He set the two cups on the kitchen table and motioned for me to sit. He'd chosen jasmine tea, which was what I usually ordered when we all went to get boba together, and I felt my eyes well up at the gesture. He was still himself, I reminded myself. He was still the same person, and our history was still what it was. This was a new layer, but it didn't erase everything else.

That meant, though, also, that I should be able to do better than this—I should have more to offer him than my silent and unsolicited presence in his kitchen.

I sipped my tea, trying to think of something I could say, but the inadequacy of everything I came up with made the words choke in my throat. After a while, he said, "What class are you ditching right now?"

"AP Bio," I said, although he should know that.

"What's happening in it?"

"Nothing important."

"Are you going to get in trouble for cutting?"

I could call in and leave a message excusing it, pretending to be my mother. "It'll be okay."

He drank the rest of his tea, then looked at the clock. "You want to watch something?"

As far as I knew, Jason barely watched TV. Most of us didn't have time. "If you want."

"Okay," he said, but then he didn't make a move toward the living room, where the TV was, and sitting there with him I could feel the past weeks roiling through me and my skin felt too tight for my body and I felt like I would implode.

I wanted to know why. I wanted to know what had happened and whether it was going to happen again; I wanted a promise that it never would. I wanted to know how specifically we'd failed, how I'd failed, and what to do next time. And maybe it wasn't fair, but I wanted him to know what this had done to me. I wanted him to understand all the ways I wasn't going to be the same again and to understand the depth of what I felt for him.

"I didn't mean to bother you," I said. "I just wanted—I just got worried."

"There's no need to worry."

"Isn't there?"

"No." He reached over, stretching his arm out and balancing on the back two legs of his chair, to drop his empty cup into the sink, where it clattered against the other dishes piled there. "I'm just not having a great day."

I sat up straighter. "What do you mean not having a great day? Are you—do you need—"

He pushed his glasses aside and rubbed his eyes. "I'm not—just relax, Beth, okay? It's just been a shitty day, that's all."

What would it be like to admit that aloud—that you were angry, that the day had worn on you, to say those things, and to feel them, without worrying how they might look to whoever you were talking to? To let the ugly emotions you harbored, your anger and dissatisfaction and irritation, seep into your words without censoring them. That was unlike him, though; usually he was so much more careful. "What happened?"

"Nothing happened."

"But you—"

"I don't really want to talk about it," he said. His voice was sharp, and tears came to my eyes. He saw, and he closed his eyes.

"I'm sorry," he said. "I'm not trying to be a jerk. I just kind of wanted to be alone right now, that's all."

That was worse, I think, hearing that—among the worst things he could've said to me.

"I'll leave you alone, then," I said quietly. I stood up. My eyes were stinging. I took a few seconds gathering my bag and then bringing my cup to the sink. I wanted him to tell me he hadn't meant it, to ask me to stay. But instead he followed me out of the kitchen in silence.

I could hardly breathe. At the door, I felt him hesitating. I said, "Jason—"

My voice came out more defeated than I meant it to. And when he looked at me, in that moment our eyes met, there was a tenderness in his expression that I don't think he consciously intended but that all the same I could feel trained on me, something that reached beyond all those ways he was tired and guarded and sad. And I thought how no matter what happened around us, and no matter what happened to us, it would always be like that for me, too, that underneath everything else would always be the way I felt about him.

"I think partly—I think I wanted to tell you something else," I said. What was I doing? My vision was tunneling, my hands going damp, but it was too late now to stop. And maybe part of me had come to say this; maybe this had been what I'd meant to do all along. "Thinking we might lose you was the worst thing to ever happen to me. I haven't been sleeping or eating, and I haven't been able to play violin. I just—I can't imagine the world without you, and I can't imagine us without you, or myself without you, and I never told you, but—" My pulse was thrumming so loudly in my ears I could hardly hear myself. This was the most, I think, that I had to give him. "I've been in love with you for as long as I've known you."

Jason looked surprised. He looked stunned, even, but underneath that, where I'd hoped to find welcome or reciprocation or who knows what, where I suppose I'd left a blank space because some things are too risky to imagine, even to yourself, there was a wall.

"I just needed to tell you that," I said. Then I fled before the silence could go on longer, and it was a long time before I heard the door close, but he didn't call after me or ask me to stay.

That night, alone at home, it felt so unbearable to be myself that I took a Benadryl and went to sleep at seven. I hoped I'd sleep twenty hours straight. I woke up at five in the morning, though, and I curled into a ball in bed and tried to breathe past the pressure against my chest. I wished I weren't so afraid of the idea of getting incredibly high or drunk.

After what I'd said, I was too anxious to message him—it would be unsurvivable if I did and he didn't answer; it could mean so many terrible things. Why had I done that? If he didn't feel the same way, and it was clear he didn't, then I'd gained nothing by telling him. Maybe I just wanted to give him that, no matter what he'd do with it. Maybe I'd never expected anything in return. Except why had I thought that was something valuable to offer him? Why had I thought it was any kind of talisman against anything—against his pain, against further disaster?

There was still a part of me, though, some stupid, hopeful part, that thought maybe he'd just been caught off guard in the moment but that he'd tell me he had feelings for me too, after all.

We had Monday off for a teacher inservice day, and so for

three excruciating days I didn't hear anything from Jason. I made sure the others had, mostly Brandon, who went to see him over the weekend. They'd gone to work out together, and I didn't think Jason would've said anything to Brandon about what I'd told him, but there was no way to know. I felt nervous and slippery whenever my phone buzzed—on some level I knew it wouldn't be Jason, but then a part of me hoped against hope it would be, and then as soon as that range of emotions had cycled out, I worried that he'd said something to one of them, that I'd upset him, or that the others would be upset with me. Maybe this would be the thing that splintered us.

I was going to pray that my other friends just never heard, but then, abruptly, on Monday morning I couldn't take it anymore and I told Sunny and Grace. They came over right away, Grace wrapping me in a long hug and Sunny asking questions to fill in the rest of the story. I couldn't tell, but I thought maybe she was hurt they hadn't known I liked him. But I'd meant for it to never matter.

"He hasn't even messaged you since then?" Sunny said. "Not at all?"

"No," I said. "I honestly don't know how I'll even look at him tomorrow." We were sitting in my living room, and I wished I could halt time and stay here in the safety of the triangle we formed. "And I don't know if he's even going to want to be around me. I just—I hope this doesn't ruin our group."

I wasn't crying, but my breathing was shaky as if I were. Grace leaned against me.

"That is definitely not going to happen," she said soothingly. "Not a chance."

"Okay, but if it does, though, you guys should go with him." He needed them more, and anyway I'd been the one to ruin things. It was beyond humiliating that I'd ever thought anything could come of what I felt for him, that of all the people in the world I would be the one he'd choose. "I don't know what I was even thinking."

We talked for a long time, through lunchtime and into the afternoon, about Jason and about all of us. Sunny told me she thought Jason loved me as much as he loved anyone, and when I said, "What's that supposed to mean?" she said, "I mean—you know how he is."

"In what sense?"

She tucked her knees under her chin, thinking. "I guess when I picture the way you give yourself to other people, I have this image where you're like—reaching straight into your heart and holding it out to someone. Whereas when Jason does, he's like, reaching behind his back or off to the side. I don't know, it wouldn't shock me if he never has a serious relationship. Not that people are supposed to, but I don't think he's aro or anything, I think he's just like, nope. It's definitely not you, Beth."

"You deserve to be *cherished*," Grace said. "Jason knows that. And you have us no matter what. Everything really will be fine."

I could tell already that as soon as they were gone, it would be impossible to believe. But for now they were here, and what had happened wasn't without its one gift: We'd obliterated the distance between us; they knew everything about me again.

Late that afternoon, before my mother got home, someone rapped on our door. I opened it thinking it would be a package delivery, but it was Jason. An invisible fist rammed into my throat.

"Oh," I said. I steadied myself and held the door open wider. "Hey. Um—did you want to come in?"

"Yeah, sure, is that okay?"

"Of course."

I led him inside. The kitchen was a mess, so I went into the living room. He sat down on the recliner by the fireplace, on the very edge of it, and he stuck his hands into his pockets, which looked uncomfortable while he was seated.

I couldn't imagine what he was here to say. It was difficult to swallow or breathe.

"I just wanted to—look, I wasn't trying to ghost you."

I looked away. "It's fine."

"No, it's not fine, it's—" He made a face, then took his hands from his pockets and leaned forward to rest his elbows on his knees. "It was a dick move, Beth, and I didn't mean—it's just been a lot lately."

"Of course. I understand."

"Yeah, but—I don't think anyone really understands. Everyone's been really easy on me, which I appreciate, but I also—everything feels so fucked up now, and I wish I could just have everything go back to normal. Anyway." He looked back at me. "Did you mean what you said? At my house?"

It was tempting to try to deny it, to say the moment had gotten the better of me, but it wouldn't be the truth, and anyway I'm sure he would've known that. "I meant it."

"Maybe we could—um." He smiled sheepishly. "Whenever I imagined this—which, for the record, I definitely have—it, uh, went a little better."

My heart had taken off and was thundering in my ears. "What are you—saying, exactly?"

"I'm saying—obviously very eloquently—I'm saying if that's how you feel, I don't know, I think maybe we should give it a shot."

"You mean like—"

"I should've like—brought flowers or something, maybe." He jammed his hands into his pockets again and exhaled. "I didn't do the greatest job thinking this through."

There had been moments in my life that had felt surreal, a little detached from reality, but this was somehow the exact opposite. This time I was hyperaware of all those banal, everyday things that rooted me in reality, like the humming of my fridge, the frayed throw pillow that was propped up next to me, the way the cuffs of my sweatpants brushed against my bare ankles—and in the midst of all that: Jason saying this.

"If you mean it—" I said, and my voice came out squeaky. I tried again. "I mean, obviously I'd—yes, I'd love—if what you're saying is—"

"Maybe let's spare ourselves this part," he said. "Let's just skip ahead to the part where we both say yes? Or—what do you say exactly?"

"That sounds—that sounds good."

"Okay." He stood up then, and he crossed the room and came and sat down next to me on the couch, and then he took my hand in his, and that was the moment when everything else around me stopped. "So—we're doing this?"

"We're doing this?" I repeated, and I stared at our hands together. *This is happening*, I told myself. *This is happening, this is—*

"So if I'm being honest, this isn't exactly how I pictured it," he said, smiling a little. "As in, when I imagined it in my head, I didn't sound like I'd never spoken a complete sentence in my life, but, um—wow. We, uh—we should've done this a while ago, maybe."

"Should we—I mean, we should tell people, right?" I said.

"You want to?"

"Did you not want to?"

He was still smiling at me, his eyes trained on me in a way that felt transformative. I was a different person now. I could feel myself expanding. All this time—all this time!—I had been so wrong about myself. I had thought I could never be enough. "Whatever you like," he said, and he reached out and brushed his fingertip very gently against my cheek.

I felt electric; I felt lit up from the inside. *Let it be like this forever*, I prayed, *and I'll never ask for anything else ever again.*

JASON WASN'T someone who'd ever liked big announcements or attention, so I said I would tell our friends. When I messaged Grace and Sunny, Grace called me immediately.

"I'm so happy for you!" she said. "It's so nice that it's a happy ending to all of this. I think you guys will be good for each other."

"Want to know something weird?" I said. "I used to always worry you guys would end up together."

She laughed. "Me and *Jason*? Seriously? I love Jason, but he's definitely too moody for me."

"You guys did go out before, though."

"Oh yeah, I always forget about that." She laughed again. "We were like twelve! I think all we did is hold hands a few times. And for our one-month anniversary he gave me a stuffed strawberry."

"Why a stuffed strawberry?"

"I have no idea. I guess he thought I would like it? Then we broke up, so I never got to see what month two would've been. Aw, but Beth—you deserve to be really happy. I'm excited. This is so cute."

Sunny called after that and made me tell the whole story in extremely specific detail. Brandon didn't answer when I called—sometimes, I knew, he'd pass out on the couch after dinner and then not wake up for hours—but in the morning at school he was waiting for me in the parking lot.

"Heard you have some news," he called across the asphalt. I couldn't stop smiling.

"Who told you?" I said when I caught up to him. Had Jason told him, unable to help himself?

"Sunny. So what's the deal?"

"The deal is—I still can't quite believe it."

"How did that even happen?"

I gave him a summary. The glow from yesterday hadn't gone away. Each time I'd told this story now, I wondered when it would start feeling real, feeling like mine.

"So are you guys like—" Brandon hesitated.

"Are we what?"

"I guess I'm just kind of—I don't know."

His tone made me pull back. "You don't know what?"

"I just feel like Jay is maybe not in the greatest place right now. I mean, speaking just for myself, I'm definitely still kind of not, and for you, I mean, I just wonder if—"

"I know he's not," I said. "Brandon, I mean—what do you think these past weeks have been like for me?"

"I know exactly what they've been like for you. They've been like that for all of us." He reached up and gathered a fistful of hair, then let it go. "It doesn't matter what I think. I'm just surprised, that's all. And, I mean, Jay's a good guy. He is, but like—I'm just worried—"

I was startled; this wasn't where I'd thought he was going. "You're worried about *me*?"

"Remember the way he yelled at Sunny at the restaurant?"

"He was just upset."

"That's kind of my point. And Sunny is—Sunny, and you're you. Not that anyone deserves to get yelled at like that, but Sunny—Sunny can kind of handle herself."

Was that what he was worried about? I was—maybe oddly—touched. "Well, you definitely don't need to worry about me. I'm not expecting Jason to be perfect or anything."

"Right, yeah." He reached out quickly and squeezed my shoulder. "Just take it slow, okay? You know. Be careful."

In those early days I was viscerally nervous before each time I saw him. I was so stratospherically happy it seemed entirely possible I'd somehow hallucinated the whole thing, and even assuming it was real, I wasn't sure about the new rules. Because they'd changed between us, hadn't they? Would we hug when we saw each other now, or would he hold my hand, or would we kiss or try to have sex? And also—what if I did something to make him change his mind? Surely it was dangerous to be this happy about anything; surely to hoard that kind of pure pleasure for yourself was to court disaster.

I'd worried a little about what it would be like with the five of us. But it was fine, at least so far. It was the five of us absorbing this new layer of history, not just me and Jason off alone.

On day three of our relationship, he called me at six forty-five in the morning. When I saw his name on the display, my heart slammed against my rib cage. He never called early like this. My hands were shaking as I fumbled to unlock my phone, and when I said, "Jason?" my voice came out panicked.

But he was, it turned out, calling to ask if I wanted a ride to school. When he arrived, he was smiling in a way that suffused the morning with warmth, that plunged away at least most of the lingering terror I'd felt from his call. In the car, all the air between us felt almost nonexistent, both in that I could almost feel every inch he moved and also in that it was a little hard to catch my breath. I wished we were going somewhere else besides school.

My mom came rushing out of the house just as Jason turned the engine back on. She was wearing slippers and no makeup, and her hair was wet. She motioned for me to roll down my window.

I closed my eyes briefly in irritation, but I did it. "What?"

"Hi, Jason," she said. "How are you?"

"Hi, Mrs. Claire. I'm doing okay. How about you?"

"Oh, you know—" I was terrified she was going to start a whole conversation, but she said, "Beth, there's a notebook on the kitchen table—did you need that for school? It has a black cover and—"

"I don't need it."

"It's not part of your homework? Or something you need for a test?"

"No."

"Oh, okay. I just didn't want you to get to school and realize you were missing it. You've all been under so much stress lately," she said to Jason. "I don't think for students there should be—"

"Is that all?" I said quickly. She still didn't know anything that had happened. Which seemed impossible, but really my mother worked a lot and so probably she made assumptions about my days when she was gone, things she had to tell herself to believe I was all right, and none of them involved me going to the hospital to visit someone I loved who had tried to die. She'd been forwarding me articles about panic attacks, though, all of which I'd ignored.

I had the window halfway rolled up by the time she finally said goodbye. Backing out of our driveway, Jason looked amused. "You seemed embarrassed."

"She's just so—I don't know. Things have been kind of bad at home." He looked at me sharply when I said that, and I said, quickly, "I mean—things are fine. It's nothing serious."

"Ah." He shifted into drive. "I always liked your mom."

"Really?" I wasn't sure why that surprised me. "That's sort of random."

"She's always struck me as a genuinely kind person."

"I guess she's kind, sure."

"You don't think that's pretty great? You can find some good in most people, but I wouldn't say most people are *kind*, per se."

"No, you're right."

He turned to smile at me. "You don't sound convinced."

"Well—" I hesitated. I hadn't planned to tell anyone—it felt so shameful—but then I'd always imagined the two of us sharing things with each other that we'd never told anyone else. And also I wanted to give him every part of me, the same way I wanted every part of him. I wanted there not to be any kind of distance or partition between us. "We've just been kind of fighting. I found out she's been taking child support from my dad ever since my parents divorced."

"Oh?"

"Yeah. And I kind of wonder—I don't know, I wonder if that's part of why I don't see him."

"Why?"

"If he resents it. Like it makes me feel like just some fallout from their divorce. Or just another bill for him to pay."

Jason winced. "Beth—that's so messed up to look at it like that."

"What other way is there to look at it?"

"Well, maybe he does it because he wants to?"

"She said they had a legal agreement. So I really doubt they'd bother going to court if it was something he'd do voluntarily anyway."

Someone else—Grace, for instance—would've tried to convince me I was wrong, that it was some kind of act of fatherly love and proof of devotion. In Grace's world, maybe, that would've been true. But Jason was just quiet for a long time, through a block of stop-and-go traffic on Creek, and then he said, finally, "Yeah, well." Then he reached out and put his hand gently on my knee. "People are shitty sometimes."

I held myself as still as I could so he wouldn't move his hand. I watched out the window as we passed by throngs of under-classmen streaming across the footbridge over the creek, and he put his hand back on the wheel when we turned onto Walnut. I missed the warmth of it.

"She thinks I'm overreacting," I said. "She was trying to make it seem like because they had some legal agreement, that's just the way it is. But I was always supposed to go see him every other weekend and she would always make up excuses for why I couldn't go, and I'm sure that was a legal agreement too."

"What kind of excuses?"

"Like I had to practice or she had to reschedule my lessons or the car was in the shop or whatever. I think she's just always been angry at him and she's never gotten over that." She'd gotten rid of all our family pictures when he moved out, and sometimes even now she still shook her head whenever we drove by and saw adults going into GameStop, sometimes looking at me like she expected me to agree. "I just don't know how she lives with it. Not just the money, but—all of it. How everything turned out."

He considered that. "I think people make bargains with themselves."

"What do you mean?"

"I mean I think you do things—I don't know, you do things you thought you wouldn't, maybe, or you put up with things you thought you'd never put up with and you look the other way."

"You think so?"

He shrugged. "I think that's just life."

I wished the drive were longer. We were at school now, but I could've stayed in the car with him forever. We went over the enormous speed bumps at the entrance to the parking lot, jostled in unison, and then when we went past the oversize cement plant-ers at the edge of the tennis courts, he said, quietly, "I remember when you told me about your parents splitting up. You remember that? We were—" He nodded toward the planters. "It was right here."

Of course I remembered. It had been a few months after I'd met them, right before he and I went into rehearsal one day, and I hadn't exactly planned to tell him, or anyone. But then Jason had asked if my parents were going to the new families orientation dinner, and I'd hesitated and then said it would just be my mother. Something about the way I'd said it had tipped him off, because he'd tilted his head and said, "Oh—are they—?"

So I'd told him how my father had left us. I remembered how nervous I'd been saying it aloud, how I wasn't sure what to make of Jason's reaction. He'd just nodded, and maybe I should've thought more about that at the time—maybe it was a signal of how wrong things were in his world, that he could so easily accept my own small tragedy. But then it was rehearsal and he didn't bring it up again and so I'd assumed that was the end of it, and what could I ask for, really? Even though there was so much more I needed.

But he'd told the others—the next day Grace had brought donuts for us to eat and she passed them out at brunch, with napkins, and Sunny had gotten me a small, pretty embossed-leather journal, and Brandon was tardy in two classes because he'd come to walk with me between periods. And I remembered realizing then how Jason had understood something in me, how he saw me more clearly than I'd known. Because if it had been him sharing bad news with one other person he would've wanted privacy, and he wouldn't have liked for anyone to spread it around. But I was the opposite. I'd wanted my friends to know because I needed not to be alone with it, I just hadn't known how to tell them—and he'd intuited that, somehow, and so he'd done it for me.

So I understood that this morning, the two of us in the parking lot, when he brought up that conversation from years ago he was making a declaration of what I somehow meant to him still.

It was a quiet promise that what I was saying meant enough to him that he'd remember these details—where we were, when it was—years later. He would make room for thoughts of me just as he'd done, in his way, for as long as we'd known each other; he would hold on to these moments and memories and take these smaller pains of mine to heart.

On our way to second period, when Jason and I had been together for a week, I finally asked him when he was planning to come back to BAYS.

"We're doing a Haydn," I said, because he'd always liked Haydn. It was noisy, conversation and footsteps and locker doors slamming reverberating off the brick walls and metal locker banks, but the ordinariness of the hallways felt transformed because Jason was holding my hand. I kept seeing people glance down to look.

"Which Haydn?" he said.

"One-oh-four."

"Ah. Kind of the obvious choice, I guess."

"It's kind of an interesting arrangement, though. I think you'd like it."

He smiled politely in a way that probably meant he was done with the conversation. But I said, "We sound worse without you there."

"Nah, I'm sure it doesn't make a difference."

"It does, though."

I recognized the way he dodged the subject, so I didn't push it, and I didn't bring up Juilliard, either. But then he called that afternoon when I was home from rehearsal.

"I was thinking about what you said about BAYS," he said. "What are you doing now? You want to practice together? I could come get you."

"And practice at your house?"

"Yeah, does that work for you?"

He came by ten minutes later. I'd tried practicing on my own a little—I didn't want him to hear how bad things had been—but had given up, and by the time he came I was mostly just scrolling frenetically on my phone. He'd said we were going to his house, but then a few streets before his, he turned.

"So, ah—I lied."

A cavern opened in my chest. He had lied about what—about me? Maybe I should've realized it was too good to be true, that if he sat down and thought about it, outside the moment, what did I have to offer him, really? "Oh—well, that's fine, if—"

"I didn't actually want to rehearse."

I tried to breathe again. "Oh. Then—"

We were at Linda Vista Park, and he pulled into the parking lot. "I just thought maybe we should try this again. By *this* I mean—" He motioned between us. "I feel like I kind of bombed the first time."

"You didn't bomb anything."

"Yeah, well—" He smiled in a self-deprecating way. "I know you think I'm always too down on my failures. So."

He opened his door, and when I got out after him he held out his hand. I took it, and we walked together across the parking lot.

When we got there, there was a blanket spread out on the grass, and it took me a second to realize this was his doing. He'd brought a small picnic: a thermos and two paper cups, a plastic clamshell of strawberries, a bag of Japanese rice crackers. I said, inanely, "This is for us?"

"It's a little better, right?" He extended a hand to the blanket, motioning for me to sit. When I did he sat down next to me and carefully opened the thermos, and the scent of jasmine came steaming out. He poured the tea into the two cups and handed me one.

"Jason—" I was not the kind of person people did this sort of thing for. Like elaborate promposals, or surprise birthday parties—I was not first in anyone's life except for my mother's. I was not someone about whom people spent time cataloguing my favorite tea or fruit or crackers, thinking about what sort of gesture might mean something to me. "I can't believe this."

He pried open the package of strawberries and held it out to me. They were white at the tops, and sour, but I ate three. I wished I could save them forever somehow, press them like flowers. Jason picked up a fallen oak branch that was lying on the grass, studying it, and then laid it carefully on the corner of the blanket like he meant to keep it, although I didn't ask.

Night fell early those days, the sun going down by six, and we lay back on the blanket and watched the sky darken over the hills. I was cold, and still a little hungry, but so happy I felt like I might break. He was lying close enough to me that our shoulders were pressed together, and my heart was beating so hard I wondered if he could feel it through my skin. All I could think was that if we turned our heads at the same time our cheeks would be touching, our lips. The silence between us felt bright and close and threaded through with all the ways we meant something to each other, all the ways we had over the years, and it glinted with possibility. He traced his thumb lightly across my palm, and a shiver went through my whole body.

I'd always wondered about people my age having sex—how it started, how you negotiated it. Did it start in moments like this? I couldn't fathom who said what or how you knew what to do and what not to, or how in the midst of remembering to register for all your SATs and struggling through enzyme catalysis and taking your PE uniform home to wash, you somehow also learned how to sleep with someone.

"We could still practice together if you want," I said, abruptly, mostly because I wondered if he'd felt my shiver, if it was more of a physical response than he'd been going for. "Like—another time. Or whenever."

He said, "Yeah, maybe, sure," but the way he said it made me think he wouldn't take me up on it.

The sky had started to darken, and in the parking lot and on the walkways, the streetlamps glowed on. I said, "I haven't been playing well lately at all."

"What do you mean?"

"I just haven't been."

He turned his head toward me. "No, what do you mean?"

"Well—I don't know what it is, but lately when I play it feels—like I lost control of it. Like before I always felt like no matter how rough something was or how bad I was at playing it I could always kind of hear past that and know what I wanted it to sound like, or even if I couldn't quite get there at first, there was always this—this sense of it unfolding if I was patient, but lately that's just gone. It just all feels like—noise."

Jason's listening had always felt different from the way most people's did: Heavier, somehow, as though it had its own presence, and it made me feel larger and exposed, suddenly aware of how much space I seemed to occupy. But lying next to him like this, both of us staring at the sky—I felt a profound safety, that there was space enough to hold all these things I was saying to him.

"You think you're burned out?" he said.

"I don't think it's that." We'd all been burned out before; you can't play as long as we had without everything coming in cycles. But there was an almost flu-like quality in a burnout, a general malaise, nothing this sudden or acute. "Because then it's just like you're bored. And this is—sharper and more I guess visceral, if that makes any sense. Like when I do play, sometimes it feels like all I actually want to do is just—saw my bow across the strings until they snap."

"What would happen if you did?"

"What do you mean what would happen if I did?"

"I don't know, if you just—let it all out."

"Like played through it? I am, it just isn't—"

"No, that isn't quite what I mean. I guess I mean what if you didn't try to fix it or beat yourself up over it and just—let it be."

I couldn't imagine what that would even look like, exactly. I said so. In my peripheral vision, I saw him smile.

"Yeah," he said, "I guess that doesn't surprise me."

And then he surprised me—he propped himself up on his elbow so that all at once we were very close; his face was next to mine. I could see the flecks of color in his eyes.

It was like standing on the edge of a very tall cliff. My heart was beating so fast I was a little light-headed, but not in an unpleasant way, and around me the park went hazy and wavered. I had never kissed anyone. I had imagined this a thousand times.

But then he stopped. My stomach clenched. Had I done something wrong? Or maybe I had just interpreted the moment wrong; I had assumed he'd want to kiss me at all when maybe that was ludicrous.

He didn't move away, though, and it struck me then that he was waiting for permission. I was nervous—what if I was reading him wrong, somehow?—but I touched my forehead against his, and then he smiled, and he kissed me.

When our lips touched, I felt like a different person. He cupped his hand gently against my head to bring me closer. I wanted to obliterate any space between us. I wanted to melt into him and somehow blur out all the sharp edges where I ended, where he started.

I read once that if you took all the atoms of everyone in the world, just the atoms without all the space between, you could fit them all into a single sugar cube: the whole world compressed into less than a square inch. I believe that, I suppose—it's hard to argue with the laws and the limits of the natural world. But that night it felt like all the history we'd shared, this life we'd built together, and what we were building now, whatever this was and whatever it would be—all that was too large and important and real to be contained by the lawn or the parking lot or the out-skirts of the park or even the city boundaries; that night, the two of us together felt so infinite.

BEFORE SCHOOL Friday morning, my father messaged me out of the blue to ask when I'd find out about Berkeley. It was the first time I'd heard from him since Christmas Eve. Usually, I would've messaged him before that, but the shame of knowing he'd been paying child support all this time had stopped me. I wanted to tell him it hadn't been my idea and I hadn't known, but maybe that didn't make a difference, and also I was too afraid to bring it up.

But I could imagine telling him I was going to Berkeley—that would be (I hoped, at least) enough to supersede whatever else had happened. He would be thrilled. Maybe sometimes on weekends he'd come up and we'd meet for lunch, or we'd walk around the campus and compare notes, or maybe go to the football games together. I'd already looked up the dates of Berkeley's Homecoming. Maybe I'd bring up the child support sometime then to apologize, or maybe by that point it wouldn't matter as much.

That weekend, Grace was going to be gone both days to watch her brother perform at a taiko festival in Stockton, Sunny had family in town, and it was Brandon's dad's birthday. I didn't want to seem greedy after the evening in the park—and really, I could probably live for years off the happiness of that—but I took a chance as we were walking to second period and asked Jason if he wanted to do something over the weekend.

"Like what?" he said.

"I don't know, like anything. I'm free all weekend. We could go for a walk or something. Or—what if we went to Berkeley?" As soon as I said it, the day began to take shape in my mind. "We could go spend the day there and visit the campus."

"And do what?"

"I don't know, just explore? We could get something to eat and just try to get a sense of what it's like for next year."

Berkeley was a lovely campus—romantic, even, beautiful old stone buildings flanked with trees, pockets of forest you could get lost in. It was what I'd always pictured a college should look like. It was right in the heart of the city, and you could spend hours wandering in and out of shops and coffeehouses and cafes, up and down side streets with clusters of cottage-like homes blooming with gardens, and there was an energy there that made the world feel safe and contained, like it had all been brought to you on a grid there on campus. I remembered walking through it with my father, how it felt like a new possibility unfolded with each walkway.

"Sure, if you want," he said. "I'm not doing anything else. I'll come get you tomorrow morning?"

Brandon called that night. I'd just showered and was getting into bed, and when I picked up, he said, "What are you doing tomorrow? You want to go get breakfast?"

"Oh—tomorrow? I thought you had your dad's birthday."

"Just for dinner," he said. "Why, are you doing something?"

"I was going to go to Berkeley with Jason. We were going to be there all day." I hesitated just a second. "Did you want to come?"

"Is this like a date?"

"It's—" I didn't know how to answer that. "I'm not sure."

He laughed. "Well, I'll pass, thanks. I don't need to be a third wheel."

"No, I didn't mean—it's probably not a date. You definitely wouldn't be a third wheel anyway."

"Nah, it's fine. I'll go bug Sunny and her cousins, maybe."

I felt a twinge as I hung up. It felt bizarre that Brandon wouldn't consider himself invited by default. This wasn't how it would always be, would it? I wished I could do both—be alone with Jason, and also be with the five of us together—at once.

I was still having trouble sleeping at night, which seemed disloyal somehow, like it ignored the current reality and left me stuck in the past Jason wanted to move beyond, and also ungrateful after he'd gone to all the trouble to surprise me with the picnic. But that night I lay awake imagining the next day. I pictured us sprawled next to each other on the grass, our hands laced together. I imagined kissing him between buildings or walking through the wooded paths. And also I imagined him falling in love with the campus in some new way—I wanted him to have something shining in his future that he could look toward, something that would lift and sustain him if he started to feel the world pressing in on him again.

In the morning, even though it was the weekend, I got up at six to make muffins. When my mother came downstairs, she looked startled, and then, watching me, she smiled.

"You look happy this morning, Beth," she said. "And the muffins look beautiful."

I was drying the dishes I'd used, and she was right: I was happy. "Do you want one? They're probably ready."

"What are they for?"

I'd told her I was going to work on a group project with Jason, which was easier than explaining Berkeley. "They're for the project."

"What a nice idea. I think it's wonderful for you to have fun hobbies. It's so good for stress." She picked one from the baking rack, blowing on it gently to cool it. "Will you be gone all day? I'll probably be home from Gong Gong and Po Po's a little after lunch."

"You're going to see them?" I didn't know why it bothered me. What had I expected—that she'd cut them off? Maybe it seemed unjust that of any relationships she could've salvaged, this was the one she'd chosen.

"For the morning," she said, and started to say something else, I think, but didn't. "Delicious muffins, Beth."

Jason was supposed to come pick me up at nine. By nine ten, he still wasn't there, and because it was unlike him to be late, I'd started to worry. Maybe he wasn't coming after all—something had happened with his parents, or he wasn't feeling well, or he'd changed his mind about Berkeley or about wanting a future in general or about me. I held my phone tightly, debating whether it was too early to message him to ask where he was. Maybe he'd just hit traffic, or forgotten his wallet and had to turn around. Or maybe I'd imagined the whole thing; maybe this was all some kind of elaborate joke.

At nine fourteen, he pulled into our driveway. I took a deep breath to try to loosen the tightness in my chest. It was fine, I told myself; everything was fine.

Jason came to knock on the door, and I checked my reflection in the hall mirror. Maybe I should've worn more makeup or done something else with my hair.

As soon as I opened the door, the evening at the park felt like a distant memory. When he said hi it was flat, and there was a feeling like a wall around him. He opened the passenger door for me, and I tried to tuck myself in quickly. When he got in, he didn't say anything, and his silence ballooned in the car between us.

"I made some muffins," I said brightly, holding up the bag. "Do you still like blueberry?"

"Sounds great," he said, but he didn't reach for one. I kept the bag aloft, awkwardly.

"Did you want one, or—?"

"Ah—maybe in a little bit."

"Sure." I put the bag on my lap. "Jason, are you—are you feeling okay?"

"Yeah, I'm fine." He backed out of the driveway. "You?"

"Of course." I sat straight and still, trying to smooth my expression. When we got to the freeway, I said, "Did you want to listen to something?"

"Ah—sure."

"Any preference?"

"I don't care."

I fiddled with his radio. My heart was thudding. What had happened? Had I done something wrong? After we'd kissed in the park, was I supposed to act differently the rest of the week, or had I done something wrong and not realized it then? Or maybe I shouldn't have told him about the child support; maybe it made me seem pathetic and burdensome, and anyway surely what he wanted from me wasn't a litany of my own relatively minor problems. Then I worried that maybe he was spiraling again; maybe these were warning signs. Maybe he'd given me a chance to find a way to him and maybe I hadn't done that, and he still felt like he couldn't tell me anything, and maybe he was descending again. My breathing seemed too loud in the car, and I tried to quiet it, to pull oxygen all the way into my lungs.

I'd wondered which way he would take us. None of the routes that made the most sense would involve the Golden Gate Bridge, but I wondered if bridges in general did anything to him now. They did to me—the thought of being on one made me feel sick. But he got onto 237, which meant we'd go around under the Bay, instead.

We hit traffic on 880 going there, and by the time we got

onto 880 we'd been driving nearly twenty minutes in silence. I couldn't think of the right thing to say. It had been a long time since I'd been to the East Bay, and I hadn't realized how stressful the freeway would be—narrow lanes, cars flying past what felt like inches from you. I tightened my grip on the armrest. I tried to think of something interesting to talk about, something that would engage him—or should I press for more details? Should I say it was clear he was unhappy and demand the reasons why?—but anything I rehearsed in my mind sounded trivial and forced. Passing through Oakland, he finally said, "I'll take a muffin now." I handed him one.

"I got batter all over the kitchen this morning," I said, trying to sound light, and he said, "Ah."

"Do you want another one? There's plenty."

"I'm good."

"Do you want some water or anything?"

"I'm fine."

It was close to eleven by the time we arrived. I was worried it would be difficult to find parking, but the lot we pulled into was mostly empty. Jason spent a long time examining the signs.

"I think it's okay," I said gently. "It's a Saturday."

"You don't think the permit matters?"

"I think it's only on weekdays."

He locked the car, but I could tell he didn't quite believe me. But that was good, right? If he was worried about getting a ticket later, it meant he was planning to be around for it. I said, impulsively, "I'll pay the fine if you get one."

He waved it off. He glanced around the parking lot. It was nestled in a cluster of buildings I didn't recognize, probably lecture halls. "So what'd you want to do here?"

"Just walk around, I guess."

"Like, all day?"

"I just thought it would be nice to see it." I had imagined us strolling through campus hand in hand, making a shared map for what our future together would look like. We could go by the music library, maybe, or the music hall, or depending on how far we were willing to walk there was the Greek Theatre and the botanical garden where my parents had had their wedding reception. But maybe I should've booked a tour, or consulted a map and made a plan. "Is there anything you wanted to see?"

"Not really."

I swallowed. I tried to keep my expression pleasant. "We could go see the Campanile."

"All right." He stood there and didn't make a move in any direction.

"Or maybe we could get something to eat first."

"Your call."

"Um—" I should've planned this better. "Maybe we can walk and see the Campanile on the way and then see if there's coffee, or maybe if you wanted brunch or something—"

"All right."

The campus wasn't familiar to me in its particulars—I didn't know where I was going. I'd thought it would be easy enough to find the Campanile, but I couldn't see it from where we were. I started walking, hoping fervently it would be the right way.

"It'll be so different next year," I said. "I think it'll be good, though, don't you? I can see us being really happy here."

"You said your parents went here?"

I nodded. "Maybe it was different back then, though."

"Sometimes I wonder if it'll be like a mini Congress Springs," he said. "How many people from school went here last year— like, thirty?"

Was that supposed to be a good or bad thing? "Well, they'd get diluted. You probably wouldn't notice as much since there are thousands of other people here."

"Maybe."

"Is that—I mean, you still want to go here, right? It's what you want?"

"Probably it's the same as any other place." He wasn't really looking around as he walked, not taking everything in. "I guess I don't really care where I end up that much."

"Um—" I heard my voice rise in pitch. "You're not—you don't mean you really don't care, right? Like you're still—"

I could tell from his expression he understood what I was asking.

"Beth, you don't need to panic about every small thing," he said, a little irritably.

"I'm not panicking, I'm just—"

"I just mean I'll get used to wherever I end up. People always do." Then he added, "You know what I hate? Everyone is so nervous around me all the time."

I didn't know how to defend myself against that. I felt my face going hot. "Everyone cares about you, Jason, that's why."

"Right, I get that, it's just—"

"It's just what?"

"Nothing."

"No, what?"

He sighed. "Forget it."

"You can tell me if—"

"I just want everyone to go back to normal."

I had to stop my voice from shaking. Did he not see how hard everyone was trying to give him that? And things had been normal, hadn't they? Sometimes, like at the park, they'd even been better than normal. "That's what we're trying to do."

"Okay, great. Let's do that, then. Just—back to normal."

We walked in a brittle silence. Would it be different at Juilliard instead? I pictured us shielded by all the skyscrapers instead of Berkeley's loose, open sky, a crush of people and motion and color and noise. Maybe it would be better; maybe it would shift whatever being here with me was doing to him. When finally I stopped to ask someone for directions to the Campanile esplanade and we found it, the stately clock tower rising above us, Jason barely glanced at it.

"My dad used to always take me to see this," I said.

He forced a smile. "Ah."

"When I was little, I thought it would be terrifying to go inside it because it was so tall."

"Heh."

"Um—do you want coffee or lunch or something? We could do a late brunch."

"Whatever you want."

It wasn't fair to feel frustrated or resentful or angry. I took a deep breath. "Let's eat something, then. I'll look on Yelp."

My palms were sweating when I took my phone from my bag. I wished I knew what to do or say to break the mood, but any possible words were forming a frantic jumble inside my mind. It was because I wanted so badly to reach for the right ones, for there to be some magic combination that would smooth things over, and it made me flail around, made everything slippery. It was like the recurring nightmare where I was onstage and had no sheet music and didn't know the piece the orchestra around me was playing.

Maybe I shouldn't have suggested coming. How much time, really, did he need to spend alone with me? It would've been better with the rest of our friends here.

"This cafe is supposed to have really good pastries," I said, holding out my phone to show him. "And they have brunch things too."

"Yeah, okay. I'll call my sister and see if she wants to eat with us." He glanced at me. "That all right?"

His sister. Why hadn't this occurred to me? Of course if he was here, where Evelyn was living, it would make sense for him to try to see her.

"Great!" I said, as brightly as I could manage, although as soon as he'd said it my stomach had plummeted. "Does she know you're coming?"

He shook his head as he held his phone to his ear. It was so last-minute, I told myself, and maybe she'd be busy. Maybe she wouldn't pick up the call.

After the hospital, I wondered if she felt differently about me now—after all, I'd tried to warn her about Jason—but it was possible that the opposite was true, that she blamed me for not doing more. I still didn't know whether she'd said anything to Jason about the time I'd called her. If she had, I thought Jason would've somehow let me know he knew, but it also seemed unlikely she wouldn't tell him; her loyalty in the situation, obviously, wasn't to me.

"Hey, Jie Jie. I'm in Berkeley. What are you doing?" There was a pause. "No, I'm with Beth. No, we just came for the day. You want to go eat something?" Another pause. "I don't know, now? I'll text you the place Beth picked."

He slid his phone back into his pocket. "She said she'll meet us."

"Great," I lied. "We can go somewhere else if she wants, too. It doesn't have to be that place."

"I'm sure it's fine."

The cafe was six or seven blocks away, which stretched long in the glare of the sunlight and in the silence, and when we got there the door was locked and the chairs stacked on the tables. All the lights were off.

"I'm sorry," I said. I felt sick. "I didn't realize it wasn't open on Saturdays. I thought—"

Jason said, a little impatiently, "It's fine, Beth. We'll just go somewhere else."

"I'll try to find—"

"That place right next door is open. I'll text Evelyn. Let's just eat there."

It was some kind of ostensibly Indian fusion buffet, decorated with the brightly colored tapestries half the stores here seemed to be selling when we'd walked by. We stood silently in the entrance while we waited for Evelyn, and as we stood there I wondered if I should offer to leave. Maybe she'd rather just see Jason alone.

She came in a few minutes later, wearing leggings and a Berkeley sweatshirt, her hair piled in a messy bun on top of her head. She wasn't wearing makeup or jewelry, but somehow she looked put together in a way I envied.

"Really, this place?" she said, giving Jason a quick, business-like hug. "If you wanted Indian food, there's a ton of good places. This is like, a place for white people."

"Eh, it looks fine," he said. "Let's just stay."

Something in Jason had relaxed when he saw her—I'd seen it as soon as she walked in, and immediately seen the way I was outside of it, too, how I hadn't done the same for him this morning or at any point in the day.

We followed a waitress, a white girl with elaborate piercings who looked like she was probably in college, to a table to get plates for the buffet. I was starving—I'd skipped the muffins in the car, although I'd eaten two before Jason came to pick me up—but I didn't want to pile my plate in front of them, so I took a small amount of each thing. The naan, inexplicably, was bright pink. (A label said it was made with beets.) Also, Evelyn had been right—everyone else in here was white.

"It's honestly kind of depressing me that this place meets your standards," Evelyn said to Jason as we sat down. He grinned. She hung her purse strap on the back of her chair and added, "You should've told me you were coming. I was supposed to meet up with people."

"Who?"

"Just some friends."

"You should've brought them. On the plus side," he said—there was a lightness in his voice; her grouchiness didn't seem to bother him in the slightest—"you get to eat pink bread."

"Where do you like to eat around here?" I said to her. I tried to make my tone casual, friendly. She hadn't acknowledged me since coming in, and I wondered whether Jason had told her we were together.

"There's a good brunch place down the street," she said. Then, to Jason: "Remember that french toast we always got when we went on that cruise? It's kind of like that, where they cover it in cornflakes."

"Yeah?" He reached out and speared a piece of tofu tikka masala from her plate, then leaned back to balance his chair on its two back legs. "You go there a lot?"

"Jason, it's literally a buffet. You don't have to eat my food. No, I don't go that often."

"What a waste. Also," he said, snagging another bite of her tofu and dodging his hand away when she tried to swat it, "this is actually pretty good."

"Ugh, don't say that. This place is kind of—" She glanced at me, then said something in Mandarin. "Don't you think?"

"Beth doesn't speak."

Evelyn raised her eyebrows at me in disapproval. "At all?"

I felt my cheeks flush. "Not really."

"Huh," she said, sitting back and appraising me for several seconds, long enough for the flush to spread through my face, down my neck and chest. Finally, I said, brightly as I could, "So, um, what are you majoring in at Berkeley?"

"Microbio. And Asian American Studies. Double major." She turned back to Jason. "This place kind of reminds me of that one place Mom used to always make us go to at the mall—you remember that?"

"Oh, where she thought they had the really nice bathrooms?"

"She was so weird about those bathrooms."

I smiled tightly, locked outside the conversation. I picked at some rice and tikka masala, and it was hard to swallow. They talked more about the food, and then about other foods it reminded them of (half the time it was Taiwanese dishes I didn't recognize, at least by name, and every time that happened I felt flooded with shame) or the places it made them think of. The language of siblings—I didn't speak that, and even if I had, I wouldn't speak theirs. A couple of times, Jason tried to pull me into the conversation, but that was worse, somehow.

"You guys want more?" Jason said, standing up. "I'm going to get another plate."

"Yes, sign me up, please," Evelyn said. "Get me like eighty pieces of their pink tortilla things. See if I can get like a whole plate load to go."

He laughed. "I'll get you the recipe so you can make it yourself."

I went with him, only so I wouldn't be sitting there alone with her. He didn't say anything to me as we were going through the line. When we sat back down, Evelyn was typing something on her phone, and Jason reached over to tilt the screen toward himself.

"I knew it," he said. "You're heartless, Jie Jie." To me, he said, "Evelyn takes a sick pleasure in leaving bad Yelp reviews. Every time we go on a trip, she insists on reviewing *everything*. Even in places where no one's ever heard of Yelp."

"Well, people traveling there will use Yelp."

"They won't," Jason said. "Your reviews just languish on the internet, lonely and—"

"Someone has to do it," Evelyn said. "Like the time we went to Italy and they would only eat the shitty Chinese food? I'm just doing my part to save other people who got trapped on those trips with their parents."

They meant Mr. and Mrs. Tsou; I understood that much of

their shorthand. Jason had told us that story too: how his family had gone with a Taiwanese tour group and he and Evelyn had had to sneak away to get pizza and gelato and pasta. I remembered how he'd been charmed by the fact that dumplings of all kinds were called *ravioli* in Chinese restaurants all over Italy.

It was disorienting to sit here and hear these glimpses of their family life as if everything between them was ordinary and fine. As if you could be that person who went on tours abroad with your wife and kids, who eschewed the local cuisine in ways that your kids poked fun at later, and all the while be someone who'd done what Jason's father had. I could understand where Brandon had been coming from when he'd wondered aloud how Jason's dad had turned into this, whether the same could be true of ourselves someday. I hated Mr. Tsou, and probably I would always hate him, but still there was something a tiny bit wrenching about the image of him trying to have a good time in a foreign country, only wanting to eat the food he knew.

I wondered if he felt that whatever he'd gone through or left behind to be here had been worth it. Maybe he felt that this country had stripped him of the things that made him himself, that it had systematically taken and decimated parts of him he'd always needed.

It was different for me, obviously, but I felt it sometimes too—that lack of concrete belonging, for one thing, like how Brandon had said once he didn't think he could ever marry a non-Asian and Jason had said casually he couldn't either, and I wasn't sure whether or not that would include me. But also I felt it in the things that living here had swallowed away from me, like how I always had to fudge my answers on those *You Know You Grew Up In An East Asian Household If* listicles so I didn't score too low, or how I never knew whether to say *they* or *we* if I was talking about Asian people.

When I was younger, I'd asked my mother once why she'd

never taught me Chinese—so many people I knew went to Saturday Chinese school, and even my father had wanted me to learn Mandarin—and she'd been dismissive. "Oh, Beth," she'd said, "no one here speaks Cantonese. It's not going to help you get ahead in life." *Getting ahead in life* was never how she framed anything, and so maybe it was more about the way she'd say things like *Chinese people* as if it both did and didn't include her, or how sometimes when we saw people flooding out of the Chinese tourist buses, she would step away from them, or murmur things like how loud they were. Or how she'd married someone who wasn't Chinese—given herself a child who was only halfway what she was.

Maybe there was a way you could lose where you came from, or where you'd never come from, and in that lose part of yourself. It was always a lowkey background hum resonating through my life. I didn't think it was quite like that for my friends, at least not in the same way, but I wondered that day if Mr. Tsou would say the same.

When we were done eating, the two of them fought over the bill, and at first I tried too, but Evelyn gave me a withering look, and I backed down, and I was embarrassed but also relieved. Eventually, between the two of them, Evelyn won. When we went back outside, the Berkeley sunlight bright even at that time of year, Evelyn glanced between me and Jason and then said, to him, "So what's your deal? Are you guys, like, going out?"

He smiled, a little sheepishly and also in a way that felt distinctly little-brotherish to me. Evelyn raised her eyebrows. "Hm," she said, studying me. I knew already I would replay that look, how it felt to have it trained on me, over and over for weeks. I regretted then not following my instincts and leaving so the two of them could have lunch together. I could see myself, could see the two of us, through Evelyn's eyes: how superfluous I was, how deeply I was failing to live up to what Jason had offered me.

I had been so happy, but maybe I shouldn't have trusted my own happiness. Maybe I should've known better. There were so many different ways to lose someone, and the deeper you went with them, the more there were.

I'd imagined us staying until evening—I'd been looking forward to seeing the sun set over the Campanile, maybe finding a romantic place to have dinner—but after we said goodbye to Evelyn and it was just the two of us, Jason said, his voice going flat again, "You ready to go?"

As soon as she'd left, that cloud had seemed to come back over him. In the car, everything I did—breathe, shift in my seat—seemed obscenely loud. I wondered if I should ask if he wanted to break up—if it would be better, somehow, if it seemed like it came from me. But what would happen if we did—would he still want to be friends like we had been? Or had I ruined that somehow too?

I wished I knew what I'd done. But maybe that was just it, maybe I hadn't done anything—maybe it was just that no matter how much I tried, I couldn't be enough.

It felt damning being in the car with him, as if being there was methodically dissecting all my failures. My stomach hurt. I was still hungry but also couldn't quite imagine ever eating again. I pictured him at home that night, alone, replaying the day and trying to superimpose it over the future we were all supposed to share. It had been a mistake to come. I should've realized it would be pushing him too far. Now when he thought of Berkeley, and when he thought of me, he would think of today.

I was afraid to imagine my own night at home. There was nothing I could conceivably do, no activity I could engage in and no conversation I could have with anyone else, that would lift this feeling from me.

When we merged onto 880, Jason said, quietly, "I was just—I think I wasn't in the mood to go out today."

"No, that's okay. I shouldn't have suggested it."

"It's not your fault. Just—we'll hang out another day, okay?"

That didn't sound like the preamble to a breakup, did it? "Of course."

I leaned my head against the window and blinked until everything flying past—the Bay, the overpasses—wasn't blurry anymore.

That Monday at school Jason brought me a small, delicate bouquet of lavender roses. It was ungrateful, but immediately I found myself wishing it had been a plant or something that would last, that I could hang on to, and I took probably two dozen pictures of the roses at home that night and looked up how to dry them.

Maybe it was just that I'd thought somehow, with this now between us, it would be easier for me to anticipate him and what he needed. Maybe I thought everything would be safer or more secure, or that I would magically become different—that I would be enough for him, or at least a better version of myself. But that didn't happen, and so often I felt that same chasm between us and didn't know how to cross it. He had given me this incredible gift, and I was squandering it.

What did happen, though, was that Thursday he didn't show up for school and didn't respond to any of my messages, either. All morning, sitting through class, holding my phone on my lap, I was frantic.

"Maybe he just overslept," Grace offered at brunch. "Or maybe he's just sick." She bit into her banana.

"Maybe," I said. I was trying to peel an orange, and my hands were trembling. "But maybe—"

"You were so worried last time this happened, Beth, but then things were fine."

Were they, though? Maybe that wasn't true at all. Maybe by showing up that day I'd averted a possible crisis—it was impossible to know.

"Why don't you call him?" Brandon said.

"Um—maybe you could?"

He raised his eyebrows. "What, you don't want to?"

"Well—I've just been messaging him a lot already."

Sunny looked like she might say something, but then she didn't. "All right, I'll call," Brandon said, and glanced around for a teacher before pulling his phone from his pocket. He ducked his head while we waited.

"Oh, hey, Jay. Everything cool? Where are you?" He was quiet a moment. "Oh, good times. All right, see you soon." When he pocketed his phone again, he said, "He had physical therapy."

"I thought he had that in the afternoons."

Brandon shrugged. "I guess it got moved."

After Berkeley, it didn't feel that simple for me—that I could just call and demand an answer, and trust that Jason would give one and not retreat into himself like he had that day. Sometimes I thought it would be so much easier to be a boy and be allowed to do things like that. Sunny was like that too, but people thought Sunny was uptight and sometimes kind of a bitch; they thought Brandon was laid-back. I said, "Do you think he was telling the truth?"

Brandon looked surprised. "You think he was lying about it?"

"I don't know—probably not, but I just worry—"

"I don't think he would've picked up if it was something really bad. Why bother?"

"Unless it was a cry for help."

Grace folded her banana peel into a neat package. "Honestly, Beth—to me he's seemed like he's been fine."

"What makes you say that?"

"He just seems like he's fine."

"Jason is still—I think he really isn't doing well. Maybe at lunch we can—"

"Oh, at lunch I'm taking Chase to Quickly," Grace said. "He's never had boba. Like literally never even tried it. Can you believe that?"

"Nothing surprises me less," Sunny said, and the way she jumped on the conversation—was she sick of talking about Jason? Did they think that was only my responsibility now? "Chase seems like he'd drink like, those Monster energy drinks."

Grace laughed. "Okay, but—"

She kept talking, but all at once, out of nowhere I was flushed with a hot, dizzy tingling. My heart wobbled and slowed as though it were caught in a spiderweb. There were widening twin circles of blankness in my peripheral vision, and they ebbed forward, growing, as my mouth went dry and there was an alarming dropping feeling in my chest and a lightness in my head.

I clutched my chest. Everything around me was like the flare in a photograph, little gleaming circles, and nothing held. *I'm going to die right here*, I thought. *Right here at brunch at school.*

"Beth, you're breathing weirdly," Sunny said. Her voice sounded oddly rounded, elongated, like she was speaking in all vowels. "Are you okay?"

"I'm fine," I managed. My throat was squeezing closed; I could barely get out the words. I tried to swallow, but all the muscles were stuck. When I looked down at my hands, they were shaking. They didn't even look like mine.

She looked at me more closely. "Are you sure? You're kind of pale."

"I think—" I could barely get enough air to talk. I tried to force a smile. "I think I have food poisoning."

"Oh, Beth," Grace said sympathetically. "You should go home!"

They were all staring at me. Brandon reached out and gently took my wrist, then pressed two fingers against it to feel for a pulse. "Your heart is beating really fast."

There were so many tests they hadn't done at the ER, so many deadly things that could be lying in wait inside my own body. My father's father had died suddenly of an aneurysm, and my mother's father had had a heart attack in his forties, and maybe whatever it was that had gone wrong in my body, whatever it was that was so obvious right now to my friends, wasn't survivable.

But I couldn't bear to have them all see me like this. I had to get out of here.

"I'm fine," I said quickly. The words felt garbled and breathless. "I'll just—" I fumbled with my backpack.

"We'll walk you to the office," Grace said.

"No, no, I'm—"

But they were already gathering up their things, already in motion, and I felt myself leaving my body, zooming out to look at the four of us gathered there: Grace's hand on my arm, Brandon slinging my backpack over his shoulder, Sunny clearing a path toward the office. And me with my hands pressed to my chest, hunched over because it felt like it used less oxygen somehow, giving myself away with each step, so exposed to them there with nowhere to hide.

We went back to the same hospital, although it was a different doctor this time, but he ran the same EKG, the same labs, and this time told my mother to take me to a therapist. By the time we were discharged and back in the parking lot, I didn't feel like I was going to black out anymore, but I was dizzy and weak and scared, and could no longer trust my body. This wasn't a one-off, and maybe it would keep happening, and who knew when. I had been in one of the safest places I knew, and that hadn't protected me at all.

In the car, my mother looked tired and sad. "Did you want to get something to eat, Beth?" she said. "We could go anywhere you like."

I shook my head. I couldn't imagine forcing food down my throat.

"Maybe ice cream? Or a drink of some kind?"

"I'd rather just go home."

She put her hand gently against my face, and then removed it, quickly, before I could pull away. When we were on Foothill, she said, "Did you want to see a therapist? I'm sure insurance would cover—"

"No."

"Maybe just to see. We could find someone you like." She took her eyes off the road to look at me. "I can look for reviews online. Maybe it would be good to have someone you could talk to."

I said nothing. We went past school. I wondered what my father would say if he knew about this, or what my friends would think of me if they'd seen me panicked and ridiculous in the hospital, the doctor coming in to inform us it was all in my head. After a while, my mother cleared her throat.

"Beth, I know how you feel," she said. "During the divorce, I had the same thing happen to me. The first time I thought I was dying. I missed a meeting with the lawyers."

Was that supposed to be comforting somehow? That this had happened to her, too, and she had gone on to survive to do what—settle into a quiet, empty house and life? Finish driving my father away except to demand money each month like I was a bill for him to pay?

"And my father," she said, "had a panic attack once when I was in my teens. We rushed to the hospital because he'd already had a heart attack and we thought it was another one, but when they did all the tests—and they did even more tests than on you— they said, no, it was just stress. But they say there's a genetic component." She turned onto Stelling, then she added, "My mother blamed him. And for me, too, I felt like it was because I was weak, or there was something wrong, but I just want you to know it's not anything wrong with you or—"

"Okay."

"If you don't want to see a therapist and you don't want to talk to me, maybe you could talk to a priest. Or maybe there's an adult at school—"

"Maybe," I said, so she would stop suggesting it. "I'll ask someone at school."

"I think that would be a good idea, Beth. I think it might help. For me, it helped a great deal to talk to my priest."

She always assumed I was so much like her. She felt, it seemed, that I was entirely hers. In the car with her there, so earnest and oblivious, I felt claustrophobic. For a second, I imagined telling her, *My friend—my boyfriend now—wanted to die and I need to make sure he never wants to again,* just for the satisfaction of the expression on her face when she realized how little she knew about me and my life after all. I wanted to shatter her illusion of sameness.

Except every time I wanted her to feel the weight of what her choices had done to me, the same thing always stopped me. When you live with someone, you're the only one who knows so many truths about them, and so you become the keeper of those truths, even if you never asked for that. How they cried in the shower every night for weeks after the divorce when they thought you couldn't hear, how they thought they had a promotion at work locked in and bought a bottle of sparkling cider to share with you in advance and then the promotion went instead to a younger man who'd just started at the job. How they would display holiday cards from the dentist's office along with the other cards, how terrified they were of moths and spiders, how much pleasure they took in strawberry ice cream, how they'd once started making online dating profiles and then stopped halfway through. How carefully they tried to hide the Christmas and birthday gifts they bought you months in advance. How, like now, whenever she drove, even on quiet roads, she gripped the steering wheel in both hands and let her eyes flicker constantly to my seat belt, checking, I knew, to make sure I was safe.

In the group chat, Sunny asked for updates on how I was, and I said I was fine, that it had been food poisoning after all, and if they didn't believe me they didn't press it. I could get away with it this once, I knew, as long as it never happened in front of them again. And if it did, maybe everything would be like it had been today about Jason: Brandon calling in a perfunctory way, duty done; Sunny skeptical, Grace making behind-the-scenes plans with Chase. They would lose interest or get tired or find me too much of a burden.

Jason was quiet all night on the group chat, and he didn't reach out to ask if I was all right. Maybe I expected too much, and I was too demanding, but waiting to see if he would and wondering why he didn't was unbearable. I was beyond exhausted with myself.

But I could wait a night. Jason and I were together; that was everything I'd ever wanted. So why did it feel like this?

I **WAS** doing a timed practice bio SAT II one evening, a few days after my second trip to the ER, when Jason called. I was in my room, the test spread out on my desk with all the pictures of my friends I kept framed and Brandon's dinosaurs we'd never put in his locker this year, and I was profoundly unmotivated; every few minutes, I kept getting bored and going back to the daily crossword I had open on my laptop. When he called, I stopped the test timer and answered.

"Hey," he said. "Did you get invited back to audition?"

Immediately, my palms went damp. I'd still been checking my email reflexively—it probably wasn't an exaggeration to say a hundred times a day—but was it possible I'd missed it? "You mean at Juilliard? Wait—did the email come? Did you get invited back?"

"I did, yeah."

From the way he said it, I couldn't tell what he thought about it. "Jason, that's amazing. I mean, I'm not surprised, but still, that's huge."

"When was the last time you looked? I would assume they'd all come out at the same time, right?"

"It's been like an hour. I'll look." I didn't want to, in a way, because for as long as I didn't, anything was still possible. My hands were shaking as I opened my email. And there it was: *Dear Beth, we are pleased to inform you* . . .

I was stunned. I wished there were a way to pin the email to my body like a badge, like a proof of worth. I was still staring at it when Jason said, "Nothing yet?"

"No, it came. I, um, I got invited back too."

He made a sound that was half-laugh, half-whoop. "I knew it!" he crowed. "I knew you would."

"I can't believe it."

"What are you doing right now? I feel like we should, like— celebrate somehow."

"Are you going to go audition?" I said. My heart was pounding. What if this was possible after all?

"I don't know. I haven't thought that far ahead. Let's go do something. Something, like—fun."

It was so out of character for him to say something like that. I said, "Like what?"

"We'll think of something. You free now? I'll come get you."

We drove up into the hills, to a cul-de-sac with four or five enormous estates set out on a plateau. (I don't know if it's what he meant by *fun*, but Congress Springs was quiet, and neither of us could think of anything else.) When he stopped the car, I took a deep breath to fill my lungs with air just to make sure I still could, which I'd been doing lately whenever any kind of tightness started in my chest. Besides still avoiding the science wing bathrooms, I'd been developing other habits to try to ward off another panic attack too—when it had happened at brunch, I'd been in the middle of peeling an orange, so I'd stopped eating oranges; in classrooms or in cars or just in situations when being trapped was more a function of social pressure, I always calculated how quickly I could escape.

It was quiet up here and more wilderness than not, and if I hadn't been with him I might've been scared, I think. When we closed the car doors behind us, it felt so loud I was worried someone would emerge from the mansions to yell at us. We walked to the edge of the cul-de-sac, and he spread out his jacket for us to sit on, even though I would've been fine sitting on the asphalt. There was a sound in the brush below us, and I jumped. Jason smiled and rested his hand on my knee.

"Just a squirrel or something," he said. "Don't stress."

"It sounded bigger."

"They sound bigger out here because they rustle the leaves, and the leaves are loud."

"I guess." Then I added, "That's kind of what being in an orchestra always felt like to me."

"What do you mean?"

"Like—no one would ever guess from the sound that it's just you in there."

From the way he smiled, I think he understood. I ventured, "You seem really excited."

"Aren't you?"

"Sure. I just—I guess I just don't understand why you aren't sure if you'll audition if you're so excited about it."

"Yeah, well—" He pulled his knees in against his chest. "It's—complicated."

"Complicated how?"

He looked out at the horizon. From where we were parked, we could see the whole South Bay all spread out below us, twinkling in the dark, our homes and our other friends somewhere down there below. For a little while, I thought he wouldn't answer me, but then he said, "You still didn't tell anyone, right?"

"No, I haven't told anyone."

"I guess I just want to keep it that way."

I suppose I wanted that too. All the same, though, I wondered:

Didn't he trust our friends? The rest of us hadn't told him about Berkeley yet, and that was the thing that felt like the strongest proof of devotion—I always wanted us to tell him, but it never seemed quite like the right time—but couldn't he feel, nevertheless, the constant steady force of care and concern surrounding him?

Maybe he couldn't, though. Maybe that was the thing.

"What if we went?" I blurted out. "What if we went together?"

He raised his eyebrows, looking, if anything, amused. "To New York?"

"I know it sounds kind of out there, but—I think we could figure out the logistics. I think we'd regret it if we never went. Just to see what happens."

"Sounds like a big trip."

"It could be just overnight. Do you think—" I hesitated. "Do you think your parents would let you? Or do you think—I don't know, do you think there's a way they wouldn't have to know? We could say we were pulling an all-nighter at someone's house to study or something. And if we did a red-eye—I mean, if it's not on anyone's radar at all because no one even knows we applied, I doubt it would even occur to anyone enough to be suspicious that we just randomly went to New York."

I thought he'd refuse right away—it was absurd, what I was proposing—but he drummed his fingers thoughtfully against the ground, considering. Overhead, something flew by us, an owl maybe. "It just feels—I don't know. It feels kind of pointless."

"Because you still wouldn't go if you got in?"

"Among other things."

"It might be worth it just to see, though, don't you think? Then you don't always have to wonder what if."

"You know what?" he said suddenly. "Sure, fuck it, let's do it."

I was more than a little surprised. In fact, I thought at first he was joking. "Really?"

"Yeah, why not?" He flipped his hand over so he could inter-twine his fingers with mine. His hand was warm and soft, and I looked at our embrace there in the near-dark and wished I could take a picture of our hands that way. "We'll do it together."

Later that night, though, I worried it was a drastic mistake, especially to go without telling our friends. Getting on a plane and flying across the country by ourselves was a huge and even alarming prospect—if anything happened, no one would know where we were—and it made me wonder at the possibility that my friends were keeping such big secrets from me.

But the point of us staying together was to be there for Jason, and so even if I didn't tell them yet, maybe I was honoring our vow in spirit, if not exactly in name. Surely if they knew they'd tell me to do it. If Jason went to New York—we could all go there with him too, as easily as Berkeley. I could find a community college if I didn't get into Juilliard, which surely I wouldn't, and then transfer somewhere close by. And my friends had applied all over to appease their parents—Sunny and Grace, I remembered, had applied to NYU, and Sunny and Brandon had both applied to Columbia, and Grace had applied to Barnard, too.

That week he and I both got our audition confirmations from Juilliard. We'd gotten the date we requested, both of us on the first Wednesday in March, and after messaging back and forth about logistics, and then deleting those messages from our phones just in case, we booked round-trip flights to New York.

I used my credit card for mine. It still had the balance from the limo plus whatever interest was accruing (I'd deleted another email saying I had a new statement; I knew the interest was probably staggering by now, but I couldn't bring myself to look). It seemed like so much money—it *was* so much money—and I'd promised myself I wouldn't use the card again. But if my balance were really dire, I reasoned, like if it were over my limit, the purchase wouldn't have gone through. I would get a job over the summer to pay everything off. And the alternative, not going, didn't seem like a real option.

I didn't want to explain the whole thing to my mother because I knew she would say no, or—more likely—she'd insist on coming. At school I nodded along when people complained about the pressure of having Asian parents, but really I knew my mother would probably be thrilled if I wanted to study violin. When the date came near, I would tell her I had to pull an all-nighter at Sunny's for a video project—I would text her while she was still at work and say I'd already come home to get my toothbrush and pajamas, and she would be upset, probably, especially the next night, when I still wasn't back, but there would be nothing she could do because I would already be gone.

I thought that since he would be auditioning, Jason would obviously come back to BAYS now. I was so sure he would, in fact, that I didn't agonize over whether or not to ask him. When he left after school that Monday I was shocked, but then maybe he'd already had a physical therapy appointment or something he couldn't reschedule—but then Wednesday he didn't come back either, or the Friday after, nor did he ever bring it up.

But—somehow, despite everything—I was playing again. I was hearing the pieces in my mind, and specific sections to work through were rising up with possibility. And that crackling noise that had been blaring through me every time I tried to play—that had quieted, or at least now there was more of everything else I could use to push that to the background.

It would take a while to find my way back, I knew. I was badly out of practice now, and I would be behind compared to other applicants who'd been working steadily all along. But this was a gift, because it had given me a purpose once more. The music wouldn't just be indulgent, it wouldn't just be something for me that I could lose myself in—it would be for Jason, too, to keep him safe.

The week before Valentine's Day, when I was doing homework at Grace's house with her and Sunny, Jason forwarded me a confirmation for the hotel room he'd booked us in New York. Sunny happened to glance up at the moment I saw the email, and she said, "Are you okay?"

"Oh—yeah." I closed my email quickly. I'd told Jason I'd split it with him, and he'd said not to worry about it, and immediately I'd wondered whether he would want or expect to have sex there.

I didn't feel ready. I wished I could talk about it with Sunny and Grace. The act of it felt a little terrifying, and altogether from a separate universe than I could imagine myself inhabiting; I had loved kissing him and holding hands, and possibly I would be content forever with just those things. But I would do whatever he wanted. All the ways you were supposed to guard and fuss over how you looked as a girl, all the things you were supposed to do and be—all of it, I knew, was in service of making sure you were attractive when it mattered, and it wasn't like the rest of you would somehow be enough to make up for taking sex off the table.

But then it was hard to say what Jason wanted. Sometimes I wondered if maybe I was entirely off base to worry about sex at all—it would be horrifying if he actually wasn't physically attracted to me after all and he thought I was the one oozing with desire. I imagined him repulsed by the things he might think I wanted, or by the fact of my wanting anything. I had googled different primers on what to do, my door locked in case my mother came home and barged in, and mostly, it seemed like it was important to make sure he believed I was enjoying myself whether I actually was or not.

I was veering between excited and petrified about the trip, and about the audition itself. The average acceptance rate at Juilliard had hovered around five percent the year before, and violin was more competitive than some of its other programs. Even at my sharpest, I doubted I had a chance, but since I'd been given one—since we both had—I wanted to do everything I could to take it.

But if Jason still thought he wouldn't go anyway, was he even practicing at home? And if so, why would he do that, cloistered away from us? I wanted him back at BAYS. It was empty without him there.

At lunch the next day, he met me at my locker as I was trying to squeeze three textbooks in next to my violin. He smiled when he saw me, and I wondered if seeing him light up at the sight of me that way could ever dull its sense of magic.

It was noisy with the beginning of lunch rush and when I asked him, impulsively, whether he was going to rehearsal today, he put his hand gently on my lower back and ducked his head down to mine to hear. "What's that?"

Maybe that was a chance for me to change the subject, and maybe I should've taken it. Instead, I said, "Oh—I was just wondering if you were coming to rehearsal today."

"Probably not today."

"Next week we're starting rehearsals for the spring show."

"Ah," he said mildly.

"We're just doing four pieces this time. There's this one section of the Haydn, though, that I keep tripping over."

"Ah," he said again.

"It's—it's really different without you there."

"Mm," he said. "Did you bring lunch today? I think I'll probably buy something. You want anything?"

"I'm good. I'll go with you, though."

"You don't have to."

"No, it's okay." I shut my locker. As we made our way to the line, I said, "I think you could catch up really quickly, if that's what you're worried about. But maybe it makes sense to just focus on the Juilliard audition pieces at home for a while, if that's what you're doing instead."

"You like the pieces you guys are doing?"

What I didn't like was how he said *you guys*. "I think you would too."

"Yeah?" We got into line, and he peered at the menu. "Have you ever had the chimichangas here?"

"I don't think so."

"You think they're anything like those taco pockets they used to have in middle school?"

"I bet it would help with the Juilliard audition too," I said. "So—have you been practicing at home? Or—?"

"Not yet."

"Do you think you will soon?"

His voice was clipped. "I don't know."

The line shuffled forward. I said, "I think it's made a difference for me. Having the audition, I mean—I don't dread playing like I used to."

"Good."

If he hadn't started practicing again yet—how long had it been, then, since he'd even picked up his violin? Over a month? Our audition was less than four weeks away, and he'd stopped using his sling, but surely injuring your arm like that would affect your playing. Was he worried that he'd somehow fail? I could see that stopping him, perhaps—that he'd be unable to accept that sort of imperfection in what had always come so easily to him.

We were at the front of the line now, and Jason ordered what he always did when he bought lunch at school, Cup Noodles and a packet of baby carrots. I said, "If you still wanted to practice together, I'm free anytime. I could do today if you wanted, or—"

"Can you just *drop* it, Beth?"

He was nearly yelling. His voice reverberated off the food service window, closing in on me from all sides. Around us, a few underclassmen turned to stare, and a sphere of quiet enveloped us. I was stunned.

My throat felt like it was going to close. "I didn't—I didn't mean—"

He dropped his voice back down to its normal volume and turned back to pay. "I just don't see why you keep pushing this when it really doesn't matter. Okay? Just let it go."

It was my fault. In all the years I'd known Jason we'd never come anywhere close to a fight, and he'd never remotely raised his voice to me. The only time I'd heard him raise his voice, ever, had been to Sunny on Brandon's birthday.

All the rest of the day I felt sick. He'd paid for his food and then we'd gone to meet the others at lunch, and he didn't say anything to them about what had happened. But really, nothing had *happened*, and in fact he was normal with me after that, and I started to wonder if maybe I was overreacting. He seemed to have moved on, to have forgiven my insensitivity, and so maybe I was the only one who spent the rest of the day and night dissecting the moment again and again. After all, it wasn't like Jason had said anything insulting, or cruel, or unkind; it had just been his tone, and maybe it was only because I had devoted so many years of my life to the altar of sound—because I wanted to find meaning in every noise—that it had felt so much to me like violence.

I wouldn't have brought it up in case it seemed clichéd or needy, but I hoped that Jason would be into Valentine's Day. He had bigger things to worry about, though, obviously, so I tried not to get my hopes up. I made him oatmeal cookies.

In the morning, he and Brandon were talking near the cafeteria when I got to school, and when I said hi, he didn't say anything about the holiday. I wondered if the cookies would make him feel guilty—if they'd seem pointed. When the bell rang and we headed toward first period together, he said, "So is it embarrassing to be into Valentine's Day now? Like super capitalist or basic or something?"

"Oh," I said. I wouldn't give him the cookies, then. I tried to keep my voice light. "Is it? Yeah, I guess, maybe so."

Outside the classroom door he touched my wrist to stop me. "Okay, well, pretend you aren't judging me." He slid his backpack around to the front and rummaged through it, then handed me a little muslin pouch. "Happy Valentine's Day."

Inside was a necklace, a delicate gold chain with a small, gold-wrapped rectangular pendant that I thought at first was some kind of glossy, burnished stone, but when I looked more closely it was something else.

"It's oak wood," he said. "I had it made from a branch I got at the park that day we went."

My cookies suddenly seemed inadequate. When I gave them to him, though, he made a big deal of saying how great they looked.

Sunny noticed the necklace right away when she met me at my locker at brunch. "Is that new?" she said, lifting it up to inspect. "It's really pretty."

"Thanks," I said, and I don't know why I didn't tell her it was from Jason. Maybe it felt like bragging, like I'd be tempting fate.

Maybe that was why, around then, I began to worry that a shift was happening with my friends—I was worried, specifically, that Sunny and Brandon and Grace's concern for Jason was waning or that we were drifting apart.

The times we'd gone to Jason's house, the time we'd gone to

the hospital—that history was going to live with us forever. But Grace was still seeing Chase—a lot, actually—and aside from Brandon teasing her now and then, we mostly weren't talking about it. Before, whenever Sunny or Grace was into someone, it had felt almost like a group project for the three of us: an endless stream of discussion, an exhaustive dissection of virtually any interaction between them and whoever the other person was. But Grace almost never brought Chase up. And that in itself—that weird shift in dynamics—was something I'd usually talk about with Sunny, but this time I didn't because I wasn't sure what she would say. Maybe she and Grace were talking about Chase, and I was being left out. Or maybe none of it bothered Sunny at all, and if that was true, maybe I didn't want to know that.

So when we were together, there was so much we couldn't talk about. We couldn't talk about Chase, and we couldn't talk about what Jason had been through, and we couldn't talk about New York or Juilliard or the plan for us to all go to Berkeley. For the first time with them things weren't as easy as they'd always been.

Grace and I got to school at the same time the Friday after Valentine's Day, and before the bell I went with her to get hot chocolate from the food cart one of the service clubs had in the mornings to raise money for a climate action fund. Aanika Shah, the junior class president, cheerfully handed us a flyer about the fund and spritzed canned whipped cream into our cups. I burned my tongue a little when I took a sip.

"Chase got me into drinking hot chocolate again," Grace said as we made our way back to the lockers. "I forgot how good it is."

"Did he not like the boba?"

"He said the pearls reminded him of boogers."

I made myself laugh. "So—what's going on with you two, exactly?"

She flung her head back and squeezed her eyes shut. It was

the way she acted in public with guys who were flirting with her—performative, kind of; dramatic—and it bothered me; it was more practiced than we ever were with each other. "Oh my gosh, Beth, that is seriously the question. I have no idea! He's so sweet, and I have so much fun with him, but I don't know if anything will ever happen."

I wanted good things for her, wanted her to be cherished and seen, but *I have so much fun with him* seemed, to me, resoundingly uncompelling. "Like you mean officially get together or anything? How come?"

"Oh, you know. I think he didn't want to do any kind of relationship senior year, and I'm still figuring out if that's what I want. Because probably we'd break up over the summer and that would be really sad. But then every now and then I'm like, wait, what if we didn't break up over the summer? Every time I bring that up, he kind of freaks out." She laughed. "I think also because I told him I'm not a low-maintenance girlfriend. Like, I would definitely want the flowers and the good-night phone calls every night."

If you had to think so hard about whether or not you wanted to be with someone, what was the point? I said, "Oh."

She finished her hot chocolate and tossed the cup into a trash can we passed by, then linked her arm through mine. "So what's it like dating Jason? You're both, like, so private."

It wasn't like I'd been refusing to tell her; we just hadn't talked. "It's good, mostly."

"We need to have a girls' sleepover or something to catch up. Is he really different with you?"

Not in the way she meant, probably. "Sometimes a little." Talking with her like this—it felt stilted, yes, but also I'd been missing her, and in some ways it would be a relief to tell her what it was really like most of the time with him, how gripped with fear I still was so often, how distant he so frequently seemed, how inadequate I felt. It was different talking about him now—before, he'd belonged to all of us equally, the way we'd all belonged to one another, but now there was more room for me to betray him.

We were in front of my locker, and Grace stopped walking. "You seem—I don't know. Are you happy?"

"Am I *happy*?" I repeated. It struck me as a bizarrely incongruous question: Jason had nearly died, and my happiness felt like the least important thing to focus on. And anyway, of all the things a relationship could be, *happy* felt a little cheap. Once I'd overheard my mother tell someone on the phone that, yes, she was happier after the divorce. "Yes."

Something in her expression changed. I said, "What?"

"What do you mean what?"

"I mean why do you look like that?"

"Nothing."

"No, what?"

She dropped her arm and pulled her hair back from her face with her pinkies and sighed a little. "I just think—it seems like you're kind of stressed out all the time, and sometimes it seems like you're still really worried about him."

I blinked at her. "Of . . . course I am?"

"But do you think that's—I mean, he seems like he's doing pretty well."

"I know, you said that earlier, but I guess I'm not sure why you think that."

"I hung out with him after school Tuesday," she said, which I hadn't known, and which gave me that trapdoor feeling in my stomach like the dip on a roller coaster. I said, "What did you guys do?"

"We just got boba."

"He invited you, or—?"

"I don't remember. We were just messaging, and I haven't seen him just by himself for a while, so I thought it would be a good time for, like, a heart-to-heart. Anyway, honestly, he seemed fine."

You got boba, I thought, *and you had a heart-to-heart*. "What did you talk about?"

"I don't know, a lot of things. Probably nothing you haven't heard. He was joking about the appointments he has to go to, like he said sometimes it's tempting to just make up crazy dreams for the therapist to see if he'll, like, super overanalyze them." She laughed. "I told him he should. Oh, and then we talked about if he'll come back to BAYS."

Felix Ni opened her locker, next to mine, and Grace and I moved over to give her room. I lowered my voice. "What did he say about BAYS?"

"He just said he didn't know if he wanted to yet. And I asked him about you, but he wouldn't say that much. It was kind of cute—like, he wanted to be a gentleman about it or something. And we talked some about Chase, because unlike Jason I have no filter. But really, Beth, he sounded good."

"But that's—"

"And you've been so down ever since it happened. I've been kind of worried about you! He's okay, and the doctors said he's going to be fine, so . . ."

"But—" That was how it was supposed to feel; how was I supposed to eat and sleep normally, like everything was fine? I waited until Felix had closed her locker and gone back out toward the rally court. The hallway felt dark and close. "Do you just not think about it because he's back now? Because that's—"

"Of course I think about it sometimes, but then what does that actually do? It's not like I sit there in class and don't pay attention because I'm just *thinking* about it. And also, I mean—aren't you relieved? It could have been so much worse, but it wasn't. I'm just so glad he's okay."

"But he's *not* really okay, Grace. It's not like it just happened and it's over because he lived."

"But—it *is* like that," she said. "That's what he wanted us to do. And I just don't think it's good for anyone to keep focusing on the past so much. He made a mistake, but now he gets another chance, and I just think we should all look forward. It's like that quote: 'Everything will be okay in the end, and if it's not okay, it's not the end.'"

I felt a yawning canyon open up between us. "I'm not like that," I said. "I can't just let go of things and assume everything's going to be fine no matter what."

She smiled, and then she surprised me—she gave me a hug, and held on tightly.

"I know," she said, finally releasing me when the first bell rang. "I know you aren't. You should try it sometime, though, Beth. Just trust that everything will be okay."

I'd always wished I were more like my friends, and frequently wished I were someone other than myself. Because I was envious, because I was insecure, because there were always so many things that seemed effortless to them that never were to me, because Grace was someone with whom Jason could randomly get boba and talk easily about the things I couldn't even bring up with him—there were many reasons why.

But that was the first time I was glad I wasn't Grace, and glad that I wasn't like her. Because there was something so cavalier in how willing she was to brush off what had happened, something that seemed a stab of disloyalty to me.

I would be better than that. I would carry it all with me, all that fear and pain. I would take it on as my own.

I'D NEVER been on a trip without my mother, and I'd never been to New York, either. We left the first Tuesday in March for our audition the next day. Our flight took off a little past one in the morning, and after a lot of back and forth, I'd decided to just sneak out that night after pretending I'd gone to bed and hope that my mother wouldn't stay up late or decide to check on me at night. Wednesdays she always went into work early for phone meetings with her East Coast branch, so I could call when we landed and she'd assume I was calling from school.

Sunny and Brandon were both still up and texting when I slipped out the back door at eleven at night, and I tried to carry on a normal conversation with them in the group chat the whole way to the airport, through the security line and finding our gate, my chest tight with guilt. I was a nervous wreck, terrified that my mother would call. She didn't, but in a way that was almost worse, because I would have to turn my phone off for six hours while we flew and I'd have no way to know if she had realized yet I was gone.

The last time I'd left the state was when we'd gone to Idaho when I was eleven to see my grandmother, which had gone badly. I'd gotten the stomach flu, and the internet speed had been too slow for my father, and my mother always thought white people there were looking at us strangely. My father thought she was imagining it. The whole flight to New York tonight, watching all the patchwork crop circles and snow-dusted peaks pass underneath us, the snaking rivers cupping the earth in their gentle curves, it felt surreal that we were going, and dangerous, too. What if I couldn't breathe on the plane, or I got a blood clot from flying and it was only Jason there? He fell asleep on the flight fairly early in—I wasn't sure what he'd told his parents—and it had the effect of making me feel like the only person left in the world. By the time we started to descend, I had grown certain the whole endeavor had been a mistake, and even when Jason woke up as we landed and then turned to smile at me, resting his hand on my thigh just briefly and whispering, "We're doing this," the oppressive, nervous haze around me didn't lift.

I called my mother once we landed, as I'd planned, to tell her I was going to stay at Sunny's that night to work on a video project, and I got her voice mail, which meant, probably, that she was in a meeting and she hadn't noticed anything was amiss. She called back almost immediately after, but I ignored it, and then a couple minutes later texted that I was in an AP bio review session before class and I'd call her later that night. Then I called the school and left a message pretending to be my mother, excusing my absence. Jason did the same, but he didn't call his parents.

It was nearly eleven in the morning, local time, once we'd disembarked and gotten through the airport. We both had afternoon audition slots, and originally we'd planned to fly back out that night, but we hadn't been able to find a good flight, and so we'd go back in the morning. We got an Uber, weighted down with our bags and our violins, and a pressure started in my chest. What if something happened to me here—a panic attack, something wrong with my heart?

As we were driving, I got a message from Sunny: *where are you? Why are you and Jason both gone??* I held out my phone to show him. "Do you think we should just tell them?"

He made a face. "I know it's paranoid, but if their parents check their phones or something—"

"What should we say, then?"

He shrugged. "Just don't write back."

I was a little bit stunned. Was that why so often I didn't hear back from him—he just ignored the messages on purpose? "Is that what you do?"

"We can talk to them when we get back."

I couldn't fathom going more than a day without responding. But I couldn't imagine saying we were in New York, either, so I turned my phone off.

It was a long, stop-and-go drive from the airport to the hotel Jason had booked, and I spent most of it trying to focus on breathing. I was worried my breaths sounded ragged or gaspy to him and that he might think something was wrong. The city kept changing out the window, but it was hard to focus on any of it and to notice very much about our surroundings when we finally got to the hotel. In the lobby, we checked in, and I worried something would go wrong because of our age, but no one asked anything, and we went to drop our things off in our room.

The room had two beds (I wondered whether he'd specifically requested them), and I sat down on one of them and tried to relax. We were here, I told myself; we'd done it, we'd pulled it off. I would think of how to respond to Sunny later.

I put my backpack on top of the dresser. I had made sure to pack my nicest underwear—which actually wasn't particularly nice, but I had one six-pack from Costco that had floral designs and a kind of sheer lace trim. It was strange to me now that I'd been daydreaming about this trip since we'd booked it. I'd thought it would be romantic and exciting, but maybe I should've foreseen that instead I would be anxious and on edge. Maybe it would be this way the whole time. Maybe I would be stiff and wooden and jumpy during my audition, too, and I would sound as scared as I was.

Jason, though—he seemed different than he had since the hospital, and in the opposite way as me. We took a yellow cab uptown to Juilliard, and on the way there I sensed in him that alertness, that kind of gentle watchfulness that made him seem like himself. And there was something hopeful in the familiarity of seeing him carrying his violin again too—how natural the movement was, how much it had always felt like an extension of him. He was nervous, the way he always was before a big performance.

It was loud when we got out of the car. The street gleamed with the glass and steel and marble of all the buildings reaching up to choke out the sun, and the sounds of traffic ricocheted back and forth between all the walls. When we walked across Lincoln Center, the streets gave way to an open plaza surrounded by performance halls, and I recognized the big, round fountain in the middle from all the pictures I'd seen online. And being there—just for a minute, as I took everything in, the guilt and anxiety I'd felt since leaving were suspended. I was here. Then I remembered the audition, and it all rushed back.

The halls were teeming with parents as we made our way to one of the designated warm-up rooms. Inside, it was crowded and frenetic. A lanky white boy who was tapping his fingers rapidly on his knees looked us up and down as we walked to find open seats. We sat next to a Black girl in a gray long-sleeved dress who was running through the same Paganini Jason had picked, No. 5. Taking out my violin, I felt sick, and I was afraid I might throw up or pass out. I tried to distract myself by listening to Jason. It was the first time I'd heard him play anything at all in months, and that familiar run of thirty-second notes from Sarasate's *Carmen Fantasy* he always warmed up with brought tears to my eyes. I tried to blink them away before he saw. When I stole a glance at him, though, I realized he wouldn't have seen anyway—he was utterly absorbed.

I wished I could listen to him longer, could try to center myself there in his playing until I felt better. But it was cacophonous in the room, and my slot was first, and I needed to prepare.

I was in the A–M audition room, and I waited outside it for half an hour to make sure I wasn't late. There were two other people waiting also, a South Asian guy with glasses and a very tall white girl, but we didn't talk. It was a small room with a music stand and a chair and a table where the three judges sat, two white men and a white woman, and alone in the room with them I felt myself blurring. I felt how little they cared about me, how impenetrable they were, and yet here I was in the face of their apathy, implying, by my presence, that I thought I deserved to be heard and watched and considered.

I was dizzy and flushed all over. I had always hated inserting myself somewhere I wasn't openly wanted.

But—and I hadn't counted on this—I felt different as soon as I lifted my violin to my chin. It wasn't how they responded, because they didn't; they told me which pieces to play and when, but they were otherwise stone-faced and didn't react to my audition. It was that when I played everything else fell away—the flight we'd taken and the lies we'd told and the huge strangeness of the city—and the room expanded, like a camera zooming out so suddenly those things felt tiny and contained and everything else there with me, the music hovering in the air, was the part that felt endless and true.

And—this never happened to me when I was playing—my eyes welled up. I don't think I realized before then how my violin let me make a home for myself, how it let me belong in places I never would have otherwise—how I could lose myself in the music and try to find myself again and how, eventually, I always did.

Usually, it's hard to feel an absence keenly before it descends on you, but there are moments in your life when you see with a perfect clarity what it will be like to lose something before you've lost it. And I felt it that day, that shock of pain that flashed all the way through me, what it was going to be like to give this up.

I'd thought after the audition that fog around me might lift, but instead it just shifted, came to rest a little lower on my shoulders, and the world around me dulled. Jason's slot was an hour after mine in another audition room down the hall, so I waited in the lobby, people streaming past with their parents, clutching their instruments.

Two white mothers were standing near me, and when an East Asian girl holding a violin case went by, the first one murmured to the other, "There are *so* many of these Chinese kids here. You can really tell they have no life, don't you think? If it were me, I'd go through last names and strike out half the Chens and Wongs right off the bat." Maybe they didn't see me, or maybe from looking at me they couldn't tell.

When Jason came out, we left and this time, since it was cheaper and there was nothing to be late for, found a subway station, and Jason lifted my case over the turnstiles for me and studied the maps to figure out where we needed to go, and we got on the train and let it carry us underground. And all the while, I think, what I was feeling, what was shrouding me, was the beginnings of grief.

"You think it went well?" Jason asked, leaning his head back against the seat.

I didn't know how to answer. What had happened in the room—the audition itself almost seemed secondary. The music had subsumed me, and it was strange to try to describe that as *it went well* or *I did okay.* "I guess we'll find out," I said. "What about yours?"

"Eh—I don't think it was the very best I could've done, but it was okay. I should've prepared more, I guess." Then he added, "It went by so fast. I forgot what that felt like."

When we emerged from the subway again, it was like another city, and with the audition over now I could absorb our surroundings in a way I'd been too distracted to do before. The buildings were shorter here—the sky closer, a blanket swaddling us—and there were more trees, and all the facades were brick and had wrought-iron gates. Our hotel was on the corner across from Washington Square Park, a medium-height brick building with pretty window boxes and a striped black-and-white awning and marble steps. We dropped our violins off back in the room, and when I turned my phone on there were twelve messages from Grace and Sunny: *where are you?? Are you okay?*

Sorry! I wrote back. *My phone was off. I'm fine!*

It was about dinnertime, and the night stretched out in front of us. Jason said, "Where to?"

I wished I could somehow go back in time and tell my younger self that I'd be here someday, alone with Jason, as his girlfriend, in New York. There was that old solicitousness to him that I'd almost forgotten about, and it felt, for the first time since we'd started dating, easy. We walked hand in hand through the park to find something to eat, the pathways curving around the playgrounds and the old leafy trees, past and then under the looming white arch. And because I liked it here, because I could still reach for and find the way it had felt to play my audition piece, my mind rushed ahead of itself, building a future for us here—maybe even just the two of us, at least at first. Maybe Juilliard would want us both and Jason would change his mind and we could make it work here somehow.

We bought slices of pizza at Joe's Pizza and ate them standing up at the high-top table outside. They were steaming hot, the crust crackling in our mouths, and delicious. After I finished, I wanted another piece, but that wasn't the kind of thing I liked to do in front of people, especially him.

"I'm going to get another piece," Jason said. "Maybe two. You want any?"

I hesitated. "No, that's okay."

"You sure?"

I nodded. My stomach grabbed at itself—I'd been too anxious to eat before the audition, and I was hungry still. I watched him go to the counter and wondered if later, maybe, once we were back, I could slip out to the CVS I'd seen on the corner and get a snack. I'd never leave the room by myself at night, though.

Jason came back with three pieces. He put one in front of me.

"You don't have to eat it," he said. "I just thought—it's good, right? And the line was really long, so I thought maybe between the time I asked and then actually ordered, you might've changed your mind."

"Oh," I said. "Thanks. I—thanks." And then I felt unsure about whether or not to eat it, and I wavered, and I think maybe some of it showed on my face, because he watched me for a second and then something in his expression changed, and he smiled, and pushed the plate toward me.

"I changed my mind, actually," he said. "I'll be offended if you don't."

And it was such a small thing. It was a slice of pizza. But it was more, too. Because you can understand the way another person needs permission sometimes, and that you can grant it without holding the power in that for yourself. And I understood that; I'd seen the opposite happen with my parents all my life and with other people, sometimes, too, sometimes with myself.

But what I wasn't sure of then was what it meant—that you cared so much, or not enough.

———•◦•———

We went back to the hotel after eating, and as the elevator ascended my nervousness, this time a kind of delicate one tinged with excitement, rose too. It wasn't really that late, and we were still on California time, and all I could think was how many good hours were left in the night. Or could be, if we used them. There were so many things he could tell me, so many conversations we could have, so many ways we could twine ourselves together.

But it was fine if Jason needed to sleep, I told myself, because he wasn't like I was and never seemed to feel the same compulsion to stretch an instant as far as it would go, and because maybe I could trick myself into pretending I wouldn't mind.

Jason glanced down the hallway, which was empty, and then checked his watch.

"You tired?" he said. "I'm not."

Our room was small, intimate in the way things always are when they're removed from your normal life and someone else is there to share it with you. My skin went hot when Jason closed the door behind him. He stood in the entryway for a while, his hands in his pockets, glancing around the room.

You can spend hours each day imagining what you might say to someone if you're ever given the chance, and then when the moment arrives, when a night stretches out in front of you, swollen with possibility, you can find it difficult to say anything at all.

"Those are really ugly curtains," he said after a while.

"I was thinking that too."

He smiled. "Got a good deal on the room, though."

He waited to see where I'd sit down. I sat on the chair at the desk—it felt less suggestive, like maybe he'd wonder about me if I sat down on one of the beds—and only then did he plop down on his bed. But he did it with a practiced kind of carefulness that made me think I wasn't just making it up that things were different tonight, that all the rules and norms that bound us were weakened. My heart was going faster than usual, pulsing in my wrists.

If he wanted to have sex, I was probably as ready as I would ever be. It couldn't be that bad, surely, and it would be something to make him feel closer to me, and also it would be something I could give him. Ever since Brandon's birthday, I'd known I would do anything, would sacrifice anything and give any part of myself, for his sake, but then there'd been nothing he seemed to want. Here, finally, was something I could offer.

How did it even happen? Did you talk about it first, or were there signals I was supposed to know, or did it just sort of— occur, like one thing led to another? It would probably be his first time too, although it wasn't something he talked about, so maybe I was wrong.

"I kind of wish our flight weren't so early," he said. "I'd be down for walking around more somewhere right now."

"We could if you wanted to."

He glanced out the window. "Eh, it's kind of getting late. And we should probably head to the airport before five."

But he didn't sound convinced, and there was a moment there where I think both of us were waiting, an instant when the night broke open and I could've said *Let's do it; let's go somewhere*, and who knows what would've happened then—maybe we would've been out until morning, maybe we would've missed our flight. But I waited too long, and I lost the chance. We sat quietly, and underneath my quiet was franticness. I was afraid now he'd just want to sleep.

"I keep worrying my mother will call Sunny or something and realize I'm not at her house," I said finally, when I needed to slice through the quiet with anything at all. I hadn't said anything more, even though Sunny had written again: *where are you???* "Have you heard from anyone else yet?"

"I'm not sure. My phone's been off." Jason got up and wandered over to the window and looked outside for a while. On the building next door there was a garden out on the rooftop, chairs set up and twinkling lights strung around. No one was on it, maybe because it was a little cold, but I wished we were out there. Then he came back and sat down again.

"I'm glad you talked me into coming," he said.

"Really?"

"I just—I feel really happy here," he said. "I guess I thought maybe I would, but then actually feeling it—I don't know. Do you wish you'd auditioned other places?"

I hesitated. "Do you?"

"I don't know. It's—complex, I guess."

"Complex how?"

"I don't know. I used to just, like—not think about the future that much, you know? Everything was kind of all laid out, so I just never thought about it. But now everything feels—kind of jumbled. But I guess I still don't like thinking about the future, so what else is new." He picked at a thread on the comforter. Outside, it was windy; the windows were thin and rattled with each gust. The thermostat was running a little too cold. I pulled my knees to my chest and wrapped my arms around them. The truth was that I didn't mind the cold, that I could see myself thriving in it. I imagined all the heavy coats I'd layer on myself, how I'd learn all those attractive complex ways of tying a scarf. Then Jason said, "My parents think I withdrew my application."

"Your application where?"

"Here. To Juilliard."

"Wait, what? I thought they didn't know you were applying."

"Yeah, they weren't supposed to. But then I left my computer open and my mom saw some of the emails. This was, uh—it was at Christmas."

I understood immediately what *at Christmas* was code for, and

I sat up straighter, my heart pounding. "What happened?"

"They—kind of freaked out. They said they were going to call the school and tell them to withdraw my application."

"But then they didn't call?"

He raised his eyebrows slightly. "I guess they were sufficiently distracted."

My face went hot. "Right, of course. But did they—"

"It's not worth talking about it."

"Jason—" My eyes were filling. Already I felt the past months reshaping themselves in my mind, and not just that but the months ahead, too. "I had no idea."

"Yeah, well." He'd found the end of the thread he was fiddling with, and he tugged it gently from the blanket. Then he said, abruptly, "What if we just went for it? If we ended up getting in?"

My stomach flipped over. "You would do it?"

"Being here—I don't know. I could see it. You know? Like walking around today, and the audition—what if it was just like that all the time?"

I felt both fragile and oddly oversaturated, and images from Christmas were flashing across my mind. I was imagining his parents finding his application, what he'd meant, exactly, by *they kind of freaked out*. My chest hurt. "I think you would be so happy here, Jason."

"Would you?"

"I could be happy anywhere."

He considered that a moment. "You think that's true?"

Was it true? What if—why had this not occurred to me sooner—what if Jason got in and I didn't? "I would love it here. But maybe—I mean, like if it didn't work out, maybe it's not being here specifically that makes you feel like this, you know? Maybe it was the audition. What if you did a music major at Berkeley?"

I got up from my chair and sat next to him on the edge of the bed. He took my hands in his, and then he pulled me down gently, so we were lying next to each other, facing one another. My heart made a funny, sad little skipped beat.

"Because you seem more like yourself this trip," I said. I could feel his breath on my cheeks. "Maybe it's just that you've missed playing."

"Maybe."

"At Berkeley you just declare the major—there's no audition. You could even double major."

"There's no audition?"

"I looked it up."

Outside, there was a screech of brakes and then a car horn, but it felt faraway, like it was coming from some other universe. Jason let go of my hands and ran his fingers gently through my hair, and I shivered.

This is it, I thought, and my stomach clenched. I tried to relax. He put both his hands on my shoulders and then skimmed them, very slowly, down the lengths of my arms, touching me so gently that it felt almost like a breeze. He took my hands in his again and shifted a little so we were side by side, pressed against each other, and I waited, tense, because I wasn't sure what came next exactly or how the mechanics of everything went. Then, kind of abruptly, he propped himself up on his elbow.

"Beth," he said, "I think—I've been thinking a lot, and—"

But he cut himself off. "What?" I said. My heartbeat was percussive in my ears.

For a little while there, the world felt so wide open, and the spaces between us so microscopic, I thought he'd keep going. But he smiled in that way I knew well, the one that meant he was done talking, and then he lay down again and rested his forehead against mine. I could feel his eyelashes brush against me when he blinked. And it was a denouement of sorts—when you play in an orchestra your whole life, you recognize a decrescendo—and so that was it, and we wouldn't have sex tonight, and I was both sorry and relieved.

I lost track of how long we lay there like that, but after a while his breathing evened out, and when I checked, he was asleep. I lay awake all night just to feel him there next to me and because I was worried that if I went to sleep I would wake up and find myself alone again, him having gone to the other bed, and that would be unbearable. I wished that after the airplane tomorrow we didn't have to go back to belonging to different spaces, that I wouldn't go home after this and sleep every night alone while he was alone too.

WE'D GOTTEN home when my mother was still at work, and I'd made sure to change and unpack and rip up any luggage tags and tickets before she came back. But the first night I was back at home, she hovered, repeating several times that it seemed an absurd amount of time to spend on a school project.

"Maybe I'll email your teacher," she said as we were eating the tomato egg and steamed bok choy she'd made for dinner. "You already have so much going on, and it just seems insensitive to pile this kind of project on too."

I almost choked on my food. "No, don't email her. It's fine. We got it all done."

"Well, when students are getting panic attacks because they're so stressed out, I just don't understand why—"

"It's *fine*," I said quickly. "Is there more egg?"

"I'll make you more."

"No, don't make more. I'll eat something else." I wasn't even hungry still; I'd just wanted to distract her. Sitting there next to her at the table, I felt like New York was written across my body, like it had to be visible somehow to her. "Actually, I think I'm full. I'm going to go take a shower."

The next morning, Sunny was waiting for me outside the math portables, and she grabbed my sleeve and said, "So did you and Jason ditch school to hook up?" When I told her that we hadn't, she said, "You go dark for a full twenty-four hours and I'm supposed to believe that? You *definitely* owe me details if it's something more interesting than you were just sick," and she seemed amused, but when I stammered out a nonanswer, she looked hurt. I was saved from the rest of the conversation only by Brandon showing up. I couldn't help wondering, though, if I'd been dating someone else, if it hadn't been Jason, if Sunny would've pressed harder. Months ago, it would've been unfathomable that I could disappear for the same two days as my boyfriend and she'd just let it go.

I'd wondered whether the way it had felt with Jason would last once we got home, and also whether, deposited back in real life, he would still feel the same way about New York. Maybe it wasn't that he'd liked Juilliard, or New York itself—maybe it was just the first time he'd been able to conceptualize the future in any real way. Maybe it was the first time he'd remembered what it was to play music.

I imagined telling my father I wasn't going to Berkeley after all. He would find Juilliard baffling, and probably he'd be so disappointed. Or, worse, if Jason got in and I didn't, how would I explain to my father why I would have to go to community college in New York? He would see it as a failure. And if all my other friends got into Berkeley, or nearby—would they give that up to switch plans at the last minute to stay close to Jason? Would they be upset we hadn't told them sooner? I knew he worried about word getting back to his parents somehow, but it was still hard to believe we had actually flown to New York and kept everyone in the dark.

The end of everything had begun to feel so close then. In AP Econ, there was a map on the wall where people could stick pushpins wherever they'd been accepted, and each new pin brought that end closer and closer. I couldn't look at it in class.

The week after we got back from New York I heard from my first college, UC Santa Cruz, which I hadn't wanted to apply to but my mother had urged me to, just in case. I'd (unsurprisingly) been accepted, but I never went to Santa Cruz anymore after our day at the Boardwalk just before my father left. It had been a waste to apply.

"I heard last year UCLA was the second UC to come out," Sunny said at lunch that day. I wanted to say *but it doesn't matter, right?* but Jason was there.

Later that week, we all got into UC Santa Barbara, which didn't help anything, and then UC Davis, which didn't help either. Grace got into St. Mary's—I'd expected she would, but it was still a relief—and Loyola Marymount and USD and BU. Sunny, who wasn't a fan of backup schools, was rejected at Harvard and Stanford. So was Brandon, but he got into Michigan and Caltech. And Jason—Jason didn't talk about acceptances much unless you pressed him directly, which I made sure not to do. Since coming back, he'd seemed better than before, but also not as good as in New York. He still hadn't come back to BAYS.

Brandon's basketball season was in full swing now. The team this year was unusually good, and Brandon was always talking about possible scenarios in which they might make playoffs. They would do things like wear their jerseys to school on game days or have team lunches or group workout sessions in the evenings. We weren't a very sports-y school—usually when we went to watch him it was like five white moms in team sweatshirts and an aggressively invested dad or two, clusters of people watching their friends play while they studied, and a handful of freshman there for the PE extra credit, probably under thirty people total—but we did have a soft spot for excellence, so people had started going to watch.

The Tuesday of spring break, Sunny and I went to see his game against Los Altos. Jason was at the dentist and Grace was in

Kauai with her family, and the gym was almost empty because of spring break. We sat near half-court, our homework for AP Econ spread on the row in front of us, behind three moms who had customized red-and-white stadium seats that said PITCHFORKS!!, where the *I* and the exclamation marks were upside-down pitchforks and the *T* was a normal one. When we'd first noticed their seats sometime last year, Sunny had said, "I'm totally getting everyone that for Christmas," and Jason had told her please do, and that the second exclamation mark really sold it.

"So are you not excited about Chase? What are we calling them now? ChGrace?" Sunny said. On our way over, Grace had FaceTimed us from the beach to say that she and Chase had finally made things official. "You didn't exactly look thrilled when she told us."

Did that mean Sunny wasn't thrilled either? I wanted so badly to be aligned in this, to be able to talk about it. I'd been simmering since we'd heard. One of the Los Altos players overshot the basket, and the ball thudded against the wall, the sound echoing against all the lacquered hardwood and metal bleachers. Brandon grabbed the ball to throw back in, springing to action when the whistle blew, and I said, "What do you think about it?"

"She seemed really happy."

My heart sank a little. "Right." I said, carefully, "I'm just worried, I guess."

"About her? Chase is pretty harmless."

"None of us really knows him that well, though." We didn't know, for instance, if he cared about our place in Grace's life, if he understood the importance of it or if he was the kind of person who thought friends should be an interchangeable collection of people you could hang out and laugh with. And you want the people you love to feel more like themselves in a relationship, not less, and it didn't seem that way.

"I've known Chase since we were like five years old. He has a labradoodle. His family makes him go to church. His car smells like a Costco."

"But you don't actually *know* him know him. It just seems—it seems so risky. And if she thinks they're going to break up anyway, and the timing—the timing is just bad." What if Grace decided she didn't want to break up with him after all, and instead wanted to go to college with him?

Brandon had the ball again. I watched him dribble with one hand, shouting directions to the other guys. He was different when he played—more aggressive, more visibly emotional—and I had the strange feeling that I could not imagine that the guy out there drenched with sweat and shouting himself hoarse, his arms muscled and pale in his sleeveless jersey, was someone I'd built my life around and would share a future with.

"Do you think they're sleeping together?" Sunny said.

I'd wondered. "Maybe. Chase seems like someone who would probably want to."

"Maybe? I don't know about Grace, though. She didn't with Miles."

"But if he wants to, she probably would, right?"

"Wait, what?"

"I mean, if they're going out—"

Sunny put down her binder to turn and look at me. "Wait, this isn't about you and Jason, is it? He's not, like, pressuring you—"

I felt my face turn red. The metal rim of the bench was pressing uncomfortably into me. "No, no, nothing like that."

"Wait, is he, though? Because it's kind of weird you said it like that."

"It's kind of weird I said what like that?"

"Like just because Chase wants to, Grace has to go along with whatever? That's—kind of rapey."

"I just meant—" I faltered, waiting for her to talk over me, but she didn't. Brandon rifled off a quick pass to Leo Lim, and

Leo shot, the ball swishing cleanly through the net. Brandon screamed something triumphantly at him, slapping his hand. We were ahead. Finally, Sunny said, "You just meant what?"

"I don't know, I guess if you're going out with a guy it seems weird to—just not, if he wants to."

She squinted at me. "Are you reading, like, housewife manuals from the nineteen fifties? What are you talking about? Because, A: Why are you just assuming only the guy wants to, and B: What the hell, Beth? Do I need to talk to Jason?"

"No—Sunny, don't." We weren't sitting particularly close to anyone else on the bleachers, but I looked around anyway to make sure no one could hear. One of the tall white guys on the Los Altos team passed the ball to one of their other tall white guys, but Leo's arm flickered out and he nabbed the ball, and then everyone stampeded in the opposite direction, a blur of red and blue. "Jason's never said anything about it. I just—I just assumed that—"

"Okay, but what would you do if he did?"

"I guess I'd say yes?"

"Because you actively want to or you feel like you have to?" I didn't answer, and she grabbed my arm. "Okay, Beth, seriously, you don't owe him anything like that, so you shouldn't feel like—"

"We all owe him, though, kind of."

"Okay, but not our *bodies*. Also, what do you mean we all kind of owe him?"

The question surprised me; it felt like it should be self-evident. "Clearly, we failed him."

"That's how you see it?"

"How do you see it?"

"Obviously I wish things had been different, but we didn't know about it. We would have done something if we could've."

There was a twist of pain in my chest when I remembered how he'd tried to sound nonchalant in our hotel in New York when he'd alluded to Christmas. "But that was the problem. We didn't know. We just assumed everything was fine, and we weren't—"

"You think it was our fault?"

"Sun—we're his best friends."

We watched as Brandon tried to take the ball down the court and lost control when one of the players from Los Altos, a short-ish white guy, boxed him in. Brandon looked enraged in a way he never did in normal life. Everything about him seemed height-ened here. One of the moms, an Asian mom I didn't recognize wearing a red Las Colinas sweatshirt, put her hands to her mouth and called, "That's all right, Brandon, keep it up!"

"You know," Sunny said, "Grace said she's been worried about you."

"She said that to me, too, but I think it's because she's kind of in denial."

"What do you mean she's in denial?"

"She thinks no one should be worried about anything."

"Yeah, I don't know if that's exactly what she thinks. It's more that she thinks you're like—I don't know, just not doing well with everything."

"I think she's just really wrapped up in Chase."

Sunny was quiet awhile. I pretended to go back to my lab notes. The tallest Los Altos player shot and missed, and a group of four freshman waved posterboards with pitchforks drawn on them. We scored again—we were up by twelve now—and every-one cheered, a small and hollow sound with so few people in such a big room. After a while, Sunny said, "I think it's because you're so like—secretive about Jason. You never talk about things. And the way you guys are together—I don't know. It feels different now."

"You mean with the five of us?"

"Yeah."

"I don't want it to feel different," I said quickly. "It shouldn't.

It's not like we're going off alone together all the time."

"Grace and I were talking—" She hesitated. "Actually, never mind."

"No, you can tell me. You and Grace were talking about what?"

She didn't look at me. "I guess like—trying to picture what it would be like next year. Like if it's going to feel like this next year."

It suddenly felt imperative to have Sunny on my side. I wished Brandon were here talking with us instead of running back and forth on the court, shouting instructions. "Feel like *what*, though, Sun? Things are the same."

"Maybe it's not you," she said. "Maybe it's more Jason. He's just kind of—still so withdrawn. I guess I just assumed it's because he's more focused on you, but maybe it's not like that."

"But that's exactly why I think Grace is in denial. I think Jason is still really not doing well, and I think he still really needs everybody, but Grace is just too wrapped up in Chase right now to see that. It's like—it's like she just wants to forget it all now that it's not convenient for her anymore."

"You really think that's where she's coming from? Because when you say stuff like you think you have to sleep with him if he wants to—that really doesn't feel like the healthiest relationship in the world."

"I'm just—" My voice cracked a little, and then I didn't know what to say. Sunny softened.

"You know you can talk to us, right?" she said. "It just seems like it's probably a lot of pressure to be dating someone like Jason ever, but especially, like, right after something so major. It's just weird to me how it feels like you're always holding back from telling us stuff."

"I mean—what do you want to know? It's not like anyone ever asks."

It was halftime, and on his way to where his team was gathered on the sidelines Brandon veered toward us. He was drenched in sweat, and he looked exuberant—we were up by eighteen now—and he pretended he was going to hug Sunny. "Don't even think about it," Sunny snapped, recoiling, and he laughed and kept going to his team, lifting up his jersey to mop his face.

We watched them huddle. The way the lights overhead were flickering, the stuffiness in the gym, the way the bleachers rattled every time someone got up and walked on them—everything was making me feel dizzy. I tried to focus on the door. Then Sunny said, abruptly, "You'll still tell me things, right? Like if there's—anything. You won't keep secrets from me just because you're with him now."

The buzzer went off, startling me, and Brandon and his teammates exploded from their huddle.

"Right," I said, over the noise of so many feet pounding against the floor. "Of course." It was maybe the first time I'd deliberately lied to her.

AT THE END of spring break, when Grace came back tanned and with Kauai Kookies for us, Jason, Sunny, Brandon, and I all got into UCSD. It was the best school I'd been accepted to so far, and if I got in there, I hoped it meant good things for Berkeley. But that Grace hadn't gotten in was a little alarming. The first day back at school, all five of us got into Irvine, which didn't seem like a realistic option, but it was so far the best place we'd all gotten into, and the path was narrowing. At least two-thirds of our class had already chosen where they were going to go next year. The map in AP Econ was teeming with all those small, cold futures.

Meanwhile, improbably, Brandon's team kept winning. For the game against our rival, Cupertino (*rival* referring to, basically, test scores, since we were both generally bad at sports), the gym was nearly packed, and a junior named Rajesh 3-D-printed hundreds of six-inch plastic pitchforks and stood outside the gym handing them out. At halftime, Brandon held up his phone and took a panoramic picture, looking emotional. His parents had both taken off work to see him come play, gamely accepting the plastic pitchforks and waving them around whenever we scored.

That night I found out I didn't get into UCLA. A few minutes later, Sunny sent a screenshot to our group text. It was her acceptance email and the party horn emoji, a dozen or so of them all in a row. My stomach clenched. Jason and Brandon had gotten in too. Maybe, I told myself, Sunny was holding out for LA being our best option, if, say, Jason didn't get into Berkeley. Still, though, I couldn't shake the dread blanketing my shoulders.

By the time Brandon had his last regular game, Berkeley decisions still hadn't come out, and the present felt as though it were being cannibalized by the future. The basketball season was supposed to end, which would be a relief because it, too, suctioned up the little time we had left, but then there was the first game of playoffs, and they won, so then there was another game of playoffs, which Brandon skipped rehearsal to go to Watsonville for. They won that, too, and then there was some complicated scenario about certain teams winning or losing certain games that would determine whether or not they would go to the championships—Brandon explained it probably a dozen times, but I could never quite follow—and at lunch the day the results were supposed to be posted, Leo and Bentley came to hold vigil with him while they waited to hear. Chase was there too.

"We're not eating until we hear, though," Bentley said, pointing first at Brandon and then at Leo. "That was our pact."

"Brandon," Grace said, "would you rather somehow curse your chances—"

"Curse them how?" Chase interrupted. "I feel like that matters to this story."

It wasn't a *story*, but Grace said, "Hmm, good question. Okay, Brandon, you eat something now and anger the Pitchfork god"— she wiggled her fingers back and forth—"or you make playoffs and the game is tied, right at the end, and you're shooting and you miss?"

"What kind of sick question is that?" Bentley said. "You're a closet *sadist*, Nakamura."

I was sitting across from Jason. Ever since talking with

Sunny, I'd been careful not to seem couple-y with him in front of the others—I would make sure I wasn't sitting next to him, and I didn't try to hold his hand or in any way reference our status aloud. He'd been quiet most of the day, and today at lunch he seemed distracted.

"Lose the game, man," Leo said. "You piss off Lord Pitchfork and you'll pay for it the rest of your life."

"So when would this theoretical game be?" Sunny said.

"This weekend."

"Isn't that our spring show?" I said.

"The game would be Saturday," Brandon said. He was beating out a constant staccato pattern against his knees with both hands. "The show's Sunday."

"The show's in San Francisco again, right?" Sunny said. "We should go up early and hang out."

"Ooh, that could be fun," Grace said. "I haven't hung out there in a while."

It was supposed to be nice in the city that day, and as Leo kept refreshing the webpage on his phone and Brandon moved on to drumming onto his empty water bottle, Chase sitting with his arm around Grace, we talked about going up first thing in the morning and wandering through some of the neighborhoods. As the plans were taking shape, the day unfurling, I watched Jason, who was meticulously peeling the pith off an orange. I reached out and touched his knee.

"Are you sure you don't want to come back?" I said. I wondered if San Francisco felt fraught to him still, if it always would. But the spring show was one of the only two big performances we had left. "You could learn the pieces by then. Everyone would be so glad to see you."

"I'll probably skip this one."

"Oh, shit," Leo said, his hand flying out to whap Brandon on his rib cage. "It's up."

Bentley covered his eyes dramatically. "I can't take it. Don't tell me. Schrödinger's results. Right now we both are and aren't in it, but as soon as we open the box—"

Brandon whooped. "We're in?" Bentley said. "For sure?" He made an exuberant stabbing motion. Brandon said, "What's that?"

"Pitchforks, obviously."

Leo laughed. "All hail." He peered at his phone. "We play St. Peter's."

"Dude, St. Peter's," Bentley said. "That's totally one of those places for rich white kids whose parents want to make sure their kids only socialize with other rich white kids. We'll crush them. Go public schools."

I thought Chase looked like he wanted to say something, but before he could, Sunny rolled her eyes. "Yes, go public schools, but also, we're basically a private school."

"How are we basically a private school?"

"Because of everyone's parents' absurd property taxes. You're still paying for your kid to go to a good school. Are they going to do that adversity score thing on college applications? Everyone here will score like, point-five."

"Oh right, Sunny has *Opinions* on college-ready adversity," Brandon said, grinning. He looked amped. "Ask her what she thinks about writing your essay about your personal traumas. Ask her about Mike—"

"I don't think you shouldn't *ever* write about traumas," she protested. "I mean, Beth's essay about Jason was great, I just think—"

A fist squeezed around my heart so hard I reeled forward. She stopped herself, stricken, but it was too late.

Across our little circle, Jason looked at me strangely. "Is that true?"

I couldn't breathe. "It wasn't—I just mentioned you in one of the questions."

"You said what, exactly?"

"Just—" Why hadn't I prepared for this possibility? I should've had some answer ready, something that would make it seem less like a violation, but as it was I was too panicked to even mash together words to form a sentence. Maybe I could've salvaged the moment somehow, except that Sunny hadn't just said it was about him, she'd also said it was about trauma. "It was just about friendship. It was kind of about everyone."

I don't think he believed me. But then he didn't say anything, and he didn't ask anything else, so I thought maybe it was all right. I couldn't look at him. My skin felt hot.

"So where's your game?" Grace said brightly, when no one else said anything. "Is it anywhere near SF? We should see if we could make a weekend out of it."

"Nah, it's in Salinas," Brandon said. He glanced at Jason, and I recognized the way he did it—it was the same way I felt when I was worried about how he might've reacted to something. "I wish we were in a league with the North Bay instead, though. We always have to do these games in like, farm towns."

"Oh, boo. We should still go early to SF Sunday, though. We could take BART. Jason, you should totally come!"

"Eh, I probably wouldn't be performance-ready," he said. He sounded all right—pleasant, mostly, like we were discussing something neutral like test answers. "I'd drag everyone down. You guys should do it, though. It sounds like fun."

"You could just come for the day too, if you wanted," I said quickly. "You wouldn't have to play if—"

His head snapped up to look at me, and he let his orange fall on the ground. "Why do you always keep pushing this so hard?"

"I wasn't trying—I just thought you might want—"

He grabbed his orange and threw it, hard, at the trash can a few feet away, where it splattered. "Just *stop*, Beth, okay? I said I didn't fucking want to go."

I'd gotten around the corner and was breathing into cupped palms, trying to prove to myself that I was pulling oxygen into my lungs, when Brandon caught up to me.

"Hey," he said, putting his hand on my shoulder, "are you okay?"

I dropped my hands. "I'm fine."

"Does Jason talk to you like that a lot?"

"No, no," I said quickly. I wiped my eyes. "It was just—I don't know why I pushed it. I know he doesn't like to talk about BAYS stuff."

"Okay, because like—that's not cool for him to snap like that. You know that, right?"

"He's just going through a lot."

"I mean, yeah, I want to give him space and stuff, and I want to be understanding, but he doesn't have to be a dick about things."

"You're his best friend," I said.

"The point being what?"

"The point being that if anyone should understand how hard it's been for him it should be you. You know he's not a bad person. Sometimes it just feels—"

My voice gave out. Brandon said, "Sometimes it just feels like what?"

"Like everyone's already stopped caring about him and I'm the only one. It's just a lot."

"Beth—that's not fair."

"I'm not trying to—I know you care about him more than anyone. I didn't mean you're not—"

"I mean it's not fair to *you*," Brandon said. "This is, like—exactly what I was kind of worried about when you said you were getting together. He really doesn't seem like he's in a great place to be in a relationship right now."

Brandon hadn't been there for the good parts—the night in the park, New York. "Why should someone have to be in a good place to be in a relationship?"

"Gee, I don't know, maybe so they don't blow up over completely innocuous questions at lunch?"

"He didn't blow up. He was just annoyed. And I would never ask him to be happy and perfect all the time. I just want to be there for him even—especially—when things are bad. Isn't that what you want too?"

Jason called me that night. My voice came out a little strangled when I answered.

"I called to apologize," he said. He sounded tired. "I should never have snapped at you like that."

"Oh—it's fine. It was nothing."

"I was just—well, whatever, it doesn't matter. There's no excuse. I was way out of line." He added, "Brandon laid into me pretty good."

"He shouldn't—"

"Nah, I deserved it."

We were both quiet a moment. I didn't know what to say. Finally, I said, "I changed your name."

"What?"

"In the essay."

"Oh. That's—honestly, I'd rather not know."

"Right, sure." That was worse, actually; it made it feel like a more shameful thing I'd done. I felt exposed and ugly, too large and sharp-edged to hide myself.

"But anyway, I'm sorry," he said. "I wish—"

He cut himself off. I said, "You wish what?"

For a moment, I thought he'd answer me. But had it ever been like that between us—that things were easy and fluid, that we could understand each other without speaking and we would just say whatever came to mind? It felt hard to remember now.

"Nothing," he said. "I'm just sorry, that's all. It won't happen again."

I believed then that in every relationship, in everything, you made a choice whether or not you were going to hold on. When something was in danger of falling apart, there was always a stopping point—the last time you could halt things before they took on too great a velocity. And I believed that because when my father left, I'd missed that point; it was only in looking back that I recognized the one day, the one moment, that could have reversed the trajectory of our loss.

That moment, with my father, was this: It was a Saturday in eighth grade, and the three of us had gone to Santa Cruz for the day. We traipsed all over town, my mother armed with sunscreen and my father with his Nikon, which he aimed throughout our visit at the painted wooden spokes of the Giant Dipper, at the reflection of the clouds in the wet sand after the waves had receded. I'd seen it happen, time and again, but I'd never quite understood how from such bright and lovely things—a candy store, a roller coaster where you screamed, happy, and the wind tugged at your hair—he'd extract small, muted black-and-white biopsies of detail and texture so you saw only the splintering wood of the ride's infrastructure, the way those grains of sand had such sharp, unsparing edges.

At the candy shop, I chose an ice cream cone with nuts, and my father had a Snickers bar. As my father was handing his card to the cashier, he turned around.

"You getting anything, Kathy?" he said.

"Oh—no," my mother said quickly. Her hands went unconsciously to her stomach, and she smoothed her shirt down over her waist. "The sugar makes my teeth hurt."

"We come all the way here and you don't want anything?"

"Oh," she said. "Well. Maybe something small. Here." She quickly picked up a small bag of taffy lying on the counter next to her and handed it to my father.

"Well, don't give it to *me*," he said.

"That's all for you folks?" the cashier said.

"Yes," my father said to the boy, a twenty-something with huge wooden ear gauges who looked bored of us, bored of the whole day. "That's all."

Later we walked downtown, and in a used bookstore he bought me *Ender's Game*, his favorite book. I read it on the way home. It was dark by then, long dark, but if I held the book up I could read by the headlights coming through the rearview window, the light spilling across the pages and making the words jump and skitter with every bump in the road.

My mother kept turning around, looking worriedly at me. "Beth, that probably isn't very good for your eyes," she murmured, and then, "Beth, aren't you making yourself carsick?" And then, the last time—"Doug, is she blocking your view?"

"Just leave her alone," my father had said—not quite angry, really; more tired, more drained. And that was it, that was the stopping point: the last moment when it was still the three of us cocooned there when we shared a destination and a point of origin and still we called the same place home. When we stepped inside the doorway later that night, my father would clear his throat and say, "Kathy—it's just not going to work."

After he left, I revised that moment over and over, gave it so many alternate endings. In one version, I defend my mother. *But I don't want to be left alone*, I say. And he understands what I mean: In the rearview mirror, his eyes meet mine, and he sees, superimposed over that reflection, what it will do to us if he leaves. He sees the father-daughter dance from which I stay home in eighth grade, the couples' gym membership my mother cancels, Mr. Irving asking me, jovially, "How come I never see your dad anymore at our concerts, Beth?"

In another version, I take his side. *Yes*, I say to my mother, *Leave me alone*. And she's hurt; she twists back around and looks out the window the rest of the ride. But we go home, my mother still quiet, and when we get back she stops nagging him about the video games, stops radiating her wounded silence around the house, and I learn to be better at the games, and he's proud and admiring. In another version, I say something funny and he laughs and the tension breaks and scatters. In another, he snaps back at her and they fight until they decide to see a marriage counselor; in another, my mother confronts him, and in another, he laughs everything off. In all my versions, he never leaves, or if he does, he comes back after a few days because he loves us, and he misses us too much.

Sometimes I still thought about my lonely, devastated eighth-grade self, so desperately clinging to all those alternate endings that would never come true. And I thought now how if I could've gone back in time somehow and told that version of me that someday Jason would ask me to belong to him, maybe everything would've felt different then. All the ways I felt broken and worthless, all those ways the world felt blown apart and all those ways I felt unwanted—maybe it would've soothed them to know that Jason, Jason whom I had always loved, wanted me.

It was more than I'd ever believed in for myself. So no matter how difficult things were, I wouldn't waver. I would understand, I would do better. I would hold on.

I HAD refreshed my email so many times the past weeks—hundreds of thousands, possibly—that it felt almost involuntary, an extension of my nervous system, and of those countless refreshes there was so infrequently anything new except for credit card emails that when the email appeared the morning of Brandon's game saying *YOUR APPLICATION TO JUILLIARD*, at first it didn't register. And then in a fraction of a second it did, all at once, and my pulse throbbed in my thighs and in the back of my neck, and I opened the email fast, before I could lose the courage.

Dear Beth, it said. *Welcome to Juilliard.*

But surely—*surely*—I'd misread. I read it four times. It was so unexpected it almost felt more real.

I did it, I thought. *They thought I was good. They want me.*

But still nothing. I was numb. I read it over and over, until the words lost their meaning, and then a message popped up while I was still staring at it.

I didn't get in, Jason wrote. *You?*

I was so genuinely unprepared for this outcome that it took me several seconds to decipher what he meant. It was impossible that he hadn't, because I had. He'd been out of practice, yes, but it was *Jason.*

I called him. "Are you okay?" I said. "What did they say?"

"They didn't say anything."

"But was it—did you put in your application about your arm, and—"

"No." His voice was flat. "That's irrelevant."

"But maybe if they knew—"

"It doesn't work like that, Beth."

I didn't know what to say. Had his audition gone that badly? Surely Jason at his best—even on an average day—was more than good enough to get in. I had spent years of my life listening to him. It wasn't just that I knew what he was capable of musically—it was also that I knew what it meant to him. Finally, I said, helplessly, "I can't believe it."

"What about you?"

"What about me, what?"

"Did you hear yet? Did you get in?"

"Oh—no. I mean, yes, I got the email too. Um—I didn't get in either."

"Well, that's bullshit."

Somehow my brain was still struggling to make sense of all the pieces, but piercing through the jumble there was a colorlessness to his voice that alarmed me. I needed to see him; I needed the reassurance of his physical presence. "Do you want to meet up somewhere?"

"I think another time would be better."

"You could come over here," I said. "Or I could go to you—I'm not doing anything right now, if you wanted to talk about—"

"It's all right. I've got some things to do here."

When I hung up, the room constricted and then expanded again with every beat of my heart, and I was struggling to breathe. Brandon would just be leaving tutoring now, and I called him three times before he picked up. When he answered, I said, "I'm really worried about Jason. I'm scared he might try again."

"Are you serious? What's going on?"

Breathe, I told myself, and I tried to iron out my voice. Where would I even start? "Um," I said, "it's—it's kind of a long story."

I told him everything—how Jason had applied, how his parents had found out, how we'd snuck to New York for the audition. How much it had meant to him, how when we were there it was the only time since Christmas he'd seemed like himself and the only time he'd seemed happy. When I finished, Brandon said, "I can't believe you pulled off secretly going to New York."

I hoped I was imagining that there was something strange in his voice. "I wanted to tell you guys. He was just so afraid of his parents somehow finding out."

"I don't know whether to be insulted by that or impressed you actually pulled it off."

"Okay, but anyway," I said, "he just found out he didn't get in. And I think having that possibility—"

"Did you?"

"Did I what?"

"Did you get in?"

"No, of course not. But anyway, that's beside the point, and the point is that I think having that possibility was everything to him. It was like an actual future he was happy about and he wanted, and I think that was something he was really holding on to, and now—now I'm just scared—"

"I'll call him."

"I don't know if he'll pick up." I hesitated. "Also—I don't think I was supposed to tell you about Juilliard."

"So do you think I should try to talk to him or not?"

"What do you think? You're his best friend."

"Well, it's your secret."

"I think we should try to go see him. Maybe we could make up an excuse and then just show up. I just feel like we should make sure he's—"

"I have to leave in like forty-five minutes to go to Salinas."

"You're still planning to go to Salinas?"

There was a long silence. "You think I should skip the game?"

"I mean—do you think you should go?"

"Did he say something in particular that's making you worry? Because, I mean, it sucks to get rejected, but if he's just disappointed and he'll get over it—"

"He didn't say anything, but—" Why was I having to explain myself? Why was Brandon not already on his way over? "Obviously last time he didn't say anything either. I don't think he would tell us in advance."

"My whole family is coming to Salinas," he said.

"But if he's—"

"I know. I know." He sighed. "Fuck."

"We could just try to go over now, and then you could still make—"

"I'm just going to call him," he said. "I won't bring up Juilliard if you really don't think I should, but I'll just call and see how he sounds. Okay? I'll call you back."

I laid my phone on the bed and lay down next to it, waiting for him to call back. I was having either a panic attack with entirely new symptoms, or some kind of neurological episode—I couldn't focus my vision on anything without it wavering, and my fingers were numb. A minute went by, then two.

"He didn't answer," Brandon said when he called back. "I tried like six times."

I sat up. There was a tingling pain up and down my left arm, which I vaguely remembered as being a possible symptom of a heart attack. "Do you think we should just go over there?"

Brandon was quiet a long time. Finally, he said, "Does it make a difference if I specifically am here? I mean, are you going to just go over anyway whether I go with you or not? Because I'd do anything for Jason, you know that, but if I just bail on the game and then it was all a false alarm—"

I was suddenly furious. "Fine," I snapped. "Go to Salinas. I won't waste more time trying to talk you into it. Have fun with your game."

But after hanging up, I didn't know what to do. I could bike to his house, or I could call someone else, but either option felt eternal and also untenable. If it was just me, and I showed up alone—what if I wasn't what he wanted? What was there about me, exactly, that would tether him back to the world? It was like that hypothetical where you're drowning in an ocean and there's a life raft on either side of you, at equal distances away, and you can't decide which one to reach for, and you perish. I would sit here, wracked with indecision, while he slipped away.

Sunny called while I was sitting there, and when I picked up, she said, "I cannot believe you *went* to New *York* without telling me."

"You talked to Brandon, I see."

"Were you just literally never going to tell me? Or—"

"Don't be mad," I said. My voice was shaking. "Also, remember how you made me promise I'd tell you if there was anything? Can you go to Jason's with me? Right now?"

She was at my house in just under seven minutes, and I loved her for that. I was shaky and hot getting into her car, and the comforting familiar smell of it enveloped me when I shut the door behind me. I was trying not to cry.

"I really think he's probably okay," she said, pulling out of my driveway, and there was something kind of stiff in her tone. "I remember reading statistics a while ago, right after, and it was something like nine in ten people never try again. It's like people get into this zone and they can't see past it, but then if they wait long enough they can think more clearly."

"Statistics never feel all that comforting."

"Yeah, maybe not. I guess someone has to be the bad ones."

I couldn't stop the images of us showing up to his house only to be too late—us finding him on the floor somewhere, us not finding him at all. "I really wish Brandon weren't going all the way to Salinas."

"It's not *that* far."

"It's over an hour."

"Well, I mean, it's not New York."

I flinched. She sighed. Then she said, with a little less heat, "I just really can't believe you didn't tell me."

"I wanted to tell you, Sun. If it had been just me, you know I would've. But Jason was just so worried that somehow word would get back to his parents. It was really awful not telling anyone."

"But you didn't have to go along with it! You really think I would've somehow told his parents?"

"Of course not, but maybe if—I don't know, if your parents were going through your phone, or—"

"My parents barely know how to use their own phones."

"I wish I'd told you," I said, which was the truth. I would've been less alone with it.

"Okay, but also, like—would you guys have gone if you'd gotten in?"

I should've lied, and I knew it, but somehow I couldn't bring myself to do it—I think even though the dream was over now, it felt too precious still to deny. "I think so."

Her expression changed. I wished, desperately, that I could tell her and all of them that I'd gotten in. They would understand what it meant to me, both the magnitude of having gotten in and also having to sacrifice that now. When we pulled onto the street before the turn for Jason's, Sunny said, "And you just weren't going to tell us? Because I was willing to give up UCLA."

"I always knew I wouldn't get in, though," I said. I had to fight to keep my voice steady. "So it was just a fantasy. When I said I would've gone—I mean, I would also, I don't know, say yes if someone offered me a spot tomorrow in the Vienna Philharmonic or something. That doesn't mean I ever thought it would really happen."

"I guess."

"I think it was something he needed to do, but that's different from making an actual plan. The plan is still Berkeley." Then I added, quietly, "I wouldn't have gone to Juilliard by myself. You have to believe me."

"All right," she said. We pulled in front of his house, and she exhaled, looking toward it. "He doesn't know we're coming, right? Should we just—knock?"

On his doorstep, waiting, there was a boiling feeling inside me, and my skin felt stretched too tight to contain everything. I felt dangerously on the verge of some kind of outburst—yelling or sobbing or breaking something. I tried to swallow it back. After a few moments, his mother answered the door in slippers and with wet hair, and she looked surprised to see us. "Oh—you come to see Jason? Come in, come in."

We followed her up the step and slipped our shoes off at the door. She was short, shorter than both of us, and as we followed her through the entry I imagined her folding up all those hundred-dollar bills, slipping them into their red envelopes to give to Jason.

Jason was sitting at the kitchen table eating a bowl of instant ramen. He'd just made it, I think—it was steaming, and there was a small pot still on the stove. He looked solid and ordinary there, and seeing him like that—my body didn't quite know how to catch up with it. My pulse was still galloping, and I felt weak.

"Oh," he said, frowning a little, "what are you guys doing here?"

"They come to visit you," his mother said. She said something to him in Taiwanese and then opened the fridge. "How nice. You want something to eat, Sunny, Beth? Maybe melon? Or—"

"Oh, no, that's okay," I said quickly. "We just wanted—"

"They just had to drop something off," Jason said. He stood up. "I'll walk you guys out."

So then we were back outside on the front step, and Jason shut the door behind him, glancing toward the window before turning back to us. He crossed his arms over his chest. "What are you guys doing here?"

"We were worried," Sunny said. "We were making sure you were all right."

"Why were you worried?"

He looked at me first. I swallowed.

"I told her everything," I said. "About New York, and—"

Sunny cut in. "Because we're your friends and we care about you," she said, "and honestly, we want to support you however we can, but I don't think *never talk about it* is some kind of one-size-fits-all solution, so. We just wanted to come and make sure you were okay."

I thought he would blow up at her for saying all that, or at me for telling her, but instead he sighed. He rubbed his temples with his thumb and forefinger. "Well, that really wasn't necessary, but thanks, I guess."

"Also, Jason—we're here if you need anything. All of us are. You know that, right? I always assumed you knew, but just in case we never explicitly said it."

He nudged her a little with his elbow in a fraternal, affectionate way. "You don't need to worry. All right?" When he looked at me, he seemed sad and tired and empty, a little bit, but also his expression was gentle. "Really. I promise. I just want to be alone."

This was the outcome I'd wanted, of course. This was the best-case scenario. It was absolutely unthinkable that any part of me would feel disappointed or anything remotely akin to a letdown. I should be only happy and grateful and relieved.

It was just that—it felt like it had all been for nothing. I had been terrified, and I had snapped at Brandon and then hung up on him, and I had, in a way, preemptively lived through disaster; I had emotionally gone through it because it had been real to me—and for what?

WE LOST the championship game in Salinas; it wasn't close. I'd been waiting to see if anyone would update me, but no one did, so I saw it on a bunch of Instagram posts. I wanted to say something to Brandon, but also I wanted him to say something first.

My mother drove me to our spring show the next day—none of my friends said anything about carpooling, and I didn't want to ask. I knew she would immediately notice that I was sitting in the first chair, so I'd told her Jason was sick.

When I saw Brandon backstage, he didn't break into his usual, easy grin, that one that always felt like home to me.

"Hey," he said, and I said, "Hi." Then I said, because it seemed absurd not to, "I'm sorry about your game."

"Yeah." He ran a hand through his hair. It was loud backstage, a stuffy room with low ceilings and faded carpet. "Sunny said everything seemed fine, though? With Jay?"

"I guess so."

He started to say something, then stopped himself. I'd almost never seen Brandon do that—he always just said what he wanted to, and if it didn't come out the way he wanted, he would fumble around aloud until he hit on what he'd meant, and he didn't mind that you were there for the process. It was something I loved about him; it was one of the ways he shared himself.

Today, though, he didn't give me that; he said only, "All right, well. Good to hear."

GRACE WAS the first one to see the email: *Berkeley!! I didn't get in* 😔, she wrote in the group chat on Saturday afternoon. I was reviewing for the AP Bio exam on my bed, flash cards taking over the comforter, and when I jumped up the cards went flying. A flash of hot-cold electricity surged through me, and my hands shook as I tried to check my email. I couldn't hit the right keys.

It's out? Sunny said, and then, a few seconds later: *I got in! Grace, forget them, you're better than them.*

Brandon had gotten in too, and Jason. But I kept getting an error message on the website—it must have been overloaded from everyone trying to log in and check. When I ran downstairs, though, the mail had come, and the letter from Berkeley was there. I tore open the envelope, ripping faster at the end so the scratchy, fibrous sound of paper tearing became a tiny crescendo.

I hadn't gotten in.

As soon as I opened it, I wished I could take it back, could go back to that moment before I knew, but the rejection had already fused to my bones. I didn't cry. I didn't move. I didn't do any-thing, actually; I lay very still in my bed trying to empty my mind, to chase away every thought that came for me. When that didn't work, I ran to the bathroom and threw up.

And then I cried, heavy sobs that I was worried my mother

would hear. I turned on the shower and got in, turning the water as hot as I could stand.

Soon I would feel all the deaths of the dreams I'd had for Berkeley one by one; soon my fears about next year and what we'd do, how we'd keep our promise now, would come corrosive as acid into my chest. For now, though, the words pounded again and again against me like the shower water: *I'm not enough. I'm not enough.*

I didn't turn my phone off this time—after Christmas I would never do that again—but I set it next to me on the desk and watched the messages roll in, and I didn't touch it. For an hour, then two hours, I couldn't bring myself to say anything. It would make it real; it would mark me, forever, as a failure. But what was I waiting for—what difference did it make? It wasn't like prolonging it let me pretend to myself, so finally I told them. Jason called within minutes.

"I'll come get you," he said. "Can I? Do you want to go somewhere, or did you just want to be alone?"

I never wanted to just be alone. He was at my house in fifteen minutes, and we went to Taro, a cafe in downtown Congress Springs where they had coffee and tea and Asian pastries. It was crowded that night, but we found a table by the door, and when we sat down, he said, quietly, "Beth—I'm really sorry."

I felt that telltale shakiness behind my eyes, but I held myself steady. "It doesn't matter."

"I know how much it meant to you, though. And I think—I mean, I know it doesn't help, but I think it was their mistake. Anywhere would've been lucky to have you."

I tried to breathe control into my voice. "Did you want coffee?"

"Right, yeah." He stood, reaching into his pocket for his wallet. "You want anything?"

There were so many things I wanted. "I'm all right."

I watched him looking at the menu in line, his hands shoved into his back pockets, all the contours of his expression and his body so familiar to me. And so close by but so distant all the same, that impenetrable wall that always existed between us, that always existed between you and another person no matter what. And maybe I already knew then, on some level, not the specific way things would fall apart but that they had to, that it's always so fragile, so fragile, the way things are held together. You blink and you disturb the whole universe.

Jason came back with a hot chocolate for me even though I'd said I hadn't wanted anything. I drank some, obligatorily, and burned my tongue.

We made a promise, I told myself. *We made a vow.* I would trust that. We could go somewhere else, all of us together.

But these moments when I felt close to him also made me feel so deeply the limits of that closeness. Later that night, he'd go back to his home, and who knew what would happen there—whatever darkness he was carrying around inside wasn't anything he felt like he could share. And I would go home and I still would've lost one of the most precious hopes of my life. The ways you love someone can feel like a shield around them, as if surely all the force of your caring creates its own gravity, but then the illusion always breaks.

"Did you tell your dad yet?" Jason asked.

I shook my head. "I still haven't seen him. That was going to be—I hoped the next time I saw him we'd go out to celebrate Berkeley together. Or something. It was stupid."

He put his hand over mine and stroked my knuckles gently with his thumb. After a while, I said, "My mom thinks he wants to see me, but he's just—maybe he's worried I'd be upset it wasn't sooner, or it's just easier to not think about. Or he doesn't come and then he feels bad, so he avoids it, and then it's this cycle."

He nodded, slowly. I lifted my cup, though it was empty already. My hands wanted something to do. Jason said, "He lives near here, right?"

"In San Jose. Kind of near Milpitas."

He took a long drink—a gulp, really—of his coffee and set the cup back down on the table. "You want to go right now?"

"Right *now?*" I repeated. My first reaction was to laugh; Jason didn't know my father, how you couldn't just show up like that. But then I thought: *Why not?* It was the opposite of what my father had done to me at Christmas. Maybe he was different now, or maybe I was different, and in seeing me he would realize he'd missed me. Or maybe, this time, I would somehow find the courage to speak to him in a way that would make him see me. Maybe it would erase all those times he hadn't come to see me, and it would be fine after that.

It wasn't logical, really. Even at the time I knew it wasn't. But maybe, in a world that imposes so many of its own rules and fates on you, sometimes you stop caring what does and doesn't make sense because that's all you can do, really, the only option you're left with, and what if something comes of it after all?

Or maybe Jason had his own reasons for wanting to go; maybe it meant something different to him. By then I was beginning to understand how both grief and fear can make a person reckless.

But also, I think, I would have gone anywhere with Jason that night.

We stopped to get gas on our way out. Jason had half a tank left, and my father's house was barely twenty miles away. But there's something about the unfamiliar that makes a place seem so far from you, especially when all the things that make up your daily life—your school, your friends, your orchestra—are so neatly contained in such a small radius. At the pump, Jason cleaned his windshield, leaving long, straight streaks across the glass. Taped to the pump was a neon pink paper with two lines of text, HUGE SALE, written on it, and someone had torn off the top right corner so that it read HUG SALE instead. On the freeway, he set the cruise control right at sixty-five and drove in the middle lane. There wasn't much traffic. It was nearly ten thirty at night.

I think it's possible that I'd never felt closer to Jason, or maybe to anyone, than I did in the car with him that night. For a long time, we drove in a full, comfortable silence, and it was the kind of silence that holds you so that at any time you can speak—you can point out a funny street name, you can say *Whoa* when a car zooms too quickly past you—and know the silence will be there still. It was the kind of silence you can have only with another person, and only with someone you love.

But as we drove, I was thinking not only of him but also of so many things that he didn't know. I was thinking about what it had felt like to watch him perform the Mendelssohn solo and to see his father in the audience, about all those days he was in the hospital while we waited for him. And because I was doing that I wondered how much he was doing it too—all those things he held that I would maybe never know.

I've never told him what really happened with that solo. But that night in his car, his headlights illuminating all those unfamiliar roads, was the time I came the closest.

"Did your mom really want you to go to Berkeley too?" Jason asked as we went by the airport. For the past few miles, you'd been able to hear the roar of engines overhead.

"I don't know," I said. "She probably didn't care as much." She'd been noncommittal when I'd said it was my first choice.

"Ah," Jason said. Grieg's "In the Hall of the Mountain King" came on the radio, and I wondered if Jason registered it, and whether I should change the station. It always made me think of Mr. Irving; once, he told us that when he was at Juilliard the tennis team used to blast the song during matches. Music had been following me everywhere—songs that meant something to me that I couldn't not hear when they were playing somewhere I was—and I wondered if it was the same for him.

"One time—" I started. Maybe he heard something in my voice—Jason reached out and switched off the radio. I cleared my throat. "One time we were in Idaho with his mother for Thanksgiving," I said, "and my mom wanted us to take family pictures for Christmas cards. It snowed, and my dad got this whole idea of writing out MERRY CHRISTMAS in binary code with rocks in this big empty field behind his parents' house for our Christmas card picture. And then we drove all the way to Kmart so he could get me black sweats and a cap so I could lie straight and look kind of like the rocks." It had been our best Thanksgiving: While my grandmother was still cooking and my mother was helping her, I went to the back and followed my father in a straight line with a red plastic bucket, handing him stones to place in the snow. Each time I handed him one, he would kneel and drop it carefully into place. As we went—there were seventy-two numbers, and it took nearly an hour—he explained to me how in binary everything was divisible by eight, how you could spell anything, or any number, with just ones and zeroes. *And you,* he'd said, craning his neck to look up at me, shielding his eyes from the sunlight, *will be a number one.*

"Binary code?" Jason repeated.

"It's really long, the code. For my birthday cakes, he always wanted my candles to be in binary, and it took *so* many candles. MERRY CHRISTMAS was too long, actually, so he wrote MERRYXMAS instead. With no spaces."

"Did it work?"

"He got all the pictures." After I'd heard the shutter click, I'd stumbled in the snow trying to get to him, asking, *Did it work, did it work?* because he'd been worried the numbers wouldn't all fit. "He's a photographer, so he had a wide-angle lens, and he used real film. But then we got the pictures developed, and the last zero was supposed to be a one, and it said MERRYXMAR. He was so upset."

I remembered that evening, the way he'd stopped short of the cashier as he rifled through the pictures, the way he'd held the picture out at arm's length, tapping against his thigh with his other hand in multiples of eight, and then how he snapped, "*Damn* it," and tossed the whole batch in the trash and handed only the receipt to the cashier.

"It's just that he has such high standards," I said, turning to watch out the window as streetlamps and warehouses flew by us. A few miles later, I added, "It's why he's so good at what he does."

It was around Vine Street that whatever recklessness I'd felt began to wear off. What if he had moved and never told me? Or maybe there would be people there with him—maybe there would be a woman—or maybe he wouldn't even be there at all. We drove slowly for a half mile down Schildpad, and then his complex was on the left.

"Big place," Jason said mildly, and that was all either of us said for several minutes.

It had been over three years since I'd been here, but it looked the same—the trellis against the side wall of the leasing center, the huge carved wooden sign that functioned as a building map. I'd been worried I might get lost inside, but I remembered everything perfectly. I remembered walking up this cement pathway with smooth red rocks on either side, carrying a backpack with a change of clothing just in case he decided he wanted me to stay over. I remembered the rusty-looking playground set near the center of the complex with the fenced-in backyards all facing it and how, the first time I'd come, he'd nodded toward it as though it were something I—at fourteen—might find appealing.

We followed the main path past four buildings and then forked left as the path wound around a cluster of potted cacti and then toward building ten. The buildings were all two-story, with sliding glass doors and large windows. It had been warm that week, and many of the windows were open. There were yellowish bulbs near the roof of each building shining little overlapping circles of light on the pathway, and every now and then we'd hear a door slam, a phone ring, or someone speaking aloud. I watched for the building numbers, and I listened to Jason's footsteps coming half a second after mine, and we rounded the corner and walked twenty more feet and suddenly there it was, brightly lit before us: my father's home.

Jason slowed as I did. While I stood frozen in place, he cupped my elbow lightly with his palm and said, his voice low, "This one right here?"

I nodded again, and in the motion when my chin dipped toward my neck I felt strangled. We stood for a long moment with our backs to the road. When a car passed by, its lights would flash on us for a moment, almost a blink, so that for a second each time we cast long, stretched shadows on the path and on the rocks.

There were no blinds on my father's windows and all the lights were on in the main part of the apartment inside, and you could see everything except for the bedroom and the bathroom. It looked mostly as I remembered, though in the instant I saw it I could feel a shift: a shuffling and a matching of the memory to the reality in front of me.

In the living area, there was a different TV, this one much larger, taking up nearly a third of the wall opposite the front door. There was a framed print above the small black square dining table, one I recognized from math class: an M. C. Escher print where a staircase appears to be infinite, to have no beginning and—more alarmingly—no end. There was a bowl on the table that contained two separate bananas and a green apple, each with a tiny produce sticker, and on the otherwise-empty counter in the kitchen there was a stainless steel toaster and a neat row of three cereal boxes, arranged like books on a book-shelf. And there, sitting in a black swivel chair I recognized, at his desk near the window, his face in profile angled toward his computer screen, was my father.

It had been so long that it was a physical sensation to see him there. Across my shoulders and my back, there was a burning feeling, like tiny fires roaring up and down the ravines of my spine.

"You know," Jason said softly, "you kind of look like him."

My father was playing a game I didn't recognize. He looked like maybe he'd gained weight; there was a new padding around his jaw and cheekbones. His hairline had receded a little, his buzz cut forming a peak. In the light of his computer monitor, he looked ghostly and bluish, and—perhaps this is fitting—this is the way he always appears in my memory, too: absorbed in some-thing only he sees, tinged with a cool, clinical light.

Jason cleared his throat. In my peripheral vision, I saw him stick his hands in his pockets. "You want to go in?" he asked, and I said, "I'm not sure."

On the way here, I'd pictured knocking, going right in, but my nerve had dissipated seeing him, and my image of how this was going to go had evaporated. My phone was warm and heavy in my pocket, pressed against my thigh. *I could call him,* I thought, and I reached down and took the phone in my hand. I could dial his number and watch through this window as he answered my call.

My father glanced up, and for a moment I thought he saw us. Jason stepped swiftly to the side, out of sight of the window, and I felt all the blood drain from my head. My heart pounded. What on earth would I *say?*

But my father held his gaze there without reaction, and I real-ized he was just thinking, letting his eyes wander the way he did sometimes when he played. My heart paused and slowed in all its rocketing.

Jason murmured, "For a second there, I thought he saw us."

"I did too."

I felt, still, a little out of breath. But why were we standing here, why had I agreed to come, if that wasn't what I wanted: to be seen by him? Surely, I thought, neither of us had wanted *this*: standing out here in the dark, watching so silently he'd never realize that I'd come. And when it had seemed he might see us, only Jason had moved: I had stayed put. Almost before I knew what I'd done, I'd pulled my phone out.

"You calling him?" Jason asked. I think, for whatever reason, he was startled. And I could have stopped there; I could have said no, and slipped the phone back away. But I said, "Yes," and with that I spoke my action into existence. I was dialing, and then I was listening to the hollow, high-pitched ringing. My heart was pounding.

Through the window, I watched my father take his phone from his pocket and study it—maybe he'd gotten a new phone and hadn't yet entered his contacts, I thought—and then he balanced it between his neck and shoulder, his head tilted. "Hello?"

It was that same voice, that voice I knew, and as soon as he spoke, all the edges and corners of the world around me dimmed and softened into something not quite real; I wasn't quite inside with him, but I wasn't outside like this either, hidden in the dark. As though I were caught in a spell, my whole body turned to something like cotton—I felt diaphanous and weightless, unrooted.

"Hi, Dad," I said. In the quiet, my voice sounded unnaturally loud and high-pitched. "It's—it's Beth."

"Beth?" His whole body straightened as he sat up, and something in me thrilled at that reaction: that his very spine responded to me, that the connection resonated through him so visibly.

"I know this is last-minute," I said. "But I'm in your area, and I thought—well, I thought maybe I could stop by and say hello. Just for a minute."

"You're in the area?" he repeated. Through the window, my father shrugged his shoulders quickly a few times and then twisted his wrists in small circles, and then he brought his hands back to his keyboard. And the familiarity of those gestures, how completely I knew them, how I even felt them sometimes as my own: they wrecked me. We shared these things, I wanted to tell him, and my throat swelled. We shared these things and so much more, and everything could be all right again; all this time, through everything, I had waited for him.

"Yes," I said. "I'm really close by."

"Well—unfortunately, I'm working late at the office tonight."

Jason heard; he sucked in his breath, and when I looked down his hands were clenched.

"Oh," I said, my voice coming out tinny. "Are you—are you sure?"

"Yes, but thank you for calling," my father said. Through the window, I saw him lean forward and peer at his screen, his fingers flying across his keyboard. He was doing that thing he always did when he was playing when his answers came just a split second delayed. "But let's set a date for soon. All right? We'll have dinner. And keep me posted on Berkeley."

"All right," I managed.

When he hung up, it broke that spell that had been buoying me, and I remembered myself, and where we were, which was outside and in the dark. My imagination was doused with images: of myself banging on his door or barging through it, of my father flooded with guilt to know that I'd watched him in his lie. I would go in, I thought wildly, and he'd have to rectify it somehow, he'd have to welcome me, I'd go in and he'd be filled with grief at the way I was feeling, at the way he'd made me feel for years, and he would finally—finally!—understand what I needed from him.

I was breathing fast, my hands trembling. And then from a neighboring home there were two quick sounds: an infant screeching, and over the sound of a faucet a woman calling, "Matt? Can you check on the baby?" And I realized in that moment there was nothing to stop me from knocking. There had never been. I could stand outside and shout things to my father through the single-paned glass, I could call and leave him messages, I could write him letters and drop them in the mail. I could learn the bus routes and come here every single day if I wanted to, and I could tell him I was here now. My father couldn't stop me from doing any of those things.

But I hadn't done them. And seeing him here like this, absorbed in his screen as I waited outside, I understood how there are parts of yourself—segments you can measure by time or by depth, by how long or how strongly they were a part of you—that you can't take back once you've offered them to someone who's made it so clear he never wanted them.

I was crying; my tears had spilled over too far for me to pretend they weren't there, and I reached up to wipe my eyes. "Let's just go," I said. My voice shook.

Jason nodded. He extended a hand toward the path, gesturing for me to go ahead. As he followed me, he placed his hand on the small of my back. I closed my eyes as we walked and hoped I would stumble, or collide with a wall, but nothing happened; Jason kept his hand there, and I stayed on the path.

But as we came back to the main courtyard, just before we turned the corner to reach the parking lot, Jason lifted his foot and kicked, a heavy slam of a kick, just past the walkway so that a landscaped pile of pocked red stones went flying. It startled me—in the stillness, the rocks skittering were very loud.

As I jerked back, my heart thudding and a few stray rocks

still spinning like tops on the concrete, Jason breathed and said, I think to himself, so quietly I almost didn't hear, "That fucking bastard."

That night we went, of course, was before I'd ever lived in an apartment of my own, before I even knew anyone else who had. And at the time I'd always felt there was something almost glamorous about apartments, and for a long time my father's seemed a sort of daring zenith in my mind.

But now there are different things that stand out to me: how the fruit on his table and the cereal on his counter were so precisely the kind of groceries you buy when you live alone; how the couch was the kind of thing you buy at IKEA right out of college, cheap and white, because you don't think about how easily and how permanently it picks up stains, all those marks of your days you don't notice until they've built up over time.

At the time I didn't quite understand Jason's reaction, though I wasn't unmoved by it. I understood, of course, that Jason knew what it was to stand before a father to whom you find you cannot speak, and—even then—I think I understood how maybe, for him, that night wasn't only about me.

But now I think there was more to it too. The barren countertops, that cold, dispassionate print, the cheap, boxy mass-produced furniture: I believe that night Jason understood, perhaps for the first time, the smallness of all these things for which my father had traded me.

We took some wrong turns getting to the freeway on the way back, and it was late. I wasn't tired, though—of everything I was feeling, tired wasn't part of it. I watched out the window as exit signs and overpasses blurred by. When I blinked, everything was clear for a moment, but when I held the gaze, my eyes filled again.

We were back on 101, and we'd reached Santa Clara, when Jason cleared his throat.

"Maybe next year," he said, "when he visits you at college, you'll tell him about this and you guys will laugh about it together."

Of course that wouldn't happen, and of course Jason never for a moment imagined that it would. But there's a particular sort of dialogue you enter when you know something's over, how you keep talking as though it isn't—not because you believe it, but because you're fantasizing about the way things might have been. You can talk about these things, you can give form and detail to their grandiosity, precisely because you know you've lost them already, or you've never had them at all.

"Yes," I said, and I forced a smile. *"Remember that time you ghosted me?"*

Jason laughed softly—a kindness. I felt my eyes welling again, because I understood: In that laughter, he was bearing witness to my loss.

I STAYED home Sunday, less because I wanted to and more because there was nowhere I could imagine going that would make me feel any different. I would be myself wherever I went. Jason called to see how I was, but I got off the phone after a few minutes—I couldn't pretend to feel better or fake an upbeat mood.

I was scared to ask him what he was going to do, to ask any of them. Grace had gotten into St. Mary's, forty-five minutes away from Berkeley, so they could all still go without me. For a while, I let myself imagine them trying desperately to work it out somehow—squeezing an extra bed into Sunny's room for me, or all of us renting out something off-campus together. (*We couldn't go without you*, they'd say. *It wouldn't be the same*.) Maybe that would be better than dorms, and then Grace could live with us too, and commute. But when I went online to look up rentals, I knew it wasn't possible; I'd never be able to come up with the rent each month, and anyway I doubted their parents would all let them live somewhere besides the dorms.

Was this what Jason felt like when he'd gone to the bridge? It wasn't that I wanted to die—I was afraid of it—but at the same time the thought of feeling nothing felt like a beckoning friend.

I'd been alone most of that day because my mother had gone to Mass and then up to see my grandparents again. She got home in the late afternoon and came upstairs right away, and knocked on my door. Immediately, I went tense—I didn't want to be around her right now, didn't want to dodge her questions.

"I brought you some leftovers," she said, and held out a take-out box. "I tried to save things that would keep well."

I said, shortly, "Thanks."

She tried to catch my eye and smile at me. "And I got some oxtail at the market while I was there. I'll make stew."

I let the box sit on my desk for a while—dim sum is so much less appealing cold—but finally I was too hungry to ignore it anymore. I was peeling the paper off a steamed char siu bao when my mother came back in, this time without knocking. There was a strange look on her face, and she was holding some kind of letter I didn't recognize. She said, "What is this?"

"What is what?"

"Why is your credit card bill over a thousand dollars? Why is there this limo ride—and this ticket to New York—"

My heart slammed into my throat. Where had she even gotten that? I'd been so careful to check the mail every day. It was a Sunday. "Were you going through my things?"

"Did you go to New York without telling me?"

"It wasn't—"

"Did you go to *New York*?"

"I—yes."

"When?"

"Um—a few weeks ago."

"When you said you were at Sunny's house?"

I looked away, which I suppose was an answer in itself. She made a choked, gasping sound and sank down onto my bed, staring at me as if she didn't recognize me. I said, "Why were you going through my things?"

"That's not the point."

"But why—"

"It came with the bills recently. I just opened them. When were you planning to deal with this?"

"I was going to pay it over the summer."

"Over the *summer*? Beth, you've missed four payments. Have you been getting phone calls? Are debt collectors calling you?"

There was a plummeting sensation in my stomach. "I thought you could take a year to pay them."

She stared at me. "No, you absolutely cannot take a year to pay them. You have to pay the minimums at the very least. Where did you get that idea?"

I didn't know what a minimum was. "I don't know, I thought—"

"And who did you go to New York with?"

"Just some people from the orchestra."

"Were their parents with you?"

"It was—it was just a quick trip."

"I have sacrificed so much to provide for you, Beth! All year I've been trying to help you with the college process, and you didn't even tell me about this?"

The way she was staring at me, the naked, baffled woundedness in her expression—I felt something cold settle around me. "You mean Dad's been providing for me," I muttered. "You were lying to me all this time."

"What do you mean I was lying to you?"

"I mean you act like he doesn't exist when all this time he's been giving you money. Why did you never tell me you were making him do that?"

"Beth, that's not—I'm not making him do anything. It's a legal agreement."

"It's a legal agreement that you set up! No one made you arrange it that way. I would've told you not to."

She blinked at me. "You would've told—that's not how it works. The judge decided—"

My throat was hot and scratchy. "Okay, well, the judge decided he was supposed to have partial custody, too, but it's not like you make him see me every month."

She closed her eyes. "Some things are easier to enforce than others."

"And you chose the one that makes me seem like a bill to him."

"Beth—I don't think you grasp how hard I've always worked to provide you with the best possible life I could. Which includes fighting for every resource available to—"

"If you wanted that, then why did you get divorced?"

"Excuse me?"

"If you really wanted me to have every available resource—"

"I have done everything—*everything*—in your best interests, Beth. Everything. All your life, as best as I've known how."

Some foundation in me trembled and shifted, like jackhammering a concrete wall so that long-hidden structures were exposed, and before I could stop myself, I snapped, "Then why didn't you try to stop him?"

I'd said it so loudly—nearly yelling—that my voice echoed, reverberating off the ceilings to descend back down on us. My mother stared at me. She said, slowly, "What do you mean?"

"Why did you let him leave you? You could've been different! But you didn't even try to change. You just let him leave."

"You think I didn't try to stay married? I went to counseling—I made your father go to counseling—we met with the priest, and—"

"None of that was what he wanted! He wanted you to be different. You were always so—you would hover around him and make so many demands on him, and—"

"Because he was my husband. He was your *father*. He was an adult, and he had responsibilities to both of us."

"But you didn't—"

Her voice was rising, going shrill. "That is in the past, and that's entirely irrelevant right now, Beth. You think this is acceptable behavior?" She dangled the credit card bill between her thumb and forefinger like it was dirty laundry. "Lying, and going behind my back, and racking up over a thousand dollars on a credit card bill? How could you *do* this, Beth?"

"Because why would I want to turn out like you?"

"What is that supposed to mean?"

"I was doing those things because it was important to my friends. You obviously don't think people should work at relationships, and look what happened to you."

She looked as though I'd hit her. She pressed a fist against her chest, over her heart. When she spoke, her voice was shaking. "I have worked very hard to—"

"To make me hate him."

"Excuse me?"

"You sabotaged our relationship. You wanted us to hate each other."

My mother was crying and not bothering to hide it. "Everything I have ever done as a mother has been for your benefit," she said. "Everything. I never wanted you to turn out anything like him. But apparently I've failed, if this is what you are."

She turned and left the room. I heard her slam her bedroom door, maybe the first time I'd ever heard her do that. I flung the dim sum into the trash. One of the har gow fell out and stuck to the side of the trash can, and I watched it glop its way slowly to the bottom, its skin tearing on the way down.

In my room that night, still feeling sick from fighting with my mother, I rummaged through my desk drawer for my compass and protractor set from eighth-grade geometry and took out a blank sheet of computer paper. I cranked the compass into three-inch circles and drew a circle for each of our names, making a careful Venn diagram overlapping on the acceptances we had in common. I shaded in each circle lightly with a colored pencil, and I drew thick black lines around our top two overlaps: UC Irvine San Diego.

It wasn't cold, but I was shivering. That promise we had made each other was sacred, a lifeline, and besides that it was everything to me. It was the most I'd ever had.

I slid the chart neatly into my binder, careful not to crease its edges. When I stood, there was a palpitation in my heart, a heavy, hollow thump like a knock on a door. I couldn't keep my mind from descending into panic over all the machinations that could be happening out in the world without me.

I was the first to our spot at lunch the next day, and I settled onto the ground and waited. The quad was mostly empty still, the lunch line snaking around the cafeteria. It was sunny that day, and warm, and my sleeves felt damp under my arms.

Grace showed up first, and then Jason, and then Sunny and Brandon together.

"I made something," I said, when they'd all sat. My fingers trembled as I reached into my binder and took out the chart I'd made, and I hoped they didn't see.

"Whoa," Brandon said, when I put it down between us. "What's this, Beth? Nice color-coding."

I cleared my throat. I was going to answer, but then I saw it in all their faces at once—they'd realized what it was.

We were sitting in our usual five-pointed circle, the crumpled bags and wrappers from our lunches in between us, and no one looked at me, not even Jason. Grace put down her sandwich, resting it on top of her brown paper bag. Brandon looked up, though not at me, and I followed his gaze to Sunny; their expressions changed almost imperceptibly, and then they both looked down again.

A loud humming started in my head. A doctor described to me once the sound an aneurysm in the brain can make, a roar that pulses in your eardrums, and that was what it sounded like—my heartbeat pounding louder and louder in my ears until I started to wonder if you could go deaf this way, or if your heart could pump yours veins so full they exploded.

A group of freshmen passed us, and then a little rush of wind lifted the corners of the chart and rattled it slightly, and still they said nothing. Sunny pushed at her cuticles. Jason reached up and took off his glasses, and then rubbed his temples with his thumb. Grace hugged her knees to her chest.

"Beth," Brandon said finally. "This is—this is really great of you to put together, and it looks like it was a lot of work. But I don't—it would've been cool if we all got into the same places, but then that didn't happen, and I just don't see how—"

"We can do the NorCal one," I said. "Or even if it isn't all of us at Irvine—Irvine isn't that far from LA, so—"

Jason started to say something else and then stopped himself when I turned to look at him. He crumpled his juice can with his fist, a cracking sound like tiny gunshots. My pulse was thunderous. I felt again how much your heart and all those other things inside could rise against you—the lungs, the intestines, the medulla oblongata. So many small disaster sites we all contained.

"I have something to say about that, actually," Grace said. She was sitting cross-legged, and she rested both her hands on her knees and took a deep breath. "I'm . . . going to Boston next year! I decided last night."

"You—what? But we—that isn't—" I stopped, the words running out, my throat constricting.

Grace wouldn't look at me, and she spoke fast. "Of everywhere I got into, it was the one I was most excited about, and obviously I'm terrified to leave home and move across the country, but I had a really long talk with my parents last night and I think I'm going to go for it, so—"

"That's great," Jason said, sincerely. "You're going to love it there."

"But the rest of us," I said. My vision was wavering, refracting and then going back into focus. "Okay, fine, Grace, whatever, but the rest of us—we can all—"

"Beth," Brandon said gently, "I just don't know if it makes sense to—I mean, Berkeley makes sense if you're doing like EE or something, but—"

I met Jason's eyes then, which took effort, everyone watching the way they were, Sunny holding herself still like she hoped I wouldn't notice her, Brandon's expression pained. "But we all promised—I'll stay here and come visit Berkeley as much as I can. I'll take classes at De Anza, and then I'll try to transfer, and—"

"What do you mean we all promised?" Jason said.

I'd been waiting for the right moment to tell him. I'd thought about it after he didn't get into Juilliard, except then it had seemed better to just not mention college at all, and there had been a hundred other times I almost did. Brandon had still gone to Salinas, Grace spent probably half her time now with Chase, but Jason would know that all this time we'd held him close; we had knitted him into our dreams and our futures.

"We made a pact," I said. "Back—right after Thanksgiving."

He said, slowly, "What exactly was this pact?"

"We'd all go to the same school next year. There was just—there was a lot going on, and we wanted to be there for you and for each other." I said it to him, but I meant it for all of them, too. "So we've been committed to that all this time. That was more important to us than any specific school or location or city or whatever, or any other—"

"You got into UCSD, though," Brandon said. "That's a really good school, Beth. You don't want to just throw that away."

"It doesn't matter," I said. "I got into Juilliard, but I'll give that up too. Because none of it means anything if it's just me there, by myself, and—"

But now they were all staring at me, openmouthed. I stopped talking. I went cold.

"You got *in?*" Brandon said. "Holy shit, Beth, you got into *Juilliard?*"

"Wait," Jason said, "you said you didn't."

My heart was pounding. I'd promised myself I would never tell him. Having the words out there dangling in front of us was like being plunged into the ocean, that icy shock tunneling itself all the way through to your bones. Then Jason laughed, incredulous, all the lines on his face softening. "Beth—my God."

"I just—I didn't—" I could feel my face draining of color. Why had I flung it at them that way? "It's just that it didn't matter. I don't mind giving it up to—"

"Are you *kidding?*" Brandon said. "Is this a joke? I can't believe you got in. You've got to be shitting us that you'd just throw that away."

I was shaking; you could see it even through my sweater. I placed the heel of my hand against my chest and pressed, trying to slow the beat. I saw again the empty third space at our kitchen table, the empty spot in the garage, the sterile walls of my father's new apartment.

"So you all were lying, then," I said. "You didn't care. And all this time whenever I started to worry but I kept making excuses and I kept telling myself you were better than that—I was wrong about you. It was never real to you, was it?"

Brandon winced. "Beth—"

"It wasn't a lie," Sunny said. "It's just that things change, and—"

"But nothing changed for me." I struggled to breathe. "It only changed because a promise didn't matter to you, and that's great for all of you because you'll go on to your perfect futures, but for me—for me this was the first time in my life that I thought I actually had people who cared about me and something real to hold on to, and—"

My voice gave out. They looked stricken.

"We do care about you," Grace said. "We—"

"Tell yourself that all you want." I struggled to my feet. "But leave me alone."

"Beth, wait—" Jason said. "Let's talk about this."

I grabbed my backpack so quickly I almost dropped it. "I'm leaving," I said, and though they blinked at me, startled, and glanced at each other—and I felt them reaching for a consensus, I felt the emptiness of a future when that kind of meaningful look would go unanswered—they didn't try to stop me.

As I kept lifting my feet to make myself keep going, even though I didn't know where I was headed and the longer I walked across the courtyard, the more it felt like the whole campus was seeing me all alone like that, I realized it was the first time I could say this: I had been the one to leave.

Jason came over that night. My mother was home—we hadn't spoken to each other—so I came out into the front yard to talk to him. When I saw him, my heart flooded with hope. He was here because he'd realized he was wrong; he had come to somehow mend it. But when I shut the door behind me and he said, "Hey, I think we should talk," I could tell from his tone it wasn't that at all.

"Great," I said. "Let's talk, then. What are you going to do? Everyone else seems to have their futures all planned out. Do you know too, and you just haven't told me?"

He looked a little startled by my tone, but he recovered. "I don't know yet," he said. "Um—with San Diego or Irvine, though, I think those aren't in the cards for me."

I gave you everything, I thought. *There was nothing in the world I wouldn't have done for you.*

"Okay," I said. "Well—I'll look into community colleges in Berkeley, then. Or—"

"I don't think you should think about it like that."

"You don't think I should think about it like what?"

"I don't think you should, like, factor in where I'm going at all. Go wherever's best for you. Also, Beth—did you seriously get into Juilliard?"

"That's irrelevant."

"How is that irrelevant? Are you kidding me? I can't believe you didn't tell me."

Why were we talking about this? Surely it was still too painful for him, and anyway, it didn't matter. "I was only going to go there if you went. It was never—"

"That's so messed up, though."

"Did you just envision us like not even bothering to try to be close next year? Just ending up on different sides of the country or whatever, who cares?"

"Isn't that kind of how it goes? I would expect you to do whatever's best for you and not give that up because it didn't work out for me."

I thought of how it had felt between us all the night of Homecoming, how I had never had a stronger sense of belonging. I realized I'd been subconsciously fingering the necklace I was wearing, the one he'd given me, and I dropped my hand. "It doesn't have to be how it goes."

"I can't believe you're seriously standing here telling me you would even think about giving up Juilliard to commute from community college or whatever so—"

"Why is that so hard to believe? If you care about someone, you'll sacrifice the—"

"It has nothing to do with caring about someone."

"It has everything to do with that."

That was the limit of his patience, apparently, with the conversation. His expression shifted then into something like anger. "Like how you apparently arranged my whole life without even telling me? What if I didn't want to go to Berkeley? And what if I didn't want you all to babysit me?"

"You always said you wanted to go there."

"Okay, well, I didn't realize I was committing my life to a secret plan when I said that, so—"

"Well, what was I supposed to do, Jason? You wouldn't let me tell anyone about applying to Juilliard."

"You weren't supposed to do anything. That's the whole point. When did I ask you to plan all that out for me?"

"But you've—"

"But I've what?"

"You've been acting like—" I cut myself off. "I've been so scared."

"I told you to just forget it. Beth, you're like—"

"But you're pretending nothing *happened*!" I said. "What do you think it's been *like* for me? What am I supposed to think when you just disappear, or you just seem really off and then you don't pick up your phone, or—"

"You're not supposed to think anything. I told you to just—move on."

"It doesn't work like that, Jason."

I was flushed all over, and my limbs felt detached from my body; I had the strange feeling that if he touched me right now his hand would go through me, like through a ghost.

Jason cleared his throat. He looked steeled and a little nervous, the way he always did before a show.

"Listen," he said, "this isn't how I meant for any of this to go. You're such an incredible person, Beth. I know it's such a cliché, but I mean it. You—you mean a lot to me."

The world started to spin around me, slowly at first, and then picking up speed. "Are you breaking up with me?"

He pulled air into his cheeks and then exhaled, scuffing the toe of his shoe against our front step. "I know this was maybe my only shot and I fucked it up. I just—I can't keep doing this."

"Is this about next year?" My voice sounded choked. "If I'd just gotten into Berkeley, would it have—"

"No. Beth—no. I swear. I just—it's not the right time. It's just me. I'm just not—it's not the right time for me."

"Did I do something wrong?" I could hear my voice going high-pitched, the tone my father always described in a woman as shrill. "I can—we can figure this out, if you—"

"It's nothing you did."

But how could he say that? All the ways I'd given of myself, all the times I'd swallowed back what I wanted to say, all the times I had tried to make myself easy for them and for him—I felt those sear across my skin. He had seen me—he had seen the most I had to offer anyone, the very best I could do—and I loved him, more than possibly anyone in my life, and none of that was enough for him.

"I tried to give you everything," I said. "And there were things I never told anyone else that—"

"I know," he said, and then at once he wasn't angry anymore; his voice dropped. "The night we went to see your dad—that was when I realized—"

I stared at him. "Is that why you're breaking up with me?"

"It's not like that," he said quietly. "Just—that night I realized—"

"Oh my God."

He swallowed. A curtain was coming over my vision. I couldn't see in the periphery; there were circles swimming wherever I tried to look. He said, "The thing is, Beth, I just—"

"Leave," I said wildly.

"Wait, Beth, hear me out. I—"

But I couldn't bear to stand there a second longer. "*Leave,*" I cried, and after I slammed the door I clawed at my necklace until the chain snapped and the pendant flew off. It flashed once in the light and then made a minute, tinny clattering sound when it hit the floor.

TO GET TO the Golden Gate Bridge from Congress Springs if you don't have a car takes nearly four hours if you're relying on public transit, and when I looked up the route on Google Maps it was so convoluted, with so many stops, I knew I wouldn't be able to do it. Surely I would have a panic attack somewhere along the way and I would be alone and there would be no one I could call.

If I didn't have the credit card, that probably would have been enough to stop me, but as it was I just got my own Uber account and walked to a corner a few blocks away from our home to be picked up. It was a Tuesday morning, and I was supposed to be in school, but in a few hours maybe that wouldn't matter.

The driver, whose name according to the app was Paul, was a white tech-looking guy (North Face fleece, fitted jeans) who was probably in his twenties. I got in, and the articles my mom always forwarded me or that you'd see girls sharing online flashed through my mind—*confirm the license plate, check for child locks, trust your instincts*. But what good were my instincts? The people I loved more than anything, the people I had built my life around, had been the ones to ruin me.

"So what are you doing at the Golden Gate Bridge?" he said, meeting my eyes in the rearview mirror.

"Just visiting."

"There's not a race or something today?"

I shook my head. I wondered whether if I told him I had a boyfriend, he would leave me alone.

"So you want to know something interesting?" he said. "Everyone thinks the bridge is like, the Golden Gate Bridge, like the bridge itself is supposed to be golden. The Gate Bridge, only gold. But then it's orange, so everyone's like, what the hell, right, that's not gold. But actually the Golden Gate is the land strait where the Bay hits the Pacific. So it's like, the bridge over the Golden Gate. That's why it's called that. Not many people know that."

What was he even talking about? People always said you made new friends after high school, that you met new people, but then you met new people and they blathered on about inane trivia about bridges while you were trapped in their car. I could feel the bleakness of my future trying desperately to winnow some kind of sustaining purpose and intimacy from a hundred stupid interactions like this one. The gap between starting over and the world I'd shared with my friends was insurmountable.

Anyway, I'd known that about the bridge. We'd learned it in California history in fourth grade.

He talked for a while about how he'd moved here from Florida to work in tech but then worried he wasn't finding himself, and he kept going as we got onto the freeway. I was trying not to listen, because this wasn't the last conversation I wanted to hold in my mind. Already it was making me feel cluttered, and further and further away from the hour last night when, sleepless, I'd thought: What if I was just like Jason?

I wanted everyone to know what they had done to me. I knew what they thought: that it was all forgivable, that they were making reasonable choices, that I would get over it and accept it and move on. They were taking me for granted in that. On the way there, I imagined what they would say when they heard the news.

I felt flushed all over, and my heart wouldn't slow down. I was starting to get dizzy.

"So what kind of music do you like?" Paul said as we slowed to a crawl in Palo Alto.

"I don't like music."

"What! That's impossible. How is that possible?"

"I just don't."

"You've never heard good music, then," he said. "You know why? I bet you listen to all the top-forty crap on the radio. All just mass-produced, commercial bullshit. I've been getting more into music theory lately—all just self-taught—and it's pretty interesting. You should look into it sometime."

"Maybe."

"If you ever learn anything about classical music, you'll gain this huge appreciation for everything else you hear. I have this really good Spotify station." He turned it on—I didn't have the energy to stop him—and we listened to the second half of a mediocre rendition of a Delibes operetta. There wasn't enough brass; it sounded a little thin.

"It's an acquired taste," he said. "Like good wine. How old are you?"

I said I was twenty. I couldn't tell if he believed me or not. He looked at me more closely in the rearview mirror, taking his eyes from the road. I wasn't quite distracted enough that it didn't make me uncomfortable. I wished I'd gotten into someone else's car. I was starting to feel sick.

Except there was nowhere better I could be. I couldn't be at home, I couldn't be at school, I couldn't be at BAYS—none of those places would ever be the same anymore. I had given all of myself, and to have that thrown back at me was so exquisitely painful I didn't know how to live with it. That was the point; that was why I was here, why I would go and stand where Jason had stood, and see if, maybe, it was easier to just not go on. It would be terrifying, and it would hurt, but then it would be over. It would be a way out.

And then the next song on Paul's playlist (Beethoven's Fifth, which if I were in another mood might have amused me) ended and the next one that came on—it took me a little while to recognize it as a take on the end of Bach's *The Art of Fugue*. When I realized what it was my throat went tight. I knew this song.

The Art of Fugue was Bach's last, incomplete work, and though I knew the story of the last part, the *Unfinished Fugue*, I'd never heard it played until a few years before at the symphony with my mother. The composition ends sharply in the middle of a measure, either because Bach died before he could finish or because—what I believed—he'd hoped others might continue it after he was gone. That day at the symphony, they'd simply stopped playing where the music stopped, and it had been stunning. You felt the loss in that abrupt silence, and even though I'd just seen them that morning and would see them the next day too, it had made me ache for my friends. And what had crystallized for me then was a specific dream: that we would write our own ending for this together. I remembered how I had messaged them at intermission to say so, and how with anyone else maybe I would've felt stupid but with them it was just another one of those promises we made: not just a promise about the future but a promise about the present, too, of the space we held in one another's lives.

I was crying in the back seat of the car. Paul studiously pretended not to notice.

It would never be the same with anyone else. I knew that; maybe it was because I would never again be able to love so fiercely and unguardedly, or maybe it's that everyone gets one great friendship in their lives, if they're lucky, and that was mine.

I didn't want it to end like this. Maybe it was too late; maybe this was already the end for the five of us, or me and Jason, but I didn't want to die sad and angry and desperately lonely. Really, I didn't want to die at all. I wanted things to be better. I just didn't know how.

"Actually," I said, and I had to say it twice to get his attention, "actually, I don't think I want to go to San Francisco anymore. If you could just drive back to Congress Springs instead."

A school and an orchestra are both places where it's difficult to avoid people you don't wish to see, not because they might try to talk to you—because mine didn't—but because they're so woven into the fabric of your day that even if seeing them is like a stab wound it will happen to you, over and over, relentlessly. You see when they're all together for lunch looking as self-contained as you used to think they were with you; you notice when one of them (in this case, Jason) seems to stop hanging out with them and sometimes you see him in other parts of campus alone.

Later that week, Sunny and Grace were walking together in the halls before the first bell rang and we all saw each other, and it was too late to pretend otherwise. Your body is slow to catch on to things, and before I could stop it, I felt that little leap of joy I always did when I saw them, the way the people you love always look so beautiful to you, and that time—it was such a chemical response—I let myself hope. Maybe they would call me over; maybe things were fixable. But Sunny said something to Grace, and they walked away.

It was, it turned out, eminently possible to feel alone on a campus of two thousand after all.

My mother came into my room Friday when I was getting ready for bed.

"I finally worked things out with your credit card company," she said. Her face was like stone. "And I paid your bill. They were going to send it to a collections agency. What on earth did you think was going to *happen*, Beth?"

"I was going to pay it over the summer. I thought it just meant you had to pay more interest."

"I can't believe you were so careless. We're very lucky they were willing to work with me. Your credit score is going to be ruined for years."

"I'll pay you back," I mumbled. I occupied myself buttoning my pajama top so I didn't have to look at her.

"And I had to cancel Asheville, so you can take that off your calendar."

I jerked my head up, stunned. "What do you mean you had to—"

"Beth, I don't have an extra fifteen hundred dollars lying around."

I thought the guilt would stop my heart. "Mom, wait, I can get a job—maybe we can still—"

"It's too late for that." She leaned over to lift the half-full plastic bag from my wastebasket and tied the top into a quick, angry knot. "Everyone's born with a different number of chances in the world, you know. You'll get more than I did. Don't waste yours on stupid things like this."

The BAYS Senior Showcase, the last major performance of the year, was that weekend in San Francisco, three weeks before college decisions were due. I was glad, for the first time, that Jason wouldn't be there, that Grace was several rows back. It would be easy enough to slip in right at the end of warm-ups and leave right afterward, and not have to see them. It would be worse to spend the time with my mother in the car, but I put headphones in, and she drove the whole way with her lips pressed tightly together, and she didn't say anything to me either, even when halfway through I took my headphones and made a show of wrapping them up to put away. Maybe on some level she knew there was a part of me that had never felt alone like this before and that hoped beyond hope she would talk to me.

I still had barely been able to play. I had been going to

rehearsals because it was easier than not going, I'd cast my ballot with the other seniors for which pieces we'd perform, though since hearing from Juilliard, going to BAYS had been physically painful. Each note throbbed in my chest. But I'd told myself that if that night there was even just a little of the old joy in it again—that would be enough. I wouldn't consign myself to San Diego or Irvine and I would find some way to make Juilliard work, and that would be how I would start over, who I would be. I would fight for it.

When we filed onto the stage that night, I tried to take everything in, to hold it close—the scuffed wooden floor, the neat rows of us. The murmur of the audience before we started, the way even after all this time my heart wobbled like a rocking chair when the house lights dimmed. The show was in a converted old stone church we'd played in almost every year, and it should've been easy; I should've been able to go on autopilot. But as soon as Mr. Irving lifted his arms to usher us into the first song, everything felt wrong.

We played Bach's Partita first. As we began the piece that night, I tried to imagine all the hundreds of thousands of people who had played this piece before me. I tried to imagine the former members of BAYS and what they might be doing now, how they'd have spouses and children maybe, houses and jobs, and I tried to imagine a younger Mr. Irving conducting it all those years before. This song could hold all those things, and tonight, I told myself, it could hold me, too.

But I didn't feel that. *This is it,* I thought. *In less than sixty minutes now it will all be over.* I could feel myself trying to speed up, and I struggled to hold the tempo. I was out of breath. I let my fingers slip into the patterns I knew, that I'd rehearsed, and waited for the discipline of muscle memory to guide me.

But maybe that was the problem. Maybe it would always be like this now whenever I picked up my violin or whenever I tried to perform, because music was the biggest lie I had ever believed. All my life, it had taught me that you could come together. It had taught me that you could, if you worked and you sacrificed, earn your belonging—you could erase the differences among yourselves and work toward oneness, toward something bigger than you, and most of all it had taught me that it could be something lasting. I guess I'd believed that if it was beautiful and true enough it would be its own end; it would sustain itself.

We were into the third movement of the Haydn, and I was sweating now, when I heard a second violin play the wrong notes behind me. It could've been anyone. It might not have been Grace. But I knew somehow that it was her, and I wondered then: Why had no one else ever had to try so hard as I did? Because wasn't that always the promise? That if I could disappear myself into those around me—if I made myself accommodating and easy, if I made myself not a burden and I smoothed over the jagged or prickly parts of myself and I didn't make too much noise or take up too much space, if I could be all the things I was as a violinist, as a member of an orchestra—if I could do that, it would save me. It would make me worth loving. I'd always thought that was the thing that made me and Jason the same, that he understood that part of me, but I'd been wrong. I'd given everything I had, and he'd dropped BAYS like it was nothing, and here was Grace casually ruining the piece everyone was trying to play together because she never could be bothered to practice more at home, and here were Sunny and Brandon, who had hurt me more deeply than I would've thought them capable of, still playing alongside me, all of us caught up in this lie where we formed one sound.

"Beth," Linde Erickson, the second chair, whispered, "what are you doing?"

Without fully realizing what I was doing, I'd stood up. I was standing now, unsteadily, not playing, in the middle of the piece. Linde whispered, "Are you okay?

I was not okay. I could only breathe in as deeply as my throat, and oxygen wasn't getting past it into my lungs. I was growing light-headed. Around me, heads swiveled to see what was going on. I clutched my bow and violin and hurried out of the row while everyone stared at me. My footsteps were heavy and loud on the stage. When I got backstage, pushing my way past the curtains, I let my bow and my violin clatter to the floor.

I made it back to the greenroom, gasping for breath, my chest squeezed tight. I sank to a crouch and tried to breathe into my palms. I tried to inhale for five full seconds. From the stage, I heard the song come to an end, and then there was a long pause.

Then I heard my name. I didn't need to look up to know who it was. Sunny and Brandon and Grace had come after me; all of them had left their instruments behind.

"Are you okay?" Sunny said. "You look like you're going to pass out."

"Does your chest hurt?" Brandon said. "Should I get my dad?"

"Maybe you should," Grace told him. "Find Beth's mom, too."

"Can you breathe okay?" Sunny crouched down next to me. "Or do you think you're going to throw up?"

Their faces, blurred a little, were alarmed. I said, "It's a panic attack. I keep getting them."

Brandon frowned. "You get panic attacks?"

"Ever since Jason was in the hospital."

"Oh, Beth," Sunny said. "You should've told us. My cousin gets panic attacks. Okay, try to breathe slower. Sit down on the ground all the way. Maybe even lie down."

"Are you hyperventilating?" Brandon said. "Do you want, like, a paper bag?"

"You'll be okay," Grace said. "Should I go get your mom? Or do you want us to just stay with you?"

They hovered there, watching me, waiting. I knew that I could give them what they wanted from me and maybe we could salvage things; we could pretend away the worst parts and tell ourselves things were the same. All I would have to do was sit up and pretend that I was feeling better, that I was all right, that I forgave them their betrayal. And then we could go back out onstage and continue where we'd left off. We could pretend to be who we'd always been.

I couldn't, though.

"Don't worry about me," I said. "I know you don't care anyway."

Sunny's expression changed. Brandon saw, and shook his head a little at her. "Sun—"

She started to go quiet, and then she changed her mind. "Beth, that's so unfair. I don't know how you can even say that."

"You don't know how I can even say that?" I kept seeing again in my mind their expressions when I'd pulled out my chart, how the future we'd planned together, once I had it written out on paper, felt to them like some kind of trap. Even now, even with the room sucked dry of oxygen and my heart struggling to pump, it hurt so much that I couldn't look right at it, like staring into the sun. "We all agreed—"

"Okay, yes, we did agree, but I just don't think it's fair to act like you never want to see us again when it was a promise you never took seriously anyway."

All those nights I lay awake worrying it wouldn't happen, all those nightmares about things ending exactly like this. How happy I was when I believed we'd stay together. "How can you say I never took it seriously?"

"I don't know, maybe because you were going behind our backs to go to New York with Jason because you were going to back out and go to Juilliard with him anyway?"

"Because I was worried about him," I managed. I was fighting for oxygen, the room speckled with flashes of light. "Even if no one else cared, I did."

"That's also completely unfair and you know it."

I couldn't answer. The pressure on my chest was so intense I couldn't believe there was nothing wrong with my heart.

"Okay, fine, so we're bad friends," Sunny snapped finally, when I didn't answer. "Not that you've been perfect either, but whatever, that's what you're saying? And that's it? You can't get past it? You're done?"

Then there were three heartbeats in a row that felt hollow, like some kind of malfunction, and I felt myself pitching forward, cupping a hand to my chest to try to still the awful beats.

I struggled to stand. Grace reached out to try to steady me, but I yanked my arm away, and I pushed past them and went out the door. My violin was still lying on the ground back where I dropped it.

I realized too late I'd gone through the wrong door, the emergency exit, and tripped the alarm. It blared so loudly I knew the audience would hear it back in the theater, but maybe music wasn't something sacred to protect anyway. The door creaked closed behind me, a weak stutter like a broken wing.

My mother decided that this time we didn't need to go back to the ER. They would run the same tests; they would find the same results. Instead, we would just go home and I could rest. In the car, she turned on the radio and drove in silence, and I wrapped myself in my sweater and tried to breathe and tried not to cry. When we got off the freeway, she turned to look at me, and she started to say something, and I was flooded with hope that she'd forgiven me and that everything between us would be fine. Then she changed her mind, and turned back to the road.

It wasn't fair, and I knew that, but I didn't want her silence anymore and I didn't want to know that I'd hurt her. What I wanted was for someone to hold me and make me believe that this would pass, all of it, that there would be something better around the bend.

ON MONDAY, I feigned illness. I had a story prepared, but my mother didn't ask about my symptoms or whether I was all right or needed anything, just called the school and then went to work. I turned off my phone, but then later I turned it back on and there weren't any new messages and I felt stupid for having thought I needed to turn it off. I felt like I was floating above my own aloneness, and it was something I could almost marvel at: This had always been my greatest fear, and here I was inside it. I couldn't stand the thought of myself.

In the afternoon, I reread my acceptance email from Juilliard to try to feel again like I had when I'd first received it: like I was someone worthy and desirable. But it made me think about having to respond one way or another to the acceptance, and then all I felt was dread.

I went downstairs to eat dinner when my mother came back that evening, but she ignored me, sitting down at the kitchen table with her laptop and immediately absorbing herself in her email. She hadn't been cooking dinner lately, and each night would pour herself a bowl of cereal.

I thought of all the things I could say to her—that I was sorry, that even though I'd meant to hurt her I also had never wanted that, that I desperately wanted to make it up to her and wanted it to stop being like this—but I couldn't put words to any of them. "Do we have anything to eat?"

She didn't look up from her computer. "There are dumplings in the freezer."

"Okay, I'll heat some up. Do you want any?"

"No."

I took longer than I needed to microwaving them, hesitating at the table. Finally, I sat down next to her. "I think I might need to stay home tomorrow, too."

"All right." She typed something. "Don't leave your plate on the table."

I went back upstairs. Eventually, I heard the clinking sounds of a spoon against a bowl, probably another meal of cereal. I lay awake all night, the pressure in my head mounting and the sick feeling around my organs expanding as the hours went by. The throbbing spread from my forehead into my jaw and neck and shoulders, and eventually my whole abdomen felt hollow, like hunger. I listened to my mother switching off all the lights and making her way up the stairs, finding her way to her bedroom in the dark, and I imagined her lying in her bed, all alone like I was, staring wide-eyed at the ceiling, and I waited—and maybe she waited with me—for morning.

I made dinner the next night, salmon I'd found in the freezer and defrosted and I steamed with oil and salt and green onions, the way my mother made it, and rice. I finished an hour before she got home, so I cleaned the kitchen too. When she came in the door, she looked surprised.

"I made dinner," I said. "Um—if you're hungry."

"Well," she said, a little warily. She set her bag on the floor next to the table. "All right."

I put a piece of salmon in a bowl over rice and brought it to her carefully. I'd made tea, too, but it was cold, so when she made herself another cup I didn't say anything. I picked at my salmon for a few minutes.

"I'll get a job this summer," I said. "To pay you back. I never meant for you to have to worry about it. And I never meant—I know how excited you were about Asheville." My throat hurt. "I'm so sorry, Mom. I thought it just meant I'd have to pay more interest later. Also, I didn't—" I felt my eyes fill, and I looked away. "I know sometimes people leave even when you try to stop them. I shouldn't have said what I did."

My mother nudged at grains of rice with her chopsticks, separating them out one by one and then lining them up neatly at the bottom of her bowl. "I tried to honor the terms of the legal agreement I have with your father," she said. "But it was—it was difficult to leave you there. Maybe you've always given him too much credit, you know. But of course I never wanted you to think he hates you."

I didn't answer that. She said, quietly, "You're very angry. You've been angry a long time."

I thought about telling her everything then—about Jason almost dying, about us going out and then breaking up. But when I tried to arrange the words in my mind I knew I couldn't say them aloud yet. I would fall apart. "I guess so."

She sighed. "Well—it's understandable. I was angry for a long time too. It wasn't what I ever asked for."

"Did you feel like you tried?"

"Yes."

And then I was crying. I hadn't meant to, and I turned away, trying to get myself under control. My mother put her chopsticks down and reached for me, cupping my chin in her hands to turn my face toward hers.

"I tried too," I said. "With my friends. I wanted—I wanted it to be different, but I did everything I could, and it was the same.

That was why I went to New York and got the limo and—"

My voice gave out. I tried to gulp down air.

My mother's expression softened. "Oh, Beth," she said. "You can't stop someone from making their own choices, you know. It doesn't work that way. And even if it did, it damages you. You can't let yourself keep giving and giving and giving to someone who stopped caring. I've always worried about you making that mistake, but I thought—well, I thought I'd set an example for you. Because if I wanted one thing for you it was that you'd always know how much you're worth. The world will tell you otherwise because you're a girl and you're not white and you're softhearted, but you're allowed to keep things for yourself, and—and to say something isn't good enough for you. You're allowed to want more. You're allowed to be angry."

She dropped her hand. She looked exhausted and sad. She was wearing one of the skirt suits that she always wore to work, and the jacket was loose on her in a way that made her look younger than she was, almost childlike. I remembered how she'd told me once that when she was a small child the one thing she'd always wanted was to be a mother.

She got up and took her plate and chopsticks to the sink, and then she stood there a moment, gripping the countertop with her hands. The refrigerator hummed and made a clattering sound. With her back to me, my mother said, "I tried to show you that, anyway. I thought I had."

By Wednesday, it felt untenable to stay home again. My mother dropped me off at school, and Sunny and Brandon and Grace were by my locker, waiting for me. I wondered if they'd waited the last two mornings too. Brandon was holding my violin.

"You left this," he said.

I said, "Oh."

"On Sunday."

"Yes, I know when." I took it from him because I couldn't not, but even just touching it I could feel my chest seizing up again, everything from Sunday night rushing back at me. I put it in my locker, out of sight. I said, shortly, "Thanks."

I should've stayed home. It hurt to look at them.

"So," Brandon said. From the way they all looked at one another, I could tell they'd rehearsed or at least heavily discussed this. I felt a hand grip around my throat. All the things I'd said about Chase, how I'd made Brandon feel for not missing his game, not telling them about Juilliard and New York—all those things I'd done for Jason that he'd never asked for, that maybe he'd never wanted from me. What could I say to the three of them now? I had tried my hardest, and so many times I'd chosen wrongly, and now it was done.

It was Grace who spoke. "First of all, are you all right? We were all so worried about you after the show. Did you go to the doctor or anything?"

"No. It's happened enough times by now that they probably wouldn't bother rerunning the same tests."

"My dad said it can straight up feel like a heart attack," Brandon said. "Sounds pretty awful."

"It is."

Then they were all silent for a little while. I could feel whatever unspoken negotiation was happening between them, and the way I was outside of it. Finally, Sunny said, "Mr. Irving said you quit BAYS."

"Yes."

"Why?"

"I just—I'm done with music." I hadn't had the courage to call him, so I'd emailed instead. I was ashamed of that. I'd also logged into my Juilliard account—I had done it three times, in fact—so I could decline and get it over with, so I could bury it. But each time I couldn't bring myself to do it.

"Is it because of the panic attacks?" Grace said. "Like, is performing really stressful?"

"It's not the performances."

"Why didn't you ever tell us it was happening? I tell you when I have, like, a headache!"

"A headache is so different." I was, suddenly, exhausted. I wished I'd walked away after they gave me back my violin. "Everyone was sick of dealing with Jason. And nothing happening to me was anywhere near as important as anything happening to him."

"No one's sick of dealing with Jason," Brandon said. "It's just that Jason honestly I think wants some distance."

I hadn't meant in the present tense, but the way he said it—I recognized that, the relief of someone finally bringing up the thing that's been right under the surface for you, taking up all the space inside your heart. I said, "What's been going on with him, anyway?"

"He's been—kind of off doing his own thing," Brandon said. He was trying not to look pained, I think, but he wasn't pulling it off. And his palpable sadness—in the face of it, something shifted in me. "I think he just needs some space right now. I think he—I don't know. We'll see. I tried to talk to him. My dad thinks—he said maybe being around us just reminds Jason of too much, or something." He forced a smile, then said, again, "We'll see."

"But we don't have to talk about him right now," Grace said. "So, okay, anyway, the three of us were talking about how you told us to leave you alone, but then we were like, wait, actually, what you said was that we didn't care. Which doesn't mean the same thing, right? So we decided what you meant was try harder."

Unexpectedly, my eyes flooded. It was true that I wanted that—you always do, I think, even when you tell yourself otherwise to try to make it hurt less.

"So," Sunny said, "will we see you at lunch?"

Grace looked uncharacteristically nervous. "Okay, well," she said, when I didn't answer right away, "here's a would you rather: we keep avoiding each other forever all of us feel like garbage all the time, like we do now, and probably regret it the rest of our lives, or we forget all this and move on?"

I think I would've let it go forever. Maybe I never would've approached them; I never would've found my way back. I was hurt and angry and also, I think, I felt guilty—but mostly it was because, before them, all I knew was that when people left they stayed gone.

"Yes," I said, and Brandon, relieved, said, "That wasn't a yes-or-no question, Beth, come on," and Grace hugged me.

I thought Grace was wrong, though—maybe the point was to not forget any of it. Because maybe in a long friendship everyone is an infinite number of different versions of themselves, and all those selves of you that you shed or grow out of, the ones you're glad you've evolved from and the ones you miss—in a long friendship there's someone who was witness to all of them, and so all those different people you were along the way, no matter what else you may have been, you were never alone.

At my mother's insistence, the last weekend before decisions were due on May 1, we took a last-minute weekend trip to UC San Diego, which was the highest-ranked school I'd gotten into, so I could see it. I felt horrible she was spending money on it, but flights had been cheap and we stayed at a Motel 6. Despite the things my mother kept trying to point out that she thought I'd like, I hated it there—I hated the vastness of it and all the cement and glass surfaces everywhere, the way sounds bounced harshly off all the walls of the buildings. I couldn't imagine people making real music there. I could see only a grim, miserable life for myself. *Did you go to the beach?* Sunny asked. *You like beaches.* But even the beach had felt all wrong, the neighborhood right behind you and a parking lot pressed up against the sand. I thought about telling my mother I'd gotten into Juilliard after all, but then she would be thrilled, and it would be such a mismatch of what it meant for me that I knew I couldn't go through with it.

I missed my violin. Sometimes when my friends mentioned BAYS or on the days they had rehearsal, it was a sharp ache of grief, but how could it ever not feel fraught, how could I ever play in front of an audience again without feeling all it was I'd lost? I had tried once since the Senior Showcase to play, but as soon as I held my violin in my hands I felt my throat start to close, and then even after I'd shoved it back under my bed it was hard to breathe and I could only sit on my bed unmoving, terrified, obsessively tracking my pulse. I had to talk myself out of calling an ambulance, and it was only because I'd messaged Sunny and Grace and Brandon, and they'd googled symptoms and promised mine seemed normal, that I didn't. It was the worst panic attack I'd had yet.

I wondered—I couldn't help wondering—if Jason would've gone if he'd gotten in. We were still using our same group chat, and every time I said something I imagined him reading it. I wished I could stop thinking about him. I wished it didn't matter to me what he did or where he was or who he was with, that I wasn't always hyperaware of his presence across campus or across a room, that it didn't feel like a punctured lung when I saw him walking to the parking lot with Annique Chang or when I heard, secondhand, that he was going to go to UPenn. I hadn't even known he'd applied there.

In our motel room in San Diego the night before we flew back out, my mother and I stayed up late watching a cooking show on TV. We were flying into SFO so my mother could stop and see my grandparents on the way. I wasn't going to go; I'd go find a coffee shop or something, or just wait in the car.

My mother missed the end of the competition—it was a sand-wich with char siu and seared blood orange that won, the one she was rooting for—because she was on the phone with my grand-mother trying patiently to arrange the visit. When she hung up, she leaned back against the headboard of the bed and closed her eyes a long time, and I said, "Why do you still go see them so much when they're so awful to you?"

"They gave me the best life they knew how to, Beth. And when people are that age, they don't change."

"Does it make you angry, the way they treat you?"

I thought she'd made excuses for them, but she said, "I sup-pose it always has, yes."

I thought of her sitting through dim sum again with them tomorrow, trying to deflect whatever they said to her. "I think you should stop seeing them," I said impulsively. "I think it's too hard on you, and you—" I felt my face go hot. "You deserve bet-ter than that."

"Beth, that's not—I—they're my parents," she said, and then she went into the bathroom to shower, and I remembered too late that anyway they were still paying for part of my tuition. They'd insisted, saying they couldn't take money with them when they died. But the way my mother had been sort of flustered—I think she was touched, and that it meant something to her that I'd said that.

Later, we'd turned out the lights and we were each in our beds. I'd been lying there awake for a while—I never slept well anymore—but I'd thought maybe she was asleep already when she said, quietly, "The thing is, Beth, I think you can—you can learn to hold on to that anger. I used to try to pray about it going away or try to push it aside. But then when I keep it—I find that it reminds me what's true and it helps me—dismiss all the other voices, I suppose. I think you can keep it as a sort of compass.

The world will always try to tell you things about yourself, and when some of them give rise to that anger inside you, you know it's those ones that aren't the truth."

I didn't know what to say to that, and then I waited too long to say anything at all. Maybe she thought I was asleep. At the airport before our flight back home the next day, I bought her a box of Milk Duds, her favorite candy, an infinitesimally small gesture compared to what I meant. For so long I'd thought of her as the one who'd been left, but I'd always failed to see the most important part, which was that she was also the one who'd stayed.

"SO IS IT like super hard when you see Jason in class?" Grace said after school when we were hanging out at Brandon's. There were just two days left before college decisions were due, and despite that, time had been unspooling slowly the past week after my mother and I had gotten back from San Diego. Grades barely mattered now, and I wasn't going to BAYS, which meant a lot of hours each day to sit at home and put off committing to UCSD, to tell myself to just officially decline Juilliard's offer so I could forget about it.

It seemed impossible that somehow, after everything, Jason and I were nothing to each other now. But I knew what it was like when people left you, how they multiplied in their absence because now you saw and felt them in all those places they weren't. I knew what it was to cycle back and forth between anger and grief and pain and shame, or to feel all of those at the same time. I knew too how you always felt like the version of yourself they'd chosen to leave, or the version you'd become because of their leaving: disposable, pathetic. Jason had tried once to talk to me in between classes, but what he'd said when he broke up with me kept echoing in my mind. The same way it echoed every time he walked into first period, every time I saw him across the halls, every time that, in spite of everything, I missed him.

"Do you ever talk to him?" Grace said. "Or do you think you will?"

"I haven't. I don't think I want to. But—" I hesitated. Grace said, "But what?"

"But it's hard to picture just never talking to him again. I don't know."

Brandon was lying on his bed, trying to spin a basketball on his finger. He said, "Is it more like you're sad or more like you hate him?"

I could hear how he was trying to sound casual—like he was interested but not overly invested in my answer. "Have you still not talked to him?" I asked.

"Nah, not yet." He dropped the ball, almost nailing Sunny in the head with it, and scooped it up quickly. "I kind of tried, but I don't know."

"What happened when you tried?" Sunny said.

Brandon glanced at me. "Is it shitty to talk about this with you? We can change the subject if you want."

The truth was that now Jason was always the vise around my lungs; at least when we were talking openly about him, I didn't have to pretend I wasn't still trying to breathe past all those bruises. "It's fine."

"You sure?" When I nodded, he said, "I just don't really know what to say. You know how he is. You can't make him do what you wish he would. So."

"What do you wish he would do?" Grace asked.

Brandon let the ball bounce onto the ground and then roll under his desk. "I guess it doesn't matter."

"No, what?"

"I mean—I wish everything were different," he said finally. "I wish we could just redo the whole year. But sometimes I think probably Jay wishes that too, but since he can't, he's just kind of giving up. And I wish he wouldn't do that. I think he's better than that."

That night after dinner, Sunny asked if she could come over to talk to me about something. By now we were back to talking constantly, and I'd told her everything about going to see my father and Jason breaking up with me. And I could mostly talk about next year, like how I'd despised San Diego or still hadn't officially decided anything, without it feeling as fraught and pointed. But I couldn't guess what she wanted to formally discuss.

When she came in, she was holding her laptop, which she set on the kitchen table and opened. I said, "What did you want to talk about?"

"I've been thinking about this a lot, and I wanted to tell you that I'll go to UCSD with you."

I stared at her. "You'll what?"

"That was the best place you got in, right? It could be fun."

"Yes, but—Sunny, are you serious? I thought you hated San Diego."

"Well, I mean, you know. It's not like I love Congress Springs, either." She shrugged. "But people manage. Anyway, it's not that far from LA. I could go sometimes on weekends."

The whole world changed around me, spun differently, like I was suddenly right side up. "I can't believe you'd do that."

She logged into UCSD's applicant portal. "We can do it right now if you want. It's due the day after tomorrow anyway."

"Sun, I—I don't even know what to say." I imagined us sharing a dorm room, having a regular spot in the dining hall, going to the beach. I imagined the others coming to visit us. All the things I'd hated about it—those were things I'd hated only when I pictured being there alone. None of it would matter with her there.

And it would be all right for her, too, wouldn't it? It wasn't that far from LA, like she'd said, and it was a good school. And maybe everything she needed from LA she could find in San Diego too—maybe she'd feel whole there; she'd be happy.

"Should I click it?" she said, hovering her mouse.

"Are you sure about this?"

"Why not? I mean, it could be kind of fun."

"Could it, though? I don't think I've ever once heard you say anything positive about San Diego."

She rolled her eyes. "Yeah, well, I'm a negative person."

"Sun, why are you doing this really?"

She looked at me strangely. "Um, for you? I thought that was obvious."

"But I mean—*why?*"

I saw in her face she understood the question I was really asking, which maybe wasn't *why?* so much as it was *why me?* "I just think we'll have fun."

"You've said *fun* like six times."

"Well, it will be."

"I bet fun wouldn't even break your top ten things you care about in your future."

"I'll reinvent myself. I'll be super fun." She sighed. "But also—I still keep thinking about you saying the rest of us would go on with our lives but that you have nothing else because no one cares about you. And—"

Without warning, tears welled up in her eyes. "It's been such a hard year and I love you so much and I just hate the thought of you feeling like no one cares about you as much as you care about them, because it's not true." She wiped her eyes roughly. "Ugh, I'm being so melodramatic. But you can't ask people *why* like that about yourself. Of course people love you. You should take it more for granted."

I reached out and nudged her hand off the mouse pad, then closed the window.

"You have to go to LA," I said.

She looked surprised. "But—"

"You've wanted that almost as long as I've known you. You're going to be so happy there."

"This isn't, like, an empty offer. I'll do it right now and click the—"

"I know," I said, and then, impulsively, I hugged her, even though Sunny was never the hugging type. "Also, Sun, I love you too."

Before that year, before all this, I would've said that what I knew about life was that there are so many different ways to lose what matters most to you. But what I hadn't known then—and maybe this has been the most important lesson of my life—was that there are also so many different ways to hold people close.

In the morning, before the bell rang, Jason was waiting for me by my locker. I tried not to look surprised.

"Hey," he said, "you feel like getting boba or something?"

I thought about saying no. It was painful to look right at him, to stand in front of him after how easily he'd discarded me. But then a part of me had been waiting for this; I was still rehearsing conversations with him in my head every night. Maybe you always stupidly fantasize that someone will say the exact right thing to make you whole again, or that you'll say the exact right thing to make them realize they need you after all. Maybe part of me would never learn to stop waiting. So I went with him.

In the car he didn't say anything except, "QQ okay?" I was nervous and self-conscious, and exhausted in a way I'd never been in my life, and I felt so badly exposed. When we passed De Anza, I said, "Brandon misses you. You should talk to him."

He winced. "I know."

QQ was mostly empty inside. The boy who took our orders got mine wrong, but I didn't say anything. After we sat down outside with our drinks, Jason checked his watch. "I don't really have to be back until fourth period. What about you?"

If I called in pretending to be my mother and excused my absence, I could be gone all day, and I said so. Then I was annoyed at myself; I didn't want to *want* to be here with him.

Jason fiddled with his straw. "You want to play poker or something?"

"Poker?" Of all the things I'd expected him to say, that wasn't one of them. "You play poker?"

"Online," Jason said. "At night, sometimes. When I can't sleep."

I thought of all those times I'd been up late at night waiting, just in case he messaged me. "I didn't know that."

He looked like maybe he was going to say more, and then he just shrugged. "Yeah."

In the drugstore next door, there were playing cards tucked behind the romance novels. They didn't carry poker chips, and after some consideration Jason bought a bag of Skittles to fill in. I pretended it was all right that I'd left school and left my heart unguarded once again just so I could stand in the aisles this way, buying playing cards. I'd thought, I realized now, that maybe he would apologize. Did he realize how badly he'd hurt me? Because I wanted him to know it. But maybe that was ludicrous; maybe he had nothing to apologize for. You couldn't fault someone for realizing you would never be enough. Maybe he just hadn't wanted to go to class.

"So," he said when we'd settled back in at QQ, the cards making a sound like pages turning as he shuffled. "Tomorrow's the day, right?"

"I hear you're going to UPenn."

"Yeah."

I thought of us both at Juilliard, both at Berkeley, how different our lives could have been. "Congratulations."

"Thanks. You, uh, you think you'll go to Juilliard?"

The wrought-iron chairs were pressing their pattern into my shoulders, the backs of my legs. "No."

"Not even a chance?"

"I can't pick up my violin without getting a panic attack, so no."

"You're getting panic attacks?"

"Yes."

"That's rough." He dealt two cards to each of us and lifted the corners of his, not looking at me. "My sister gets those too. So you're not playing at all?"

"I can't."

We played through the end of first period and into second, the sticky candies staining our palms and fingertips and my pile dwindling. You could, it turned out, have imaginary conversations with someone who you were with; I started so many sentences in my head. I was agitated in some unrecognizably hot, unruly way.

Jason looked half-focused at first, but as we continued he seemed distracted. He folded his hand once, giving me a small mound of candies, and said, "Nice one." Then, as he watched me sweep them into my pile, he said, "Did you tell your mom you got in?"

"No."

"What about your dad?"

"Oh, totally," I said, sharply, before I could stop myself. "We talk all the time. You of all people know how close we are."

He looked up at that; that one landed, I think. I could feel something ratcheting up between us. Jason leaned forward.

"Beth," he said, "maybe it's not my right, but I have to say this. I think you're making a huge mistake."

I sat back in my chair and crossed my arms over my chest. I was exhausted. What else did we have to say to each other; why had I even come?

"And why's that, Jason?"

He shrugged and opened his eyes wider momentarily, a show of exasperation, and when he did, something unleashed in me. It took a few seconds before I recognized the feeling, but then I did: It was rage. How could he look at me that way? *I* was the one who should feel that way; I was the one who'd been betrayed. There were whole oceans of anger inside me that I'd always tried to map for myself instead as hurt or fear or shame.

"I think it's a mistake," he said, "because you've put so much into your violin all these years, Beth. You really have."

"What does that even matter?"

My voice was shaking with an anger that was totally disproportionate to what we were talking about, and he must have heard it; it was a conscious choice he'd made to pretend otherwise. He said, "Well, listening to you play . . ." He paused, searching for words. In the sunlight, I could see the tiny shadows his eyelashes cast, the downy hairs on his forehead. I was out of breath. My skin felt too weak to hold my hammering heart safely inside my chest.

"It makes me feel like I know you better," he said. "I know that's not true for my playing. And I've never heard that in anyone else we've played with either."

How could he sit here and say these things to me? I decided then, abruptly, that I wouldn't leave without making sure he understood what he'd done to me. I wanted it to haunt and accuse him every time he tried to look away.

"And, you know, after—" He looked down again, and he swallowed. Then he started to say something and stopped himself, and he exhaled and drummed his fingers against his knees. "Um, after I—when I was in the hospital, one of the things I missed most when I was in there—this is going to sound stupid, but I missed sitting next to you and hearing you play. There's always been something about that that's felt so—well—centering to me. Like being with you in a way that just lets me be."

That antiseptic smell of the hospital and our feet squeaking on the tile and Jason lying there so wholly past our reach—all at once when he said that I was funneled back there. And I felt myself deflate, my anger furling in on itself like a sea anemone.

I knew then I wouldn't say anything. Because it *would* haunt him, I knew that, and I didn't wish to destroy him. I could shield him from my anger; I was strong enough to bear it on my own.

He picked up the deck of cards, leafing through their edges roughly with his thumb. "I don't think it's possible to play like that unless it's something you really care about. You care more about music than anyone I know, Beth."

"Obviously I *care* about it. Do you think the only thing that matters is how much someone cares?"

I regretted saying that immediately. It felt cruel in a way I hadn't intended—of course he knew what it was to care about music, for that to not be enough. He let it go, though. Instead of whatever he could've said, he looked down again and then swept the cards into a single stack and shuffled them.

When he laid the first three cards down, I bet high. I had a queen and a king, and I doubted he had the two and six he'd need for a straight. After he turned over the last card, he pushed a handful of candies into the middle of the table and flipped over his hand.

"I don't have the straight," he said, "but I have two eights and I know you're bluffing."

I slipped my cards back into the deck without showing him; he was right. "I think you're cheating," I said, and he smiled, in a way that made me think if the mood between us were different he might have laughed.

"No," he said, "it's just that you're a bad liar, Beth."

He looked down at the table and gathered the cards into a neat stack. And then—I almost missed it—his expression changed. It was the only time I ever saw him look that way: defiant and tender and sorry and wistful and maybe a little afraid, too, all at once, and I wondered in that moment if some truth or core of us, underneath all those ways we were damaged and all those reasons we both had to be angry, was good. Or it could've been; it almost was.

"Jason," I said, before I could stop myself, "even if deep down I thought everyone else would leave, I thought it would be different with you." I swallowed; there was a lump like a tumor in my throat. "I thought—"

For a long time I thought he wouldn't answer me. He was slumped down in his seat, and it made him look wearier, and older somehow.

"Me too," he said finally, quietly. "I thought it would be different too. But—I couldn't. I can't."

I had the strange feeling that we'd never move past this moment, that I would sit here like this with him forever, everything he said buzzing and humming always in my ears. It was well into third period now, and the shopping center was beginning to fill for lunch, dozens of engineers with their jeans and North Face, their clip-on employee badges.

"You know," Jason said finally, "I was really shocked when you said you got into Juilliard. Not that I'm surprised you were accepted," he added quickly, carefully. "That part doesn't surprise me at all."

"Mm," I said tightly. Of course, I thought, of *course* this was when Jason would watch himself—mind his tone, carefully select his words. But that wasn't what I wanted from him.

"But also—you do this all the time, Beth. You talk yourself into selling yourself short. And you give people more of yourself than they ever ask from you, and I know I didn't handle that well and I think you deserve better than that, and I think if you turn down Juilliard you're going to regret it for the rest of your life."

It turned out I had to speak carefully too; if I didn't, I was afraid I might yell. "Why does it even matter to you?"

"Oh, come on, Beth," he snapped, his patience finally dissolving. "Because I *know* you."

I looked at him sitting across from me, the candies scattered across the table in little pops of color like a still life, and I felt then how much I was going to miss this. Because he did know me; he knew me better than most, maybe sometimes better than I knew myself. And maybe that was everything.

He was wrong about one thing, though: I always was an excellent liar.

Or maybe even that's untrue; maybe it's just that it's taken me so long to learn to be more honest with myself.

MY FATHER came to my high school graduation. I hadn't expected him—I hadn't invited him, even though my mother had asked if I wanted to—and it was so jarring at first I had to look again to make sure it was him. We'd all poured from the bleachers onto the lawn when the ceremony was over, and he'd waved me over to where he was deep in conversation with Sophia Grace Parada's father, who, he told me excitedly, was his coworker.

"We were just saying it's lucky the launch finished right in time for summer," Mr. Parada said to me, smiling. The way he said it, as a father who made certain assumptions about the other father he was talking to, filled me with a cold anger. "I was so worried we were going to have to cancel our vacation. What about you guys—you have any summer plans?"

"I wouldn't know if he does, actually," I said, aloud, to both of them. "This is the first time I've seen him in a year and a half." Then I left without saying anything else to him, without taking the grocery-store bouquet of carnations he was holding.

I saw him once again after that, off to the side, scrolling through his phone the way you do at a party where you don't know anyone and occasionally glancing up, holding the carnations still, and in that moment all I could feel toward him was a flicker of pity. Because there was such a high energy right then, all the emotion swirling around and bouncing like sound waves among everyone we knew, all of us laughing or crying or cheering or hugging or some combination, that this was the center of the universe, and all I could think toward him was—*You could have had all this. You could have been a part of it.*

And then it was all over; it ceased to exist.

At the last minute, Jason got off the wait list at Dartmouth, and he decided to take it. I heard it from Brandon—since we'd cut class together, Jason and I hadn't spoken. Sunny was going to UCLA, and Grace to BU, and Brandon, ironically, to Berkeley. I'd committed to San Diego, and even after I had, I still couldn't bring myself to decline Juilliard's offer even though, as a courtesy, you were supposed to as soon as you knew. Instead, I just never logged back in, and I ran out the clock. My mother bought me an embroidered sweatshirt from UCSD.

I stopped listening to any kind of instrumental music, and then for a while I stopped listening to music at all. I missed it. It wasn't just missing—it was a form of grief. It was easier to not think about it.

That summer, though, I had to pay my mother back. I applied for close to a dozen different jobs—at QQ, at a summer camp—but I never heard back from any of them. The second week of summer break, Mr. Irving called me to say a private teacher he knew was going on maternity leave, and he thought I would be perfect to recommend to parents as a summertime substitute for their younger children. If he held my quitting BAYS against me, he didn't say it. It was an absurd amount of money—one that made my stomach squeeze with guilt at my mother having paid these rates (more, surely) for all my own lessons—and I didn't have other options, so I agreed.

I had six students. Near the middle of August, around the time Grace broke up with Chase and left for Boston, one of the girls, Luna, brought Shostakovich's *String Quartet 8 in C Minor,* a song Mrs. Nguyen had given me to learn near the end of eighth grade. To me it had always been a difficult, anxious, angry piece, at parts nearly incandescent in its fury, but also somehow one that had made me feel less alone. When I'd played it for her, though, Mrs. Nguyen had frowned at my interpretation, urging me to play more gently, more softly, and then I'd been ashamed.

Luna, who was eleven, told me she despised the piece. (I liked her prickliness; it made me think she'd be all right in the world.) But her playing, annoyed and uncertain as it was, sparked something in me. I wanted, suddenly, fiercely, to bring back to life for myself those familiar measures she was fumbling through. I wanted to resurrect their anger, hold it close.

But I imagined picking up my violin again and my skin went clammy. There were a lot of things I still avoided—oranges, taking Uber—but those meant less to me. How was I going to do this for the rest of my life? All at once, I was ravenously, furiously jealous of Luna, that music meant none of this to her, that she had it all ahead of her still.

I knew from Brandon exactly when Jason was leaving for New Hampshire. It was mid-September, two weeks before I'd leave for San Diego, and even though we hadn't spoken I was dreading his departure for reasons I couldn't quite name.

That morning around eight, a little after my mother had left for work, there was a sharp rapping on my door. Luna was coming but not for another hour and so I thought maybe she'd gotten the time wrong, but when I opened the door it was Jason. He was holding his violin case.

"Hey," he said. He was a little out of breath.

"What are you doing here?" I thought about pretending I hadn't been keeping track, but he'd probably know better. "Aren't you supposed to be on a plane soon?"

"Technically I'm on my way to the airport. But, uh—" He lifted his violin. "I thought maybe you'd play something with me."

"You thought maybe I'd play something with you," I repeated. I don't know why I thought fleetingly that he'd back down, that he'd realize how absurd this was, but he didn't. He stood there, waiting. Finally, I said, "I told you I can't."

"I heard you say that, yeah."

"Okay, so—"

"I think you can, though," he said. "If you don't *want* to, that's a different story. But I just thought—"

The sun was shining behind him, so I had to squint. I sighed. "Do you want to come in?"

There were still so many things we could've said to each other, but there wasn't time, and once he was inside Jason took out his violin and went right away into the living room, where I sometimes kept my music stand. It was in there now, the last piece I'd practiced at home lying open on it, Reger's *Serenade in G*. He motioned toward it with his bow. "You like this one?"

I did, actually. When I looked out the window, his mother's car was idling in our driveway, and Evelyn was sitting in the driver's seat, waiting. I said, "Is your sister—"

He waved it off. "She's fine. She's covering for me. So if you—" Then he lifted his eyebrows just slightly, a question.

I could have said no. I almost did. But maybe I answered with the version of myself that no matter what, would always feel something for him, that wanted to play with him one more time.

It hit me as soon as I lifted my violin, that crushing pressure in my chest like my heart was giving out, and immediately I thought I should've said no. He raised and then dipped his shoulders and chin, which had always been his signal to start, and my hands were shaking so hard I kept missing notes. I hunched over because sometimes that made me breathe better, like I could hoard oxygen that way, but it didn't help. I was scared—I was so scared—that this time it wasn't actually a panic attack at all but some dire medical emergency and all these symptoms were warning signs.

I struggled to focus on the music, and then wondered if, later, I would wish I had listened to my body and gone to get help instead. I felt like I might suffocate.

Jason lowered his bow and stopped playing and watched me.

"I'm not—"

"No, keep going," he said, and I did.

I played the next two pages while Jason watched. I was damp with sweat and out of breath, and through it all the awful clutching in my chest never went away or got better.

I did it, though. And I could feel how maybe the next time would be easier. Or maybe not, maybe that wasn't true, but I could feel at least that there would be a next time.

When I put my bow down, my face flushed, Jason clapped. I tried to catch my breath as he put his violin away and stood up, and I stood—shakily—too.

I wasn't sure what to say. There was so much, but I knew he had to go. For a second, it seemed like maybe we'd hug, and then Jason held out his hand instead.

"Well," he said. His eyes were clear and watchful and guarded and maybe, if I was reading him right, a little sad. He smiled, his real smile. "It was a pleasure."

I watched him walk down the driveway, and I watched his car until it turned a corner and I lost sight of it, and then I went back inside.

I had learned in all my years performing that afterward you remember the music, not the audience. That day, though, I'd remember both.

I hated San Diego: the hordes of strangers, the spindly, acrid-smelling eucalyptus trees and the pale brownness of all the shrubs clinging to canyon walls, the relentless sun. There were probably thirty or forty people from my class at Las Colinas who'd gone there with me, but it wasn't anyone I was close to and that made it worse somehow, seeing them around campus, an uncanny valley of my life.

The new symptoms started in my first week there. I would awaken feeling like something important inside me had shifted out of gear, and everything would look blurry. And then my vision would clear and simultaneously my skull would explode in a throbbing, crushing pain that left me weak. Each beam of sunlight was like an ice pick, burrowing itself deep inside my skull and wriggling around in the soft matter of my brain and down my spine and into my stomach until I was violently ill. It felt like I was dying every time. When I could see again, my hands would shake violently as I'd google things like *how to know if you're having a stroke* or *brain aneurysm symptoms* or bus routes to the nearest emergency room. There were a lot of days I couldn't make it to class. I missed all my midterms except for Victorian Lit, which was a paper, and in the two classes where my professors were understanding and let me reschedule, I missed the makeups, too. My roommate, Maria, was a pleasant girl who joined a sorority early on and then was almost never there, and one night when I was curled in a fetal position in bed, trying to make it to morning, she sat up and peered at me.

"Are you okay?" she said. "Why are you breathing like that?"

"I'm just not feeling well," I managed, "but I'm fine," and she rolled over in bed and murmured, "That sucks. Maybe it was something you ate."

I talked to Brandon and Grace and Sunny, but they were all

doing well and there were only so many times I could tell them that I wasn't. I barely talked to Jason, although I wished often— and maybe perversely—that he'd call me. When I thought of him I was still sad and still hurt, but not angry, and I wondered if he thought about me. I wondered if he'd felt like this. I was so nonfunctional that it was astonishing to me, in retrospect, how much he'd managed to hold himself together; I could barely leave my room. Sometimes Sunny would come see me, a process that necessitated a train, a shuttle, and Ubers on both ends and one I tried to do myself so many weekends, but every time I was too scared I'd have a panic attack on the train. She'd tell me about everything happening in the Queer Asian American Alliance she'd joined and try to fill me in on her new social constella- tion, the roommates and parties and classes. And she'd talk about Dayna, who'd ended up at UCLA too, and how she felt most like herself around them, like so many silent parts of her were all in concert now, and how she was starting to hope in the possibility of being together. I think sometimes she tried to hide it around me, but Sunny was so happy, and so I'd try to be happy for her too and to hoard all those details of her days the way I used to. I'd try to tell her she was being ridiculous whenever she worried she wasn't caring or brave or brilliant enough for Dayna, but my mind felt like a sieve. Sometimes we'd go to the beach or take the shuttle to the mall or eat at one of the places near campus, but a lot of times I couldn't make it out of my room and she'd lie in my bed next to me while I tried desperately to breathe normally, to hold on. Once, when it was close to midnight and I'd spent the past few hours yo-yoing between whether or not to go to the ER and could finally trust that I'd survive the night, she said, "Why don't you leave?"

"It's going to be like this anywhere I go."

"I mean, maybe, but also maybe not, right?"

I dismissed it at first, but after that whenever I thought about

it that *maybe not* was a beacon for me. Maybe I had made a mistake in coming here. I'd made a choice I regretted, and I had tried
to stick it out and make it work, and it wasn't. But I believed now
that one thing didn't have to define you; some things you got to
leave behind. I stayed until the end of the quarter, and I lived
through all those moments when fear felt like it might consume
me, and then it didn't and there I was on the other side of it.
When the quarter ended, I unenrolled, and I went back home to
reapply for music schools the following year.

Mr. Irving helped me prepare my audition tapes, and I'd spend
mornings with him in the music room off his garage. At first
I was clumsy; my body had forgotten. I had to relearn how to
hear things again, how to sift through things like pain and rage
and loss and from them cull what I could transfer into sound.
But Mr. Irving was patient—we both were—and things came
back, deeper, I think, and richer than before. His husband, Keith,
a jazz pianist, would tiptoe in exaggeratedly to listen as I played.
When I put down my violin, he'd applaud loudly and then offer
us lemonade. At night, my mother would come in to listen to me
practice, and sometimes we'd stay up late to talk.

I applied to eleven programs this time, was invited to audition
at all eleven, and received offers of admission to nine. This time I
got a partial scholarship to Juilliard, and maybe it would always
feel fraught and weighted with history for me, yes, but still, I
wanted it. When I told them, Grace sent me a package of cookies
shaped like musical notes and Brandon posted a picture of me
with the caption *so fucking proud,* which was especially touching
given that no one in his new life—all those people in all the pictures he posted of parties and hikes and birthday dinners, who
always commented on his posts—had ever met me. Jason, who I
almost never heard from, wrote to say how happy he was for me.
And Mr. Irving was ecstatic—he teared up when he found out—
but I think my mother was the most overjoyed of all.

At Juilliard, playing felt electric with possibility. I was lonely sometimes even when I was with people, though, and everyone was so stunningly talented I often felt inadequate. But one day in Colloquium the teacher mentioned how normal it was to have impostor syndrome and afterward, London, who lived a few doors down from me, said, "I thought she was going to say, everyone here has impostor syndrome *except* for London, who we can all agree is a legitimate hack," and we all laughed and it was a little better after that.

The panic attacks visited me there still, but less often, and when they did they were less familiar, a loud noise I could grit my teeth through. Sometimes when I was playing or sitting in class or going out to explore the city with friends I caught myself feeling that I belonged here, that I was enough. One night a little before Thanksgiving I was coming back to the dorms from practicing with my string quartet. There were never open practice rooms, so we'd waited over an hour and we were all cranky, but then the way all the parts had come together had been so transcendent I was still so absorbed in it that I was nearly back to my dorm before I realized it was raining. And then two things happened in quick succession: I registered that I was soaked, and I felt for the first time that maybe I'd be able to erase the feeling I'd carried with me since I was fourteen, that everything—everything—I could ever be or accomplish would be asterisked by how easy it had been for my father to walk away from me.

So maybe I was different now. But it turned out that in spite of that I still wanted the same things I'd always wanted: to play music, to hold on to the people I loved.

I was most of the way through my first semester when my mother called to tell me she'd had a minor heart attack, and I flew home immediately to be there for her bypass surgery. I'd barely finished messaging my friends when Brandon drove back from Berkeley. His father took off work, and they came with us to that first day of appointments, his father asking dozens of questions to the cardiologist and surgeon and then turning back to us and translating the medicalese.

The night before my mother's surgery, Sunny came home and woke up at four to wait with me in the hospital. She showed up armed with a box of donuts, two cups of coffee, and a packet of personalized crossword puzzles she'd made me. It must have taken her hours. A week or so later, I found that packet in my suitcase, stuffed into a side pocket with a sterile mask and a Ziploc bag of stale almonds, half the puzzles filled in, in my handwriting. I stared at it—I couldn't remember filling them out, somehow coming up with my audition piece for BAYS or the name of the land where *The Adventures of King Brandon and Prince T-Rex* took place. But I can perfectly picture Sunny—both tense and patient, bossy in a way I would've needed in that moment—coaching me, directing my thoughts away from the operating room with all its scalpels and monitors and needles and onto those neat, ordered squares, as she waited with me all that day.

And Jason flew back too, without telling me he was going to. There was a knock on the door when I was back at home my mother's first night out of the hospital, sitting alone in the kitchen while my mother slept, and he was standing outside, holding flowers.

"For your mom," he said, and handed them to me. "I don't have to stay if you don't want. But I thought maybe you'd want company."

It was the first time I'd seen him since we'd left for college, but the surgery had drained me and he was right, I did want company. I hadn't eaten all day and was starving, and so Jason and I went to get pho at the place on Stelling that was open late.

I know a little more now about what it's like to feel close to death, to peer out at the horizon and watch for its approach, and I know this: even though Jason survived, I still lost part of him that day he nearly didn't. I wasn't there for all the ways he pieced himself back together after that, and by the time I saw him that day back in Congress Springs, he'd changed.

But then, of course, though it's harder to track in yourself, I'd changed too.

We talked a long time that night. It was funny, being there with him—it felt at once the same as it used to and also it didn't. I asked him if he still played violin at all, and he told me how he'd gotten to know a group of people who met once a week at a house full of seniors that had a piano. Everyone brought something to eat or a six-pack of beer and an instrument of some kind, and they played jazz.

"I didn't know you liked jazz."

"Yeah, me neither." He laughed. "Well, it's probably not fair to call what I'm doing *jazz*. I'm terrible. The whole thing is pretty chill. One guy just brings a tambourine. It's not the kind of deal where anyone cares if you're good or anything." He tore a leaf of Thai basil from the tangle of herbs in half, then another one, then placed them on the small plate in front of him. "It's—really different. Sometimes there are parts of you where you worry if they were gone there'd be nothing else left over. But then it turns out there is." He looked at me. "Some things, anyway," he said, looking away again. "Not everything."

Did he mean something by that? Maybe I was reading too much into it; surely he wasn't talking about me. "Do you ever miss BAYS?" I said. "It's funny because now I play, like, all day, and the teachers are mostly really amazing, but sometimes I still miss it."

"What do you miss?"

"Playing with you guys, mostly. And Mr. Irving. But also

some people at Juilliard are really competitive. Like whenever you play, you can tell they're sizing you up or like, scheming how to make sure to stay ahead. Not very many people, but it's definitely there."

"Yeah, you've never been like that," he said. "I think the thing I miss most about BAYS is how music then was like—it helped drown out a lot of other stuff. You know? When I was playing, I could try to make that louder than like, whatever else was repeating over and over in my head."

"Does anything do that for you now?"

"Yeah, you know. You figure out ways."

"You seem good," I said. "You seem—happier. More settled."

"Yeah, I think I just had to get out," he said. "For a while I thought I'd just literally never come back home, but then the guilt got to me. First-generation problems, I guess. But it's easier now that I'm gone. Also, I've been seeing this therapist."

"Really?" I was surprised. "Like, of your own volition?"

"I'm trying to, you know, be better. Get better. All that." He signaled to the waitress for another glass of water, thanked her, and then drank half of it in one gulp. "We talked about you."

"Oh."

He grinned at me. "You're not going to ask what?"

"Would you tell me if I did?"

"You really think I'd bring that up and then not tell you?" He saw my face. "Okay, fair enough. But yes, that was an opening."

"Okay. What did you talk about?"

"Mostly about how fucked up it was last year with us."

"Well," I said, lightly. "I'm so glad I asked."

He laughed. Then he sobered. "Do you ever think about all that?"

"Well—" I paused. "Yes. A lot."

"Really?"

"I mean—did you think I wouldn't?"

"Yeah, I guess I thought probably you would. But I never really heard from you, so I thought—I don't know. I didn't want to force myself on you. I guess I hoped you were off being happy instead."

"That would've been nice."

"So—no, then?" he said. "I'm sorry to hear that."

He drank the rest of his water, slowly this time. The only other people in the restaurant were a family sitting by the door, a mother and father and three school-aged kids, and Jason watched them.

"I've thought about this a lot," he said. "After Christmas, I guess I thought if we went out, that would like—fix everything. It sounds stupid now. I told myself if I was with you I could just move on and forget everything. But then it was—it was kind of the exact opposite. It's funny," he said, "because I know you never thought of yourself as like, this angry person, and I know you were always so careful about it, but I guess I always felt like we had that in common. So it wasn't fair what I was asking of you. Like—I wanted you to be angry along with me, but then also I wanted you to feel like everything was great. Except then when I was with you, that was like, the one place I felt like I actually wanted to just like talk about how shitty everything was, except I also just didn't. And I knew it was messed up, but I kept thinking it would just get better on its own."

There was a ring of condensation on the table from my cup, and he reached out and wiped it away gently with his thumb, not looking at me. "But then we went to see your dad that night," he said, "and after that I couldn't do it anymore."

"You know," I said, and then I almost stopped myself—it had been long enough that when I'd seen him on my doorstep I hadn't thought we'd get into all this. But then here we were. "I regret a lot of it and I shouldn't have tried so hard to fix you, and I'm not blaming you, because you can't help needing whatever you need and all, but just—that night at my dad's and how you would see that and then decide I wasn't enough for you, either, after all—I don't know how you could imagine I wouldn't think about—"

"Wait, what?" he said, leaning forward. "Beth, no—that wasn't—that's not what happened at all."

"You've said twice now that was why you broke up with me."

"When did I say that?"

"Just now, and when you—"

"I never said that. Is that how it came across? Fuck, Beth, I'm sorry. I never meant that. All this time that's what you thought?"

"What was I supposed to think?"

"Definitely not that. It had zero to do with not thinking you were enough. What happened was I guess that night I realized—I realized how shitty it is to start something with someone when you know you can't live up to it. Especially when it's someone you love."

I felt the word make its way through me—a flush on my face, a tingling ribbon down my spine, and then an ache through my whole chest. It's possible, it turns out, to miss someone who's sitting right in front of you.

The waitress turned off the neon OPEN sign in the window. The family at the other table signaled for the check. After a while, I said, "I wish you'd told me that last year."

"Yeah, well." He tilted back in his chair so it was balancing on its back legs, a gesture so familiar that for a moment I felt us rein-habiting each other's worlds. But the feeling passed. He looked a little older—his cheekbones had hollowed out so that the shadows on his face cast differently, and there was still a scar along his fore-head from when he'd almost died. He ripped his napkin into little strips, then looked back up at me. "I wish a lot of things."

Afterward I was planning to move back for my mother's recovery. She would need round-the-clock care at first and then significant assistance as she regained strength and fought off complications, and I couldn't bear the thought of her dependent on some health aide who was just putting in hours and watching the clock. I could take a leave of absence or just drop out, but my mother would have none of it. I didn't want her to be alone for months, though, and so she suggested she would come to New York. The idea felt fantastical, but then Brandon's father made some calls and got her in to see a cardiologist he'd known from med school, and then Mrs. Nakamura had a friend who had a rental in New York, in Midtown, and she found someone who could rent my mother's house while she was gone too. So when she was cleared to fly, my mother came to New York to recover.

I stayed with her most nights. She was weak, easily fatigued, but the cardiologist was pleased with her progress. And it was easier there, somehow, between us, like in a new place we were unfettered from all our ghosts. Sometimes we'd stay up late talking. One night, when the table was littered with the remains of the Vietnamese food we'd ordered, spring rolls and bánh xèo and pho with tendon and tripe, I finally told her about Jason.

"I wish you had told me," she said, reaching up to wipe her eyes. "I wish you hadn't felt like you had to carry that alone."

She meant well, I knew that. But she was wrong to think there was anything she could have done. And anyway—I'd never been alone.

When she got better, she started going out during the day to wander slowly around the neighborhood, sometimes shopping at the produce markets even though she was scandalized by the grocery prices here. She told me she'd always dreamed of living in a big city. She'd cook dinners, and sometimes she'd steam a whole salmon or simmer a whole chicken and then press me to invite my friends from school to come cram into the apartment and eat home-cooked food.

I missed her fiercely when she went back home. But I'd been

giving private lessons to rich children in Manhattan and saving whatever I could, and when she was strong enough, I bought us tickets to Asheville. We had an incredible time.

My mother's illness made the rest of the world recede for a while, like a tide, so that I only ever saw people there on the same shore. Which meant my mother, and those who made it a point to be there with me.

I'd thought Jason would disappear back into New Hampshire, but the opposite was true. The day I'd gotten back to New York he had revived our five-person group chat, and he and I started talking again too.

It was different this time: he was doing better now, and I was too. I always told him what pieces I was working on; I sent him posts and headlines, the things people said in class or on the subway, that made me feel rage and despair about the world. Once I called him when I was having a panic attack outside a restaurant where I was supposed to meet friends. I called him when my father messaged me out of the blue one evening to ask if I could teach violin to his manager's daughter via video chat as a favor to him because he thought it would help him get promoted and then was so furious I couldn't sleep.

It was funny, sort of—now we could talk about anything. Most of his old walls weren't there and when they were, I knew what was on the other side; I was less afraid of his anger because I was less afraid of my own.

Sometimes, because this was what I'd always hoped it could've been like, I wished we could start over. But he would've said it, I thought, if so—he had so many openings. The truth was that it was better now because when he'd left and healed over, he'd healed over from me, too.

That was painful, sometimes incredibly so, but the past is

immutable, and anyway I was always so busy. When I was play-ing I thought often about what Jason had told me about letting the music drown out other voices, and I worked on that. Because you hear so many, ones that might want you to think you're worthless or undeserving or cursed. The amount of freedom I had at Juilliard was staggering—maybe it always is when no one knows you—and I could try on different selves like new clothes.

I met Tag near the end of my first year. He was extraordinarily talented, a second-year in the acting program, and he thrived on all the posturing and social competition and networking whose inner workings eluded me. It wasn't that I hadn't known people who were ambitious, because everyone in Congress Springs was ambitious, but Tag expected things from the world in a way that was so new to me, and in a way that was exciting and fun. When I was with him, the future was all expansive possibility.

You're going out with someone named Tag? Brandon said when I told them. *Who names their kid Tag? Are white people okay?* In fact Tag was half Chinese; his mother was from Beijing.

He's hot!!!! Grace said. *I just stalked him on Instagram!!! So preppy!! Is that your new type??*

Part of me wondered if Jason might react in some negative way. He didn't, though, which meant I'd read our closeness cor-rectly as strictly friendship, and not some prelude to something else.

I'd thought we'd talk about Tag more, that even though they weren't physically here somehow he'd become a part of their lives too, but I don't know why I thought that. Sunny was going out with Dayna now—she'd written a piece and asked them out at the same open mic night Dayna had taken her to years ago, and I'd been so excited I made my roommates watch the video—and still Dayna and I had never met. There were always a million pictures of Brandon at different parties. Grace always said, "We need to catch up!" and then we didn't. We'd been to hell together, with Jason, but maybe those are the things that draw you close and it's the mundane that lets you drift apart: different locations, different obligations. Maybe that was growing up, but I was sad about it still.

Tag was from Litchfield, Connecticut, a two-hour drive away, and one weekend over the summer I went home with him for the first time. His house had a full basketball court on the lower floor, and his mother wore shoes—tan Louboutins—inside. We went for a drive through the rolling green hills dotted with enormous white colonial mansions like Tag's so they could show me the town, and his father explained how you could tell how old a house was from the number of panes in its windows. It was beautiful and also exquisitely boring, and when we got back to his house, Tag cut a star out of paper and handed it to me and said, "Your medal for surviving that." Later that night, I idly googled his parents, out of curiosity, and there were articles about how they were major donors to the GOP.

We were supposed to meet up with some of Tag's high school friends that night, but after dinner he changed his mind.

"You're tired?" I said. We were lying together on the couch in the finished basement, where there was a TV, a pool table and a foosball table, and a bar.

"Nah, I just don't need to hear about who's running whose mom's art gallery or whose dad's hedge fund now. The world is big! Move on!" He slipped his hand around my waist. "I always think it's weird how you're so into high school still."

"What do you mean I'm so into high school still?"

"It's one of your quirks. You live in probably the most vibrant place in the world and there are literally thousands of people you can meet who are probably going to be culturally important, and yet you'd rather Whatsapp people you went to Homecoming with." He jabbed my waist with his finger. "It's not everyone who'd come all this way just to be the same person."

"I'm not the same person."

"Would your high school self have dated me?"

"No."

That made him laugh. "Touché."

"Also," I said, "I think that's a stupid framing."

"You think what's a stupid framing?"

"That people somehow lose their value when it's been x years or you move x miles away."

He sat up and looked at me. My voice had been shaking. "Are you *angry?*"

I'd never seen Tag angry—he found it unseemly and also unnecessary, a waste of emotional investment. "I just think you're wrong."

"Okay, then we differ. There's no need to be angry over it."

I was starting to think that anyone who paid attention had anger embedded in her, like an earring backing. "Okay," I said, and he lay back down, and after we left Litchfield I decided to end things with him. It was friendly enough; it was just that, maybe for the first time, I was able to want more for myself. What we were together wasn't enough for me.

And then something happened after Tag and I broke up: Sunny told me that when we'd started going out, Jason had been devastated. I asked how she knew—was she just imagining it?—and she said he'd called her. I was shocked.

That had been a while ago, and since then he'd dated someone else too, so maybe I'd missed my chance. But the truth was that I still loved him, maybe would always love him, and so—nervous, hopeful—I went to go see him.

It was a five-hour ride to get to Hanover and I was worried I'd have a panic attack, and then actually I did. But I was on a bus, and the road kept flying past, so I made it. Jason met me at the bus stop and I saw him through the window before he saw me. His hair had gotten longer, and he had that little almost-smile that used to mean he was being his public self. I hadn't told him why I was coming in case I decided to back out, but seeing him there, I knew I wouldn't change my mind. After everything, he felt like home to me.

But then it was different in person. We went back to his dorm and I met all the people I'd only heard about—no one was quite how I'd imagined them—and then we walked around campus together and we were both trying too hard. We kept talking over each other, and he didn't ask about breaking up with Tag and it felt out of place to just blurt out why I'd come, and it took effort to think of the right things to say.

I'd been planning to tell him at dinner, maybe, but then we ate with some people from his dorm. One girl, Kathleen, seemed attuned to him in a way that made me wonder if there was anything there between them, and I waited for some kind of signal from him (*don't worry, it's not like that with us*) but it didn't seem to occur to him to send one, and why should it? There was a knot in my stomach. I'd come all this way, though, so then I told myself I'd talk to him after dinner, but then we went to hang out in Kathleen's room (rugs and plants and certainly-illegal candles all over) and when we finally went back to Jason's room one of his two roommates was there.

"You seem happy here," I said, as I was folding my clothes to put in my backpack. "Your friends are nice."

"Yeah, they are," he said. For a second he looked like he'd say something else, but then he didn't. He didn't seem like someone who felt unfinished, or who was looking for more. He wedged himself on the floor between his bed and desk so I could sleep in his bed, and he fell asleep right away.

I think I might be too late, I messaged Sunny when I was still awake a few hours later. I was lying on his lofted extra-long twin bed, my chest aching.

Noooooo, she wrote back. *What's happening?? Did you tell him yet??*

I'm really not getting that vibe from him. I think he's moved on. Then I added, *The stupid thing is I think maybe if I'd been ready after my mom's surgery I think he would've been too. I just waited too long.*

You waited exactly the right amount of time, Sunny said. *You're ready when you're ready.*

I guess.

So are you just not going to say anything? she said, and I wrote back, *I don't know.*

I think you should, Beth. If it's what you want, you owe it to yourself to try.

Sometimes the people who know you best can speak into your life—they can illuminate all its shadowed parts for you to see. But I wasn't quite sure if that was still true with us, whether that was the kind of adage Sunny would tell anyone or whether she still knew how to be exactly right about me.

In the morning I had only a few hours before I had to catch my bus back. If Jason found it strange I'd come all this way just to have dinner with his dorm mates and sit around in someone's room, he didn't say it. We were going to get coffee and go for a walk before I had to leave, but on the way to coffee we saw flyers about a string quartet playing at the Hopkins Center. It was free and open to the public, so, spontaneously, for old times' sake, we decided to go.

It was probably a third full when we got there, a medium-size hall that felt familiar in the way all concert halls do when music's been your life since you were small.

"They're not going to be as good as you, huh?" Jason said, grinning. "You still go to small-time gigs like this? It's weird I haven't heard you play in so long. I don't even know how good you are now."

"Probably about as good as you'd hope someone would be if her single mom worked her whole life to send her someplace like

Juilliard," I said. "That's right, though—the last time we played together was that day you left home."

The quartet came onstage with their instruments, arranging themselves on the chairs. By the time it was over, I'd have to go catch my bus. I said, "Sunny told me you called her when I was going out with Tag."

"Oh." He raised his eyebrows. "Well. I'll be honest, that's, uh, not a conversation I expected to have right here in"—he glanced down at his chair—"seat 34G in the Hopkins Center for the Arts. But yeah, I mean, I won't lie to you."

I tried to keep my tone conversational. "I had no idea you felt that way then."

He didn't correct my *then*. "Yeah, I know you didn't."

"Why didn't you tell me?"

"Why didn't I tell you?" He had the same conversational tone; we could've been discussing the bus route. "I mean, you'd just started going out with someone else. And I didn't want you— just with our history, and just knowing you—I could see it feeling like pressure if I said anything. Also, I mean, what was I going to say? Hey Beth, that went so great the first time, can I interest you in some more emotional unavailability and the occasional freak-out? I wasn't exactly sitting there with pocket aces." He said it lightly—he even had a small smile—but then he glanced at me, and sobered. "I should apologize, though. I shouldn't have said anything to her. I wasn't trying to send some roundabout message to you."

So maybe that was a closed door. But I thought of going back having only said all this to each other, and I knew I had to try.

"Do you ever think—" My heart was pounding. "Do you ever think about trying things again?"

He turned in his seat to look at me more closely. "Do you?"

"I do."

His expression changed. "Are we having this conversation?"

he said. "I thought you were just annoyed about me calling Sunny. I didn't realize we were, you know, actually doing this."

"I wasn't annoyed. I was just trying to find a way to say I wish I'd known earlier, because I would've wanted to try again. I know a lot went wrong, but I think we could be better than we were before. And I also think we could be better than—whatever was passed down to us."

The ceiling was probably forty feet high, but it seemed to be pressing down on me as I waited for him to answer. He swallowed and looked at the empty chairs in front of us, and then something changed in his expression, like he'd made some kind of decision. There wasn't anyone close enough to be listening, but he ducked his head next to mine.

"Do you remember the Mendelssohn piece we played for BAYS? That one with the solo audition?"

Of course I did. I said so. Jason rubbed at his knuckles with his thumb.

"I'd always planned to tell you this," he said. "But then you were with Tag, and then when you said you were coming, I didn't think—well, whatever, the point is that when I heard you play it that day we auditioned, I thought, *I am never going to feel about another person the way I feel about Beth.* There was a lot I turned out to be wrong about. But that part—I think I was right about that."

Onstage, the quartet tuned. The conductor raised her arms. Jason didn't look up.

"I told myself I'd never say anything before I could make any real promises. And I know people change, and I can't ask you to wait forever while I work through all my shit, so maybe by then it'll be too late. And if it is, I get it, that's fine, but if I'd somehow had another shot and fucked up that one too, it might've been the thing I always regretted most. And that's saying a lot."

We'd moved closer to each other in our chairs. The lights went dim.

"Do you think you ever will be able to make those promises, though?" I said.

"I think so," he said. "I'm working on it."

"And you'd—I mean, you'd want to?"

"You know how you told me earlier I seemed like I was happy here?"

"Yes?"

"I almost am. I mean, it's good. But when you said that all I could think was how if we could try again, and get it right that time, I think I actually would be."

Sometimes you can believe in the heart of another person. And sometimes, I think, you can also believe in your own—that it's stronger than you realized, that it can hold multiple things at once, like anxiety and also hope, the future and also the past. It can hold space for another person without forfeiting itself.

The music started, Maconchy's String Quartet No. 3. It was a piece we'd never played together; it was strange to realize, after so many years, how many of those somehow existed still.

"Well," I said, "whatever version of yourself you are then— give me a call. Whoever I am then will want to meet you."

I'd been right: It was never quite the same playing without Jason, without the rest of them. I was a better musician than I had ever been in my life, but still sometimes I missed when we had all played together.

At the end of my second year, I successfully auditioned for a solo at an end-of-year gala at Tully Hall, and when I mentioned it in our group chat, Sunny said, *let's all come to New York!!!!* I wrote it off as the sort of thing people say, and assumed if I didn't push for it or arrange it somehow, it wouldn't happen, but then a few days later she sent me flight information. They were all coming, the four of them.

I couldn't host all four of them in my dorm room, and they'd wanted to get a hotel, so I was going to stay with them while they were there. It would be the first time since we'd all left home that the five of us would be together at once, and I was anxious about how it would go. We still messaged, still kept up on one another's lives and days, and Jason and I tried to see each other every few months. But it was always different in person, and maybe they'd get here and we would reach for those ties that had always tethered us to one another and this time our hands would close around empty air. Maybe it would shatter my illusion that we hadn't truly grown apart. Maybe, as we were all moving into new futures yet again, it would feel like a requiem.

For the recital, I prepared Bach's *Unfinished Fugue*, for which I'd composed a new ending. It was the one I'd heard in the car the day I almost went to the bridge, and every time I played it I remembered what it had felt like then, who I'd been in that car, and I felt as though I'd kept a promise to myself. I hoped it wouldn't be the only part of everything I got to keep.

Brandon's flight was delayed, and Jason's bus hit traffic, so they'd arrive midshow and we wouldn't all be together until after. Grace arrived first. She walked into my room like she'd been in it a hundred times and handed me a bouquet, peonies and greenery she told me she'd bought on the way at Trader Joe's and had arranged herself and then tied with a silk ribbon she'd packed expressly for that purpose. "I know it's supposed to be after," she'd said, hugging me, "but obviously I already know you're going to be amazing, and also I wanted you to see it before it wilts." It had been the longest since I'd seen her, her life the most hidden from me, and she was so different. She was making plans for law school and volunteering for a congressional campaign, and she was happy in a way I could see now she'd never been in Congress Springs. She felt bigger to me, more expansive. But maybe it always goes that way the first time you move away and make a new life of your own, when you stretch out the corners of your own personal map of the world and tack them down in new places you learn to know.

That night, knowing they were all out there watching, I let myself hope. I wasn't there for the ways they rebuilt themselves, and they weren't there for all the ways I did either. But I hoped a foundation you'd laid years before could hold firm enough to bear the weight of so many new layers, so many new selves. And I hoped too that you could build something vital and lasting even if all you'd had to offer was the damaged parts of yourself, even if you weren't yet whole.

I played my very best. I was glowing afterward, my professors and classmates catching me backstage to congratulate me before I had a chance to go out and see my friends. The four of them were outside waiting for me, and when they saw me, they clapped.

"Holy *shit*, Beth," Brandon said, and Jason said, grinning, "I feel like I need to write you a thousand-word text about what you just played."

They talked about the performance for several minutes, but I could feel a silence hovering, and then it descended. We stood there arrayed on the sidewalk, five people who had shared a life and now no longer did.

Then Grace said, "Oh, guys, I keep forgetting to tell you what happened to me yesterday. You'll never guess." She paused dramatically. "I was home yesterday and it was the middle of the day, like two p.m., and someone outside our building was smoking pot right under our window and it just *reeked* inside, and I went outside to tell them to move and guess who it was?"

We couldn't guess. Grace said, "It was Eric Hsu!"

"Oh my god, Eric *Hsu*," Sunny said. "What's he even doing now? Besides smoking outside your window?"

"He goes to MIT, but I guess he's dating someone at BU.

Okay, but literally, isn't being at MIT but then also just randomly smoking outside someone's window in the middle of the day, like, *exactly* where you would've expected his future to go? I told every single one of my roommates and none of them got why it was so funny to me and I was like, ugh, I need to see my friends."

We were laughing—too loudly; people were looking at us— and Sunny said, "God, I've missed you guys." And I knew then it was all right, that it would always be; we would go out into the world and find our way back to one another still.

We decided to walk all twenty-eight blocks back to the hotel since we couldn't all fit into one taxi. We talked about all the things we were doing and all the things we wanted to do, like Grace's environmental law and Sunny's studying abroad, Brandon's volunteering at the hospital and Jason's switching to a sociology major. We talked about all the ways we wished the world were different, all the ways we'd try to change it. I imagined us like a sunburst, all of them and all the ways they'd touch the world radiating out from the single point of our beginning together.

I was the last one awake that night, back at the hotel, after we'd stayed up talking until three. I listened to the four of them breathing, and I felt all the weight of the past between us like an anchor. And in that room, in the way the night felt suspended like the morning was never quite going to come, it was as though all the things we'd been remembering and revisiting together had formed a little pouch around us, had pulled a drawstring to cordon us off once more into this old closeness. I thought about the ways we'd made it to the other side, and I thought about the ways things reverberate across the years, and I thought how one of the enduring gifts of the past is that it's yours to keep.

And then, that night, was the thing I'd thought was gone. Lying awake, sensing their presence around me it felt, just for a moment, like being back in BAYS in those rare times when we were able to give ourselves over completely to the music, when we were able to draw on all our moments of practice and all our repetitions and all our intimacies with a piece so we inhabited it, so it flowed through us and we could feel the percussion in our pulses. I felt it there again that night, the way it always was with Mr. Irving holding us in the moment, all of us suspended in that same stillness, holding our instruments carefully and watching, waiting. And all at once, and just for a moment, I was back there, back up on that stage looking out, the weight of what we'd just played all around me in a way that happens so rarely, a way that so consumes you that when the song ends—a song you've grown to know, one you've crafted and built—you sit there, blinking in the lights and coming back slowly to the world, and you find that the song, in its closing, has opened up a whole new silence for you to fill.

RESOURCES

This book discusses suicide, abuse, racism, mental health, and micro-aggressions. If you find yourself struggling, while you're reading or at any other time, please reach out to one of the resources listed below. You deserve help, and the world is better with you in it.

National Suicide Prevention Lifeline (available 24/7):
1-800-273-TALK (8255).

Crisis Text Line (available 24/7): text "hello" to 741741.

The Trevor Project hotline,
for LGBTIA youth in crisis (available 24/7):
1-866-488-7386, thetrevorproject.org

National Alliance on Mental Illness helpline
(M-F, 10am-6pm ET): 1-800-950-NAMI
or nami.org

Visit
https://www.nimh.nih.gov/health/find-help/index.shtml
for more resources on mental health and suicide prevention,
and for a list of action steps to take if you're concerned
about a friend or loved one.

National Child Abuse Hotline:
1-800-422-4453, childhelp.org

ACKNOWLEDGMENTS

Adriann Ranta Zurhellen first read this book in 2011, and has believed in it and championed it tirelessly ever since. Adriann, thank you for always holding this book in your heart and seeing it into the world after all these years.

I'm grateful to my wonderful editor, Kendra Levin, for her work on this book—for caring so deeply about these characters and for always pushing them to deeper and more interesting places, and especially for making room for female anger.

Thanks to Lizzy Bromley and Akiko Stehrenberger for such a lovely face for this book. Thank you also to Katrina Groover, Amanda Ramirez, and the whole team at Simon & Schuster BFYR for their efforts to turn this story into a real book, a process that seems magical to me still.

I'm indebted to the mentors who worked with me on early drafts of this book—Nona Caspers, Sarah Shun-lien Bynum, Maxine Chernoff and Peter Orner—and to the MFA community at SF State and the friends—Toshio Mori, Patti Wang Cross, Mary Taugher, Cindy Slates, Ami Sheth, Traci Chee, Jean Znidarsic, Diane Glazman—who read and offered feedback. Thanks to others who read early and encouraged me—Colleen Dischiave, Jen Ireland, Andrea Heggem, and Reneé Euchner.

Thank you also to my grandmothers, Marjorie Gilbert and Helen Loy, and my great-aunt, Mary (Junnie) Young, for sharing so many of your stories with me, so many of which have shaped our family history and also my own life and my imagination.

If this book had been published when I first started working on it, it would've been one of extremely few YA novels by and about Asian

Americans, but today it'll join a rich literary tradition. I'm grateful for the work of authors who paved the way, such as Malinda Lo and Cindy Pon, and for the efforts of We Need Diverse Books and the writers, agents, editors, librarians, booksellers, scholars, and readers who work toward a literary landscape that greater reflects our diverse reality. I feel privileged every day to be part of the YA community and I'm especially thankful for the friends I've made in it and for the Bay Area crew.

I have been working on this story since 2006—it's seen me through most major transitions in my life and has been around long enough that the original manuscript had landlines and no cell phones—and it's been many different versions of itself, but at its heart it has always been a story about friendship and was written in tribute to some of the most important friendships of my life. Thanks to the incredible friends I've been blessed with, and especially REA, for all those ways we've tried to figure out the world together. Also, Tim, thank you for resurrecting all our old group emails and reminding me of the core of our friendship at a crucial time in the writing when I'd forgotten entirely what I ever wanted this story to be about.

Thanks always to my parents, BreTT and my constellation of extended family for their support and encouragement. Thanks to my beautiful children, who make me laugh and give me hope for the future and let me witness the magic of storytelling in all its many forms, who steel me for our collective responsibility to write better stories for the next generation.

And thanks always to Jesse—you are the reason I get to live so many of my dreams.